Acclaim for Katherine Sutcliffe

Notorious

"This is by far the best historical romance I've ever read. Sutcliffe has really outdone herself this time with this masterpiece novel, and I can't recommend it highly enough."

—*Rendezvous*

"Seething with deep emotions and brimming over with plot twists and masterfully crafted characters, this is a spellbinding page-turner!"

—*Romantic Times*

"*Notorious* has everything I expect from a Katherine Sutcliffe novel: breathtaking action, an exquisite hero, vivid and evocative prose, and an exploration of the boundaries of the romance genre. You can't go wrong with *Notorious*."

—*The Romance Journal*

"*Notorious* is dark and dangerous. This is absolutely one of the most compelling historical reads of the year!"

—Jill Barnett, bestselling author of *Sentimental Journey*

"The incomparable Katherine Sutcliffe is in top form with her trademark blend of passion, pageantry, and thrilling romance."

—Susan Wiggs, bestselling author of *The Mistress*

"Katherine Sutcliffe is a marvelous talent and a treasure of the genre!"

—Laura Kinsale, bestselling author of *My Sweet Folly*

"Pure entertainment!"

—Kat Martin, bestselling author of *Perfect Sin*

"Ms. Sutcliffe confided in me that she had written her previous novel, *Whitehorse,* from the heart. In which case I can only surmise that *Notorious* was written from the soul. *Notorious* is poignant, powerful. I found myself reading feverishly."

—Heidi Katros, *Winter Haven News* Chief

Hope and Glory

"Devoted fans of historical romance know that Katherine Sutcliffe is one of the best writers of romance in bookstores today."

—Harriet Klausner

"Moving, emotional, and powerful, *Hope and Glory* is a wondrous novel about redemption and the power of love. As always, Katherine Sutcliffe wields her pen with care, bringing to life memorable characters and an unforgettable, not to be missed romance."

—*Romantic Times*

"Katherine Sutcliffe pens a passionate, potent tale! Horrors of war give the book a gory, realistic tone. Meanwhile, a fortune-telling hag and Hope's visions lend subtle and credible foreshadowing to this very compelling story."

—*Publishers Weekly*

Renegade Love

"*Renegade Love* is Katherine Sutcliffe at her best. You'll be mesmerized by the intense passion in this hard-hitting, emotion-packed tale that smolders with raw sensuality. Ms. Sutcliffe slowly builds sexual tension until it boils over in the explosive and tender love scenes. This is a keeper."

—*Romantic Times*

Jezebel

"Sutcliffe has given us some of the great damaged heroes of recent years . . . a fine writer."

—*Publishers Weekly*

Devotion

"An exemplary romance—perfect in every way. Flawlessly plotted and written . . . this is one of the most exciting romantic stories in years."

—*Publishers Weekly*

KATHERINE SUTCLIFFE

FEVER

SONNET BOOKS

New York   London   Toronto   Sydney   Singapore

An *Original* Publication of POCKET BOOKS

A Sonnet Book published by
POCKET BOOKS, a division of Simon & Schuster, Inc.
1230 Avenue of the Americas, New York, NY 10020

Copyright © 2001 by Katherine Sutcliffe

ISBN: 0-7434-1197-8

First Sonnet Books printing July 2001

10 9 8 7 6 5 4 3 2 1

SONNET BOOKS and colophon are trademarks of Simon & Schuster, Inc.

Front cover illustration by Lisa Litwack; photo credit: Kevin Dodge/Masterfile

Printed in the U.S.A.

Acknowledgments

My sincerest thanks to my editor, Caroline Tolley, for her wonderful enthusiasm for my work—and for being so very, very nice. Not to mention patient. Caroline, you're a dream editor come true!

A very special thank-you to Paolo Pepe who so beautifully captured the heart and passion of *Fever* in this wonderful cover. Thank you, Paolo, so very much! After fifteen long years of covers, I finally succeeded in getting one that actually depicts my story. Bravo!

And to two wonderful friends and talented writers who held my hand through the writing of *Fever*, who encouraged me every step of the way: Linda Campbell and Melanie George. Ladies, friends, I couldn't have done it without you.

FEVER

FEVER

Prologue

A CONVENT IN FRANCE, 1853

On normal, sun-kissed days she found in this isolated place a sense of peace and contentment. From this lofty summit, placed at one angle of the more bleak walls, the brooding figure of the Mother of Sorrows looked down with eroded eyes. Here, the profound silence would be broken only by the cries of the rooks swooping in black flocks or the screeching calls of gulls as they hovered over water.

Today, however, she sat like a Turk, legs crossed within the folds of her skirt, the tips of her naked toes peeking from beneath the tattered hem as she leaned against the gray sculptured stone at her back—a grim gargoyle with big teeth and extended wings.

The escalating wind whipped her hair so it lifted like red flames around her head. It stung her cheeks with cold and watered her eyes. Below the bell tower where she perched atop the creaky cupola that trembled with each blast of driving wind, France spread in vast undulations of deep green and desolate cliffs that plunged toward a whitecapped sea. More closely lay the graveyard, girdled within the ancient and crumbling dry-stone walls: dark tombs and weathered headstones whereupon sea fowl took shelter from the advancing storm.

Ah, but she despised the cold. Never in the last nine years of enduring this cloistered existence had she grown accustomed to the chill that made her stone cell feel like a tomb even on the brightest, warmest days. But she thrilled to the thunder and lightning that would frequently roll in from the sea like a goliath serpent spitting fire bolts and roaring with fury.

Turning her face toward the dark heavens, Juliette watched the play of flashing lights behind the clouds, felt the first rush of her heartbeat as the rumble rolled through her body. The tower trembled. The rafters, burdened by the weight of the old bell, a gift from the pope himself, groaned like a body dying.

Cautiously, she stood and braced her feet apart. The wind slammed her. She caught her breath and raised her hand to shield the force of the first driving spears of rain from her eyes. She inhaled the musty smell of wet earth and awaited the tingle of electricity in her body.

There! It vibrated up her spine and crawled over her scalp, shot along her arms and down her legs as the tongue of fire streaked through the clouds and lapped at the horizon with a spray of blinding white sparks and flames.

Dear God, how she loved the force of it. The smell of it. The taste of the rain on her tongue, salty as the sea spray. As always, with the tumult came the images in her mind: flashes of color, of faces, laughter and screams. Fire and rain. They made her tremble. Breathless. Her heart beat thick within her breast and the blood in her head rushed with the violence of the driving, crashing waves against the coast.

Spreading her arms out to her sides, facing the wind, she

closed her eyes. For that brief moment she imagined herself lifted by the current, risen high, higher, tossed upon the draft like down, carried beyond the crags, beyond the white-tipped waves to a place that shimmered pure and golden amid riotous gardens.

"Juliette! Come down from there this moment! Juliette! Someone help us! Quickly before she is incinerated to an ash. Dreadful, ill-tempered termagant. Bane of my existence."

She heard them scramble over the ledges, grunt as they slid upon the rain-slick stones—the village idiots—the deaf-and-dumb eunuchs the Reverend Mother employed to manage the grounds. Juliette knew damn well that had they the slightest stirring of manhood in their pants, the dour, mule-faced Reverend Mother would castrate them with their trowels—if she hadn't already.

Two of them gaped at her as they clambered onto the tower, their hair and clothes dripping, their jaws slack and eyes dull of intelligence. The Reverend Mother, framed by the windowsill, rosary clasped in her hand as if to fight off the devil himself, glowered up at her with the determination of one prepared to exorcise whatever demon possessed Juliette.

A man stood at her side. Tall and imposing—distinguished, she thought, as a tremble of thunder passed through her. Dark hair streaked by gray. Mouth curled in sardonic pleasure—appreciation? Amusement, certainly. But something else. She felt it as certainly as the rain beat upon her face. As certainly as his gaze penetrated the gray haze and locked upon her own.

Her lips curving, she returned his smile.

Her mother, Maureen Jarod, had been a whore. Not *just* a whore. A demimonde. A prostitute. A very expensive prostitute, according to her father's solicitor, Lester

Roswell, a diminutive man with a thatch of yellow hair and spectacles thick as bottle glass. A prostitute who won the heart of a handsome young planter, Jack Broussard, who thought by lavishing his wife with love and wealth he could change her lascivious ways.

Alas, once a whore always a whore.

According to solicitor Roswell, Maureen's healthy appetite for lavishness had financially destroyed her husband. Her appetite for men had broken his heart.

And, according to the solicitor who had peered at Juliette with the look of a man who had come face-to-face with a ghost, Juliette was a mirror image of her dead mother.

Which explained a great deal—acknowledgment of which, though helping to somewhat alleviate her pain and confusion over her father's odd behavior toward her, had planted a hard core of germinating resentment in Juliette that grew more bitter each time she thought of her father's pitifully broken heart.

Oh, yes, it explained a great deal.

Why her father had buried Juliette in a convent the moment she developed breasts.

Why Jack's face had gone white as milk and his entire body had shaken as if with ague the last time he'd visited her. What tenderness he might have shown toward his daughter was fast replaced by unbridled fury and hatred the instant Juliette had glided into the room, radiant with the prospect of flinging herself into her papa's arms, certain she could convince him to remove her from this depressing and constrictive environment if she was enchanting enough.

She had been certain she could make him love her, eventually.

That had been three years ago. Now her papa, Jack

Broussard, was dead eight months—blew his own brains out with a pistol, according to the Reverend Mother, who had a penchant for dramatic details—especially when it meant that her father's soul would forever burn in Hell because of his suicide—leaving Juliette orphaned. And penniless, but for, according to the solicitor, her father's gold wedding ring and a decaying property buried in the Louisiana swamps that she would inherit when she turned twenty-one—unless she married first.

Considering she was barely nineteen, reptile-infested swampland was hardly going to help her now.

And marriage? That wasn't likely as long as she was sequestered in a convent, the only civilization within a hundred miles being a village full of inbred imbeciles whose greatest thrill in life was training cocks to kill one another.

Such straits would have distressed most young women, she supposed. But Juliette, thanks to her mother's scandalous reputation and her father's eventual abandonment, was not like most young women—much to the consternation of the Reverend Mother, who stood in the distant shadows, quaking in her white woolen gown and winged cap, her thin lips moving in silent prayer for Juliette's damned-to-hellfire soul. One would have believed the devout old woman to be staring straight into Lucifer's eyes the way she shook.

Obviously this was serious business. One was not escorted to the Mother's apartments unless something was afoot—bad news, corporal punishment. The chamber felt as cold and hollow as a crypt and skirted the cloister and song school where the other young ladies, mostly younger, were collected in that moment heralding God's miracles like a chorus of harping magpies.

Juliette, doing her best to ignore the bone-aching cold made all the worse by the draft of wind whipping around the cavernous room, raised one eyebrow at the Mother and curled her stiff lips, tipped her chin and drew her shoulders back, which lifted her generous breasts in a way that made the man circling her stop in his tracks and suck in his breath.

Max Hollinsworth—her godfather—caught her chin between his fingers and regarded her features with something just short of amazement glittering in his dark blue eyes. Handsome. Monied. Distinguished.

And his breath smelled heavily of spirits.

"By God," he said breathlessly. "You're . . . exceptional, Juliette. Even more beautiful than your mother, and I thought her to be incomparable."

"She's willful and spiteful and profane," declared the Reverend Mother, her voice dropping to a conspiratorial level. "I vow she's possessed. You've seen it for yourself, *Monsieur.* Her soul craves hell's fire and tumult. Is she not the vision of sinful temptation?"

Her eyes narrowing, Juliette shot her a look that caused the Mother to step back and clutch her rosary.

Hollinsworth raised one black eyebrow as his gaze drifted from Juliette's face, down to her breasts that were normally bound as flat as possible by lengths of coarse linen under her dress. Today, however, they filled out her bodice to the straining point, thanks mostly to the sodden material of her blouse.

"Indeed," he murmured, amused. "Perhaps, Juliette, you share more with your mother than just her pretty face, *oui?*"

"She has the heart and soul of a harlot," the Reverend Mother announced. "Thrice she's strayed to the village at night. We found her at cockfights, wagering with coins she obtained from heaven knows where from doing heaven knows what."

"True?" Hollinsworth smiled into Juliette's eyes.

"Yes," Juliette replied with a curve of her lips.

"Where did you get the coins?"

"I stole them, *Monsieur*." Cutting her gaze to the Reverend Mother, she added, "From the chapel coffer. I was owed it. Having spent the last years on my hands and knees scrubbing floors, sweating in that wretchedly hot kitchen under the supervision of dour women who pleasure in wielding strops in the name of God, I felt I was due compensation—as meager as it was. Then again, all the coins in their coffers couldn't compensate for the misery I've been forced to endure the last years in this place."

"Ah, yes, you have your mother's dauntlessness. Her obstinacy. Her . . . fire. It was what your father loved about her."

Shifting her gaze up to his, Juliette laughed—a husky sound deep in her throat that brought hot color to Hollinsworth's face. A swelling began in her chest that replaced the shivering of her body with a flash of emotion as vibrant as the lightning dancing beyond the stained glass. The antipathy she experienced in that moment for the mother she no longer remembered robbed her of breath and caused her eyes to burn with a heat that made her doubt her own sanity.

"*Monsieur* Hollinsworth," she replied through her teeth, "I'm well aware of what my father loved about my mother. I assure you, it wasn't her dauntlessness and obstinacy."

For a long moment he remained speechless, unblinking, unmoving; the color drained from his high cheeks, leaving his flesh pale and tainted with spider veins. His eyes held hers in a strange, discomposing way, as if he were staring at her again through the curtain of rain that beat continuously on the stained-glass window.

"Do you know," he spoke suddenly, shattering the quiet as he looked over his shoulder at the Reverend Mother, "that

Juliette was born during a storm much like the one raging now? The child born of thunder and lightning be born of high spirit, fierce temper, and a splendid passion for . . . life."

"Child born of the tempest is born of evil," the Mother declared righteously. She pointed one crooked finger at Juliette. "Her own father recognized it—turned cold and pale as a corpse when he saw her. She has her mother's wickedness, I vow, and the sooner she is gone from this holy place the better."

Thunder crashed in that moment and lightning illuminated the colored windowglass of a crucified savior that towered over the Reverend Mother's stooped figure. Juliette stared at her, forgetting the storm and the man who stood so close the smell of his breath triggered images of the drunken farmers on their knees yowling at blood-spattered cocks. Even now the strop marks across her back throbbed with heat—punishment for failing to show the proper respect during vespers.

She has her mother's wickedness, I vow . . .

Wicked? Yes, too often she felt wicked to the marrow of her bones. Wicked with the hatred for the martyred shrunken woman before her, wicked with resentment she felt over her father's abandonment—wicked with hatred for a mother who destroyed everyone who loved her.

Yet, it wasn't the shame of that wickedness that made her face burn and her knees shake, but the acknowledgment that buried at the heart and soul of her was an ember of dreaded wickedness begging to be fanned.

Prurience too often heated her blood.

She swallowed, but did not look up into Maxwell's eyes—as if by doing so she would reveal the weakness of her character. "Tell me why you're here, *Monsieur*. My father never mentioned you."

"I'm not surprised. We were the closest of friends, like brothers, until your mother's death. After that . . . your father retreated into himself. He returned to France. We lost touch. Perhaps he simply wished to put his old life, and memories, behind him."

"Obviously."

She did her best to ignore the humiliation heating her face. God forbid that she would allow the Reverend Mother to see her suffer. 'Twould give the old woman too much satisfaction.

Max took her chin in the crook of his finger, tipped back her head until she was forced to look in his blue eyes that assessed her closely.

"Tell me, Juliette. What, if anything, do you remember of your childhood—before your father moved to the Continent?"

"Nothing."

His eyebrows lifted. "Nothing at all?"

There were memories—few, of course. Snatches of sound and images that were as difficult to grasp as vapor. They frightened her. Through the last many years, she had awakened in the night, shaking violently, body sweating, her flesh feeling as if it were on fire—Reverend Mother's purgatory, no doubt.

Occasionally, there were others—a glimpse of masculine features that, if she hung on long enough to the dream, would quench the fire and replace her terror with an equanimity that eased her racing heart. It was those indistinct features her mind reached for when desperation and unhappiness consumed her.

She shook her head. "Nothing, *Monsieur*. I was only four at the time of my mother's death."

"You have her eyes as well," he said softly, as if drifting in thought. A shadow of something flickered through his expression. His look became distant, briefly, before he appeared to fight his way back to the present. When he touched his hand to a tendril of hair near her cheek, his fingers trembled.

"Your hair . . . like rich fire. When your mother rode over Belle Jarod it was as if sunlight drenched her in flames. She refused to wear a bonnet, of course. She liked her hair down. The wind would lift it like banners behind her. Your father would sit for hours and brush it, until it shone like new copper. She would rest her head on his knee and grow languid with pleasure."

Juliette frowned. "How very romantic. Surprisingly so, considering that apparently my mother's favorite pastime was adultery."

With a lift of her chin, she added, "*Monsieur,* perhaps your memories of my mother are fond, if not fanciful. However, for me, she's the cause of my father's despair and the reason he'll forever writhe in hell—according to yonder lady of compassion whose judgment of fallen souls is as sanctimonious as Maureen Jarod was promiscuous."

The Reverend Mother gasped and pressed her rosary to her bosom.

Juliette narrowed her eyes and smiled.

Hollinsworth allowed her a short bow and laughed. "Whether you wish it or not, you have your mother's tact as well as her beauty. Very well. We'll dispense with the reminiscing and get down to business. I've come to take you home, Juliette."

She stared up into his smiling face, refusing to acknowledge the stumble of her heartbeat. In that moment, it seemed that her entire soul expanded with exultation and caused her legs to grow weak. Surely she had misunderstood him. Were the Mother not looking on like a fierce old crow she might have pinched herself to determine if she were caught up again in one of her confused dreams.

"Pardon, *Monsieur?* I don't understand—"

"As your godfather, it's my responsibility to provide for you now that your father is gone. Holly House, my home in Baton Rouge, is in dire need of a woman's laughter since my wife died, so I can hardly deny that this mission is solely altruistic. My son Tylor is grown. My days are long and often lonely. I hunger for laughter. For youth . . .

"You'll want for nothing, my dear. We'll buy you pretty dresses and combs for your hair. Lavish bonnets. Soft slippers. Ribbons that match the green of your eyes. You'll be the most beautiful woman in Louisiana. And the most pampered. We'll throw soirees in your honor and young men from across the state will flock to Holly House to woo you."

He turned away, paced to the window, gazed out through the rain-speckled panes to the churning green ocean beyond. "My home is comfortable. Your room has a view of the river. There are servants to feed you, to dress you—no more scrubbing floors on your hands and knees. God forbid."

Disbelief thrummed between her ears like the wine she tippled during her secretive late-night jaunts to the village cockfights. Dare she believe him? To show even a whit of the hope rapping at her chest would be too brazen, surely.

"I couldn't possibly," she heard herself say breathlessly, aware her hands had clutched her damp skirts as if preparing herself for a fall. "You're a total stranger to me, *Monsieur* Hollinsworth."

"What choice do you have?" His mouth smiled. His eyes did not. "Alas, your father left you destitute, I'm afraid. You think the drab, cold walls of this convent are dreary. There are far greater horrors than these, *ma petite.*"

"Whoring like my mother, I assume." She gave him a dry

smile. Her throat felt tight and her eyes burned. The old
desperation squirmed inside her—the sensation of being
lost, adrift with no harbor within a thousand miles. "I need
time, of course. To reason on this sudden twist of fate."

"Of course." His voice was kind, his smile patient. The
reality occurred to her then that there simply would be no
thinking about it.

Thanks to the stroke of a pen and a sprinkle of holy
water nineteen years ago, she had become, upon her father's death, the ward of a total stranger.

One

BATON ROUGE, LOUISIANA

Boris Wilcox, glaring through the strands of his limp snow-white hair, teeth bared and blood streaming from his broken nose, slammed his fist against Chantz's jaw a third time. His frustration mounted as the gathered crowd, bathed in beer and sweat and obviously in Chantz's corner, whooped like maddened savages and roared their encouragement. They punched the air with their fists, slapped their hats against their thighs. The ear-splitting racket caused the horses in the livery stalls to spook and roll their eyes.

Chantz stood his ground, legs braced apart, boots planted in the livery sawdust as he flashed Boris a smile that was as intimidating as it was arrogant.

Boris swept the back of his hand over his mouth, smearing blood and drool across his chin that was already swollen and purple as a new turnip. "Boudreaux, I'll knock yer teeth through the back of yer head before I'm done. See if I don't."

"So you say, Wilcox." Chantz laughed and blinked sweat

from his eyes as Boris stumbled over his own feet and staggered as he attempted to straighten. "I'm just amazed you've managed to win as many fights as you have, considering you punch like a girl."

The crowd hooted again, scaring a three-legged tabby from under a moldering pile of damp hay.

"My money's on Chantz," someone shouted, followed by a scurry of men placing their final bets on the outcome of the match.

His heavy brows drawing together, Boris raised his fists. His six-foot-two-inch body shook to his muddy boots. Chantz knew well enough that Wilcox had a lot riding on the fight—he'd wagered a good portion of his employer's supply money on his winning—normally not a bad risk. However, Chantz suspected that Boris was going to have some explaining to do when he returned to his employer with nothing to show for his money but a busted nose and a few missing teeth.

"Big talk, Boudreaux. Especially from one stupid enough to think Fred Buley is gonna approve of his daughter bein' courted by a fatherless white-trash boy who ain't got a pot to piss in."

The jeers and hoots dwindled. The men surrounding Chantz and his opponent pressed close, eyes fixed on Chantz's face that began to heat. Suddenly the swirling cloud of sawdust closed off his throat and burned his eyes. He felt the others' gazes fixed on his face, their anticipation crackling like air before a lightning strike.

Boris grunted a laugh and spat blood on the ground. "Looks like I hit a nerve." He wagged his busted fists at Chantz. "What's wrong, Boudreaux? Surely you don't believe you really stood a chance with Phyllis Buley."

He threw back his head and brayed with laughter, then

focused his small round eyes again on Chantz. "We all seen how you mooned about like a blue-tick hound ever'time you seen her ride by in her daddy's carriage. You didn't really think she was serious when she batted those long lashes at you, did you? Why, she's just toyin' with you, boy—havin' fun. Heard this mornin' Horace Carrington declared himself. They's gonna be married come September."

Hooking his fists up toward his chin, Boris grinned. "Face it, Chantz. You just ain't got a lot to offer. That prize cock between yer legs might be good enough for mud daubers like your mama, but it ain't ever gonna buy you a smidgen of class."

Boris lunged and swung.

Chantz stepped aside, drove his fist into Boris's ribs, lifting the reigning boxing champ off his feet and sending him stumbling through the cautiously silent spectators who parted like the Red Sea out of his way. Chantz hit him again, felt the man's ribs snap like old pinewood—again—driving his knuckles into the soft underside of Boris's jaw—again—drilling the man's shattered nose like a battering ram.

Boris hit the ground with a groan, his head resting in a pile of fresh horse manure that steamed around his ears.

Anger a red haze, Chantz went for him again only to be suddenly hauled back on his heels, hands clutching his arms and braced against his shirtless, sweating chest as several men dropped to their knees and slapped Boris's smashed face in an attempt to revive him.

"Is he dead?" a voice, high pitched with excitement, shouted.

"If he ain't, he aught t'be," came the solemn response.

Someone flung water from a tin pail over Boris's face. He sputtered, thrashed like a man drowning before gagging and gasping and clutching at his nose with a howl of pain. He blinked glassy, swollen eyes at Chantz as he struggled to sit up.

Chantz pointed one finger at him and said through his teeth, "You ever call my mama a mud dauber again, Wilcox, and I'll kill you. That's a promise."

Bud Bovier, owner of the Bovier Livery and promoter of the weekly boxing matches, slapped a wad of money into Chantz's hand and shoved him toward the door. "You best git while the gittin's good, Chantz. I ain't havin' nobody killed in my livery, no sir."

Grabbing Chantz's shirt from the ground, Bud tossed it at him. "Go take out your anger someplace else. Buy you a bottle of whiskey and one of Meesha's girls."

Lowering his voice, his heavy brow furrowing with concern, Bud added with a touch of sympathy, "Take no mind to him, buck. Half the time Boris ain't got the good sense God gave a mud bug." He forced a smile. "Get on now. Ain't none of us here care to see you hang over a bastard like Boris. He ain't worth the horse dung in his ears right now."

Outside the livery, his jaw suddenly throbbing like hell and the coppery taste of blood in his mouth turning his stomach, Chantz plunged his head and shoulders into a trough, hoping the cool water would assuage his fury before he kicked in the livery door and tore into Boris again with something more life threatening than his fists.

He wasn't certain what made him madder. Boris's insult to Chantz's mother and his heritage, or the news that Phyllis Buley—the woman whose legs he'd crawled between the previous night and every time she came scratching at his door—the woman who vowed she adored him and couldn't live without him, was about to marry someone else. Not simply someone else. Son of a bitch Horace Carrington.

He kicked the trough, then the hitching post, causing a sorrel mule to turn its long sad face toward him and flick its ears.

Son of a bitch Horace Carrington.

Speak of the devil . . .

Lights from *La Madeleine* spilled out the double glass doors and the broad window, illuminating the highly polished brass fittings on Carrington's rig whereon Nathan, a Negro driver in red livery, sat, cap pulled low over his eyes as he napped in the heat.

La Madeleine supplied the only upscale eating establishment in town—the finest food outside of New Orleans. Or so Chantz had heard. Not that he would know personally. Even if he had the money to waste on French cuisine served on bone-china plates, the proprietor, Nelson Barlow, required his customers to "dress accordingly" inside his establishment—and Chantz didn't own a suit. Hell, he was doing good to manage a decent pair of boots every few years. In fact, he suspected that folks paid more for a room for one night at Barlow's *La Madeleine* than Chantz did for a month's worth of sorry beans and the weevil-infested cornmeal Charlie Johnson of Johnson's Mercantile sold to his less esteemed customers.

His hand crushing the prize money in his pocket, Chantz considered waving it under Johnson's nose and demanding clean cornmeal for a change.

To hell with it. Money was just too damn precious, and besides, he didn't mind a few weevils in his corn pone. As his mother always said, "We need all the meat we can get. Besides, the damn bugs add a bit a flavor to the bread."

He put on his shirt, blotted sweat and water from his face with his shirtsleeve, ran his fingers through his hair in an attempt to tame it back from his eyes—not that it would do a damn bit of good. The heavy dark mass had a life of its own. It spilled in a wave over his brow and loose curls over his collar. Most men slicked their hair back with Macassar oil, but Chantz would have none of that. God forbid that he bow to decorum . . . fatherless bastard that he was.

The threat of more rain rumbled overhead like a portent of Chantz's intent as he moved toward the hotel, mud sucking at his boots and the afternoon humidity thick as cane syrup in his nostrils. More than a few heads turned to watch him pass—most knowing that when Chantz got that look in his eye, trouble would soon erupt. Just last month the sheriff had hauled him into jail because he'd punched Silas Stuckshead hard enough to send him flying through the dry-goods window. Certainly it was a sorry state of affairs when a man could publicly thrash a Negro child yet Chantz was the one dragged to jail for stopping the brutality.

Women up and down the wooden walks, attired in their town dresses of silks and taffetas belled over hoop frames, tittered to one another behind their ornate fans and batted their lashes at Chantz as he slogged ankle deep in the mud toward *La Madeleine*. While most of the time he found amusement in their flirtations, today they only incensed him further. Because, just like Phyllis Buley, not a one of them would publicly acknowledge that they would be more than happy to let him slide between their sheets at night.

The hotel lobby—lush with carved paneled walls where hung massive paintings depicting French hunting scenes, tapestries, and portraits of royalty—smelled of stale cigar smoke and floral perfume. There was burgundy velvet upholstered furniture piled with rug-covered pillows, and massive frilly-leafed ferns in wicker stands cluttering every corner. Crystal chandeliers imported from Versailles hung from the ceilings. The highly polished wood floors reflected the sparkling prisms like mirrors.

The scattering of hotel guests all turned to watch Chantz, hair dripping sweat and trough water, boots tracking on the floor, cross the lobby toward the *salon de cuisine*. As he paused at the sheer-draped open French doors and swept his gaze over the patrons sitting at white linen-covered tables with candles and glittering crystal and silver, the murmuring of quiet conversation faded to a heavy silence. Anticipation hovered in the air as thick as the mud on the soles of Chantz's boots.

The maître d', with a horrified expression, stepped in front of Chantz, blocking his entry. "*Monsieur,*" he purred with a thin smile, "I'm afraid there's been some mistake? You're looking for the saloon, *oui?*"

"No," he snapped, shoving the man aside. "I'm looking for Phyllis Buley."

He found her then, sitting stiff as a rake handle across from her fiancé, her lovely face beet red and her brown eyes glazed with horror. She would not, of course, meet his eyes. To do so would be a form of acknowledgment, and he highly suspected at that moment that the *last* thing she wanted to acknowledge was that Chantz Boudreaux had ever been born.

His lips curling, Chantz moved toward her.

Horace Carrington slowly stood, spilling his napkin

to the floor. His normally pale complexion bleached whiter—his lips as blue as if he'd been submersed in ice water. As his high brow shimmered with sweat, his pale blue eyes narrowed with threat. Chantz and Horace had stood toe-to-toe enough times that Chantz knew that if pressed hard enough Horace's temper would snap like dry tinder.

A hand slammed onto Chantz's shoulder, stopping him in his tracks. Fred Buley, Phyllis's father, smiled up into Chantz's eyes. Except there was no friendliness to the thin curl of Fred's mouth. And the grip on Chantz's shoulder burned into the muscle like a dagger blade.

"I wouldn't, Chantz," Fred said softly, still smiling, his bushy salt-and-pepper eyebrows drawing together.

To the spellbound spectators it must have seemed like two old friends were passing pleasantries. But Chantz recognized there was no pleasantness whatsoever in Buley's narrowed eyes. His breath smelled of the expensive bourbon he'd been drinking with his meal—a great deal of bourbon, judging by the way he slurred his words. The blue-steel color of his slicked back hair added to the effect of his gray eyes that were speaking volumes, as was the flush of anger on his jowls.

"You may be a touch on the wild side, friend, but you're not stupid. I like you, Chantz. And I know that you and my boy Andrew are quite friendly. But that won't stop me from cutting your throat if I thought you had more to say to my little girl than congratulations on her betrothal to Mr. Carrington."

Fred smoothed the front of Chantz's wrinkled shirt, then reached into his coat and withdrew a pair of Cuban cigars, tucked them into Chantz's hand. "You run on now. Folks here spent a great deal of money to enjoy their food. We wouldn't want to spoil it for them, would we? *Would* we, Chantz?" The smile again. "Good fellow. *Good-bye,* Mr. Boudreaux."

Chantz cut his eyes to Phyllis again, prim in a pink silk gown with a high collar of fine lace snug around her throat, her brown hair partially swept up with ringlets and pink ribbons spilling down her back. She looked demure and fresh as a peach blossom. Hardly the same vixen who had, the previous night, made love to him with an expertise that would shame most of Meesha's girls.

Then he looked to Carrington, still standing, fists clenched as inconspicuously as possible at his sides, jaws knotted like cypress knees. As a boy, only son of one of the wealthiest planters in the area, Horace had been a prissy little snot who got his jollies from verbal and physical cruelty to man and animal alike. As an adult, he was worse. Cruelty had become ambition to Horace . . . not to mention recreational. Chantz wondered what Fred Buley would think if he witnessed his future son-in-law hanging from wrist irons in Meesha's Pleasure Palace while naked women beat his privates with willow whips.

Hell, the two of them deserved each other.

As Chantz turned on his heels and left the salon, an explosion of excited conversation erupted behind him. Bud Bovier was right, he thought. He needed several stiff bourbons and Meesha's raunchiest whore.

The Pleasure Palace, a three-story clapboard structure painted purple with lemon-yellow shutters, was located on a bluff overlooking the river, far enough from town so when business heated to the boiling point the township wouldn't be offended. River traffic was good. Boats could dock right at Meesha's doors and clients could slip in and out of the establishment without showing their faces.

There were no boats today, however. Thanks to continued rains the river was up and fast and growing more dangerous by the hour. Chantz suspected that another couple of days of such torrents and his employer would be faced with another crop disaster. Life at Holly Plantation would, once again, become intolerable. He was damn glad Max Hollinsworth hadn't yet returned from France to see his farm sink like a leaky ship for the second time in four years. Of course, there was His Royal Pain in the Ass Tylor Hollinsworth to deal with. But Tylor was too damn stupid and lazy to care one way or another about his father's farm.

Meesha's raunchiest whore was a six-foot-tall quadroon beauty, Virginia, but the way *she* drawled it made her sound real nasty—especially after Chantz had imbibed half a bottle of the house's finest Irish whiskey purchased with the money he'd won by pounding Boris Wilcox to a pulp.

With his fingers twisted in Virginia's hair, his eyes closed and his teeth clenched and his body sweating, Chantz worked his hips hard against Virginia, who sprawled facedown across the plush bed.

Looking over her shoulder, her dark-as-night eyes admiring him as her full lips pouted, Virginia said, "You is a sweet, sweet person, Chantz, but you gots a fire in you tonight. Tylor Hollinsworth been diggin' at you agin, honey man?"

He shook his head and as Virginia rolled to her back, he sank down on her, slid his body back into hers, more gently this time. She sighed in pleasure. Her legs curled around his back as he rocked her, easy at first, then faster, until their skin shone with sweat and the smell of the act scented the air like a rich aphrodisiac. She ground her pelvis up and hard against him, swirled her tongue inside his mouth, clenched his buttocks in her long fingers until control shattered. The bed battered the wall, the sheets tore from the mattress. Her head falling back and her mouth open, Virginia clawed at his back as a cry rushed up her throat.

With a last deep thrust, Chantz spilled himself; each throb inside her was a sublime finale of the tension that had built in him throughout the day. He collapsed on her, his face buried in the crook of her neck that smelled like magnolia blossoms—sweet floral heat that made him think of sultry summer mornings . . . and something else . . .

Someone beat on the wall, and a woman's voice called, "Chantz Boudreaux, you in there?"

" 'Course that's Chantz!" another shouted. "Who else in this town bangs the damn plaster off the walls!"

Virginia's arms slid around him as she chuckled. "You is in fine form tonight, honey man. You is the only one who do that for me. I thank you for that."

"Phyllis Buley is getting married," he said against her throat.

"I heard. Horace Carrington. Meesha says she's gonna wrap up a pair of wrist irons and a blindfold and give it to Miss Phyllis for a weddin' present." She turned Chantz's face toward hers, and smiled into his eyes. "She done broke your heart, Chantz?"

He rolled to his back and stared at the ceiling and tried to reason exactly what he was feeling. Mad, mostly. He was good enough to scratch Phyllis's itch when she got one, but not good enough to spare even a glance at in public. Thinking of the money in his pants, he imagined buying himself a suit, wondered if Phyllis would be so quick to turn up her nose at him then, then he realized it would take more than a suit to impress a woman like Phyllis Buley, soon to be Carrington.

Fine. One of these days he would have enough money saved to buy his own piece of land—the money he'd won

today would help. There wasn't another overseer in the
state as good as he at raising up tall, sweet cane; even if he
had to plant and harvest by himself, he'd turn that goddamn sugarcane into a gold mine. One of these years, the
Buleys and Carringtons and all the others who looked
down their pompous noses at him would be doffing their
hats and moving off the sidewalk out of respect as he
passed.

Virginia left the bed and walked to a basin. She bathed
then moved the basin to the bed and began to gently clean
Chantz with a silk cloth and warm water. Her gaze moved
lovingly over his body.

"You been fightin' at Bovier's agin, ain't you? Dem is
some mean bruises. You gonna hurt tomorrow. Who you
done beat up now?"

"Boris Wilcox."

Her eyebrows shot up and she tutted. "He a mean man,
Chantz. Don't be foolin' with him."

"He called my mother a mud dauber."

"They is worse than bein' called a mud dauber."

"No there isn't." He left the bed, walked naked to the
window that looked out over the moving brown water of
the Mississippi.

Lights glowed from the tarpaper shanties perched on
the bluffs and banks of the river. The people who built their
houses with tarpaper and mud were shiftless, filthy, lice-
infested individuals who survived by thievery and a fair
amount of throat cutting. They robbed the planters blind
of crops and stock and were known to spread disease, including yellow fever.

No, there was nothing worse than mud daubers . . . except the yellow plague itself.

Virginia moved up behind him. Her hands slid over his

back, traced the ridges of his muscles, eased down to lightly
brush his buttocks. "One of these days, Chantz, you gonna
get what is comin' to you. Be patient. Man as honest and
hardworkin' as you will be rewarded."

"I'm not getting any younger, Virginia."

"What are you, thirty? Honey man, you just movin' into
your prime. Some day soon you gonna find yourself a
fine young woman and settle down—beget you some
young'uns—"

"No." He shook his head. His chest suddenly felt tight
and the familiar hot anger coiled in his belly. "No way in
hell would I bring a child into my world. I won't have him
looked down on because he lives out back of the big house
instead of in it. I won't have my son ridiculed by the likes of
Horace Carrington. And I sure as hell won't have him eating bad cornmeal and wearing other folks' hand-me-
downs because his father was born under the bed instead of
in it."

"You just too damn proud for your own good, Chantz.
Not to mention angry. You got too much fire burnin' in
you—"

"You saying I don't have a right to be angry?" He looked
around at her. His jaw worked.

Her dark eyes searched his. "Ain't a man or woman with
any conscience in this town who don't recognize your right
to be angry and respect you for the honorable way you've
handled yourself. You've grown to be the best damn overseer in Louisiana. You take good care of your mama. And
you're a good friend to the other planters. I hear 'em talk,
Chantz. Most of 'em regard you highly. Very highly."

He grinned. "Obviously not so highly as to let me court
their daughters."

"Phyllis Buley ain't worth you. She might be prettier

than most, but she got the heart of a rattlesnake. You want that kind of woman raisin' your babies?"

Sliding her long arms around his waist, she breathed into his ear and said in a low and husky voice tinged with a touch of sadness, "I dread the day you find the right woman, Chantz. 'Cause if you love as intensely as you crave respect and success, I won't ever get to hold you in my arms again. Honey man, that is gonna be the saddest day of my life."

Chantz smoked one of Fred Buley's cigars as he headed back to Bovier's Livery to collect his horse and supplies. The night was made blacker by the clouds lying low and threatening more rain. The streets were empty, the businesses dark, but for the hotel where Chantz paused to look through the high, wide windows into the *salon de cuisine,* at the diners dressed in their finery and enjoying food that looked more like works of art than something to load in their stomachs. The smell of baking bread drifted out to remind him that he hadn't eaten since breakfast.

His body was starting to suffer from the pounding he'd taken that afternoon from Boris Wilcox, who was no doubt hurting a hell of a lot worse than Chantz. Son of a bitch deserved it, for more reasons than his calling Chantz's mother a mud dauber.

Recent rumors had been circulating that Wilcox had become involved with the paddy rollers, a group of cutthroat poor white men who helped subsidize their sorry lives by coercing slaves into pilfering pigs, calves, sheep, wheat, and corn—anything they could get their hands on, including household items, believing that in turn the rollers would help them buy their way out of bondage—or escape to the North. The paddy rollers sold the stolen goods at the market for a tidy profit. Those same rollers then took sadistic delight in chasing down the runaways they were supposedly helping with blood-hungry dogs in order to collect the rewards.

If Wilcox ever messed with Holly workers, the beating Chantz had given him earlier would pale in comparison.

The men moved out of the alley darkness so fast Chantz barely had time to look around before he was grabbed by the hair and shirt collar and slammed against the Mercantile brick wall. The night exploded in white light and pain that ripped through his head like a lightning strike. Fists drove into his back and ribs, kicking the air out of his lungs. Then he was spun around—knuckles cracked across his cheek, sending him careening backward over several empty hogsheads where he landed facedown in the mud.

He struggled to lift his head, to think—too damn much pain, he couldn't breathe—

A booted foot crashed into his side with enough impact to lift him off the ground and fling him onto his back. Again, harder, so he writhed and twisted in an attempt to escape the pain and the kick he knew was coming. Rolling onto his belly, he tried to rock onto his knees.

"That's it," a voice laughed. "Crawl, Boudreaux. That's where scum like you belong. In the dirt on his belly."

Then someone grabbed a fistful of his hair, yanked back his head, and hauled him to his knees.

He heard himself groan as the impact on his face snapped his head back. His body floated backward, hit the ground like dead weight, arms useless as unconsciousness crawled through his brain, and pain like sharp teeth tore through his head. He tried to fight it—attempted to open his eyes that were blinded by mud and blood.

Hands clutched at his clothes, dug into his pockets

"What the devil is going on back there?" someone shouted from the street.

"Get the hell out of here," a voice near him urged . . .

He floated on pain.

"Chantz? Good God, what have they done to you? Chantz? Can you hear me?"

He struggled to open his eyes, glimpsed Andrew Buley's hazy, shocked features hovering over him. Twisting his muddy fist into Drew's shirt, he managed through his bleeding teeth, "Son of a bitch stole my money."

Two

He thought the roaring was in his head.

Chantz slowly opened his eyes, anticipating another stab of intense pain between his temples. How long had he floated in and out of consciousness? One day? Two? There were vague memories of Andrew Buley hauling him in a wagon to the shanty in the woods where Chantz buried himself when he needed a place to escape . . . or meet women—the women like Phyllis Buley who wouldn't be caught dead with him in public.

The roaring again, like constant thunder. The bed under him vibrated.

Gritting his teeth against the pain in his side, Chantz struggled to sit up. The bare room spun around him and the effort to breathe sent a knife blade of heat through his chest. He recalled, then, what had happened to him. Recalled lying helplessly on his back while someone dug the money from his pocket. Boris Wilcox? Horace Carrington? Tylor Hollinsworth?

He would find out, of course, if it was the last thing he ever did.

He finally managed to stand. Pain cut up under his rib so sharply the breath rushed from him. The open doorway rocked from side to side like a boat on troubled water. He staggered toward it, gripping his ribs, swallowing the copper-tasting old blood in his mouth.

The shanty's small main room consisted of a fireplace with hook and iron pot for cooking, a sideboard, a crude table, and two ladder-back chairs with husk seats. Chantz plowed into the table, knocking a tin cup to the floor, leaned heavily on it until he could collect his balance enough to focus on the door.

The table beneath him trembled like a terrified rabbit.

Realization crawled in his throbbing head, and a flash of panic speared through him. He stumbled to the cabin's door and flung it open. Heat drove him back momentarily as he did his best to focus on the surreal world outside the shanty. Briefly, he wondered if he was hallucinating again.

Dense black and green clouds boiled just over the high tree-tops, turning the daylight into a sickly dim haze. The air felt ominously still and thick with impending rain. More rain, by the looks of the saturated ground and the waterlogged branches of trees drooping toward the earth.

Chantz stepped from the shanty and moved unsteadily along the wheel-rutted tracks, his boots splashing through standing water. Breaking into a slow run, he followed the ruts to the road that was pitiful during the best of weather. Now it was a mire of mud that sucked at his feet as he followed it around the bend and—

The roaring cacophony vibrated his eardrums as he stared out at the roiling brown water that was fast eating up the earth in its wake. The deep crack of snapping timber punctuated the violence and power of the driving, boiling force, followed by an explosion of thunder and a sudden wall of wind that nearly knocked him from his feet. With it came rain driving fiercely, skewering his skin like needles. He couldn't breathe, and he was forced to turn his back to the wind and brace his legs to keep from being driven into the water.

That's when he saw the woman.

Surely he was imagining things—hallucinating again, thanks to his brains being beaten to a pulp. He blinked and, shielding his eyes from the rain, focused on the water again.

Caught like flotsam amid a dam of brush and timbers, she floated facedown in the yellow, turbid waters of the storm-driven Mississippi, her dark red hair like a silken web around her head. The raging currents had stripped the clothes from her body. Her flesh glowed like moonlight, pale as alabaster, against the swirling mud.

"Jesus," he whispered.

No chance in Hades she could be alive. He'd be stupid to risk wading into that torrent, especially in his sorry condition. Although she was caught up in a brake of snagged-up brush, he knew the dam could and would give at any moment.

And if she wasn't dead now, she would be.

He cursed.

Rain drove into Chantz's back as he stumbled to the water and waded in up to his chest. Debris slammed into him with the force of a mule's kick, driving him under. Suddenly the world became a rushing brown wall that sucked him deep and clawed his face with tree branches. He fought them, lungs aching, legs kicking; he planted his feet and lunged upward. His head breaking the water, he gasped for air and searched for the woman—there!—his hands reached for her, tangled in her hair, drew her toward him until he could wrap his arms around her.

Hauling her out of the water and onto the shoal, he collapsed to his knees. The woman sprawled beneath him, facedown, skin pale as pearl, hair a fiery skein of wet silk in his hands. Her flesh felt warm, still. He pressed his dark hands against her slender back and began pumping, cursing.

"Breathe, dammit. Breathe."

She moved. Just slightly. Moaned.

"Breathe."

She vomited, then gasped. Her arms thrashed, as if she were still fighting the water. "I won't!" she cried. "I won't do it, damn you. You can't make me!" With a violent shudder, she lay still again.

Blinking the rain from his eyes, Chantz carefully rolled her over, swept the tangle of hair from her colorless face. Blinked again and covered his eyes with one hand—he'd never believed in specters, or haints, as Rosie liked to call the undead, but damn if he wasn't looking at one now.

The vision of the young woman's flawless, stunning features sat him back on his heels. The driving rain felt suffocating; focused on the churning river of water and mud, the thought occurring to him that maybe he'd died in that goddamn alley. Maybe he was on a spiral straight to hell and this face was the first to greet him: a succubus. Temptation personified. The embodiment of seduction. The female serpent of Eden who drove intelligent grown men to a fever pitch of sexual stupidity.

But Maureen Broussard was dead, fifteen years ago this summer.

The woman groaned again.

His gaze flashed down her naked body. His mouth

turned dry and his skin hot, despite the bite of the cool rain and wind that whipped the roaring water into white peaks.

Chantz, gritting his teeth against the pain in his own abused body, lifted the woman into his arms, tossed her over his shoulder, and made his way, stumbling, along the washed-out road-bed to the shanty nestled under the sprawling oak trees. He carried her into the bedroom, dumped her on the bed, and flung a sheet across her, backed away as if her presence were as threatening as a timber rattler prepared to strike.

Sinking back against the wall, he closed his eyes and waited for the pounding of his heart to ease.

As thunder shook the house, memories stirred. He hadn't pondered on them for years; though, occasionally, when he rode by the blackened ruins of the deserted old plantation on the high grounds overlooking the river, he would briefly allow himself to recall the occurrence that had crumbled the grandest house in the area. Not just the area, but one of the finest homes in Louisiana. Belle Jarod. Jewel of the River Road. A palace built by a man's obsession and love for a woman who would ultimately bleed him dry of his last dollar and dignity and shatter his heart, not to mention his sanity.

Chantz frowned and walked again to the bed. He lit the lamp next to it, then stood staring down into the woman's face. His skin warmed.

It wasn't possible. Maureen Broussard was dead. Max Hollinsworth had buried her. Or what was left of her after the fire that burned most of Belle Jarod to the ground. Max wasn't a man given much to any emotion but spite and meanness, but in this instance he'd fallen to his knees and blubbered like a baby into his hands. Chantz had always wondered why. Because Max had truly been in love with his best friend's wife? Or because he was burying his only hope of getting his greedy hands on Belle Jarod?

Knowing Max, it was the latter. Then again, Maureen Jarod Broussard had a way of looking into a man's eyes and upending his soul. She had been a whore with a tempter's body and an angel's face.

Something stirred deep down as Chantz studied the woman's features. Only, he realized as he stood there with the roar of the river trembling the house that this was no woman. Not yet. She was an eyelash flutter from crossing that finite line into womanhood. Oh, she had the body, all right. The mouth that could tempt a saint. The smooth as marble flesh that made men think of lapping sweet rich cream. But there was yet a softness about her features that made him think of the young women who attended the St. Elizabeth's Academy for Young Ladies in New Orleans, the ones who coyly smiled and batted their lashes at him when he rode by.

Again, his mind tumbled back to that sultry afternoon, not unlike this one, his lazing under the sprawling, twisted old oak while the oppressive heat of the day made his clothes cling to his skin, while the whirring of cicadas in the grass and trees pulsated like a slow heartbeat in the heavy air.

He and Max Hollinsworth had been returning to Holly House from Baton Rouge. Max had risked one last visit to Maureen, thinking her husband, Jack, would not be returning from New Orleans until the next day. Sitting there in the sweltering heat, listening to the deep growl of thunder from an approaching storm, Chantz had heard them laugh. Saw Maureen dance through her bedroom balcony door dressed only in a shift, so thin she might as well have been wearing nothing, her torrent of dark red hair pouring over her white breasts and shoulders.

She had looked down and seen him there, under the tree, and her ruby lips had curled, her lashes had lowered.

She'd leaned over the balcony rail, giving him an unob-structed view of her scantily clad bosom.

"Why, Chantz Boudreaux, you're becoming quite the handsome young man. You got a lady friend, Chantz?"

"No, ma'am," he'd answered, and her smile had grown and her eyes had narrowed.

"That's too bad. Come see me sometime and I'll give you a few pointers on what it takes to charm a woman off her feet."

Then he'd watched Max Hollinsworth tear away what little clothes she wore and mount her right there against the wall. And even as Max thrust himself into her, she had turned her eyes down to Chantz's and smiled.

Jack Broussard had found them that way.

Juliette. Could it be? All grown up, a woman herself now? The child who had clung to his neck and screamed for her papa as flames licked so high into the sky it seemed even the thunderous clouds blazed with them.

Had Juliette come home, back to Belle Jarod, at long last?

Returning to the main room, Chantz prodded at the embers in the hearth and tossed in a handful of tinder. The flames soon fingered the twilight shadows, as lulling as the drone of rain on the roof.

There had been times over the last years when the slight-est hint of smoke had roused those best forgotten memo-ries. Mostly he remembered the silence and the stillness, like those moments before a lightning strike. Remembered the expression on Jack Broussard's face during those mo-ments after he'd found his wife and best friend together—his eyes pools of pain. More pain than anger . . . initially.

The thought had struck Chantz in that moment of look-ing into Jack's tormented face, as Chantz stood in Belle's open front door with storm winds scattering leaves around his legs and over Belle's cypress floors, that if loving a woman could so unman a man then he would have to think long and hard about doing it. He'd reminded himself as he grew older, most men didn't love their women like Jack loved Maureen. Then again . . . there weren't a hell of a lot of women like Maureen. None, as a matter of fact, and that was probably a damn good thing. Man simply wasn't created with enough willpower to resist her kind of temptation.

Chantz located a bottle of whiskey in the sideboard, tucked behind a tin of coffee and a jar of Rosie's kraut.

Taking a long drink straight from the bottle, he turned his eyes again to the bedroom door.

Surely he would return to that room and discover he had dreamed that he fished Maureen Broussard from the river. No, not Maureen. Couldn't be. He'd helped Max bury Jack's wife under the old live oak overlooking the grand spread of cane Jack and his Negroes had sweated over all summer.

Could it be . . . Juliette? The exquisitely beautiful child with untameable hair and flashing eyes like green fire?

Chantz took another deep drink and sank into a chair.

He could still recall the day he'd first discovered that there was more than friendship going on between Max and Maureen. Rosie, Maxwell's cook, had been occupied by kitchen duties, and Chantz, only fourteen at the time, had been summoned up from the field and ordered to "occupy" the little girl while Max and Maureen discussed "business" in the house.

Juliette had been a handful. Although Chantz was no stranger to children, often overseeing the Negro children while their parents worked, Juliette had tried his patience to extremes. She'd been saucy, rebellious, and so full of excess energy he had been hard pressed not to lock her in the storehouse. She'd managed to fall down Holly's steps before he could catch her, severely cutting her knee, and although her lower lip had pouted in a charming way, not a solitary tear had fallen. Chantz had hauled her in his arms to Max's office with the intention of summoning her mother, but the sounds he'd heard through the door had frozen him in his tracks.

So he'd carried her off to the kitchen located a distance from the house where Rosie had clucked and tutted and murmured under her breath that "somebody gonna git killed one of these days over that hussy woman."

Juliette hadn't so much as whimpered as Rosie ministered to her injury, and Chantz had rewarded her with a piece of ho'hound sweetened with molasses candy. She'd rewarded him with a kiss on his cheek and a *"Merci, Monsieur."*

His head and body pounding with pain and whiskey thrumming in a slow heat through his veins, Chantz could almost feel Juliette's lips on his cheek again—except those lips didn't belong to a child any longer. Far from it.

Damn, he was tired. He'd come to this deep-woods shanty to spend a few days alone. Rest and solitude went a long way toward extinguishing the temper that more often than not these days got the better of him. He'd had it up to his throat with Tylor Hollinsworth. One more slur out of his mouth and Chantz was going to drive his fist through Tylor's teeth. Or worse. And that's what had started to bother him the most. His hatred for the soft son of a bitch was going to prompt him to murder if he didn't get control of himself.

But Tylor Hollinsworth was going to be the least of Chantz's problems. Judging by the looks of that river, Holly House Plantation, and its crops, were going to be several feet under water. Max Hollinsworth had been scrambling to recover from the flood that wiped him out two years ago.

This disaster could put him in the poor house, and he was going to want to take out his anger on someone . . . and that someone was usually Chantz.

No doubt about it, plenty were going to suffer under Max's tirades. The thought of it made Chantz turn up his bottle and drink until it felt as if his throat and stomach were going to ignite.

Christ, he wanted to sleep. He needed a bed. The whiskey pooled like thick molasses between his ears, and if he didn't lie down he was going to fall down.

But there was a woman in his bed. A naked woman. With the face and body of a whoring witch who was probably burning in Hell at that very moment for her wicked ways—who had no doubt dragged a few souls down with her—other women's husbands, mostly.

Tossing the empty bottle aside, he returned to the bed. She slept still, her face turned toward the lamplight, her long lashes like rusty feathers upon her smooth cheeks. There had only been one other woman put on God's earth with a mouth like that, a cupid's bow pink as a pomegranate, the tips slightly turned up making her look always as if she were about to break into a smile. And the chin—obstinate. The brows sweeping as egret wings.

"Open your eyes," he said softly, a bit drunkenly, he realized as the room shifted dizzily. "Open your eyes and I'll know for certain if you're Maureen's little girl."

They would be turbulent, of course. Stubborn. Challenging. Lustful. At odds with her angelic features. Sparkling pools of heartbreak.

The bed creaked as he eased down beside her, stretched his body out, groaned as his head rested on the goosedown pillow.

The woman shifted, rolled, and nestled against him. Her

lips parted with a soft sigh. Her eyes opened, briefly, a flash of color that reminded him of the deep rich green of magnolia leaves. Then she drifted off again.

Chantz listened to her breathe, felt the warmth of her body ooze through him, easing the raw pain of his injuries. As the rain drove harder against the roof, he closed his eyes and returned to that sultry summer afternoon, with the heavy scent of jasmine in the still air, and saw Maureen on the Belle Jarod balcony, peering down at him, smile and eyes like temptation personified . . .

Only it wasn't Maureen, but the woman next to him whose soft, tangled hair coiled over his chest. Whose complexion glowed pale as magnolia blossoms. Whose full naked breasts were like china globes in the golden light.

And it wasn't Max Hollinsworth who took her against the wall. But himself.

For a blurry, confused moment Chantz thought he'd dreamed the whole thing: the incident in the alley . . . the flood that was surely, in that very moment, washing Maxwell's sugarcane into the Gulf of Mexico . . . fishing a red-haired siren out of the water.

No such luck because the siren stood in the bedroom doorway draped in his only clean shirt, hair a fiery shadow around her pale face. There was no mistaking those eyes. They were enormous and flashing with challenge. On any other woman her red lips would look sullen. On this woman, however, they were as alluring as the sweet meat of a ripe plum. And her legs . . . long and slender beneath his shirttails. Apparently she didn't care in the least that her knees were showing.

Stiff and sore, Chantz raised up on one elbow, watched as she approached him, cautious, her hands fisted and pressed to her breasts as if the act would somehow hide the way she filled out his shirt. She appeared mesmerized by him and studied his face as if she expected to discover the meaning of life in his eyes.

"Hello," he said softly.

She jumped and backed away a step, tipped her head to one side, and studied him intensely.

"You want to tell me what you were doing in the river?"

She shook her head, no.

"Can you talk?" He grinned.

Her expression became as dark and turbulent as the storm crashing over the cabin. Still, she advanced, stopped by the bed so the light of the oil lamp cast her profile in soft gold. Her hand reached out. Fingertips brushed his hair, touched the swelling on his brow, lightly traced the curve of his cheek, hesitated briefly at the laceration she found there—she frowned—then continued to his chin that needed shaving.

He caught her wrist; although she flinched and acted as if she would attempt to flee, he held on.

"Shhh," he soothed her, and eased his grip on her arm. "I'm not going to hurt you."

Lifting her wrist to his mouth, he pressed the soft, pale underside to his lips, as if he were attempting to calm the child he had once held, her face smeared with soot and flushed by heat, eyes streaming with tears and rain. Then he had made a funny noise with his lips against her wrist—as his own mother had done when he was a child and frightened—then her light, melodious laughter had bubbled up through her whimpers and her tears had dried.

But he made no funny noise now. She was no longer a child, after all. Far from it.

He brushed the delicate pale place with a kiss that made

her gasp. Made her soft lips part. Made her eyes that were full of lamp fire grow wider and brighter.

And something shifted in his chest: an unfamiliar emotion that made his senses expand to a keen pain that brought a rise of sweat to his flesh and robbed him of breath.

"Juliette," he murmured, "you've grown up."

The sound of her name drew a harsh breath from her. A look of shock followed by fear twisted her features and she lunged away, breaking his hold on her arm. She spun on her heels and fled the room. The next thing he heard was the front door slamming open against the wall and the drone of hard rain.

Chantz rolled from the bed and ran to the open door. He struck out through the rain, stumbled, clutched his side, forged through the night darkness in pursuit, sliding in the deepening mud and splashing through broad puddles. What the devil was she about? If she wasn't careful she would find herself in the river again. He sure as hell didn't intend to dive into the swollen Mississippi in the dark.

The growl of the roiling water magnified. He ran harder, his heartbeat quickening as he lost sight of her amid the trees—hell, maybe she was a ghost after all—then she reappeared, just a flash of white before dissolving again into the darkness.

"Stop!" he yelled. Useless. The rain and river drowned the sound of his voice.

He saw her then, at the bluff's ledge, shirt whipped by the wind and gnashed by the rain. Christ, she was going to jump—

"Juliette, don't do it!" he shouted.

The sound of his voice brought her head around. She stared at him like a terrified doe, as if with the slightest provocation she would bound off the precipice into oblivion.

"Get the hell away from there!" he told her.

"Stay away from me! I'll jump!"

He moved toward her. She backed away, until little more than air kept her from plummeting toward the river. He froze and looked hard into her frightened yet determined eyes.

"Why are you doing this?" he demanded.

"I won't go back. You can't make me!"

"Go back where? What are you talking about?"

She looked over her shoulder, at the water below.

He moved closer. Closer. Stopping short as she turned her eyes on him again. Her white face looked sad. Hopelessness weighed on her slender shoulders.

"I would rather be dead!" she cried, and tottered. Her arms flailed.

Chantz lunged, snagged the shirt in his fingers.

Her weight drove the air from him as they hit the ground and rolled, over and over, coming to rest at last in a tangle of pine needles and jasmine vines.

Her fists pounded him. *"Je vous maudis! Allez à l'enfer!"* she cried, and drove her knee hard into his groin.

Gritting his teeth against the knife-blade pain that ripped through his loins, Chantz pinned her arms to the ground and wedged his knees between her thighs.

"Be still," he said through his teeth. "Behave before I give you a reason to—stop squirming, dammit!"

Her struggling suddenly stopped. But for the rapid rise and fall of her breasts she lay motionless, her gaze fixed on his, her head resting within a cloud of crushed pale jasmine flowers that scented the air intoxicatingly sweet. Rain beaded on her pale face and ripe lips like tiny dark diamonds.

Most young women in her position at that moment would be fainting of humiliation and fright. Not this one. Damn if she didn't act as if his body on hers was the most natural thing in the world. Damn if she didn't challenge him with her eyes and the pout of her soft mouth that he ached to kiss in that moment even more than he cared to breathe.

Cursing, he rolled away, struggled to his feet, and pulled her up with him. She swung. He ducked. She kicked. He sidestepped, caught her foot in midair and flipped her backward so she sprawled in a puddle.

Had he been a gentleman, he would have averted his eyes. But he wasn't a gentleman any more than she was the daughter of a nun. So he stared. And she stared. Rain ran down her face and body and pooled beneath her where the ends of her hair floated with the jasmine blooms.

Finally, and with a guttural curse, he reached for her again, locked his fingers around her wrist, and hauled her onto her feet.

She followed begrudgingly, feet dragging, occasionally sinking her heels into the mud only to have her arm yanked hard enough to nearly topple her. As they neared the shanty's open front door she gave one last heave against his hold then surrendered. He shoved her into the shanty then kicked the door closed behind them. The dim light of the lantern shimmered off her drenched body and turned his shirt transparent.

"Sit," he ordered her, and nodded toward a chair. When she looked frantically toward the door once again, he pointed one finger at the tip of her nose. "Forget it, sweet cheeks. I'll hog-tie you and hang you from a hook. I'm not a patient man and you've exceeded my endurance. Next time you run out that door I'll chase you down and toss your butt in the river myself and good damn riddance. Any woman who would stoop to kneeing a man who is trying to save her life deserves to be bait for gators."

Her eyes flashed. She swallowed a retort, then turned her back to him and glared into the fire.

"Sit!" he shouted, making her jump and grab a chair which she plunked in front of the fire. She dropped into it and drew her knees up to her chest. Despite the warmth of the night, her body began to shake.

"I'm waiting," he said as he dragged his muddy shirt off over his head.

Her head tipped slightly, and she glanced at him over her shoulder. Her eyelashes, spiked with rain, lowered as she acknowledged him, shirtless, hands on his hips as he regarded her through his dripping hair.

With a lift of one eyebrow, she said, "I'm not accustomed to conversing with half-naked men."

Sweet Mary, she even sounded like her mother. There was a touch of roughness to her voice that made a man think of forbidden passion in clandestine meeting places.

His mouth curled. "I'm more than accustomed to conversing with naked women, so if you would care to give me that shirt you're wearing I'll be more than happy to put it on—wouldn't want to offend your sensibilities, after all."

Her cheeks flushed with hot color. Yet, she did not look away. Her perusal took a slow journey down his body, hesitated at his muddy booted feet, then back up again, to his mouth, then his eyes. An intensity passed over her features, then, with effort, she turned away and gave him her shoulder.

"Where am I?" she asked in a monotone.

"I fished you out of the river. And you're welcome, by the way. Now I want an explanation. Who the blazes are you running from and why?"

"I hardly think that is your concern, *Monsieur*."

"The hell you say."

She flashed him a slanted, angry look. Glimpses of her mother again. He'd seen Maureen's tantrums turned on Jack Broussard enough to know there was a firebrand lurking within.

"Juliette, when a woman contemplates throwing herself into a raging river, there had better be a damn good reason for it."

"How do you know my name?"

"Don't change the subject."

"I didn't ask you to fish me from the damnable river, did I?"

He flung his shirt as hard as he could toward the fire.

She flinched, drew her shoulders back, and looked stiffly around at the shanty. "This house is rather pitiful, isn't it? I assume you're poor?"

"Actually this is my summer home. I have a château in Biloxi where I keep a staff of twenty and a stable of imported warm bloods."

She smiled at the fire. "I doubt it. There's nothing remotely refined about you. Except perhaps your boots. Those breeches are of coarse material as is this pitifully thin shirt I'm wearing. Your skin is much too dark, which means you spend most of your time out of doors. You're a farmer, perhaps. A farmer who too often works with his shirt off." Turning her eyes back to his, she added, "A gentleman of breeding would not have that sort of musculature."

"You've seen a great many gentlemen with their shirts off, have you?"

That, of course, wouldn't have surprised him, not if she was anything at all like her mother morally.

"You're a ruffian," she told him. "Judging by your injuries, and the scars on your knuckles, you like to fight. You probably participate in those dreadful bare-knuckle punching matches where men smoke and drink to extremes and place wagers on who will knock out whom first. Where is your wife?"

"Not married." His eyes narrowed.

Her lips curved and she looked back at him again. "I'm not surprised."

He frowned. "What's that supposed to mean?"

"I find you . . . raw. Too hard. Too . . . fierce."

"And you're an ill-tempered, ungrateful spoiled brat who needs her bottom smacked."

He moved to her side, his face burning, not just from the pain of his "dreadful bare-knuckle punching" but because she could so easily determine by a glance what he was.

Lifting a tendril of her damp hair, he curled it around his fingers. "You look like a whore I once knew," he said in a soft, husky voice meant to taunt her. "She had hair like this. Like blood fire. Wild, untamable curls that she would occasionally try to twist up in coils and pin with pretty combs that her lovers brought her from Paris and London. Didn't do her much good, though. That damn hair had a life of its own. Sooner or later it would fall like hot-copper threads over her shoulders.

"She had skin like yours. Smooth and pale as polished pearl. She enjoyed showing it off. Wore her dresses cut so low the whole of Louisiana held its breath when she walked. She had a mouth like the heart of a sweet ripe plum. I heard that one kiss of her lips would ruin a man. Make him crazy with a need to own her.

"She finally snared herself a wealthy Frenchman. A man who didn't care that she'd bedded most of the men in Louisiana and Mississippi, too. He had the crazy notion that he could change her. He built her a house fit for a queen. Spent a king's fortune on clothes and jewels and

horseflesh to occupy her afternoons while he was out overseeing his cane crops.

"But when a woman is born to hunger for a man between her legs, no amount of pretty threads and dazzling
jewels are gonna keep her from prowling. And prowl she
did. Right up until the day her husband came home unexpectedly and found her with another man."

Silence, but for the snap of burning kindling.

Her shoulders looked rigid, as if she would disintegrate if
he so much as touched her. He caught her chin with the tip
of his finger and turned her face toward his. Her green eyes
were glassy; tears streamed down her white cheeks, wet
threads painted gold by the firelight. Her lower lip quivered.

In that moment he felt awash with the same hunger that
must have driven a thousand men mindless with the ache
to have her mother—not just to bed her, but to possess her,
body and soul. The craving rushed through his blood like
white heat, worse than any niggling of lust he had ever experienced for Phyllis Buley and those like her who thought
toying with a man of low birth with dirt under his fingernails was exciting and dangerous.

His hand slid around her head, tunneled through her
tangled hair; he drew her out of the chair and against him,
so close he could feel her warm breath against his mouth.
Her body heat curled over his damp skin like slow moist
tongues of fire.

She didn't move, didn't breathe, just stared up into his
eyes, hers wide and unblinking. Her body felt fragile and
tense and trembling. Her breasts within the thin barrier of
his shirt pressed against his naked chest, and he felt her
heart beat against his.

Reason flurried in his brain, and he did his best to rouse
that child image of a pouting little minx eating ho'hound

candy and skipping in the sunlight like a vibrant butterfly, but that pretty picture coalesced into the supple warm body in his arms, stirring up sensations that made him hard and aching in a way he had never ached. Desire felt as out of control as the river rampaging beyond its boundaries eating everything up in its path.

He drew her closer. She struggled, briefly, until his hands twisted her hair so tightly she could but stand, frozen, her eyes burning into his. "What the devil were you doing in that river, Juliette?" His breath touched her lips and she shivered.

"Going home," she said in her faintly husky voice. "To Belle Jarod."

"Darlin', there is no Belle Jarod to go home to, or didn't your daddy ever tell you that story?"

"I'll live in a shanty—"

"No you won't. You're not a shanty kind of woman, Miss Broussard. But you didn't answer my question. Why were you out in this storm—"

"Because I like it," she declared with a defiant flash of her eyes. "I enjoy the power. It makes me feel vibrantly alive."

"I think you're just a little bit crazy. I think you'd look God right in his eyes and defy Him to his face, if you could. Is that what you're doing when you're playing with lightning, Juliette? You challenging God to strike you dead?"

"What I do with my soul, *Monsieur*, is no concern of yours."

Her lips parted with a murmured French curse as she fixed him with a look that was as damning as it was challenging. He suspected he could tear out her hair by fistfuls and she wouldn't shed so much as a tear just to spite him.

Thunder rolled and memories stirred—long forgotten. Her face blurred into another, sweating and panting upon bloody sheets, her screams as piercing as the lightning thrusting through the boiling clouds.

"You were born on a night much like this one," he told her, his voice soft and distant even to his own ears. "My own mother was there, bathing Maureen's brow with rose-scented water. I stood outside the door, watching it all. I was eleven at the time but I had already seen at least fifty babies born but never ever to the anticipation of this one.

"I'd never seen a man as proud as your daddy. He'd invited his closest friends to share in the occasion. While they laughed and slapped one another on the back and raised fluted crystal glasses of French champagne in celebration, not just for the birth but because that summer had brought Jack the finest crop of cane in the parish, thunder and lightning shook Belle's foundation like it was made of tarpaper.

"An old slave name Mavney crouched between Maureen's legs. She was seventy at the time, little more than a bag of bones, with hair white as dogwood petals. She'd pray in one breath. The next she'd roll her frightened eyes toward my mother and swear there was a curse on Maureen's soul for the devils to be dancing so fiercely over the house."

Chantz touched Juliette's full lower lip with his finger, traced the curve of it, feeling again the odd sentiment that had sluiced through his chest as Mavney lifted the bloody child in her hands. The night had fallen still and quiet, heat pulsing the air. She'd slapped the babe hard, waiting for the squall of life. Nothing.

"That's when lightning struck the tree at the top of the hill," he said into her eyes that were as spellbound as they were beautiful and willful and roiling with emotion that he could feel heating her body pressed against his. "Light speared through that room so heated and brilliant we were blinded. Until her dying breath Mavney declared that bolt of lightning speared right into that child, filling her with a heart and spirit of restlessness, fire, and devilment.

"Now here you are again, Juliette, all grown up, dancing in the dark with lightning, devilment a tumult in your eyes."

Lowering his head over hers, his voice a low scratch in his throat that felt so tight he couldn't breathe, he whispered, "I got a feeling that all hell is about to break loose again, and damn if I don't already have one foot in the pit. Then again, I've walked the fine line between heaven and hell all my life. Why should this be any different?"

He tipped his mouth over hers, hesitated, still looking into the dark green spheres of her eyes—waiting, waiting for what?—then he moved his lips over hers with a pressure that forced back her head.

A trembling passed through her. Her hands fluttered then flattened against his shoulders. And although her lips parted allowing him to sweep his tongue inside her, she did not kiss him back. Her eyelids slid closed. A whimper escaped her. She went heavy in his arms as if every bone in her body had liquefied. He was forced to slide one arm around her waist to keep her on her feet.

His mind whirled, intoxicated as hell, not by the whiskey he had imbibed earlier, but by the taste of her on his tongue. A sense of desperation overcame him, as if he'd unwittingly stepped with both feet into that hell pit and realized too late that his soul was doomed. But not only that. Mavney had been right. Whatever bolt of lightning had streaked into that babe's body that storming night burned there still. It jolted him with an intensity that gripped his heart and sent fire streaking through his blood.

Releasing her suddenly, he stepped away.

Slowly, her eyes opened and fixed him with an intensity that held him paralyzed and fighting the insane need to reach for her again. Deep color flushed her face, and for an infinitesimal moment a vulnerability flashed in her eyes that left him feeling as if Boris Wilcox had gut punched him again.

Then she slapped his face, rocking him back on his heels.

Spinning on her bare heels, she ran to the door, flung it open. The rain slashed the trees and ground and the roar and tremble of the river made the tin cup on the floor vibrate with staccato plinks.

Did she expect him to stop her again? he wondered with a mounting sense of frustration and anger—her slap burning his cheek like fire. The wet wind whipped her mass of fiery hair around her shoulders and molded his shirt to her body. The words were there, on the tip of his tongue. Gritting his teeth he forced them back and told himself to let her go. To the very pit of his soul he knew she was trouble. With the taste of her still in his mouth, warming his blood like fine bourbon, he knew if he stopped her now he was a lost man . . . if he wasn't already.

Yet . . . she didn't go. Very slowly she turned. Her face shone with rain spray and the fine tendrils of her hair clung to her cheeks red as claw marks upon her white skin. She looked, he thought, like a soul sentenced to die.

Then she closed the door against the rain.

" 'Tis irony," came her voice, slightly tremulous. "I've loathed my mother these many years for what she was, for the grief and humiliation she caused my father. She broke his heart. Shattered his sanity. I was a constant reminder of her to him, and I hated her with fresh vigor each time I looked into his eyes and watched his love for me eclipsed by her memory."

Her hair, damp and windblown, tangled with pine needles and the crushed blooms of the jasmine in which they had tumbled, spilled over her shoulders as she moved toward him, releasing the buttons one by one on his shirt. It slid off her shoulders, down her arms, catching at the bend of her elbows. Her breasts were high and full and painted by firelight, her nipples like dusky rosebuds. Chantz felt his mouth go dry. His crotch grew tight—so damn tight he thought he would explode.

Stopping before him, she turned her wide eyes up to his. Her lower lip trembled. Tears shimmered. "Now I find myself desperate enough to sacrifice my body not to mention my self-respect. . . . And I wonder now what might have happened in my mother's life to drive her to such an indignity.

"I'll do anything," she admitted in a broken whisper. "Anything you ask if you'll take me away from here. Far away. I have no money with which to barter, *Monsieur*. But surely there is a way—to convince you?"

She pressed her trembling body against his, rose on her tip-toes and brushed her lips against his—warm, wet, tasting like her tears. As her hands twisted into his hair and drew him into the kiss, he felt as breathless as if he had plunged again into the dangerous river current.

Groaning, he wrapped his arms around her, body hard and inflamed, control obliterated. She tore her mouth from his and gasped, eyes wide and head fallen back, her expression one of bewilderment and surprise; soft French words he could not understand sighed through her lips.

A wave of aching tenderness rolled through him, and something else . . . The same emotion that had speared him before, warm and protective and . . . possessive.

Pulling her arms from around his neck, he eased her

back, gave her a little shake, then slid the shirt up her arms and over her shoulders, pulled it closed over her breasts. Cradling her chin in the crook of his finger, he tipped back her head so he could look into her confused eyes.

"The next time you offer yourself to a man, darlin', it better be out of love, because nothing is worth this indignity."

A ghost of gratitude touched her eyes. Suddenly she flung herself into his arms again, her own locked around his neck and her warm breath falling against his ear. "*Merci, Monsieur.* Thank you." She kissed his cheek—warm moist lips pressed against his skin.

His arms curled around her, tightly. His eyes closed. His heart stuttered . . . his body ached.

The door exploded open.

Chantz flung Juliette away as he was hit across the face with the butt of a rifle, spinning him against the wall where he slid to the floor. Beyond the scuffling of feet and the shouting of men's voices, he could hear Juliette screaming. Struggling to sit up, to shake off the pain and the unconsciousness that yawned beneath him, he focused on the blurry face above him, blinked as it grew sharper. Son of a—

Tylor Hollinsworth, a wet coil of dark hair spilling over one blue eye, grinned down at him. "I declare, Chantz, I don't know whether to shake your hand or kill you."

"Leave him alone!" Juliette screamed. "He hasn't done anything—"

"On one hand, you've managed to capture my elusive little bird of a fiancée. On the other, I find you with your filthy hands on her body—and her half-naked. What am I to think? A stupid mistake like this could cost you your job, you know, not to mention your life. I can't imagine *what*

Daddy is going to say about this. He won't be happy, as you can well imagine."

Juliette squirmed and kicked at the brute of a man with his arm locked around her waist.

Fiancée? Tylor Hollinsworth's fiancée? Juliette?

Damn. Oh damn.

Three

"Will I ever grow accustomed to this heat?"

Juliette paced the length of her bedroom, over the cypress floor blotted with bright rag rugs—peach colored like the paint on the walls. Aside from the heat, the room was surprisingly lovely and comfortable. The bed was tremendous, each one of its four posts bigger than her waist; the beautifully pleated tester had soft, sheer rose-colored curtains tied back with dark green cords and tassels.

As Juliette mopped her throat and chest with a damp cambric kerchief, her temper mounted and her patience grew as frail as the diaphanous mosquito *baire* draping from the frame over her bed. She wore only a thin shift that adhered to her flesh with sweat and humidity. Pausing at the open French windows, she regarded the terrain of brown water. The distant slave shanties appeared to float on the river, as did the trees and the outbuildings. Hounds sprawled atop their kennels, panting in the heat.

Dear God in Heaven, wasn't it bad enough that Maxwell

Hollinsworth had lied about his reasons for bringing her back to Louisiana?

Just exactly how was she supposed to react to the news that Chantz Boudreaux worked as her godfather's overseer? The man had seen her naked as the day she had been born, for heaven's sake. Not only that but she had offered herself to him as flagrantly as the slatterns who entertained the drunken brutes at cockfights. Not only that but she had allowed him liberties. And what discomfited her most, it had come as natural to her as breathing. Even worse . . . she had enjoyed it. As the Reverend Mother had declared with her fire-and-brimstone promulgations no woman worthy of Heaven would welcome such acts except to beget with her husband and that was allowed only with the greatest indifference to any and all bodily responses.

Obviously, the Reverend Mother had not shared time with Chantz Boudreaux.

Oh how she craved to share time with him again. Lord help her. The tiniest thought of him made her heart race and her mind feel light as goose down.

And that would *never* do. The very *last* thing she needed was to allow anything to confuse her reasoning. If she intended to rectify these sorry circumstances in which she found herself, thanks to her naïveté, she needed a clear head—and that meant no Chantz Boudreaux . . .

"Doesn't the wind ever blow in Louisiana?" she demanded as she slapped a mosquito on her arm. "Do these insects ever stop buzzing and biting? I'm going mad, Liza. I swear I am. I thought that dreary cold convent was bad, but I would happily trade a good thrashing from the Mother right now for this deplorable situation in which I'm shackled."

Glaring at the comely mulatto whom Maxwell had assigned as her step-and-fetch-it, Juliette frowned. "Imagine

their thinking I would marry Tylor Hollinsworth. I don't
know Tylor Hollinsworth, and even if I did I would refuse
to marry him on principle. The insufferable brute drunkenly forced himself into my bedroom and, looking me over
as if I were a horse to be purchased, announced I am more
than fit to marry and mount.

"I know what they want. They want Belle Jarod. They
shan't have it. Do you hear me?" she shouted so loudly Liza
covered her ears with her hands. "If Tylor Hollinsworth
were my last hope for marriage and children I still wouldn't
marry him!"

Liza shook her head and raised her eyebrows. She wore a
thin gingham dress and a white tignon around her head.
Her shoes were bound together by frayed bits of rope. Soft
tendrils of dark brown hair fell down her slender neck and
around her temples. A sheen of sweat caused her light
brown skin to look slightly rosy. Juliette thought her fasci-
natingly beautiful, like pale chocolate.

"If I's you, Miss Julie, I'd keep my voice down. Max been
sweet talkin' his bourbon since dawn. He ain't a man to be
crossed even when his mood ain't been soured by mash. I
'spect Tylor is gonna feel the back of his daddy's hand over
what he done yestaday, if he ain't already. Now Chantz been
dragged into this mess."

Liza plucked the cambric from Juliette's hand and moved
to the washstand with a solid marble top, dunked the kerchief into the hand-painted china basin of cool water, gave
it a wring, and handed it back to her. The amused expression that had curled her brown lips turned concerned.

Juliette clutched the cloth so tightly a stream of water
trickled through her fingers. "Mr. Boudreaux saved my life.
He was a perfect gentleman—"

"Miss Julie, Chantz Boudreaux might be a lot of things,

but gentleman he ain't. He be ever' gentle-bred woman's daddy's worse nightmare." She chuckled and plumped the feather pillows on Juliette's bed. "Come on now. Ladies nap in the aftanoon. Take away some of this heat."

"I don't want to nap."

"You don't wants to nap. You don't wants to eat. You don't wants to marry Tylor Hollinsworth. What do you wants to do, Miss Julie?"

"I want to go to Belle Jarod, and . . ."

She pressed the cool cloth to the pulse in her throat, moved again to the window. Black-skinned children splashed through the flood waters, carrying long knives and slapping with sticks at submersed shrubbery.

"What are they doing?" she asked, inviting something other than Chantz Boudreaux to occupy her thoughts, however briefly.

Liza moved up beside her. "Snake huntin'," she said. "Turtle huntin'. Whatever they can scare up."

"Snakes?"

"Big ones. Brought up by the floods. You don't gots to worry much. Maxwell be puttin' young'uns in each room for the next few days to snake watch."

Juliette glanced around the room and bit her lip. "I don't know what appalls me more. The possibility that there could be snakes curling up in my bed or that Maxwell would put children in charge of hunting them."

Grinning, Liza leaned against the window frame and regarded Juliette's profile. "I'm thinkin' you don't wants to talk about snakes at all."

Juliette looked into Liza's eyes that were dark as coffee. How odd it seemed, to be standing here discoursing so freely with another woman. Friendship with other girls had not been encouraged at the convent—especially with her.

"I'm thinkin'," Liza ventured softly, "that you gots Chantz Boudreaux on your mind. You can tell me, Miss Julie. What went on in that shanty with Chantz?"

"Nothing." She shook her head and focused harder on the children as they waded through the muddy water, slapping their sticks at bushes.

"That ain't what Tylor say. He say he found the two of you—"

"It was an innocent embrace, Liza. Nothing more."

Juliette turned away, mopping her nape with the linen. Water ran down her back, making her shiver. She walked to the dressing table and regarded the collection of seed-pearl combs for her hair—gifts from Maxwell. They were aged but pretty and had belonged to his wives, as did the silver-backed brush and hand mirror. There was an ornate jewelry box as well. When she opened the lid tinkling music filled the air and on the bed of deep purple velvet were earbobs and bracelets, one of ebony wood carved in the shape of entwined snakes. It had ruby eyes.

Sunlight through the window reflected from the facets of a cut crystal perfume bottle. Lifting the stopper to her nose, she closed her eyes and inhaled the deeply floral scent of sweet magnolia. Something stirred in her memory and in the pit of her stomach. Touching the damp tongue of the stopper to the pulse in her throat, she slid it down to the hollow at the base of her neck.

"Does he have a lady friend?" she heard herself ask.

"Chantz?"

She nodded, drawing the stopper down to the valley between her breasts.

"Women come and go. Chantz got one deep and true love, and that be sugarcane. That man could grow cane outta rock."

Liza joined her. Juliette dipped the stopper tongue back into the perfume, then touched it to the moist skin below Liza's ear. A gold bead of liquid slid down her neck.

"When I still lived with my father, I would occasionally find him sitting in the dark with an open bottle of perfume. He called it Midnight Magnolia, and when I asked him why he had it, he told me that it reminded him of his home in Louisiana. If I lived to be one thousand I would never forget the scent of it. Once, just before he sent me away, I sneaked into his room and took the perfume, dabbed it on my wrists thinking that I would please him. I didn't, of course, because it wasn't Louisiana he thought of when smelling Midnight Magnolia. It was my mother. I think that was the first time he truly looked at me and realized what I had become."

Juliette set the perfume down and walked to the open French doors, turned her face into the sun. The scent of magnolias mingled with that of muddy water and the aroma of cooking food from the kitchen in the distance. She felt tired, suddenly, and dispirited. She wanted to focus her thoughts and feelings on her anger over her godfather's ruse, of having been virtually shanghaied and sold into the slavery of marriage to a man who, on first sight, had repulsed her to the point of nearly throwing herself intentionally into the flooding river.

There were so many problems to sort out—yet her mind continued to shift to those moments the night before, when she had awakened to find herself curled up against a man she had never before witnessed. But even that had not had the effect on her that his touching her had. Something had awakened in her. Something that she had desperately attempted to ignore the last years. His kiss had ignited a fire that even now made her flesh burn and her heart race as if she'd just run as fast as her legs would carry her from the village to the convent, scrambling up stone walls and diving onto her mattress before dawn crept over the horizon.

Liza took her arm. "Best you rest now, Miss Julie. You got dress fittin's later—"

"I don't want those dresses, Liza." Juliette flashed a hard look toward the scattering of brightly colored and extravagant frocks tossed over the backs of chairs. "They belonged to dead women."

"They wasn't dead when they wore 'em."

"What is that?" She pointed to a ribbed contraption with crisscrossed laces.

"That be a corset, Miss Julie. To hold in your waist proper." Liza assessed Juliette and shook her head. "Not gonna do you much good. You not big as a minute anyhow."

"It looks torturous." Juliette shook her head and frowned. "I shan't wear it. I shan't wear those dresses either. Bring me my convent garment."

"You mean that pitiful gray sack of cloth you be wearin' when you come here? Maxwell done burned that quick as you took it off. 'Fraid you gonna be stuck with them lot of frilly rags whether you like it or not."

She followed Liza to the carved four-poster bed draped with sheer net that did little to keep the mosquitoes from her at night. As she sank into the goose-down mattress, Liza tossed a white sheet across her. Juliette reached for her wrist, holding her as she turned to leave.

"Do you have a man friend, Liza?" she asked sleepily, suddenly too tired to care that her question was far too personal and was again leading her back to the very source of mental and emotional conflict that made her unsettled.

Liza smiled a little. "Yes, ma'am. I gots me a fine man, Miss Julie."

"Are you in love?"

She nodded. "I 'spect I am."

"How do you know?"

Liza sat on the bed and regarded Juliette's face. "You just know, I reckon. I suppose when you can't think of spendin' your time with nobody else. When you feel all filled up with commotion—"

"Has he kissed you?"

"Yes." She nodded, her smile widening and her dark eyes shining like polished onyx.

"Has he . . . *touched* you?"

Raising one eyebrow, Liza tipped her head to one side and appeared to consider her question.

"I'm dreadfully brash, aren't I, to ask such a thing when we hardly know each other? Except . . . I've never had a friend, Liza. Never a confidante in my entire nineteen years."

"Never?"

"I didn't dare confide in the girls at the convent. The Reverend Mother rewarded anyone who would tattle on our sins with an extra hour of sleep in the morning. Subsequently no one trusted anyone. I'd very much like us to be friends, Liza. Do you think we could?"

Liza gave a short laugh and scratched her head. "In case you ain't taken a good look at me, Miss Julie, our skin ain't exactly the same color."

"Is that supposed to make a difference?"

"Lord, girl, you *are* naive." Liza placed her dark rough hand over Julie's pale soft one.

Juliette grinned. "Does that mean yes?"

"That mean we both gonna take a while to think about it."

Liza pulled away and walked toward the door.

"It's dreadfully sad and frightening to be a prisoner, isn't it, Liza?"

Stopping, her back to Juliette, Liza didn't turn for a moment. Finally, she looked around and her eyes were dark hollows of emotion. "I be a slave, Miss Julie. You're not."

"But we're both women, and at this point in my life I'm as imprisoned as you."

A smile of understanding touched Liza's mouth.

"They can't force me to marry Tylor, Liza. I won't. I'll throw myself in the river, this time on purpose."

"Careful, now. There might be no Chantz Boudreaux there to fish you out again."

As Liza quit the room, Juliette rolled to her back and focused on the netting overhead. She tried to fix her mind on her sorry situation—but couldn't get Chantz out of her head. Not just the image of him, wounded and bleeding on the dirt floor of the old shanty, but those other sensations as well. His hands had been hard and powerful, both cruel and gentle on her body. He had kissed her and she had felt . . . overwhelmed by emotion.

How would she ever face him again?

Jeremiah, a barefoot Negro boy no more than eight years old, wearing a sleeveless bleached muslin shirt and pants, cinched at the waist with a rope, sat in a chair in the corner of the high-ceilinged room and pulled a rope attached to a punka overhead. The big fan did little but stir the hot, wet air and cause the flies to buzz angrily. And the mosquitoes. The drone of their humming had been constant as Juliette lay tossing, turning, and sweating in her bed.

The miserable humidity made her drowsy and incapable of concentrating on Max Hollinsworth, whose annoyance at her running off into the storm was thinly veiled by his attempts to pacify her own anger. The man pacing, wearing a rumpled, sweat-stained shirt and smelling of sour spirits, could hardly be compared to the soft-spoken charming godfather who had occupied her during their journey from France with vivid descriptions of Louisiana that likened it to the Garden of Eden. Max Hollinsworth had filled her with such grand dreams for her future—thrilled her with images of gay soirees and lazy picnics under sprawling oaks overlooking the Mississippi River. He'd encouraged her fantasies of rebuilding Belle Jarod to its former glory. He'd inspired her with such hope . . .

Yet, the ugly reality stretched as far as she could see—muddy water and snakes and humidity so thick she felt as if she were breathing through a damp linen. According to Tylor, Belle Jarod had burned nearly to the ground thanks to the fire that had erupted during the confrontation between her father and her mother's lover—the fire that had killed Maureen Jarod and destroyed everything her father had worked for.

Max drank from a tall glass of bourbon. His blue eyes, however, never left Juliette, with her mass of hair anchored to the top of her head by the seed pearl combs that she despised to use but had little choice. While her voluminous hair might have been welcome in the cool convent to help keep her warm, here it felt as miserably heavy around her shoulders as wet wool.

Then, of course, there was the cursed garment that she had been instructed to wear that had belonged to his second wife, Mabel or Myrtle or some such, a long-sleeved green silk with lace and ribbons that drooped from her shoulders, pitifully too big. The scalloped décolletage plunged far too daringly over her breasts, forcing her to clutch it closed with one fist. Never would she have imagined that she would long for the drab gray frock she was forced to wear at the convent. And, oh, for the chill of those dreary shadows and walls. The Reverend Mother's severity in that moment would have been a welcome respite from the biting insects and suffocating air that made her lungs feel like sodden cotton.

Max moved to his desk and sat on the edge, drank the bourbon, watching her over the lip of the glass. Sweat trickled down his jaw. Although his mouth formed a semblance of a smile, the emotions crawling in his dark blue eyes appeared to be anything but friendly.

Despite what her father had become the latter part of his life, Juliette couldn't imagine his entrusting her well-being to one as ruthless and mendacious as Max Hollinsworth. Then she acknowledged with a despairing, infuriating sense of growing helplessness that she hadn't known her father at all.

"I understand you spent time with my overseer," Max said in a falsely neutral tone that sent caution up her spine. His eyebrows lowered and his voice dropped an octave as he added, "Chantz Boudreaux."

Fresh anger rushed through her, adding to the cloying heat of the clothes scratching at her skin. The memory of Chantz lying in a heap on the floor and Tylor Hollinsworth standing over him made her empty stomach turn over. For all they knew, or cared, he might have died—or could be dying that very moment. The possibility made her throat close and her heartbeat quicken with a desperation that made her feel frantic to see him again.

"He saved my life," she declared with shaking voice. "He didn't deserve the viciousness that was inflicted on him by your son and his companions."

Max shrugged. "How could you blame them? They enter the hovel and discover you in his arms, barely dressed. Chantz has a . . . reputation, shall we say. Besides, such behavior between a man of his social status and a young lady such as yourself is highly frowned upon."

"That's ridiculous." She shook her head. "I'm virtually

destitute, as you've pointed out. I'm hardly in a position to look down my nose at Chantz Boudreaux or anyone else."

"Need I remind you that your father was once highly regarded. The most successful planter in Louisiana. Some considered him the royalty of sugarcane. Belle Jarod was the finest home in the South, Juliette. She sat like a glistening jewel on the *cyprière* above the river. From her wide galleries you could look down on fifteen thousand acres of the tallest, greenest, sweetest cane outside of the West Indies.

"Most speculated that Jack had a special talent for growing cane. Perhaps. But I suspect he could contribute most of his success to his dirt . . . and the fact that he never flooded. Not like the rest of us. Belle Jarod sat just high enough to stay mostly dry when the river rose. While we waded through water up to our knees and watched our crops wash away or rot, Jack sat up there like a king and tallied his profits. Profits, I might add, that mounted every time we had a flood. Less cane meant higher prices. While we grew poorer, Jack grew richer. He was lucky that way. Seems everything he touched turned to gold."

"Obviously not," she pointed out with a lift of one eyebrow, "or I wouldn't be standing here now, would I?

"Touché." Max finished his bourbon and put down the glass. His cheeks looked flushed. Whether from anger or the liquor, she couldn't determine.

Setting her shoulders and lifting her chin, Juliette said, "You want Belle Jarod. And the only way you'll get her is through me. I'm well aware of the law. When I marry all my property, including Belle Jarod, will revert to my husband."

His dark eyes regarded her intently, first her face, then down, over her body. A weary yearning settled over his features; he ran one hand over his brow, and sighed.

"I can hardly vow that I wouldn't give my soul to own

Belle Jarod. My heart is broken each time I ride by her barren fields and her crumbled walls. A wealth of dreams and prosperity died in the fire, Juliette. Her beauty, her magnificence haunts me even now . . ."

He stood and swept up his empty glass, refilled it with bourbon from a bottle on a table near a window. His back to her, he looked out over his submersed property, scattered with piles of driftwood and debris. The neatly trimmed boxwood hedges and brick-lined paths were buried under a foot of silt.

"I loved your father. Never doubt that for a moment. He was a good friend to me. Carried me through troubled times. Laughed with me. Wept with me."

He laughed dryly. "Never once did he ask for anything in return. Not even the money he loaned me. I once told him he was a candidate for sainthood. I'm afraid it wasn't a compliment. His tolerance and philanthropy, not to mention his damnable trust, infuriated me. It seemed everything I did or succeeded at could never measure up to his most simple act of humaneness."

He turned and looked at her. His face appeared as gray as cold ash. "When Solicitor Roswell contacted me about his death, I suffered, Juliette. Now I see you standing there and I'm reminded of how I failed him. I'm reminded of it each time I look in your . . . extraordinary eyes."

A sad smile turned up his lips as he walked to her. "Let's begin again, Juliette. I trust, once you've grown to know us better you'll be more inclined to act reasonably. I'll spare nothing to ensure your comfort and happiness."

"And in return—"

"The mistress of a plantation like Holly House . . . or Belle Jarod, has tremendous responsibilities. Aside from overseeing the house slaves—"

"There will be no slaves on Belle Jarod, *Monsieur*. I find the practice barbaric. And I'm far more interested in learning the process of growing cane than I am in the waxing of tables and the polishing of custors."

"A woman has her place, Juliette. That place is in the house. And as long as you're living under my roof, you'll do as I say. You'll find I'm an easy man to get along with as long as you remember who is in control."

He drank again and his eyes narrowed. "A woman like you must be kept on a tight rein. Give you a little slack and you'll bolt like a hot-blooded filly with the bit in her teeth. You won't respect a man who allows you to dominate him. I told your daddy as much, but he wouldn't listen. Thought he could tame Maureen with flowers and sweet talk. Maureen hungered for power more than she craved his money and all the sparkling baubles it could buy her."

He put the glass down and moved toward her.

Juliette turned her face away, so her gaze fixed on Jeremiah. He stared at her with big eyes, their whites slightly jaundiced.

"The dress suits you," Maxwell said as he circled her. "We'll have Emmaline fit it, of course. She'll be along directly. You'll need some pretty things, what with our guests arriving. We can't have Phyllis Buley showing you up, now can we? Fred thinks there isn't another young lady in Louisiana who can challenge his daughter for looks and charm, and maybe there wasn't. But now you've come home and there won't be a man, eligible or not, who won't believe you to be the prettiest female in this state."

He caught her chin and tipped her head so she was forced to look in his eyes. She wanted to slap his hand away, but something in the pressure of his fingers warned her that to push him in that moment would not be wise.

"You've a great many lessons to learn, my dear. The first is to always look at me when I speak to you. The second is to obey me. Should I tell you that you're to wear your hair up, you'll wear your hair up. Should I require you to wear a certain dress, you will wear it. When I behest you to keep away from Chantz Boudreaux, I fully mean that you are to keep away from him. Now, I'm willing to overlook this last unfortunate occurrence with my overseer—a certain amount of tolerance should be rewarded him because he saved your life. But should there be any further fraternizing between you beyond the normal requirements of his duties as my employee, then I will surely be forced to administer swift retribution."

He smiled into her eyes. "Do you understand me, my dear?"

Juliette swallowed. Some internal heat brought a rise of sweat to her face.

"Massa Max!" came a child's excited voice, followed by a banging on the closed door. "Massa Max, you best come quick. Boss Chantz be back, and he be hurt somethin' bad!"

Without so much as a thought for her actions or the directive her godfather had just given her, Juliette grabbed up her overly long skirt and exited the room with no backward glance.

Max looked around as Tylor entered the office through the gallery doors. His son's face, shapeless and fair and without character—so much like Max's dead wife's—looked petulant and flushed by the heat and the liquor he'd been drinking. His clothes were soiled and wrinkled and sticking to his body by large patches of sweat. He looked as if he'd been sleeping off his drunk in a barn.

"Tylor, you disgust me," Max declared in a weary voice.

"I'm not in the mood to be belittled, Daddy. You gonna let her just fly out of here like that on her way to flutter all over Chantz barely a minute after you told her to keep away?"

"I might remind you that if it wasn't for Chantz, Juliette would be dead right now, thanks to you. I might remind you that if you hadn't acted the imbecile, she wouldn't have run out of this house and wound up in Chantz's arms. When are you going to grow a brain, Tylor? When are you going to show a little responsibility, not to mention maturity?"

"When you get over being in love with a whore." Tylor grunted a laugh, and added, "Maybe you didn't haul Juliette out of that convent for me to marry. Maybe you got designs on her yourself."

Max backhanded Tylor hard enough across his cheek to send him careening over a table, crashing it to the floor along with the lamp that shattered and spilled oil in a thick yellow pool on the floor. His hands sliding in the slick, mephitic fuel, Tylor scrambled back to his feet, his mouth bleeding, his face white. His brown hair spilled in Macassared coils over his eyes.

His fists shook as he sneered. "Nothing more pitiful than watching an old man make a fool of himself over a young woman, Daddy. She'll make you into a laughing stock. And you can mark my words, Chantz is gonna be trouble where she's concerned. The problems I might have caused ain't gonna hold a candle to what he's gonna stir up.

"I wouldn't be surprised if he ain't already had her, not the way they were clutching at each other when I found them. Since when did you ever know Chantz not to crawl between a woman's legs when it was offered—especially one who looks like her?"

With a snide grin, he added, "You think she would have run out that door like she did if either of us had come crawling out of the woods on our bellies?"

"Get the hell out of my sight, Tylor, before I lose my temper."

"I hate to be the one to break it to you, Daddy, but that ain't Maureen who just ran out that door much as you would like her to be. You can drape her in fancy satins and silks and dress up her hair with Maureen's combs and bathe her in Midnight Magnolia, but she ain't ever gonna willingly walk into your arms . . . or your bed.

"You're an old man, Daddy. And she's already known Chantz's touch. We both know neither of us can compete with him. Especially me. Remember? Tylor, why can't you shoot as straight as Chantz? Tylor, why can't you ride a horse as well as Chantz? Grow cane as well as Chantz? Hell, the only thing different between Chantz Boudreaux and God is Chantz can't walk on water."

Tylor drew himself up and wrist-wiped the blood from his lip. He motioned toward the empty glass on the desk. "Pull your head out of your bourbon bottle long enough so you can think clearly for a change. She's on to us, Daddy. No way in hell are you ever gonna get your hands on Belle Jarod, assuming that's what you want to get your hands on, of course."

Tylor held Max's gaze for a long tense moment, then left through the gallery door, crunching the shattered glass under his boots.

Max closed his eyes, anger and whiskey making his body shake. He heard the bell ringing then.

He made his way out the front door, stopped on the gallery, his sight sweeping the brown water terrain that covered his land so he couldn't tell where the earth ended and the river began. He might as well have been standing on the deck of a goddamn boat.

His Negroes came from every direction, slogging as fast as they could through the high water. All converged on

Chantz where he had collapsed to his knees beside his horse. The respect and loyalty the blacks showed Chantz set Max's teeth on edge.

Now there was Juliette, stumbling toward Chantz as well. The hem of her green skirts floated on the water surface. Her hair, full of fire and wild silken waves, fell from the combs and cascaded over her shoulders, and for a moment he thought . . .

"Juliette!" he barked, and watched her freeze.

Chantz lifted his head. His blue eyes focused first on Max, then shifted to Juliette, who slowly turned back to Max at the sound of her name.

Max stepped from the porch into the water. He watched a spark of hot anger ignite in her eyes as he approached.

"If you want to help Chantz," he told her in a flat tone as he caught her chin in his fingers and stared hard into her eyes, "get back in the house and forget him. Do you understand me, Juliette? Forget him."

four

With the sun beating down on him and the pain in his chest making breathing next to impossible, Chantz watched Juliette struggle back to the house, dragging her wet skirts. Then he shifted his gaze to Max who plowed through the water toward him like a maddened buffalo, teeth bared and eyes glazed by bourbon.

Gritting his teeth, Chantz attempted to stand. Too damn weak. The heat and pain in his chest pressed him down.

"Boss," came the gentle voice, and Chantz looked around, up into his gang driver, Louis's, face. Louis stood seven feet tall with skin as blue-black as a raven's wing. The man had the patience of Job and the strength of ten men. He smiled kindly down at Chantz and said, "I be helpin' you if that's awright. Give me your arm, Boss. Right here 'round my waist. Gonna lift you right up now. Careful. You ain't lookin' so good, Boss."

"I've been better." Chantz groaned and caught his breath as Louis eased him to his feet. He ran his hand over his face, swiping at the sweat and humidity streaming into his eyes.

Max shoved his way through the workers. "Where the

hell have you been, Chantz? My goddamn plantation is sinking into the river and you're off carousing with women and getting yourself half beat to death."

Chantz shifted his gaze from Max's irate face to Juliette. She stood on the gallery, watching, hands buried in the folds of her water-stained skirts. Then Tylor exited the house and joined her. He leaned against one of the six fluted columns stretching across the front gallery, smoked a cigar, and grinned.

His eyes narrowing and the heat of pain replaced by the hotter flame of anger, Chantz stared hard enough at Tylor that the smirk slid from Tylor's lips.

"Get your ass down to those levees and start rebuilding before the next rains come and my whole damn house is washed to New Orleans."

Chantz forced his attention back on Max. The whites of Max's eyes were shot with red and his breath stank heavily of bourbon. Max was a mean drunk. And crazy. Chantz knew from experience that the slightest provocation could send him over the edge and anyone within punching distance would experience the repercussions—not just Chantz. Max would lay a whip against the back of man or woman just for spite if he was drunk and mad enough. Judging by the look and smell of him, he was definitely drunk and mad enough.

"I hold you personally responsible for this catastrophe, Chantz. Had you made certain the levees were properly constructed this fiasco would have been avoided. Now over half of my crops are ruined."

"I did what I could with what I had," Chantz snapped, doing his best to keep the contempt and escalating anger out of his voice. He hurt too damn much to put up with Max's tirade and the fact that Juliette was watching Max verbally ass whip him didn't help. "Maybe if you weren't so stingy with money, Max, we could build a levee that would hold."

Max shook his fist in Chantz's face. "Maybe if you didn't insist on feeding, clothing, and housing these slaves like they're white folks I'd have the extra money to invest! Tell you what, Chantz, maybe if I withhold half of your salary over the next year I'll have the money I need to spend on this plantation."

Max stepped closer and, glaring into Chantz's eyes, said in a quieter voice, "If I wanted this farm run by an idiot, Chantz, I'd put Tylor in charge."

With the sun beating down and the gnats and mosquitoes swarming around his head and shoulders, Chantz shoved free of Louis's hand on his arm, and moved into Max's face.

"You calling me an idiot, Max?"

"Stop this. Stop this right now!"

Chantz looked around.

Skirts hiked nearly to her knees, her gray-streaked brown hair hanging in damp tendrils around her face, Emmaline Boudreaux, Chantz's mother, waded through the murky water, her face pinched with concern and growing irritation.

"Stay out of this," Chantz told her.

"You're in enough trouble as it is, Chantz. For God's sake, look at you. You're half dead on your feet and looking to get in another fight. And you . . ." She turned on Max, thrust her sweating face up to his, and declared, "You would cut off your nose to spite your face, Max Hollinsworth. Chantz is the best overseer in this state and you know it. If you didn't know it, you would have fired him long ago. You know if you fired him there would be twenty other planters on his doorstep by nightfall offering him a job."

Frowning, Chantz opened his mouth—

"Hush!" she snapped, red faced and shaking. "I don't want to hear another word out of either of you—two grown men so damn stubborn and full up with pride you've gone soft in the head. Chantz, you get to the house right now so Rosie can see to those injuries. Louis, you give him a hand 'cause by the looks of him he won't make it that far on his own. As for you, Max Hollinsworth, it would serve you right if Chantz quit you."

"If you got something to say to me, Emmaline, you best do it in the house," Max said through his teeth. "And you." He pointed at Chantz. "You should count your lucky stars that I don't have you tied to a pole and whipped . . . boy. Don't think for a second that I won't if I find you in the company of Juliette again without a chaperone. Now, I want you down to those levees in an hour or you're finished at Holly House. The other damn planters can have you and good riddance."

Rosie, her head bound in a red tignon, clucked and tutted as she wrapped Chantz's chest tight enough to nearly cut off his breathing. "Lawd, Lawd, you is a mess. A real mess. I ain't ever seen no man who could get himself into such trouble. Massa Max 'bout ready to pop when he find out you be with Miss Julie. As I live and breathe, that woman is bound for trouble. Best you stay away from her, Chantz. Far away. She got her mama all over her. Um hm. She the kind of woman who'll git a man killed quicker'n he can swat a fly."

Chantz groaned as Rosie made one last yank on the bindings and tied them off. There was no point in arguing with the woman. Juliette Broussard was trouble, all right. She was trouble even if she wasn't involved in Max's plans. When word got out that Maureen Broussard's daughter was back in Louisiana, there wouldn't be a man over the age of twenty who wouldn't come sniffing at her skirts. If they weren't old enough to have been seduced by Maureen herself, they'd been seduced by her legend.

"Yassa, you best git your mind off that child. Man who gits hooked up with the likes of her is gonna suffer. Puts the ruttin' fever in a man. Makes him crazy."

She plunked her big fists on her wide hips and frowned. "When it come to women you gots enough problems, Chantz Boudreaux. You and Miss Julie gits together and there won't be enough left of either of you to use as chicken scrap. 'Sides, you gots enough problem, what with Massa Max frettin' so 'bout his crops. That man is just plumb crazy anymo'."

The door opened and Emmaline stepped in. Her face looked white as the muslin strips around Chantz's chest. She always looked that way when she'd gone nose-to-nose with Max. Her gray eyes were a little dazed and her thin body trembled. She'd pace throughout the night and drag out the bottle of brandy she'd stolen from Max Christmas Eve two years ago. She'd pour herself one, maybe two fingers, depending on how hot the fight had become with Max. One finger made her tipsy. Two made her smashed. By the look on her face this was going to be a two-finger night.

Stopping just inside the door, she stared at him hard and said, "The levee can wait until tomorrow. You're to spend the remainder of the day in bed. Resting."

"When are you gonna stop fighting my fights for me?" he asked, flinging a wad of bandage into Rosie's medicinal basket.

"When you stop antagonizing the hell out of him," she replied angrily. "My God, Chantz, you're more like your father every day. Look at you. Willful. Spiteful. Full of fight. Always fight."

"Not always." He slid from the bed, carefully straightened, and walked to the dresser where he kept a bottle of whiskey. He reached for a glass and shot her a dark look.

"What happened between you and Juliette Broussard, Chantz?"

"Is that what this fit of pique is about?" He shook his head and splashed whiskey into the glass. "Did the son of a bitch ask you to find out if I seduced the young lady?"

"By the looks of her, I suspect it was the other way around."

He grinned, tipped his glass to her, then drank.

Rosie humphed and said, "I is gittin' while the gittin' is good. If there be anything left of you two when the fur stops flyin', I'll bring supper."

Rosie mumbled to herself and headed for the kitchen, water swirling around her skirt hems.

Chantz stretched out on the bed, propped his shoulders on the iron headboard, and drank the whiskey. He watched his mother pace, her face grow red with heat and anger.

"That young woman is trouble, Chantz. Stay away from her."

"That you talking or Max?"

"We both know why she's here. Max couldn't get Belle Jarod through Maureen, now he'll do it through Juliette."

"Maybe." He drank, then wrist-wiped his mouth. "She doesn't strike me as the type who would allow herself to be manipulated. Besides, I got the idea she wasn't too thrilled over the prospect of marrying Tylor." His mouth curled. He said in a lower voice, "I suspect she's as smart as she is beautiful."

Emmaline stopped pacing and glared at Chantz. "And if she's anything like her mother she'll have Max, Tylor, *and* you dead by the time the dust settles. I won't have it,

Chantz. I won't have you getting killed over the likes of Maureen Broussard's daughter."

"If I was inclined to get myself killed over a woman, it would have happened by now."

"I'm certain Jack Broussard must have felt the same way, until he set eyes on Maureen Jarod. She destroyed him, Chantz. His dignity, his fortune, his life."

Chantz left the bed. He picked up a cloth and wiped the sweat from his face and throat, walked to the door and looked out over the brown water landscape. The avenue of slave shanties was elevated high enough so the flood didn't reach into the houses—at least this time. Children sat on the steps, dangling their feet in the water, squealing and pointing at fish and frogs that their parents rushed to net. They'd be eating something besides corn bread and smoked pork tonight.

"I'm not as naive or as stupid as Jack Broussard," Chantz finally replied, directing his gaze toward the big house. The image returned, of Juliette rushing out of the house and into the water before Max stopped her. Then he recalled her body, naked, perfect, curled against his in the bed as she slept—recalled the taste of her mouth.

Emmaline moved close. "I don't like that look on your face, Chantz. I haven't fought tooth and nail to see you grown only for you to get yourself shot over the likes of Juliette Broussard. Tylor is itching for an excuse to kill you, Chantz."

"If I don't kill him first."

"I'll kill him myself before I see you hanged over that sorry, lazy, worthless human being."

She gripped his arm and her voice became frantic. "I want us to leave this place, Chantz. I've wanted it for a long time, but especially now that she's come. There are a hundred planters out there who would hire you this quick." She snapped her fingers.

"I'm not going anywhere." He shook his head, his gaze still fixed on the house with its flowing gallery and white columns. It shimmered in the sunlight, hazy behind the steam rising off the water. "Not yet," he added softly.

"Damn you, stop this madness, Chantz. Walk away from Holly House and put Max Hollinsworth behind you. He isn't worth this pain you're putting yourself through."

"You should have thought about that thirty years ago." He turned his hard blue eyes on her.

Her tired eyes filled with tears as she drew back her shoulders. "You've become as hateful as Max. And hard. Detestably hard."

Chantz gave a cold laugh. "Thirty years of being called bastard white trash will do that to you, I guess."

"Accept it. I have, finally. He's never going to acknowledge you, Chantz. Get out of here while you're still young enough to start over. Buy you some land. Marry you a nice girl. Take all the rage you expend on Holly Plantation and grow your own sugarcane."

He turned on her then, his anger rising. "I'm not going anywhere, damn you. I've worked this goddamn sugarcane since I was ten years old. I took over the overseer job from a thieving inept old drunk who couldn't find his way out of his bed much less to the cane fields. I tripled Holly's profits in five years. I designed those sugar boilers so our sugar yield doubled with half the effort expended, and I sit here in this piece of shit shanty and watch that damn house grow and watch Tylor Hollinsworth lazy around on his fat butt waiting for Max to drop dead so he can inherit what I've sweated blood and tears to build. And you suggest that I just walk away?"

"You can't make him love you, Chantz." She touched his arm.

He snatched it away.

"I learned too late that he just don't have the capacity for it. Not anymore. Not since Maureen came into his life," she said wearily.

"I don't give a damn whether he loves me or not," Chantz said through his teeth. "I just want him to look me in the eye one time and acknowledge me for what and who I am. I want to understand why—"

"I've told you a hundred times, Chantz. A thousand times. Why won't you just leave it alone?"

"If I'm gonna be denied my birthright, I have a right to know why."

Emmaline walked away. Her back to him, she hugged herself as if the room had suddenly turned freezing cold. "I was young and foolish and he was . . . handsome and dynamic and, believe it or not, charming as hell. Much like you, when you want to be. When you're not simmering in anger and inviting the world to take a swing at you. Back then there was a kindness in him still. And a gentleness." She smiled at the memory. "He was easy to love. Too damn easy. Such a handsome man, and those blue eyes . . .

"The affair was passionate and brief while he was in Charleston on business. He was long gone by the time I discovered I was carrying you. When my father, the only family I had in the world, learned of my condition, he disowned me.

"I came to Holly House and discovered Max had married. My decision to remain here at Holly House was made out of stubborn spitefulness. Not to mention desperation. What was I to do, a young woman on my own with a baby? I had no money. And I was angry enough that I wanted him reminded every day of his life that he ruined me. He provided me employment and a roof over my head, such as it is, in exchange for my never telling Sarah, his wife, that you were Max's firstborn."

She turned to face him, chin squared, thin body rigid. "Do you think it's been easy for me, Chantz? I was forced to sew her pretty clothes and me wearing little more than rags. I wiped her brow and held her hand while she was giving birth to Tylor. I watched Tylor given everything Max's money could buy and there you were living on infested cornmeal and wearing hand-me-downs. I sometimes dreamed of killing him, but I held on to the hope that someday he would wake up and see what a fine son you are, or could be, especially when it became obvious that Tylor was worthless and lazy and had no interest in Holly House."

"And you loved him still." Chantz watched resignation settle in his mother's eyes. "You hoped he would come to love you again as well."

"He never loved me, Chantz. He never loved poor Sarah, nor did he love his second wife. Max Hollinsworth has loved only two things in this life, and those were Maureen Broussard and Belle Jarod."

She laughed and shook her head. "I'll never forget the day Jack brought Maureen here to meet Max. I'll never forget the look on Max's face. He loved her the instant she turned those big green eyes on him and smiled. He was . . . thunderstruck. Thank God poor Sarah died soon after. She didn't have to witness the onset of his madness as he fell deeper under Maureen's spell.

"After Maureen was killed I thought that would be the end of it. But it wasn't. Then the bitterness set in, and the guilt. What humanity once lived in his heart, little as it was, was extinguished.

"Chantz, honey, if you stay here you're going to turn out

just like him. Mean and bitter and angry. I already see it in you. Now that young woman shows up here not much younger than Maureen was when she married Jack, a mirror image of her mother, and you've got a fire burning in you for her. Don't deny it. I know you better than you know yourself. I saw how you looked at her out there, the same way as Max looked at Maureen that first time. Those eyes don't lie, Chantz. They're predatory and right now they're fiercely hungry. Please. For me. Promise you'll leave her alone."

Drinking his whiskey, Chantz moved again to the open door. His mother knew him too well. Right now, even if he wanted to, he couldn't shake his thoughts from Julie Broussard, or the idea that Tylor Hollinsworth, his goddamn good-for-nothing half brother, might well get his hands on yet another piece of good fortune all because Max Hollinsworth wouldn't acknowledge Chantz's being his firstborn—not that it would make any difference if he did, thanks to the law. The only hope Chantz had of inheriting Holly was for Tylor to die and Max to suddenly get a conscience and confess his parentage. But while Chantz might fantasize about putting an end to Tylor with a well-placed bullet between his eyes, there would be nothing short of a miracle to sway Maxwell. Max Hollinsworth was not a man to acknowledge his mistakes . . .

Chantz had long since given up any hope of getting his hands on Holly Plantation . . . but Juliette was another matter.

Juliette might balk now at the prospect of marrying Tylor, but when faced with the reality of her situation, that could change. The thought of her walking hand in hand into the sunset with his sorry brother made a dangerous anger flirt with his thoughts.

He stepped from the house, into the steam of the day. The bandages were tight and hot around his chest and the humidity made the cuts on his face throb. His pants clung to his sweating legs as he watched the children and their parents chase catfish with nets. Dragonflies with iridescent wings darted through the air while dark clouds of gnats hovered over the water.

The sun would go down soon. The snakes would come out then. Lots of them, due to the waters that drove them out of the swamps and forests. Then the gators. Last flood, worse than this one, brought one old bull right into shanty row. Only a last-minute effort by a horrified parent had kept the hungry gator from snatching a baby right off the threshold of his mother's shanty.

"Boss Chantz!" the children cried, and threw up their hands in greeting.

Simon, a boy of nine years born with a clubfoot and frail as a reed, danced and splashed and held a giant frog in both hands. His sister Liza stepped from the house and, seeing Chantz, smiled and waded into the water.

Chantz felt the tension leave his shoulders as he watched Liza approach. She had a tall, slender body with nice curves accentuated by the thin soft cotton of her blue dress. Her sparkling black eyes were concerned, and there was a hint of flush to her cheeks that were as golden as rich molasses. A coil of chocolate-brown hair spilled over her brow, and she brushed it back with her hand, frowning.

"You tangle with a bull gator, Chantz Boudreaux?" she asked, tipping her head to one side. "You a real mess. Can't be havin' your nice face messed up, can we?"

"Try telling that to the thugs who jumped and robbed me." He grinned and lowered his voice. "You're looking pretty, Liza. Going somewhere?"

"I'm hopin'," she replied with a sly grin. "If you tell me it's all right."

"Be a shame to waste that full moon tonight, I guess."

"I'll wear that dress you brung me last week. Thought I'd wear my hair up like this." She swept the heavy mass off her neck and anchored it with her long fingers at the top of her head. Her smile widened. "I understands that men likes to see the curve of a woman's neck."

"Drives us crazy." He smiled and drank his whiskey.

Liza sighed and her lashes lowered. "The crazier the better. That's what I'm sayin', Chantz Boudreaux."

Emmaline stepped from the house and stared, first at Chantz, then at Liza. Then she marched off toward her own house, a smaller version of Chantz's: white clapboard nestled under a live oak dripping with Spanish moss.

"She don't look too happy," Liza said. "And I can't say as how I blame her if what I'm hearin' is true. That you is bustin' your breeches over that Broussard girl, and her to marry Tylor. We don't need you to be gettin' yourself killed, now do we? We gots enough to worry 'bout 'cause of this water."

Chantz looked away, toward the big house.

And there stood Juliette, on the upper floor gallery. She had released her hair and it fell in heavy waves, nearly to her waist. The humidity in the air made it look alive and wild, windblown when there wasn't a breath of wind to be felt in all of Louisiana in that moment.

Liza touched his arm briefly, then stepped away. When he forced his gaze back to hers, he found her solemn. The sparkle had left her eyes.

"I 'spect the rumors I've heard are true if the look on your face is any hint of what is stirrin' inside your pants. I'm startin' to feel frightened, Chantz. I heard stories about her mama—"

"Her mama is dead," he said, cutting her off.

"And you're gonna be too if you fool with her."

She was right and he knew it. Something unsettled and unsettling had begun to coil around inside him since he'd pulled Juliette out of the river.

After Tylor had dragged her kicking and screaming out of that shanty, Chantz had lain on that damp dirt floor, hurting and wanting to rip Tylor apart with his hands; the thought of Tylor with Juliette had filled him with a hot, gnashing hatred that even now made him consider murder.

"I've been summoned to the house again," Liza told him. "You have somethin' you want me to pass on to her?"

His eyes narrowing, Chantz finished his whiskey, watched as Juliette reentered the house, gliding as gracefully as a willow frond on water.

"When I've got something to say," he said in a low, rough voice, "I'll tell her myself."

Juliette paced as the pendulum of the squatty little clock on the escritoire ticked back and forth as impatiently as her heartbeat. Again it whirred, struck—once, twice— hummed and clicked and again struck up its monotonous *tick tick tick* that made her want to scream. Finally, she grabbed the satin lace-edged pillow from the bed and tucked it around the clock to smother the sound, only to frown as the muffled *tick tick tick* shot through the silence like a gun.

With a sigh, she tiptoed to the French door that stood open, allowing in the croaking of rain frogs and the stagnant decay of swamp water. The air felt moist and hot against her face and her jaws ached with the restless clenching of her teeth the last hours as she recalled Chantz's collapsing to his knees and Maxwell's apparent indifference.

Surely by now Maxwell and Tylor had turned in to bed.

She struck off down the gallery, her bare feet silent upon the worn wood planks, carefully descended the curving staircase to the floor of water that oozed, warm and thick, up her shins as she held her breath and waded through the dark, her gaze fixed on the distant glow of yellow light from Chantz's window.

If you want to help Chantz, Juliette, stay away from him.

Dear God, what was she doing?

She had to know . . . must assure herself that he was all right—that Tylor's unconscionable brutality had not done him terrible harm. Rosie and Liza had been little help after dinner—as if both had taken a pledge to avoid the topic of Chantz Boudreaux whether she chose to or not.

She must assure herself that the emotions swimming around in her chest were simply not justified—that she had become swept up in some idiotic fairy-tale ideal where dizzy-headed young women fell in love with handsome strangers—

Poppycock! All of it. She didn't believe in fairy tales. And she certainly wasn't the dizzy-headed type of young lady who could be easily swept away by the flash of a man's intensely blue eyes . . . or the touch of his hand . . . or his kiss. Or the fact that he had risked his own life to save her from the flood.

She stubbed her toe against a rock, then something brushed against her ankle that made her jump and high step as fast as she could down the path, splashing, causing the hounds in the pen to bark frantically from atop their houses. After what felt like eternity, she reached Chantz's porch steps, breathing hard and fast in the heavy air, her body, what wasn't drenched from her splashing through the floodwater, moist with sweat that crawled over her scalp and dripped down the back of her neck.

At last, drawing in a less than steady breath, she eased up

the steps to the porch, where the long finger of yellow light spilled through the open doorway, peeked around the doorpost into the small room—at the empty bed where the sight of twisted sheets made her stomach feel strange—where was Chantz?—then around the small room. Papers and envelopes littered an ancient desk bracing the far wall. Its pigeonhole compartments overflowed with papers as well. Against the other walls tired, rickety shelves sagged under the burden of wornout books with leather spines.

But where was Chantz?

"Looking for someone?" came *his* voice.

Startled, she turned to find him leaning against the house, shirtless but for the bandages around his chest, his pants slung low around his hips. A thin cigar drooped from the corner of his lips.

She opened and closed her mouth, took another deep breath that made her chest ache. Suddenly she felt ridiculously silly—and dumb. Whatever had possessed her to come traipsing down here in the middle of the night, especially with Maxwell's warning ringing loudly as bells in her ears?

"I must have been wrong about you, Miss Julie." The words were slightly slurred and hardly friendly. She eased toward the steps again. "Lying in my bed last night, my face throbbing like hell, I imagined that you had more than a lick of common sense in your pretty head. Now I have to question my normally good judgment, because any woman who would venture out at night to see a man who is likely to have imbibed the better portion of a bottle of bourbon isn't thinking straight."

"I . . ." She swallowed and backed toward the stairs. "I was concerned. I feel dreadful over what happened—"

"This?" He removed the cigar from his mouth and pointed it at his temple. "I'm certain Tylor is pleased at the idea that he very nearly bashed in my brains. I, on the other hand, have experienced far worse."

"I'm sorry." She bit her lip and narrowed her eyes to better see him in the dark.

"Sorry?" His smile flashed, then he moved toward her. "If you really gave a damn about my welfare, Miss Julie, you wouldn't be here right now. Maxwell is a man of low tolerance. Much like myself. Our patience can be tried only so far before we snap." He snapped his fingers, making her jump. "Are you aware of what the punishment is for a man like myself to be caught with a young lady like you? Aside from losing my job, Max would have every right to strap me to a post and whip me to within an inch of my life. But then, you strike me as the kind of woman who enjoys flirting with the forbidden. Am I right, sweetheart?"

"Yes," she heard herself say, her cheeks warmed by the confession.

Leaning one broad shoulder against the porch post, his weight shifted to his right hip, Chantz smoked the cigar and looked down at her where she tarried on the step just above the water. "I'll bet you gave those nuns hell, didn't you, darlin'? Woman with your body and eyes and mouth . . . Christ, they probably spent half their lives on their knees praying for your soul . . . or theirs."

"Are you insulting me, Mr. Boudreaux?" she demanded with a lift of her chin.

"I'm giving you fair warning, Miss Julie. You're much too young and naive to toy with a man like me. I don't take lovemaking lightly, but I'm not stupid, either. You're gonna be trouble for somebody and I'd just as soon that that somebody not be me."

Drawing back her shoulders, her face in full burn, she

declared, "I came here to ascertain whether you were suffering—"

"Oh, I'm suffering all right."

His voice came out low and husky. He moved down the steps. She backed again, down into the water before bracing her feet and refusing to budge further. His body heat rushed over her—and his scent—bourbon and tobacco and sweat. Still, it was his eyes that made something roll over inside her. Something exhilarating. Something dizzying. The feelings confused and excited her, and though her mind shouted for her to run as hard as she could back to the big house away from Chantz Boudreaux, her heart simply wouldn't allow it.

"I'm suffering all right," he repeated, his mouth curling at one end as he flicked ashes into the water. "Every time I think of you with Tylor Hollinsworth I hate him with new vigor. I want to kill him even more than I want to make love again to your mouth. I want to shake my fist in God's face and demand to know why a man as lazy and worthless as Tylor should be gifted with a plantation like this . . . and a woman like you while the rest of us work our fingers to the bone every day and are forced to make do with . . . scraps."

"I'll never belong to Tylor Hollinsworth," she assured him as she searched his shadowed face.

Stepping into the water, catching her chin in his fingers, Chantz looked deeply into her eyes, his body tense and wary, as if he could sense something hectic and unabandoned in her behind the calm of her voice.

"Never say never, darlin'. Life is hard and sometimes we have to compromise whether we like it or not. What seems important to us now might look different in the light of day. The choices we made yesterday, we might eventually come to regret . . . that doesn't mean they weren't right at the time."

"Are you regretting having saved my life?" she demanded, holding her breath.

A gentleness passed over his face and suddenly his eyes looked immeasurably sad and weary. His hand dropped to his side and he looked away. "Yes," he replied thoughtfully. "I regret every act of fate that took me to that riverbank at that exact moment. Another three minutes and you would have been . . . gone. I wouldn't be standing here right now feeling like a condemned man. I'd be contemplating the upcoming harvest, maybe imagining asking a young lady at church to a picnic down by the river. I'd think about rebuilding that levee or frog gigging with Louis. I wouldn't be pacing the grounds tonight, my body burning with bourbon and the ache to take you in my arms again."

A smile touched her mouth. Slowly, she climbed the step until she stood eye-to-eye with him, lifted her arms and wound them around his neck, her breasts brushing against his bare chest—heard his indrawn breath and felt his body brace against his instinctive response to reach for her. She pressed her lips to his bruised temple, breathed upon it warmly, then softly, so softly kissed the corner of his lips.

Five

Juliette tried to disregard the unsettling emotions brought on by the mention of Chantz's name. More disquieting was that Liza had become so astute at reading those emotions the last days. Then again, she mused with a sense of ever-increasing frustration, she was not, nor had she ever been, adept at hiding her thoughts and feelings, much to the Reverend Mother's dismay. In the case of Chantz Boudreaux, however, the increasingly disingenuous denial wasn't simply an effort not to flinch when Maxwell or Tylor mentioned his name, but to ignore the ever-increasing tumult in her heart when she thought about him.

"Why must you insist on bringing Chantz's name up to me at every opportunity?" she declared between her teeth as Liza propped her knee against Juliette's rump and heaved back with the corset laces. The air in Juliette's lungs expelled in a rush that made her chest hurt. As Liza yanked again, nearly unsettling her from her feet, Juliette frowned and looked over her shoulder. "The last week you've found every excuse to drag him into our conversation."

" 'Cause I think you likes to talk about Chantz."

"Poppycock."

Her face grew warm as she mentally acknowledged the truth of Liza's words. The fact that a woman who hardly knew her could so easily read her thoughts—even more discomposing, her emotions—made her feel . . . naked.

She walked to the cheval mirror where she regarded her trussed figure. The corset thrust her breasts high and forced her shoulders back so she stood as straight as Rosie's broom handle. She made a face and propped her hands on her hips, her gaze wandering to Liza's in the mirror. Those dark eyes regarded her with a steadiness that annoyed her.

"Poppycock," she repeated more forcefully. "The man rarely crosses my thoughts, Liza. I don't recall that I *ever* bring up his name."

"Don't gots to. I seen you hangin' on every word Maxwell say when he talk about Chantz. Don't think that Maxwell don't see it, too. Ever'body see it, Miss Julie. You go flush as a strawberry."

"You're imagining things. Besides, I wouldn't waste my time dithering over a man who surely doesn't give me a thought."

She frowned at her reflection, at the high color in her cheeks. A niggling sense of disappointment battered her heart as she acknowledged that she was, indeed, wasting her time dithering over a man who obviously didn't give her a thought. Since the night she had braved snakes in order to see him, he hadn't so much as looked her way when passing. No doubt he thought her an irresponsible ninny. Worse . . . a child.

Liza smiled and mopped her damp brow with a rag. "Chantz got a levee to build. I 'spect he ain't thinkin' of too much aside from keepin' these grounds from floodin' agin.

Best you fix your thoughts on keepin' Maxwell and Tylor happy."

"Maxwell appears happy enough. I've done everything the last days to pacify him besides lick his boots."

"And I'm askin' myself why."

Turning on her heels so suddenly her hair flew around her bare shoulders, Juliette said, "Because he's right. Because I need to know everything there is to know about running a plantation. I want to know how to manage this house and the storehouses and the kitchen and stables. I want to know how a sow farrows and chickens roost and how Louis hammers out a horseshoe from a piece of hot iron. I want to know how to dip wicks and cook and skim soap. And when I'm done with budgeting cornmeal and pork to the families, I want to know how to plant cane and make it grow and harvest it and mill it and boil it and haul it down that damn river to New Orleans."

Liza sat on a tasseled, velveteen ottoman, her hands folded in her lap. "Lord have mercy, girl. I be worn out just listenin' to you. Come to think about it, you gots a twinkle in your eye today. I 'spect you're gonna need it what with the Buleys arrivin' tomorra," she added under her breath.

"I've been thinking, Liza."

"Oh, Lord." Liza tucked a coil of hair behind her ear and shook her head. "We in for trouble. I seen you think enough the last days to know somethin' gonna git stirred up."

Juliette dropped to her knees before Liza, took her brown hands in her own, and smiled up into her eyes. "We're going to Belle Jarod, Liza. I'm going to rebuild her and plant cane and—"

"You gonna do this all by yourself?" Liza smiled.

"Where there's a will there's a way. I'm going to learn everything there is about running a plantation—"

"Can't do it by yourself, Miss Julie. You seen how many slaves Maxwell got workin' here. Over a hundred in the fields—"

"I don't want to hear all the reasons I can't do it. I want to hear all the reasons I can."

Her lips turning under, Liza shook her head. "You just dreamin', Miss Julie. You got no money. No slaves. You not more than a splinter of a girl. You don't know nothin' 'bout nothin'. You ever harnessed a mule to a plow? Cut cane until your hands bleed and your shoulders ache so bad feels like hosses be pullin' you apart?"

"I'll learn, Liza, just like my mother learned."

"She learn from walkin' at your father's side for how many years?"

Liza smiled kindly and laid her hand on Juliette's head, stroked her hair as if she were a pet tabby. "Best you can do is find yourself a wealthy husband—"

"Then I'd be no better than my mother, marrying a man for his money—"

"It's what women do."

"Not this woman. When I marry, Liza, it'll be to a man I love. It'll have to be, because Belle Jarod will then become his. Everything my father worked for, fought for. All his hopes and dreams, his sweat and blood. He built that house out of love, from the ground up. Do you know that every brick that he made to construct the walls of that house had my mother's initials engraved on it? He would roll over in his grave if I simply handed Belle Jarod over to just anyone."

Juliette walked to the French door. Dusk settled like a gray mist over the trees and buildings. The air smelled musky and sweet at once. Not so much as a breath stirred.

Odd how the heat no longer bothered her. Or the humidity. The smells that had once filled her with confusing and disturbing sensations now invigorated her with a yearning that made her chest ache.

She leaned back against the doorposts. Her fingers toyed with the strands of corset ribbon as she closed her eyes and imagined Belle Jarod as Maxwell had described it. The snatches of images, gleaming and colorful, that haunted her dreams were taking shape—a child's memories that thrilled and frightened her.

"Papa told me once," she said softly, "that they would throw a *fête champêtre* every spring, just as the dogwoods bloomed. They would roast pigs and calves on spits and the gentlemen would escort their ladies along the *parterres* lush with pink azaleas and daffodils and jonquils. Mama would weave flowers in my hair and fit me into a dress identical to hers."

As Juliette released a weary sigh, she looked back at Liza. "Papa had every right to despise her, didn't he? She destroyed it all—their marriage, Belle Jarod—for the sake of a sordid affair."

"Love make us do foolish things, Miss Julie. Hard to think right when your heart is flyin' wild in your chest. Somethin' come over you that kick good sense right out your head. Now come here and sit. We gonna do somethin' special with your hair tonight."

Juliette dropped onto the stool and, with pale shoulders sinking, stared at her reflection in the mirror. Her complexion glowed with heat and her skin shimmered with moisture. Her eyes looked too large for her face. Her mouth too red. She had lost weight. Her cheeks looked slightly sunken, accentuating the high curve of her cheekbones.

"I don't think it's a good idea to dress me up, Liza. The

last thing I need do is to encourage Tylor or Max. The more unattractive and discreet I am, the less likely Tylor will be to bother me."

"Miss Julie, you could never be unattractive and discreet, even if you plastered mud on your face and shaved your head."

Liza lifted a handful of hair and admired it. "You gots such pretty hair, Miss Julie. Like garnet." Bending over Juliette's shoulder, Liza held the long, coiling tendrils of Julie's hair up next to her own face and smiled into her reflected eyes. "What you think, Miss Julie? Would I make a right fetchin' redhead?"

Juliette smiled as she admired Liza's face. Liza's skin looked as golden as topaz. Her shoulder-length mass of dark brown hair framed her sculpted facial features in curls. The niggling thought that Max Hollinsworth most likely was Liza's father invited another cold stone of resentment for him to settle in her chest. That a man would treat his own daughter barely better than a beast of burden filled her with disgust.

"Liza," Juliette said earnestly, "you're one of the most beautiful women I've ever seen. My red hair isn't going to improve upon that. Not in the least."

Liza's eyes widened. A hint of color touched her cheeks. "You're very kind, Miss Julie."

"Kindness has nothing whatsoever to do with it. You're exceptional, Liza."

As Liza began brushing Juliette's hair, Juliette watched her in the mirror. Liza's eyes were without their normal sparkle. Her expression gave her a drawn appearance that caused Juliette to frown.

"I didn't mean to upset you," she said.

Liza gave her a watery smile. "I'm touched is all. I never expected you to be so nice. Most mistresses aren't, you know."

"I'm not your mistress, Liza. And for your information, I find the bondage of human beings an abomination of the highest degree."

"I wouldn't be lettin' Max or Tylor or anyone else hear you talk like that. You liable to find yourself *tossed* into the river next time.

"Holly House slaves are lucky to have a man like Chantz overseein' this plantation. We got it much better than most. Chantz don't tolerate much in the way of meanness from Max and Tylor. More than a few of us owe him our lives."

"There you go bringing up his name again." Julie searched Liza's face, a startling suspicion suddenly biting at her. The sharp pang made her press her hand to her bosom and catch her breath. "Are you . . . enamored with him, Liza?"

"With Chantz?" Liza's head fell back and she laughed, a full, deep sound of genuine humor. "Me and Chantz? Lord, girl, you gots that wrong. Real wrong. I gots me a man, but it ain't Chantz."

Julie turned and grinned up at Liza. "Who is it?" she teased. "You can tell me. We're friends. You said so. I shan't tell another living soul, I swear it!"

"I'm not tellin'." She winked. "But I'll say this. Aside from Chantz Boudreaux, he be the finest lookin' man God ever created. Kind and gentle, with kisses warm and sweet as new cane syrup."

Her hands falling still, Liza looked away, toward the open French doors leading to the gallery. The pleasure that had briefly touched her cheeks with color turned into something else, a yearning that reached into Juliette's own heart and squeezed. Watching the emotion roll over Liza's face brought tears to Juliette's eyes and she waited breathlessly for Liza to continue.

Liza spoke softly, with a catch in her voice. "I loves that man so deep, Miss Julie, I sometimes think I gonna die from the pain of it. I thinks about him mornin', noon, and night. I feel crazy with it sometime. He just fill up my head and heart so fierce that I wants to scream."

"That's wonderful," Juliette said breathlessly. "Who is he, Liza? Tell me, please."

Frowning, Liza pulled out of her dreamy state and shook her head. "I can't. I'm sorry."

"Will you be married?"

Stiffening her back and setting her chin, Liza took Juliette's shoulders and forced her to turn back toward the looking glass. She began brushing again, harder, her expression intense and almost angry.

"Won't be no marriage. Not for us. Now I don't wants to talk about it no more. Tonight we're gonna talk about you. We gonna put your hair up just so with those pretty pearl combs that Max give you. Emmaline gonna be up here soon with a pretty dress that she been alterin' to fit you these last days. That peach silk gown with the bib of Cluny lace? And the lovely green silk petticoat she was hemmin'. You're gonna look like an angel, I declare."

Judging by the distressed expression on Liza's face, Juliette mused that prying out further information of Liza's sweetheart wouldn't be easy or wise.

"Emmaline doesn't care for me." Juliette winced as Liza accidently pulled her hair.

"Emmaline don't care for most folks, Miss Julie. And when it come to Chantz . . ." She lowered her voice and met Juliette's gaze in the mirror. "She fiercely protective of him. You should know that."

Averting her eyes, her face warming again, Juliette sat straighter in her chair and clasped her hands in her lap.

They felt damp and unsteady. Once again the mere mention of Chantz's name vibrated along her nerve endings, making her feel edgy.

"You don't gots to deny what you're feelin' over Chantz. Not to me. You wouldn't be female if you didn't feel rattled by him. Can't rightly put my finger on what it is that bothers women so. He be sweet on the eyes, for sure. But then they is lots of nice lookin' men, I guess. None so hard as he is, though. He a hard man. Body and soul. He love hard and hate hard and fight hard. Got a way of makin' a woman feel like a woman. Understand what I'm tryin' to say?"

"Yes." Juliette shivered as a drop of sweat slid between her breasts. The taste of him returned, and his scent, curling through her body like slow smoke. "Extreme masculinity," she said in a tight voice, "makes us aware of our own femininity. Our own frailty."

Liza reached for the combs on the table. "He be reckless. Aside from his pride and temper it be his only shortcomin'. He see somethin' he want and he takes it."

Her finger lifted Juliette's chin and Liza gave her a troubled smile. "He a man who been told no too often in his life. He ain't much got the patience for it no more. Here now, you're lookin' a little pale."

Liza lightly pinched Juliette's cheeks so they bloomed with color.

"Just so you know, Chantz be havin' supper with you all tonight." She chuckled. "There you go again, lookin' all aflutter. Once a week Max bring him into the big house. They have a meal and talk business. Most prob'ly be about the levee and the impact the flood will have on the crops. Tylor will sit there and mope and snarl an occasional insult at Chantz. Chantz will do his best to ignore him, then eventually he'll start to get mad. They exchange words and Chantz will leave before he finally breaks down and murders Tylor."

Liza stepped away as she admired Juliette's hair, swept up and back from her face by pearl-encrusted combs. Loose wisps curled at her temples and around her nape. Long coils hung over her shoulders—ribbons of fire against her pale skin.

A slow smile curved Liza's lips. "Men gonna have a hard time talkin' business tonight, I 'spect."

"Did I hear my name mentioned?"

Tylor stood in the open French door, his hands tucked into his trouser pockets. Juliette gasped and covered her thinly clad breasts with her hands. Liza stepped between them, blocking Tylor's view.

"Git outta here, Tylor Hollinsworth. What you thinkin' by saunterin' into a lady's room?"

His mouth curved and his eyes narrowed, giving him the look of a fox in a hen house. "There hasn't been a lady on these premises since my mama died, you know that. Hell, Daddy don't blink twice at a woman unless she's a whore. And speaking of whores . . ."

Tilting his head to one side, causing a thin dark thread of hair to spill over one blue eye, he directed his gaze from Liza to Juliette, who glared at him around Liza's hip.

"I hear the Buleys will be arriving tomorrow. They'll be wanting to meet our Juliette. I suspect they'll have a great deal in common."

"And what might that be?" Juliette demanded with a lift of her eyebrows.

Liza stalked toward Tylor. "I said git. I'll be callin' your daddy if you don't. You got somethin' to say to Miss Julie, you can say it over supper."

"I suspect I'll be hard pressed to get Miss Julie's attention, what with Chantz being there."

"Out!" Liza flapped her arms at Tylor and he raised his eyebrows, set his heels.

"You never know, Andrew Buley is just liable to fall in love with Juliette. I'm sure Fred would welcome the prospect of getting his hands on Belle Jarod."

Liza grabbed the doors and closed them in Tylor's face. She snatched the curtains across them, stood with her back to Juliette and her hands fisted full of the chintz material.

Juliette watched Liza closely as she turned from the door. For a long moment Liza didn't meet her eyes, and when she did there swam a shadow of something like fear in their dark depths. Not just fear, but anger. They assessed Juliette in a manner that made her flush with discomposure.

"Tylor's a jackass," Juliette pointed out with a dry laugh.

Liza nodded, rubbed her palms up and down her skirt, then headed for the bedroom door.

Juliette jumped from the ottoman and grabbed her arm. "What's wrong, Liza?"

"Nothin.'" Liza shook her head and forced a smile. "Nothin' at all. Tylor just git on my nerves is all."

There came a knock at the door.

Emmaline entered, her arms full of the peach silk dress and green petticoat. She stopped short at the sight of Juliette, hair upswept and body clad in nothing more than shift and corset.

Liza tugged her arm away from Juliette, and as she walked by Emmaline, her step slowing, she said, "What's wrong, Emmaline? You look like you just seen a ghost."

Juliette thought of chasing after Liza with some flimsy

excuse to detain her. The emotions glittering in Emmaline's eyes as they assessed her sent a shiver of nervous anger through her. Merciful heaven. It was enough that she would be forced to face Chantz over supper.

Taking a fortifying breath, she faced Emmaline, her shoulders squared and chin set. "It's time we clear the air, Emmaline. Obviously, you don't like me. Would you care to tell me why?"

If Emma felt fazed over Juliette's directness, she didn't show it. Without a flicker of emotion, she replied, "You're going to be trouble for my boy. That's why. It's written all over you. You're the kind of woman who makes men stupid."

"That's ridiculous."

"You have that look in your eye. That tilt of your head. The way of looking at a man from under your lashes. The way of holding yourself, shoulders back and head up as if presenting your body like it was God's gift to mankind."

"Nothing happened between Chantz and me, regardless of what you choose to believe."

"Nothing?"

The heat in the room pulsated as intensely as the drone of the night insects whirring in the dark beyond the house as Emmaline's gray gaze drifted down over Juliette's body, making Juliette feel naked and embarrassed. She could deny to the world that anything had happened between her and Chantz, but she knew in her heart that it could have. Almost did. Something about the man had crawled into her blood in the instant he kissed her.

"Something has my son restless, Juliette. And bothered. Very bothered. And a mother's instinct tells me it's got nothing to do with broken levees or lost crops or the catastrophic consequences that Max will face over this flood."

Emma tossed the dress over the back of a chair, then proceeded to help Juliette into the petticoat. Her hard, rough hands slid down the seams, though Juliette sensed Emmaline's attention was focused more on her than on the garment. Next came the dress—soft peach silk that draped low on the curve of her shoulders and fit snugly through her small waist that was accentuated with a wide band of green satin the same shade as her eyes. The skirt, trimmed with quillings of green silk, had a cut-away hem which revealed the petticoat ruffles beneath.

Her eyes softening somewhat, Emmaline regarded Juliette with a wistfulness that extinguished the hot anger that had been building in Juliette. The woman looked haggard, suddenly, her thin shoulders burdened.

"You're a beautiful young woman," Emma said. "I know you can't help being what and who you are. I only pray that God gave you the conscience that he never gave your mother."

Her cold hand reached out and took Juliette's in a painful grip. "Leave my son alone, Juliette. He's been hurt too damn much. More than you could ever know. Planters in these parts wouldn't think twice about hiring Chantz if Max let him go. They'd fight over him, if the truth be known. But not if the reason Max let him go was over you. Planters are funny that way. They'll tolerate their overseer drinking, lazing, lying, cheating, thieving, but they won't tolerate him messing with their wives and daughters. While the lot of immoral bastards might keep their mistresses, they don't want to think if they ride away from that house their overseer is gonna slip in through the back door and into their bed. A man with that reputation would never find work in Louisiana again, I don't care how good he is at growing cane."

Emma stepped closer, and the grip on Juliette's hand sent a spear of dull pain up her arm.

"I hope I'm wrong about you, Juliette. I hope we're all wrong. For your sake as well as ours. For my son's sake. I hope when Maureen Jarod Broussard was buried, her wanton, wicked, deceitful heart and spirit were buried with her."

Juliette woodenly turned toward the cheval, regarded the reflected image that made her body flush.

Pray, what had become of the drab mouse of a young woman she had been a few short weeks ago? As she stared at the scandalously low décolletage that exposed most of her breasts that shimmered pale as milk glass in the lamplight, Chantz's words flashed through her memory—the ones with which he had so spitefully described her mother that stormy night in his cabin—her dresses cut so low the whole of Louisiana held its breath when she walked.

"I won't wear it," she heard herself declare in a dry voice. "It's . . . disgraceful."

"You'll wear it. Because Maxwell wants you to wear it." Emma touched the wisp of hair coiling around Juliette's nape. "Maxwell always gets what he wants . . . eventually."

Her gray eyes meeting Juliette's in the glass, Emma said, "Only one thing I know of that he never got that he wanted with a desperation that has nearly broken him. Then again . . . he might get it yet. Time will tell, I guess."

Juliette stared after Emma as she left the room. She felt desperate for air. Desperate to tear the indecent gown from her body and burn it. Yet, as she focused again on her reflection, how the cut of the gown accentuated the smallness of her waist and cupped her breasts in a way that flaunted her femininity, a rush of hot thrill raced through her. Not just from the sudden self-awareness that in a manner of a few short weeks she had grown from a naive child into a woman, but from the idea of presenting herself in such a way to Chantz.

With an angry cry, she ran from the room and onto the gallery, leaned against the balcony rail and turned her hot face toward the night sky and its vast panoply of stars that glistened like diamonds on black velvet. But even here she could find no respite from the unnerving emotions that were rushing their way into her mind and heart. Emmaline's words rolled over and over in her thoughts:

"For my son's sake, I hope when Maureen Jarod Broussard was buried, her wanton, wicked, deceitful heart and spirit were buried with her."

Dear God, how many lives had Maureen Broussard destroyed? How was she to live down the reputation of a woman who apparently had the soul of a she-devil?

But worse than that, and what frightened her most: How else could she explain the scandalous emotions and physical reactions that took hold of her body every time she so much as heard Chantz Boudreaux's name? Even now they were there—racing wildly through her, making her breathless, trembling, flushed—had been there since the moment Liza had told her that Chantz would be joining them for supper.

Suddenly she *did* care if her hair was coiffed and her dress was pretty. She *wanted* him to look at her appreciatively with those burning, oddly haunting eyes. She *wanted* him to desire her. She craved it with every fiber of her being.

The memory of the Reverend Mother came back, not for the first time, of course; she often thought she could hear the woman's susurrant chanting as she lay in the dark, awakened from her troubled dreams of burning.

Perhaps those dreams were simply her mind's way of preparing her for the eventuality of her soul burning in Hell. Perhaps there were times when the prayers and exorcisms murmured by priests and obsessive nuns could actually prove futile. Perhaps there were times when the wickedness ran too deeply, corrupting the very heart of the soul beyond redemption.

Surely, if her soul could have been cleansed of her mother's legacy, the years spent under the Reverend Mother's ceaseless barrage would have done it.

Obviously, it had all been for nothing. Because something had roused inside her the last days—something strong and dark and pulsing . . . and uncontrollable. And growing more so by the hour.

Closing her eyes, she took a deep, unsteady breath. That's when she heard the hounds howling.

They ululated like mourning souls in the night. A dozen of them, heads turned to the sky, filling up the stillness with a moan that sent a coldness through Juliette's veins. Odd how the sound intensified the stillness and heaviness of the air that seemed to crawl over her exposed skin like claws.

"Miss Julie?"

Startled, Juliette jumped and turned.

Standing in the doorway, Little Clara, Rosie's nine-year-old granddaughter, bestowed on her a wide, mostly toothless smile. Her hair jutted from her head in spikelike braids, each tied with a sliver of pink ribbon Julie had given her when she discovered the child admiring them in her armoire.

"Granny say you gots to come to suppa now. Boss Chantz be here and food 'most ready." Her smile widening, Little Clara shook her head. "You 'bouts the fanciest lady I ever seen. Massa Max gonna pop his eyeballs clean outta his face. I reckon Boss Chantz gonna be all amudlycockle agin when he see you."

"Amudlycockle?" Juliette smiled and lowered herself until eye level with the mischievously grinning child. The stiff skirts and petticoats mushroomed around her. "What is amudlycockle, Little Clara?"

"You know. Fidgety. Granny say he got a piss ant in his britches. Git that way ever' time he see you. Go sore as a boar in a patch of high thistle. That what my granny say and granny, she ain't ever wrong 'bout nothin'."

Six

The day had been hellish, what with the repairs to the levee and the waters still standing ankle deep, making the hauling of timbers and bricks and the trenching of mud enough to drive even Louis to his knees. The last thing Chantz wanted or needed tonight was to be subjected to Max's drunken tantrums and Tylor's insults. Then, of course, there was Juliette.

The prospect of sharing her company had put him in a foul mood since noon, since Max had sent word that Chantz was to meet with him tonight. Hell, he'd made a point of staying as far away from Juliette as possible the last days—since she'd shown up on his doorstep in the wee hours of the morning looking like some child angel with moonlight in her eyes. She had pressed her soft mouth against his and he'd felt . . . gut punched. He'd wanted to shake some sense into her and curse her for her naïveté. But he hadn't . . . only because if he'd put his hands on her in that moment his restraint would have shattered.

It might shatter yet, he acknowledged as he glanced

around the foyer, at the expansive walls and high ceiling where an imported chandelier glistened with a hundred candle flares. There were massive portraits on the walls—austere men with glowering blue eyes and exotic faces—Spanish, according to his mother, several generations removed. Chantz's own flesh and blood, and he didn't even know their names.

No doubt about it, there was very little patience left in his reservoir of endurance at the moment. Something was going to snap soon. If he was kept standing here in this damn foyer for another twenty minutes it was liable to be Max's neck.

Little Clara came bounding down the curving staircase and threw herself against Chantz. She beamed him a snaggletooth smile and dove into his pants' pocket with one hand, her big dark eyes twinkling in excitement.

"You done brung me some ho'hound, Chantz?"

He frowned hard and shook his head. "No ho'hound tonight, Little Clara. Rosie tells me you've been naughty. You know I don't oblige naughty girls with ho'hound candy."

"I done put that frog in the chamber pot cuz I didn't have nowheres else to put him. 'Sides, you just pullin' my leg. You gots me ho'hound. You always gots me ho'hound if'n I been bad or not."

She plunged into his other pocket, giggling as she withdrew the chunk of hard mint and molasses candy. "You's an angel, Boss Chantz," Clara declared, pressed a big kiss on his hand, then scampered through the nearest door.

Chantz grinned, shook his head, and looked to the top of the stairs.

Juliette stood there, awash in peach silk, still as an alabaster statue. For a long moment, she didn't move. Her green eyes didn't blink. Slowly then, she descended, one hand resting lightly on the smooth walnut banister, the other lifting the hem of her skirt just enough so he could glimpse her ankles. Another time he might have found the flash of that dainty foot arousing. But he had already seen a lot more of Juliette than her ankles. It was that image in his mind that made him hard . . . again. Made him brace his legs apart in an effort to contain the sudden overwhelming desire to storm up the stairs and do something idiotic.

At last reaching the floor, hand still resting on the banister, Juliette glanced right then left, as if desperate for a means to escape him. Finally, and with apparent difficulty, she stood straighter and forced her gaze up to his. Her skin shimmered and flushed. Her lips parted slightly, and he heard her draw in an unsteady breath.

"Mr. Boudreaux—"

"I prefer Chantz," he said in a voice that came out sounding low and rough. "Besides," he added with a sardonic afterthought, his gaze drifting down over the pink skin above her daring décolletage, "I think we've seen enough of each other to dispense with formalities."

A flare of something ignited in her eyes. "You needn't remind me, you know. A gentleman would at least attempt to dismiss the occurrence from his memory."

He curled his mouth and narrowed his eyes. "In case you haven't paid close enough attention, Miss Julie, I'm not a gentleman."

"Regardless." She shook her head, causing her hair to loosen slightly from its combs, threatening to spill. "I've been remiss in thanking you for your help. You saved my life. I've struggled these last days in an attempt to think of some way I could show you my gratitude."

"I could think of ways. But I suspect they would get me killed," he added.

"Chantz."

She took a step toward him, then drew herself back. Her hands clasped together. When her eyes met his again, hers were warm and intense in a way that made the gnawing start in his belly again. His body responded, turning hard enough to make maintaining his control next to impossible.

"I acted very foolishly," she said softly. "You could have easily taken advantage of my unfortunate behavior. Yet you didn't." Forcing a smile on her pink lips, she said, "Perhaps you should give yourself more credit. There could be more gentleman in you than you think."

"I don't think so, *chère*." He laughed, but there was no humor in it. "Believe me, if I had it to do over again, nothing that I would do to you could be remotely misinterpreted as gentlemanly."

"My dear Juliette!" Max exclaimed as he strode into the foyer, not so much as glancing toward Chantz. "My God, don't you look beautiful. The dress is splendid on you. But then I knew it would be."

Juliette forced her attention on Max.

"Rosie has our supper prepared. I hope you won't be too wearied by our business conversations."

Max turned a dark fleeting look on Chantz. "Come along, Chantz. I'll try not to keep you long. I'm certain you must have better things to do with your time."

Staring at Max's back, Chantz said through his teeth, "I've got better things to do than stand around in a foyer for half an hour."

Dragging one hand through his dark hair, Chantz closed his eyes and willed back the savage anger that made him shake. It wasn't the fact that he'd been kept waiting for half an hour and him so damn bone tired he could have lain down on the hard cypress floor and easily slept—Christ, he hadn't had a decent night's sleep since he'd fished Juliette out of the river and discovered her eyes and body would haunt him every waking and sleeping minute. It wasn't that Max couldn't find enough politeness in him to speak when entering the room. It wasn't even because Max talked down his nose at him like he was less consequential than dirt.

It was her. Seeing her. Smelling her. Remembering what she felt like in his arms. It was watching her glide down those stairs like a vision, her hair a dark fire cloud around her head and her breasts smooth and pale as ivory.

It was watching her walk off on Max's arm.

If he was smart, he'd turn on his heels and leave the house now. Tell Max if he wanted to talk business tonight he could come see Chantz. Max could swelter in that sorry box of a house that was so damn hot Chantz would lose his appetite. Too damn hot to even sleep. Too damn hot to do anything at night but lay sprawled nude across his bed and think about Juliette Broussard and how her naked body had felt curled up against him those hours after he'd fished her out of the river.

By the time he reached the dining room everyone was seated—a serene setting to be sure, despite the undercurrent of hostilities. The room was warm and mellow in the light of a large Dresden lamp on the mantelpiece. Candles flickered in two tall hurricane shades on each end of the table. In a cut-glass crystal bowl in the center of the table, Rosie had arranged a centerpiece of pink japonica and delicate magnolia fescata. As always, the fine linen tablecloth was white and spotless.

Max sat at one end of the table, Juliette at his right. Tylor sat at the opposite end of the table. Rosie had placed Chantz directly across from Juliette.

Rosie was placing a large platter of fried chicken on the table as Chantz entered. She turned her broad, sweating face toward his and her eyes regarded him in a way that made him feel ten years old again. There was warning in that look to behave or suffer the consequences.

Tylor, slightly slouched in his chair, regarded Chantz with a smirk as he reached for his nearly drained glass of bourbon. "Well, well, look what the cat has dragged up again. Daddy, when you gonna do something about these damn river rats?"

Rosie bent over his shoulder as she placed a bowl of potatoes and asked, "You wants a drink, Chantz?"

He glanced at Max who already had the flushed appearance of one who had been imbibing for a while. "Water only. Somebody here should stay sober or we'll never get anything accomplished."

"The voice of reason speaks again," Tylor declared, lifting his glass in the air. "Where the hell would we be without the mighty Chantz Boudreaux's sage advice?"

"The poorhouse, I suspect," Chantz said. He looked at Juliette. She averted her eyes. The soft glow of the lights made her complexion look like the china on which they were eating. Her hair shimmered with a radiance like slow heat.

"Thanks to this flood, we're liable to be there soon enough," Max joined in. Sitting back in his chair, he appeared to be more interested in watching Juliette pick at her food than he was in eating. "I hope you'll pardon us, Juliette, if our conversation becomes a bit heated. We often have our differences of opinion. I considered carefully before including you in this discussion. I'd hate for you to form the opinion that we're all ill-tempered heathens. But your education in the running of a household such as Holly House is important, especially if you entertain the idea of reconstructing Belle Jarod."

Max turned his gaze on Chantz as he reached for his

bourbon. "The last week Juliette has proven to be quite the astute pupil. Soon she'll be overseeing the running of this house as capably as any wife."

"Or daughter," Juliette stressed, flashing Max a look that wiped the smug grin from his face. "And speaking of Belle Jarod. When do you intend to drive me out to see it?"

"In time, my dear. Obviously there are more pressing matters to attend to. Such as the reconstructing of a levee that will keep my land from drowning every two years. Over the last few days my overseer here has had the task of putting together a plan that will satisfy those needs once and for all. I trust, Chantz, that you have a satisfactory strategy for accomplishing that?"

"Why, of course he does, Daddy." Tylor planted his elbows on the table and leaned toward Chantz. "Why wouldn't he? He's God's gift to sugarcane, after all. I'll bet ever'time Chantz takes a piss on the ground a cane shoots up ten feet tall."

Juliette put her fork down with a loud plink against the china plate. She lifted her gaze directly into Chantz's and this time did not look away. Her eyes burned as hotly as the sudden blush of color on her cheeks.

"That'll be enough, Tylor," Max said. "I fear you're upsetting Juliette's sensibilities."

"I suspect it would take more than a crude word to affect Miss Julie's sensibilities, Daddy." Tylor grinned and flopped back against the chair, lifted his glass, and cut his gaze to Chantz. "But then I suspect our overseer would know better than either of us just to what lengths we could go before insulting the young lady."

"Careful," Chantz said in a measured tone, shifting his gaze to Tylor's slack, beet-red features. "I'm fast losin' my patience with you tonight."

Tylor snorted and drank and smeared the back of his

hand across his mouth. Fat drops of sweat ran down his temples. The harder Chantz stared at him the more he sweat. Little by little the hot beet color drained down his cheeks, leaving the flesh of his face looking like damp bread dough. His eyes became pale blue sockets.

"That'll be enough from both of you," Max declared irritably. "I didn't call this meeting tonight to listen to the two of you go at each other like a pair of bull gators. Behave yourself, Tylor. I won't have you discomfiting Juliette. If you've got a problem with Chantz, just keep the young lady out of it."

"If you've got a problem with me, Tylor," Chantz said through his teeth, "we'll take it outside."

Max grunted and glared at Tylor. "We both know that isn't going to happen, Chantz. If he had the guts to take you to task he would have done it long ago."

Sinking deeper into his chair, Tylor finished his bourbon and shouted, "Rosie! Where the hell are you? My goddamn glass is empty!"

Little Clara ran into the room carrying the bourbon bottle, her cheek bulging with ho'hound candy. "Granny be down at the kitchen fetchin' cake. I be pourin' you a drink, Massa Tylor." She grabbed for his glass, knocking it into his lap.

Tylor snatched the bottle from her hand, then shoved her hard enough to send her flat on her butt. Before Chantz could react Julie jumped from her chair and slapped Tylor's cheek hard enough to nearly topple him.

Tylor lunged to his feet.

Chantz jumped up, knocking his chair back to the floor while Juliette stood toe-to-toe with Tylor, her small hands knotted and shaking in anger.

"You're despicable, Tylor Hollinsworth. While I might

be forced to listen to your taunts and jeers toward Chantz and your snide insults at me, I won't tolerate your cruelty toward a helpless child!"

He gave a short laugh and curled one hand into a fist.

"You don't frighten me, Tylor. I'm not a little child you can bully. If you strike me, you'll rue the day you were born. And while I'm at it, if I'm to act as mistress of this house, according to your father, I hereby lay down this rule: You will *never*, for any reason, put your hand on a child again in this house. Furthermore, I will not tolerate your infantile tantrums, vulgarities, or drunkenness at this table."

Max roared in laughter.

His face sheet white, his bloodshot eyes bulging, Tylor turned his focus on his father, who reared back in his chair and howled in hilarity. "Son of a bitch," he slurred. "You gonna let her talk to me like that, Daddy?"

Catching his breath, Max reached for his bourbon and nodded. "By God, Juliette, you've got the heart of a lioness. I'm damn impressed. You're exactly what Holly House needs, a woman with spunk and backbone; something neither of my wives had—obviously, or Tylor wouldn't have turned out to be the pitiful excuse for a man he is today."

Tylor flung his napkin on the table. "I don't have to stand here and tolerate this. The lot of you can go straight to hell."

He stormed from the room, slamming doors as he went.

Chantz watched as Juliette relaxed. Chagrin crept over her face and a twinkle of something that looked deliciously like mischievousness brightened her eyes. Her lips curved. She glanced at him askance as she turned to Little Clara, who gaped at her in awe.

"Lawd," the child whispered. "I ain't never seen no white

lady behave like that. Miss Julie, that be somethin' to be-hold. Lawd, lawd. I gots to go tell my granny what you done. Ain't never seen nothin' like it."

As Clara ran from the room, Juliette sank into her chair. "I apologize. I fear I allowed my temper to get the best of me."

As Chantz righted his chair and sat, Max smiled; his eyes were intense with emotion. "You're your mother, all right. I never knew another woman with her spirit for bucking the shackles of convention. She'd stand toe-to-toe with any man and give as good as she got."

"If that's an attempt to compliment me, Max, I'm sorry to say that you failed horribly. I hardly aspire to follow in my mother's footsteps."

"Despite what you've been told, Maureen was astute and competent. In your father's occasionally long absences she ran Belle Jarod with an iron fist and a lust to succeed equal to or greater than your father's. There were times I'd seen her working right there along with the slaves, on her hands and knees, giving each ratoon a kiss for luck before burying it in the soil. Jack used to say she was the reason why his cane was so damn sweet. How could it not be when touched by her lips?"

"Please." She shook her head, her gaze focused on her plate of food, forgotten during the last heated minutes. "I don't wish to talk about her. *Ever.*"

Whatever force had burned in her during her confrontation with Tylor was now, apparently, extinguished. Chantz watched her relax in her chair, once more the demure, somewhat nervous and troubled young woman whose odd, naive sensuality excited him as intensely as the passion of her anger had those moments ago. In her ferociousness her hair had slid from the pearl-backed combs—

a disarrayed mane the color of rich claret. The light shimmered within the wild curls like sparks.

Chantz forced himself to look away from her, into Max's hard eyes that watched him with the sharpness of the knife in his hand.

"The levee," Max said in a monotone, his lack of inflection as telling as the threat in his eyes. "I trust you have a viable plan to remedy this sorry situation in which we find ourselves."

"Yes." He nodded and shoved his plate away, no longer hungry. The hell that had broken out moments ago was nothing compared to what was about to transpire, he reasoned.

Sitting back in his chair, he released a weary sigh. "I made a few calculations. The base of the new levee would be three hundred feet, the berm thirty feet, the new borrow pit two hundred and fifty feet. This means, of course, that the new levee would have to be moved back nearly three hundred feet from the line of the old one.

"The men would need to move an average of one thousand yards of earth a day for four months, rain or shine, if we hope to remedy our sorry situation before the winter rains begin. An impossibility, as I see it. And there is one other factor that must be considered . . .

"You have only one recourse if you want to guarantee that your sugarcane will remain dry when the river rises." Forcing himself to look directly into Max's eyes, he said, "The levee would pass directly through this house."

His lips thinning, Max said, "I beg your pardon?"

"Rough calculations estimate the cost of such a levee would run ten thousand, give or take, basing the numbers on what Owen Howard spent two years ago to construct a levee capable of holding the river. Of course, that doesn't include the reconstruction of the house at a different location. Nor does it include the cost of labor."

His hands curling into fists, Max leaned toward Chantz, his nostrils flaring and his face red and sweating. "Are you trying to destroy me, Chantz? Is that what this is about? You want to drive me into the ground? I suspect that would please you to no end, wouldn't it?"

He raised one eyebrow. "Max, had I wanted to destroy you these last years, all I need do is walk away. You wouldn't get another man in this state to work for you. No one else would tolerate your drunken abuse or Tylor's stupidity. Aside from that, your slaves would riot. They'd scatter to the four corners and leave your cane to rot in the field. You wanted my opinion and you got it. To save Holly Plantation you'll have to sacrifice something and that something is this house."

Max came out of his chair, slowly, leaning on his hands, his body trembling. "My father built this house with his bare hands—"

"Your father built this house fifty years ago, Max. The river has changed since then. Hell, it's changed radically in the last ten years. Unless something is done soon, half your cane fields are gonna be under water in the next five years."

"Just how am I supposed to pay for this?"

"Convince Tylor to curtail his spending. He's run up quite a gambling score at Dietrich Hall. Then you might consider selling your apartments in New Orleans. There's also the expenses of your outrageously lavish soirees twice a year."

"I have a goddamn reputation to live up to. People expect certain things out of Maxwell Hollinsworth."

Chantz laughed and reached for his water glass. Juliette,

her food completely forgotten, looked at him with an expression of dismay. The idea occurred to him in that moment that the impending disaster threatening Holly House wouldn't just affect Max. Faced by the inevitable catastrophe, Max would look at Belle Jarod with a new and desperate vigor. She knew it, too. A shadow of panic darkened her eyes.

A door burst open suddenly and Simon limped in. His eyes were wide and he struggled to breathe. Chantz left his chair and caught the boy as he collapsed just inside the room.

"Boss Chantz." Simon gasped. His entire body shook so hard his teeth chattered. "Dat paddy roller be down at Louis's—be huntin' a runaway."

Chantz swore aloud, and as Juliette fell to her knees beside Simon, he told her, "Stay in the house."

"What's happened?" she asked as Max stormed from the room.

"Bounty man," Chantz said. "Keep Simon here and calm him down. And I mean what I said, Juliette." He pointed one finger at her. "You stay in this house."

A pack of hounds lunged against their ropes, frenzied by the chase and the tension crackling the air. Chantz shoved his way through the press of black bodies crowded around Boris Wilcox and his companions—two of whom pointed a rifle at Louis's head while two others wrestled a terrified Negro man into the mud. Louis's frightened eyes, reflecting the torchlights held by Wilcox's posse, widened as he saw Chantz. Tessa, Louis's wife, rocked on her knees, weeping as another woman did her best to calm her.

"What the hell is going on here?" Chantz demanded as Wilcox turned to smirk in his face. "Get those damn rifles off my man, Wilcox, or—"

"Or nothin'," Wilcox snapped, standing his ground. "We tracked that runaway for two days and found him hid in that shanty yonder. Hid by this man, here." He pointed at Louis. "You know the punishment for assistin' a runaway, Boudreaux."

Chantz looked first at the hog-tied man on the ground. His body was heavily scarred from previous whippings. There were lash marks on his back that were several days old, just beginning to scab over and heal. As he turned his horrified eyes up to Chantz's, Chantz felt dread turn over in his chest.

"He be my brother, Boss," came Louis's voice. "I can't turn him back when he come to my door. He the only family I gots, Boss. I gots to help him. I gots to."

"Maybe if Horace Carrington didn't beat the hell out of his workers, they wouldn't bolt at every opportunity," Chantz said as he turned back to Wilcox.

"Ain't my business or yours what Carrington does with his slaves, Chantz. My business is huntin' em down. Your business is punishin' the one who helped him and we ain't leavin' here until we see that it's done." Stepping closer, Boris added through his teeth, "If you don't inflict rightful discipline, I will. As Carrington's representative, I got the right."

He glanced around, into the resigned faces of the Holly slaves. The dense air smelled of fear that mounted as Tessa howled all the louder, rocked all the harder. The fire of blazing torches exaggerated the heat that in that moment felt as if it were boring through Chantz's skin.

Max stepped forward then. "That man is my gang driver, Wilcox. I can't have him out of commission—"

"You got no choice, Max." Wilcox shook his head. "Example's got to be made. You let this man get away with harborin' runaways and next thing you know they'll all be doin' it. Punishment is fifteen lashes." He shoved the coiled whip toward Max. "He's your property. Now git to it."

"I'll do it!" came the eager voice.

Tylor shouldered his way through the crowd and snatched the whip from Boris's hand. "I'm sorry to say that some of us ain't got the backbone it takes to lay leather to flesh. Well, I do. Strap that man up, boys! By the time I'm done with him, he'll turn in his own mother."

Cold fury rushed through Chantz. There were ways of whipping a man guaranteed to strip the flesh in a fashion that made the pain next to unbearable—and Tylor was damn good at it. The sadistic little bastard took pride in it.

"What's wrong, Chantz?" Tylor waved the whip under Chantz's nose. "Think you can muster up the backbone to do your job as overseer of this plantation?" Tylor glanced at Boris. "I doubt it. I ain't seen him pick up a whip but once in the ten years he's worked as overseer."

"I don't need a whip. They're eager enough to work hard and respect rules when they're treated right."

"Obviously he didn't respect the rules this time, did he?" His eyes narrowing, Tylor shoved the whip against Chantz's chest. "Whip him, Boudreaux, or I will."

The night became silent but for the pulsebeat of insects and the croak of frogs in the river.

Tessa crawled on her hands and knees and wrapped her thin arms around his legs. She turned up her tear-streaked face. "Lawd, Boss Chantz, don't be whuppin' my man. Don't be doin' it. He love you, Boss. He love you so hard, don't be whuppin' him, I begs you!"

Liza rushed over and pulled Tessa away. She hugged

her close, her dark, troubled eyes turning up to Chantz as she rocked and crooned comfort words into Tessa's ear.

Chantz turned to Louis.

"Sorry, Boss." Louis shook his head. "He my own flesh and blood. You woulda done the same 'cause you a good man and take good care of folk." He put a big hand on Chantz's shoulder. "You do what you gots to do, Boss. Best it be you. Won't hurt so bad. Ask only one thing. Don't be strappin' me up."

Louis pulled his shirt off. He dropped to his knees and braced his hands on his thighs.

Chantz looked at Liza who gripped Tessa in her arms. "Get her out of here," he ordered. His voice sounded deep and unsteady, his throat tight with anger. His mind scrambled for any way out of the dreaded situation, but it all boiled down to Tylor and the whip in his hand. Tylor would kill Louis without compunction.

He waited until Liza got Tessa in the house and closed the door. Then he took the whip from Tylor, his own eyes reflecting his disgust as Tylor smirked. Sweat rose as did the sickness in his stomach. He felt his heart squeeze severely and his body began to shake. Bracing his legs apart, he let the eight-foot twist of braided leather loose so it coiled on the ground between his feet. "You ready, Louis?" he asked gently, his voice rough and unsteady as he looked into his friend's eyes.

Louis nodded and braced. "I ready, Boss."

The torchlight danced over Louis's broad, sweat-slick back.

But for the muffled whimpering of Louis's wife from the shanty, silence hung thick as the humidity in the air.

With sweat burning his eyes, Chantz turned back to

Boris. "What will it take for you to walk away right now and forget this?"

Boris's lips curved and his eyes narrowed. "Do it or Tylor will . . . boy."

With the final crack of the whip, Chantz flung it as hard as he could at Boris's feet. Legs braced, he said, "Now get the hell away from here."

The men mounted their horses, one by one peeling away to ride off into the dark. Tylor hung back as Maxwell returned to the house. He looked at Chantz, then down at Louis, spat on the top of Chantz's boot then pivoted on his heels and walked away.

Chantz turned and fell to his knees, took Louis's sweating face in his hands and searched his agonized face. "Damn you, Louis. Damn you. Look at me, you bastard." He shook his friend, self-disgust making his stomach roll. "What the hell did you think you were doing? Why didn't you come to me—"

"Didn't want you involved, Boss." Louis shook his head and averted his eyes. He grimaced.

Closing his eyes, his hands curling around the back of Louis's head, Chantz took the man in his arms, pressed Louis's head to his shoulder, and swallowed back the grief in his throat. "I'd rather have taken the damn whipping myself, Lou. You know that."

Louis nodded and his big hands came up to grip Chantz. "I know you loves me, Boss. I know you do."

Tessa came running from the shack, and Chantz backed away, stumbled to his feet, blinded by tears and sweat and the absolute fury he felt at Boris and Tylor. He wanted to storm up the path and haul Tylor out by his lank hair. He wanted to beat the meanness out of him. He wanted him to suffer—

Juliette stood in the dark, beyond the torchlight, despair on her face, her body trembling. Chantz stopped short as he saw her. The sick in the pit of his stomach rose up his throat.

"Chantz," she cried, her hand reaching for him.

"Get the hell away from me," he choked. "Do you hear me, Juliette? Just stay the hell away from me."

Seven

The emotion in her heart and head was not unlike the swirling, dizzying sensations that had rocked her upon hearing of her father's suicide: shock and heart-sinking despair. Followed by righteous anger that a man would be whipped for sheltering his own brother . . . that a man would be *forced* to whip his friend in order to protect him from a far worse cruelty at Tylor or Boris Wilcox's hands. What fury she had first felt for Chantz participating in the punishment had fast evaporated when recognizing his disgust, when witnessing his pain, him holding his friend in his arms as if Louis were a broken child . . . of the tears in his eyes that he'd tried desperately to hide when coming face-to-face with her in the dark.

She had spent the remainder of the evening in her room with the doors locked. Rosie had attempted to coerce her out with rice pudding and lemonade. Liza had tapped gently but unconvincingly. Then Little Clara came tiptoeing and volunteered a chunk of ho'hound if Miss Julie would stop crying. Juliette had unlocked the door for the child and both had curled up together in the middle of the bed, sucked on hard candy, and watched lightning bugs dance like fairies in the dark.

The next two days she avoided going out-of-doors altogether, which annoyed her all the more. Rosie had promised to teach her how to dip wicks for tallow candles, which she did in a cauldron over an open fire.

Once she glimpsed Chantz and Maxwell standing nose-to-nose on the whistle walk, Maxwell shouting into Chantz's face about the escalating cost of repairing the levee. Chantz hadn't so much as flinched in the heated wave of Maxwell's anger and Juliette had found herself mesmerized once again, caught up in emotions she had never before experienced . . .

By the end of the first day of the Buleys' visit she would have gladly traded a few lashes of Chantz's whip for the visual and verbal cuts administered by Mrs. Buley and her daughter Phyllis, who was pretty, but far too prissy. And rude. Juliette's irritation mounted as Phyllis refused to so much as look Juliette in the eye. When Phyllis spoke to her—if she spoke to her at all—it was with barely more respect than she showed Liza, which was precious little. Liza insisted that Phyllis was jealous of anyone who would likely rob her of the gentlemen's attention. Perhaps, Juliette mused, but she got the feeling there was more to Phyllis's hot glances than met the eye. And as far as Hazel was concerned, no doubt there were far too many recollections of Maureen batting like moths in her memory. Every time Juliette opened her mouth, Hazel glared at her as if Juliette had launched a full-scale war to seduce her husband. As if she would. Fred Buley resembled Simon's bullfrog.

Hazel Buley was thin as a beanpole with hair black as the jet earbobs she wore. Her brows were fixed in a deep vee between her brown eyes, giving her the appearance of a perpetual scowler. Not that Juliette blamed the woman for any unhappiness she might harbor. To spend one's life with a man who not only resembled Simon's bullfrog but erupted frequently with the most foul-smelling flatulence, so that Juliette was forced to cover her nose with her scented kerchief, would depress most women to their coffins.

Upon their arrival the Buleys had swept through Holly House like they were royalty, sending servants scurrying and Rosie to the kitchen, grumbling under her breath. For the last day Rosie had practically worked herself to a frazzle. Phyllis demanded her eggs poached for breakfast while Hazel wanted hers scrambled. Then there was Fred Buley who continually sent back his fried eggs because the yolks were too runny or too hard, and who wanted his grits sweetened not salted.

Finally reaching the end of her tether of patience, Juliette had stood from her chair and declared at the top of her voice, "What difference does it make if the damn eggs are poached or scrambled or the grits are sweet or salted? If you're hungry enough you'll eat. If not, I suggest you take a lounge on the gallery and pray that your dinner is more to your liking."

Maxwell had glared at her with a cheek full of biscuit, his face red as the strawberry jam on his plate. Tylor howled in hilarity and Rosie dumped an entire platter of brawn in Hazel's lap.

For the next half-hour Maxwell, upon ushering her into the privacy of his library, as quietly as possible, considering his irritation, pointed out to her that the Buley family was one of the most respected families in Louisiana and should they decide to could spoil her chances of ever being accepted into their polite society. She, of course, pointed out that there was absolutely nothing "polite" about the Buleys and if they were an example of "polite" then she would certainly hate to come face-to-face with crassness.

On the other hand, Juliette found Andrew Buley, Phyllis's older brother, handsome and charming and without the pretentiousness of his family.

She frantically wondered how she would survive the three long days of acting as hostess to Max's guests. With mounting despair, she realized that she must certainly harbor yet another of her mother's infamous traits.

Chitchat bored her to tears. So did stupid people.

Idling for hours in the gallery shade, fanned by the overhead punka while flies buzzed and hounds panted and drooled puddles, filled her with a restless annoyance that made her feel explosive. Had Liza not lingered in the background, diverting her attention each time Fred Buley leered at her from behind his cigar, she would no doubt have further embarrassed Max and totally humiliated herself.

But therein was a problem as well. Apparently Phyllis and Hazel found sport in Liza's fetching. By the time they all finished their midday meal and sprawled on their gallery lounges, Liza had run herself ragged. Her clothes were drenched with sweat, which wasn't surprising, considering the heat felt close to boiling. Juliette, however, kept a keen eye on her friend, who sat on a hard chair near the door wagging a palmetto fan at her face. Something had been amiss with Liza since the evening she had confronted Tylor in her bedroom. Occasionally she glanced at Juliette with a shadow of some underlying emotion swimming in her dark eyes.

"I declare," Phyllis sighed as she cooled herself with an ornate fan of dyed blue pigeon feathers that perfectly matched her dress and silk slippers. "I can't recall such a hot spell so early in June. I'm simply exhausted."

"Feels like rain again," Fred mused as he smoked and

looked out on the Holly grounds that were finally drying. New grass had sprung up in thick thatches and the children, too young to work in the cane fields, were scattered over the grounds, nearly to the river, bent and plucking weeds that they tossed into willow baskets. "How's the rebuilding of that levee, Maxwell? Making any progress?"

"For whatever good it will do me," Max replied, smoking. "Chantz said if I'm to guarantee flood protection I'd have to tear down this house and construct a dam right here where we sit. Can you imagine? I told him he could go to hell. Man's crazy as a betsy bug if he thinks I'm moving my house."

Andrew, his long legs crossed and his white shirtsleeves rolled nearly to his elbows, turned his brown eyes on Juliette where she sat with her hands clasped in her lap and her mind drowsy with boredom. Andrew had obviously taken after his mother, slender with refined features and brown hair that waved slightly around his temples and nape. He had a kind look in his eye and an easy way of speaking that took the edge off her discontent at having to wile away her time watching hounds pant when she would rather be off in the kitchen meddling in Rosie's business.

"Chantz is a smart man," Andrew pointed out, smiling at Juliette. His eyes narrowed slightly as she sat straighter with the mention of Chantz's name. Her face turned warm and with frustration she realized it had nothing to do with anger. "He's got a good eye for detail, not to mention sugarcane. Might behoove you, Maxwell, to listen to him."

"I would expect that coming from you, Andrew," Max said, frowning. "You're his friend."

"Yes, I am. Therefore, I know what Holly Plantation means to Chantz. He's a man who takes great pride in his accomplishments. Those cane fields are his accomplishment. Correct me if I'm wrong, but when the sugar finally settled last season, you sent as many hogsheads down the river with half the cane as some planters did with full crops."

Tylor mopped his face with a kerchief and curled his lip. "Why is it ever damn conversation somehow gets on the topic of Chantz Boudreaux?"

Andrew flashed him a less than tolerant smile. "Perhaps if you took a more active role in this plantation you'd find yourself the topic of conversation. Not much to say about a man who does nothing more than sit around all day swatting flies. Then again, maybe Max should count his lucky stars. I suspect by the time you finished asserting your authority over your daddy's slaves there wouldn't be enough of them capable of harvesting the cane, much less cooking it."

Phyllis stopped her fanning; her eyebrows drew together. "Mr. Carrington tells me that one of his runaways was discovered here at Holly a few nights ago, sheltered by that monstrously big Louis creature. Chantz was forced to whip him for it."

Again, Andrew looked directly at Juliette, his expression serious. "A terrible thing for Chantz. He respects Louis mightily. The feeling is mutual. But far better to have been by Chantz's hand than Tylor or Wilcox."

Juliette left her chair and walked to the ledge of the gallery. Drawing in a shallow, unsteady breath, she said, "The whipping of a human being is unforgivable."

"I'm certain Chantz would heartily agree with you, Miss Julie."

She looked around, straight into Andrew's eyes.

"I understand," Phyllis said somewhat dreamily as she fixed her gaze on the brown moving river in the distance, "that compared to most, when it comes to punishment, Chantz has a gentle hand. There is a certain talent few men possess that enables one to apply light pain that leaves the skin burning, but not cut."

Phyllis pressed a lace-edge kerchief to the hollow at the base of her throat. Her voice dropped. Her eyes became sleepy. "Funny, isn't it? On the surface Chantz doesn't seem like the sort of man who could be gentle."

She fluttered the fan at her face and moistened her lips with her tongue. "There is nothing remotely gentlemanly at all about his appearance. Everything about him exudes energy and anger and barely restrained power. The man virtually sucks the very air out of the room when he enters it. How he can possibly contain all that ferocity to show the slightest hint of gentleness astounds me."

"Been a long time since Chantz last whipped a man." Andrew looked out at the river. "Only one other that I know of—"

"Cost me eight hundred dollars," Max pointed out angrily. He walked to the far end of the gallery, hands on his hips. "I haven't forgiven him for it. Every time I ride by that grave, I get mad all over again."

"Man who rapes little girls deserves what he got, Max." Andrew narrowed his eyes and shook his head. "I suspect Chantz would do the same again, given similar circumstances. You know what he's like when it comes to children. Got a protective streak in him wide as that damn river."

Hazel looked around at Liza. "Fetch me some water, Liza. All this chatter about whippings and Chantz Boudreaux has made my throat feel like river mud. Can't we talk about something else, gentlemen?"

Yes, please, Juliette thought. Anything besides Chantz Boudreaux.

Wearily, Liza stood and entered the house. Juliette noted that Andrew's gaze followed her before he forced himself to focus again on the water. His face looked darker and intense.

"Heard tell there have been a number of deaths in New Orleans," Fred said, then puffed on his cigar. "Down along the river district. City is holding its breath that we're not looking at a new outbreak of fever."

Hazel huffed and puffed out her breasts with self-importance. "River wastrel. Those dreadful mud daubers and foreign shipmen. They're all crawling with one form of disease or another. We shouldn't be too hasty in jumping to frightening conclusions."

"Still, we won't be making any jaunts to New Orleans any time soon, just to be on the safe side. Damn fever take off through the city and the outcome would be catastrophic. Last major outbreak killed five thousand."

Phyllis sniffed and shrugged. "That was years and years ago, Papa. We're far too sophisticated now for such a disease to annoy us."

"Long as it stays in the river district I shan't give it another moment's thought." Hazel's lips thinned and curved as she slid a look toward Juliette. "God has a way of cleansing the scurf from society when need be. He smites them with His heavenly sword by disease or . . . fire so that the righteous may prevail."

Juliette stared into Hazel's face until dark color crept into the woman's sallow cheeks. With a lift of one eyebrow, Juliette said, "I take it you're a very religious woman, Mrs. Buley."

"I attend mass every Sunday," she replied.

"Then you're aware of Matthew seven one. 'Judge not, that ye be not judged.' Or as Thomas Browne, noted physician wrote sometime in the late sixteen hundreds, 'No man can justly censure or condemn another, because indeed no man truly knows another.'"

"Amen," Andrew declared, cutting off whatever remark his mother was prepared to make. Her mouth snapped shut like a trap; giving Andrew a glower that made him grin, she then turned her pointed chin toward the river and sniffed.

"We could discuss my wedding plans," Phyllis chirped, allowing Juliette a smile that was just short of smug.

"Again?" Andrew covered his yawn with the back of his hand.

"It's going to be a garden affair with five hundred guests. We'll have a barbecue, and did I mention that Marr Engles is designing my gown?"

"Yes," Andrew said. "Several times."

"It's not every day I get married." Phyllis dabbed her hanky to the beads of perspiration on her brow. Her dark eyes flashed toward Juliette, no doubt to determine if she had sufficiently grabbed her attention. "Marr is from New York where he was the finest couturier outside of Paris."

"Until he ruined himself," Fred pointed out with an edge to his voice.

"He married a Negro," Hazel said in a low voice. "Can you imagine?"

"She was a quadroon, Mother," Andrew corrected with a touch of annoyance.

"Doesn't matter." Hazel set her chin determinedly. "Color is color. Makes no difference whether she's black as spades or pale as fresh cream. There are simply some things that are not condoned. One is marrying a woman of color and the other is . . ." Hazel snapped her mouth shut.

"Marrying a prostitute," Phyllis finished as she fixed her attention on a pair of young boys attempting to balance their wicker baskets on their heads. "I'm not sure which is more shameful."

Juliette stared at her.

Andrew cleared his throat and uncrossed his legs. "I understand there's trouble again with that old bull gator."

"Mean, hungry son of a bitch," Tylor remarked nervously. His brow creased as he sat forward with his elbows on his knees. "I heard him last night—"

"There you go again with stupid talk," Max interrupted.

"I tell you, Daddy, I heard him. 'Round midnight. 'Bout froze my blood. There's fifteen feet to him or I ain't sitting here. Bull that big could bite a man in two like that." He snapped his fingers.

Max shook his head. "You'll have to excuse Tylor. He has an inordinate fear of gators."

"Not just any gator. *That* gator. He's crafty and he has a taste for humans. Once they get a taste of a man they just ain't satisfied with anything else."

"You're not serious." Juliette leaned against a column. "You don't really mean there's a creature that eats people skulking up and down the river."

Fred nodded sleepily. "Took his eighth last week. Came right out of the water and plucked one of Bartholemew's slaves out of a boat while he was fishing."

Tylor left his chair and started to pace. His gaze swept the river. He wrung his hands.

As Liza returned with a glass of water and handed it to Hazel, Andrew looked up at her and grinned. "You know what they say about fear and gators, Liza?"

She shook her head, her cheeks turning dark and her lips curving as she stepped away, self-consciously pushing back a strand of hair spilling over her brow. "What do they say about fear and gators, Mr. Andrew?"

"Fear is like an aphrodisiac to a bull gator. The scent of it lures him in. Makes him hungry. If I was Tylor, I'd be real careful about how much fear I show. Considering we're on the tail end of gator mating season, I suspect that bull will be eager to sweet-talk about anything he can wrap his mouth around. Why, I'll bet he's lying out there right now swimming in the scent of Tylor's fear. Next thing you know, it'll be crawling up those stairs tonight—"

"Shut your mouth," Tylor shouted with such vehemence his voice cracked. "I ain't afraid of that damn bull. I'm just respectful of him."

"I'm glad to hear it. Then you can join us in the hunt. We'll need all the hands we can get."

"Hunt?" Liza asked. Her face suddenly intense and her dark eyes sharp, she stared at Andrew and said, "You got no business huntin' bull gators. You best be leavin' that up to Chantz."

"Speak of the devil." Andrew grinned and pointed.

Chantz rode his big bay gelding up the drive. He didn't bother to use stirrups. His calves in boots to his knees held the animal's lathered sides just snugly enough to maintain his balance. He wore a wide-brimmed straw hat cocked low over his eyes. His shirt was mostly unbuttoned, exposing a plunge of glistening copper skin.

Andrew moved up beside Juliette, leaned against a column, and glanced down at her. "You're looking a little flushed, Miss Julie. Maybe you should lie down awhile."

She shoved a heavy coil of hair behind her ear, sank harder against the column, only vaguely aware that Phyllis Buley had moved up beside her, between her and Andrew. Her gaze fixed on Chantz, Juliette felt the air steam her face and the heat of the sun-baked porch sizzle her bare feet.

Chantz rode the gelding close to the gallery, removed his hat, and blotted his forehead with his shirtsleeve. His hair looked black with sweat. It tumbled over his forehead and around his ears in damp waves as he turned his blue eyes up and rewarded them all with a curl of his lips that made the blood rush from Juliette's head.

She tried to look away from his face—those blue eyes made all the bluer by his sun-darkened face and black hair—but she realized in that moment that she might as well tell the Mississippi to stop moving. The pull of the man straddling the tired animal, his face streaked by dust and sweat, was as powerful as the river tow.

"Ladies," Chantz greeted with a smile. "You all look cool and pretty this afternoon." His gaze locked on Phyllis and he raised one eyebrow. "Miss Buley. How are the wedding plans coming along?"

Unblinking, Phyllis stared down at him, silent so long that Juliette frowned and narrowed her eyes, assessed her profile closely. The woman whose complexion had glowed with heat since her arrival at Holly House appeared, suddenly, as sickly yellow as Rosie's tallow candles. And her eyes—fairly glittering with a kind of intensity that electrified the air.

Realization struck Juliette.

Phyllis Buley was sick in love with Chantz!

It was as obvious as the temperature was sweltering.

Phyllis drew in a breath and replied, "Very well, thank you. It promises to be the finest wedding Baton Rouge has ever seen. I'm a very lucky woman."

His grin stretched and the horse shifted under him. "Well, if nothin' else you'll have a fine plantation to show for it."

Andrew made a noise and Phyllis's spine went rigid.

"What's that supposed to mean?" she said in a tight voice.

"What he means," Andrew said, looking down at his sister, "is that if you're marrying for reasons other than love, you damn well better get something out of it."

Her face flushed with anger as she turned on Chantz

again. "I'll have you both know, I adore Horace Carrington." Eyes narrowing, she added, "He's the kindest, most considerate man I've ever known. The fact that he owns the largest plantation in the area has nothing to do with it."

"That'll change soon enough," Andrew pointed out as he turned his focus on Juliette.

She forced herself to shift her attention from Phyllis. Thank God for the column at her back or she might surely have collapsed in a pool of her straw-colored cotton skirt. Fixing on Andrew's eyes, she struggled to breathe normally as Andrew added, "Belle Jarod is the largest plantation in the area. Now that Miss Julie has come home, I suspect the old place might yet rise from the ashes."

Lifting her chin, Phyllis said in a flat tone, "She won't get very far without a husband. Besides, what could she possibly know about planting—raised in a convent all these years? She'll need a husband with money—"

"Or muscle." Andrew cut her off. "Land is there already. House is there. Or most of it, what didn't burn. The mills are there. Heck, with a few months' work to clear the grounds and plant, this time next year Miss Julie could be looking forward to her first harvest."

"Do you think so, Andrew?" Juliette forced a smile.

"Absolutely." He nodded.

"Andrew tells us that you're gator hunting tonight, Chantz." Max planted himself in front of Juliette.

Chantz nodded. "Bartholemew is offering a reward to the man who kills that bull."

"Tylor is joining us." Andrew grinned as he thumbed at Tylor whose face was slowly turning the same sickly shade of green as the moss draping from the trees.

Chantz laughed. "He'll make good gator bait, I guess."

Juliette squeezed between Phyllis and Max, neither of them willing to give an inch. She finally shouldered Max hard enough so he was forced to step aside.

"Tell me about a gator hunt," she said. The words were more like a challenge than a request. She dared him to look her in the eye with the same smoldering intensity as he'd regarded her that night on his porch steps. She'd know right then and there if her suspicions were right—that there was a good reason for Phyllis's moon-calf expression. A woman didn't look at a man with such blatant longing unless something had passed between them. As Juliette set her shoulders and curled her fingers into her limp skirts, she thought with a fresh blaze of heat over her cheeks that she must surely look as pitifully desperate as Phyllis.

Chantz looked away, shook his head, put his hat back on so it cast a shadow over his eyes when he finally focused on her. "I'd hate to upset your sensibilities again, Miss Julie. Most women find the process of gator hunting distasteful and alarming."

Her lips curved, another challenge. "In case you haven't noticed, Chantz . . . I'm not most women."

Phyllis gasped and went stiff as the column at Juliette's back.

Chantz shifted in his saddle, causing the horse to move to better balance his weight. His jaw looked chiseled of granite and dark with a day's growth of beard. Silence pulsated the hot air. Even the hound stopped panting, his face drooping and his eyes peering up at Juliette from under folds of loose skin.

Of course, she wasn't like most women. She was Maureen Jarod's daughter. What other woman would dare stand here with her naked toes curled over the edge of the hot plank gallery flooring, her hair allowed to spill around her face and shoulders, her body radiating a challenge to a man who personified the forbidden?

"Well," she said, her cheeks burning, "are you going to answer me or not?"

"Folks meet at dusk," Andrew offered, though Juliette continued to look down into Chantz's shadowed eyes. "On the banks of the deep bayou. That's where he lives. Not in the big river. Too open. Too fast. He likes the marshes where the water is still and a little stagnant. More trees and reeds the better. Especially now. He's rutting. He'll stay close because he's territorial. He won't like interlopers be it another gator or a man. Could be what happened to Bartholemew's slave. Could be he boated too close to a nest or a pod and the bull reacted.

"Men go out in their boats at dark and bait the water and banks with animal and fish entrails. Bloodier the better. Louder they stink, the better. They come back in and spend the next few hours around bonfires. They eat. Sing. Dance . . . pray."

Andrew's voice dropped, barely above a whisper. While everyone else leaned toward him, rapt by his story, Juliette continued to be held by Chantz's gaze. What, exactly, did she see there?

" 'Round midnight everything goes real quiet. Firelight dwindles. Night gets so heavy you can feel it weighing down on you. River sounds begin to thump at you like a heartbeat growing so loud you want to cover your ears. Something primitive crawls into your blood then. Makes you do things that come morning will cause you to question your sanity. You become the bayou. Earth. Stars. Water. Animal.

"Suddenly there is silence and absolute stillness. Not so much as a cricket chirp to be heard. Then, somewhere out in the dark, comes the low grunt of that old bull. Sound like you won't ever hear again. Starts deep in his belly and rolls up through his snout like a growl of thunder.

"Men reach for their weapons and take to their boats, one to paddle, the other to hold the torch high. It's the light from that torch that will give the bull away. While his body is submerged in the water, those two eyes will reflect the firelight like mirrors. You give the water a pop with the flat of the oar. Then watch that bastard move in real slow, attracted by the slap of the water, the torchlight, the smell of fresh meat and fear. Oh, there is plenty of that, all right, especially when that old bull sinks out of sight. You know he's coming up somewhere, you just don't know where or when. So you take your lance in both hands and wait. You usually got only one chance. If you don't time it just right you're either dead or you can give up the hunt until another night."

Andrew eased down the gallery, toward Tylor who stood with his back to them, his hands knotted into white fists as he stared out at the river. The shirt clung to Tylor's back with patches of sweat. His body visibly shook.

"One chance," Andrew said quietly. "Got to get him in his soft underside. Just the moment he comes scooting out of that water to make a grab for you, you take that sharp lance and drive it deep and fast into his throat—'cause if you don't, those big jaws are gonna open right up and chomp!"

He slapped Tylor's ribs hard. Tylor yelped and toppled off the porch, landed in a mud puddle and came up spitting and glaring at everyone who howled in laughter. His face, or what they could see of it behind the spatters of mud, was colorless as a corpse.

"Gotcha," Andrew laughed.

"You're a cruel bastard, Andrew Buley!" Tylor coughed and slung mud from his hands.

"What's wrong, Tylor? I thought you wasn't scared of that old bull."

Tylor turned on his heels and stormed away.

Chantz shook his head and rode away. Juliette watched him go, then turned her attention back to Phyllis whose gaze remained fixed on Chantz, her countenance hardly belonging to a woman looking forward to her wedding day. She looked, Juliette thought with a sinking heart, like a woman desperately in love with Chantz Boudreaux.

Eight

When Juliette scaled the stone wall secluding the convent from the village at the bottom of the dale, as she rushed through midnight shadows to watch and wager on cockfights with ale-swigging men whose foul curses made her ears burn, she considered that the Reverend Mother could be right about her character—except she had prided herself on the fact that while she might find a certain spiteful pleasure in defying decorum where cocks and ale were concerned, men had been another matter.

She had vowed to herself, since she was old enough to understand her father's reasons for despising her, that she would remain chaste before marriage—unlike her mother. And afterward . . . faithful and loving and devoted to her beloved husband—whoever that might be.

That, of course, was before she woke up with her arms and legs wrapped around Chantz Boudreaux, drowsily gazing into his sleeping features. That was before she knew what a man's hard body felt like under her hands. Before she'd ever touched hair so thick and soft, that coiled around her fingers and lay upon her pale skin like a silken shadow. Before the scent of a man had filled up her raw senses and intoxicated her blood.

Before sensations, dormant until that moment, surged to life and plunged her into a whirlpool of dark prurience.

Before the thought of a man occupied her every hour— her every dream—and made her heart ache so fiercely at times she thought she would surely expire.

"She's paced the length of the gallery a hundred times since supper." Juliette peeked out her door, toward Phyllis's shadowed figure at the far end of the upper gallery. "I've never seen such blatant emotion on a woman's face as when she looked into Chantz's eyes this afternoon. It was positively indecent."

Liza, looking at her own reflection in the mirror, shrugged as she pulled her hair up and fixed it with Juliette's pearl-backed combs. "I has, Miss Julie."

Juliette looked at her, her brows drawing together.

"You get that same expression ever'time you look at him."

"There you go again." Juliette frowned harder, her nervousness beating at her stomach like butterflies.

"You tellin me you ain't a little jealous over Miss Phyllis and Chantz?"

"Then you admit there's something between them."

Liza removed the combs and reached for a hair brush. "Was somethin' between them and you didn't answer my question."

"Is he in love with her?" She held her breath as a knot of emotion formed in her chest. What, dear heavens, would she do if Liza confirmed her suspicions?

"I suppose he had some kind of feelin's for her. He ain't the type of man to waste his energy on women he don't care for."

"Were they intimate?"

Liza shrugged. "You tell me. Would a woman with nothin' more than an occasional flirtation with a man be stalkin' in the dark like a cat in heat?"

She repeated, "Is he in love with Phyllis?"

Liza appeared to consider her choice of words before responding. "Don't matter if he was, do it? She be marryin' Horace Carrington in a few months."

"I have to know, Liza."

Liza's head slowly turned and her eyes narrowed, not just with speculation, but realization. Something akin to panic ignited in her features.

"Lord have mercy," she said cautiously. "I can't believe it. Chantz Boudreaux might be tomcat enough to mess with the likes of a woman like Phyllis, but it ain't like him to bother no innocent. There's been plenty who tried. Come Sundays at church they flock like sparrows, titterin' and flappin' their pretty fans and battin' their eyelashes anytime he glances their way. He don't pay them no mind. Then here you come and suddenly Chantz ain't Chantz no more. Short tempered. Surly. Restless. And stupid. Lord have mercy, he done gone and got stupid."

Juliette averted her eyes. Her face burned.

"Somethin' done happened between you," Liza said. "What has that man gone and done?"

"Nothing." Juliette shook her head. "Only a kiss . . ."

"Only? Kissin' don't make a body shake like you is shakin' right now. He be puttin' his hands on you, Miss Julie?" Liza dropped onto the ottoman as if her legs had turned to water. "He ain't—"

"No!"

Exhaustion overwhelmed her. She wanted to pound her head against the wall—knock some sense back into it. She could deny it all she wanted—to herself, to Liza—but she'd known the very moment she'd looked into Phyllis's star-struck eyes and felt the bitter, biting teeth of jealousy; she had become infatuated with Chantz Boudreaux.

No, not simply infatuated. The emotions rolling over and over in her chest were far more disturbing than a simple infatuation.

Slumping against the wall, Juliette closed her eyes. "He kissed me and I liked it. God help me, it's all I think about any longer. I toss and turn in my bed all night counting the minutes until daylight, thinking of excuses to see him again."

She sighed and shook her head. "I've become my mother, Liza. I've become the very woman I loathed all these years for her despicable behavior. I don't know what came over me. The urges . . . my mind screamed one thing and my body did another."

Liza shook her head. "Lord knows I ain't one to preach, but, Miss Julie, you can't be foolin' with him. You'll get him whupped, or worse."

Liza's voice turned rough, the tone slightly bitter. "You gots a whole lotta problems to deal with now. Like the hungers that's gonna take you over, Miss Julie. The needs that make you do things that a rational woman wouldn't even consider."

Arms crossed tightly over her bosom as if holding her emotions in check, Liza rocked forward and back. Her dark eyes reflected the lamplight like glowing coals. "You think if Phyllis Buley could control herself she'd be riskin' her reputation by foolin' with Chantz?" She gave a harsh laugh and shook her head. "You can tell yourself a hundred times a day that it's gonna stop. But it don't ever stop, Miss Julie, once it starts.

"Look at you, your face flushed and your body sweatin'

and your eyes full of sufferin' cause you is thinkin' of him with another woman. What you gonna do if he find someone else he loves more? Someone prettier . . ."

With a soft whimper, Liza covered her face with her hands.

Juliette ran to her. "Liza! Liza, whatever is wrong with you?" On her knees, Juliette tugged Liza's hands from her face. Tears smeared her cheeks and her lips quivered. Her entire body appeared to convulse in an attempt to hold in her distress.

Turning her face away, Liza shook her head. "Don't you be botherin' with me now, Miss Julie. You gots enough to worry 'bout, what with you all in a tizzy over Chantz and Maxwell grumblin' 'bout you not hostessin' proper." Liza swiped her hand over her sweating brow. "Lord, it's hot."

Juliette rushed to the basin of water and dampened a cloth. As she gently placed it on Liza's forehead, Liza's dark, troubled eyes watched her.

"Reckon I'm more tired than I thought. I declare but Hazel Buley have me runnin' from sunup to bedtime. Liza, fetch my slippers. Liza, fetch another lump of sugar for my coffee. Liza, I hear a gnat buzzin'. How am I suppose to sleep when there's a gnat hummin' in my ear? Liza, my feet are dreadful hot. Fan them for me." Liza managed a dry chuckle. "Her damn feet smell like skunk. It's no wonda I spent half the last three days bent over a chamber pot."

Juliette bathed the sweat from Liza's brow and forced a smile. "Have you told Andrew you're with child?" she asked softly.

Liza sat up straight and pushed the cloth away. Fear flared in her eyes and her face contorted. "What you talkin' 'bout? Tell Mr. Andrew what? Soon as I get the Buleys

tucked in for the night Rosie gonna ply me with her cura-
tives. I'll be right as rain come mornin'. "

Juliette caught Liza's hand and squeezed it. "Liza, I think
you should—"

"I gets this way every summer. Neva could tolerate the
heat much, even as a child. Rosie give me somethin' to thin
my blood a touch and I'll be just fine. Just fine. Now I don't
want to be talkin' 'bout me no more. Understand what I be
tellin' you, Miss Julie?" Liza stared at Juliette hard, her face
tense and her fingers curled around Juliette's hand so
tightly it throbbed.

Juliette nodded.

"Good." Standing, Liza took a deep breath and blotted
the tears from her cheeks. "There now. All better. Won't be
no more talk 'bout Mr. Andrew—"

"I would never take him from you, Liza."

Liza's head snapped around and she regarded Juliette so
fiercely, her body so rigid she appeared honed from ma-
hogany.

"That's why you've been acting so strangely since the
Buleys arrived, isn't it? You've been jealous."

"I seen the way the men look at you and I can't blame
them. Man would have to be blind not to think you is the
prettiest woman in Louisiana." She smoothed her hands
down over her limp skirt. "I ain't exactly precious, am I?"

A smile touching Juliette's mouth, she took Liza's face
between her hands. "I told you already. You're one of the
prettiest women I've ever seen. Only difference between us
is all these fancy clothes Maxwell forces me to wear."

"Case you ain't looked lately . . ." Liza grinned. "They is
more different between us than clothes." More softly, she
said, "How come you know 'bout me and Andrew?"

"Your adoration for the man might not have been so

blatant as Phyllis's for Chantz, but any woman with eyes could see the two of you adore each other. His every glance at you was a caress, Liza."

Liza's shoulders slumped. "I try to keep it from my face when he's near," she said with a shadow of sad resignation in her voice. "It's just so hard."

She turned her dark eyes back to Juliette's. "I know what it's like to crave the touch of the forbidden, Miss Julie. I know the look a woman gets when the need fills her up, and the frustration gets so hard to hold back you wants to explode. I see it in my eyes ever' time I looks in the glass. You spend half your life cussin' him for doin' that to you, the other half thankin' Almighty God that you be fortunate to experience the kind of passion that most women won't ever have the pleasure of knowin'. "

She laughed to herself. "For all her high and mighty airs, I can't help but pity poor Miss Phyllis. She no better off than me. Both in love with a man we can't have. The kind of man who gets in the blood and won't ever leave. The kind of man who fill up your head with crazy thoughts so you can't reason no more."

Liza took hard hold of Juliette's shoulders. "You know what I'm sayin'. You feelin' it too. Rosie call it a fever. And it is. Right down deep in the pit of my belly. Sometimes I feel like I'm just gonna go right up in a lick of smoke. Don't tell me it all in my head like Rosie do. You got it yourself for Chantz."

She felt weary of denying it to herself. "I'm afraid," she admitted, her voice little more than a whisper. "I don't know myself any longer, Liza. I can't control my thoughts, or my body. I lie here at night listening to those hounds bay and the night birds cry and thoughts of Chantz start a slow undulation here." Pressing her hand low on her belly, Juliette closed her eyes. "I'm ashamed to say I liked it when he kissed me. I hadn't meant to. I didn't expect it. Sometimes I think if he doesn't kiss me again I'll simply fade away."

Forcing a smile to her lips, she sat back on her heels. "Aren't we the pair? Both all tangled up over men—"

" 'Cept you don't gots no baby in you." Liza looked at her hands in her lap. "I heard what they say today, the Buleys, 'bout that dressmakin' man marryin' color. Can't happen. Can't be spoilin' things for Andrew. Don't know what I was thinkin' to go fallin' in love with that man."

Her shoulders shrugged and she sniffed, grinned, and tucked a lock of hair behind her ear. "I just so happy when I'm with him, Miss Julie. I don't think nothin' 'bout nothin' 'cept how good it feel for his arms to be around me."

Juliette stood and reached for the hair brush on the dresser. She began to brush Liza's soft hair, sweeping it up and holding it with the seedpearl combs. She met Liza's eyes in the mirror.

"You want to look especially pretty tonight, I think. The sky is bright with starlight. The air heavy with the scent of magnolias." Juliette reached for the tiny pearl earbobs on the dresser, then held them up to Liza's ears.

Liza's eyes widened. "Oh, Miss Julie, I couldn't!"

"Of course you could." She applied the jewelry to Liza's ears, then she hurried to her wardrobe and rummaged through it, pulled out a pale blue gown trimmed in white eyelet lace. "You'll look absolutely fetching in this gown, Liza, and he'll—"

"No!" She jumped up, one hand over her mouth and her eyes huge. "I couldn't possibly—"

"It doesn't suit me, Liza. Since Maxwell gave me these clothes I can do anything at all I want with them. I'm thinking you need a fine dress like this."

Liza stared at her, her hand still covering her mouth.

Juliette smiled. "You're going to look so pretty in this dress that Andrew might never leave."

"Juliette is quite a woman." Andrew poured whiskey into a glass and flashed Chantz a smile. "I don't remember Maureen clearly, but clearly enough that the moment I saw Juliette I felt as if I'd seen a ghost."

Drowsy from his warm bath, Rosie's ham and beans and hot water cornbread, not to mention his second two-finger portion of bourbon in the last half hour, Chantz stretched out on his bed, his back propped against the headboard.

The last thing he wanted to do in that moment was talk about Juliette Broussard. Hell, he had enough on his mind the last days. His workers were frying in the heat and suffocating from the humidity. Max rode him constantly about money—then comes Phyllis finding every excuse possible to present herself in his line of vision. Once he might have actually given a damn. Now—

"Baton Rouge is all abuzz about Juliette," came Andrew's voice. "Soon Holly House will be swarming like a beehive with men callers. She won't last long, not with her looks. Then, of course, there is the prospect of latching on to Belle Jarod."

"I really don't care to talk about Juliette."

Andrew dropped into the only chair in the room and took a deep drink of bourbon before adding, "I suspect whoever sets his sights on Juliette will have a hell of a time of it, however. By the expression on Maxwell's face when he looks at her, any man who thinks he's going to walk hand in hand into the sunset with Miss Julie will do it over Maxwell's dead body. Just a friendly warning, Chantz . . . as if you didn't know already that your daddy has ulterior motives for the young lady."

Laughing, he added, "And they haven't got a damn thing to do with Tylor. Why, I suspect Tylor would rather crawl into bed with that bull gator than with Juliette Broussard . . . or with any woman for that matter."

Chantz smoked the fine cigar Andrew had given him and regarded his friend closely. "You one of those bees, Drew?" he asked with a curl of his lips.

Andrew frowned and drank again. "I suspect my daddy wouldn't mind my getting my hooks into Belle Jarod. Hell, I wasn't born yesterday. There was more to this visit than my mother and father simply desiring to idle away the days discoursing on gators. Despite Juliette's less than illustrious parentage, most mamas would welcome such a woman into the fold if it meant their son came into fifteen thousand of the finest acres in Louisiana, not to mention a palace that, with a little work, could be restored to its former grandeur."

His eyes turning dark and troubled, Andrew ran his hand through his hair and sank deeper into the chair. "But we both know that isn't going to happen, and we both know why."

"Because you're in love with my sister."

"I don't know how I can keep this up, Chantz." Andrew shook his head. "I'm thirty years old. I should be married by now with a passel of children. Instead I'm still sneaking around to shanties in the woods, to my best friend's house at midnight like some wet-behind-the-ears adolescent up to mischief." Andrew left his chair and paced. "What the hell am I supposed to do?"

"Leave Louisiana and take her with you. Marry her."

"You think I haven't thought of that? You think I wouldn't like to? Can you imagine my mother's reaction? Oh by the way, Mama, I'm getting married. To a slave. But never mind that, Maxwell Hollinsworth is her daddy so you need only be half horrified."

Chantz watched his friend through a stream of cigar smoke. "We both know that if your daddy discovers your relationship with Liza there's gonna be problems, regardless. While he might applaud your skirt sniffing at Liza as a recreational pastime, if actual emotions enter in he's gonna demand that Maxwell haul Liza to the market."

"Don't I know it? There isn't a night goes by that I don't wake up from that nightmare. Always me watching her dragged across that platform, ankles shackled, presented like a damn broodmare to ham-fisted animals like Boris Wilcox."

There came a knock at the door. Chantz rolled from the bed and answered it.

Liza smiled up at him, then shouldered him aside and rushed into the house. Andrew stared as she twirled on the balls of her feet so the skirt of the blue dress billowed around her ankles.

Laughing, she glanced at Chantz. "I'd say the cat got his tongue, Chantz. What do you think? Do I look as pretty as I feel?"

"Prettier," Andrew declared, his voice tight with breathlessness. "My God, Liza, you're about the prettiest woman I ever saw. Honey, where did you get that dress?"

"Juliette give it to me." She twirled again, her eyes sparkling. "She let me borrow these earbobs, too." She gave her head a shake, causing the pearls to rattle. "And will you look at these combs? You like my hair up like this, Andrew? Do I look sophisticated? Do I look pretty enough to walk arm in arm with you down Chartres Street in New Orleans?"

Chantz slammed the door. Suddenly the bourbon he'd imbibed the last hour and the heat that had baked his body all day felt as if it had settled into a hot core in his belly. He glared at Liza with his jaw working and his teeth clenched.

The smile slid from Liza's lips. She backed toward Andrew, her lower lip pouting. "I know what you gonna say, Chantz. I don't want to hear it—"

"You're gonna hear it anyway. What the hell were you thinking dressing like that and coming here? You act like a woman who is trying to get caught—"

"I'm actin' like a woman who wants to look pretty for the man she loves!" she declared with a tip of her head. "Just because my skin ain't as white as yours, Chantz Boudreaux, don't mean I don't want to feel like a woman once in a while."

"We'll see how much a woman you feel like when you're hauled to the market and sold for the price of a good slab of meat."

Her eyes widened and glazed. She sank back against Andrew who wrapped his arms around her.

Chantz swallowed his anger and took a steadying breath. He looked hard into Andrew's brown eyes. "I should never have gotten involved in this. I should have stopped it long ago, for all the reasons we just discussed."

"It's just a dress," Andrew said softly, nuzzling Liza's nape with his lips. "Lord," he whispered, "you smell like honeysuckle, sweetness."

"Just a dress." Chantz shook his head and forced himself to look away. "I'll remind you of that when we're watching Liza sent down the river. I'll remind you of that when she ends up in the hands of a man like Horace Carrington or Boris Wilcox. Because in case neither of you have noticed recently, not every overseer is as tolerant as I am. For God's sake, look at her, Drew. She's a beautiful woman. The man who lays down his three hundred dollars for her won't have cane cutting or cotton picking on his mind."

Chantz left the house, stood on the steps in the dark, did his best to will back his anger, not to mention his mounting frustration. Regardless that Max was Liza's father, he wouldn't give a damn about sending her down river. Hell, truth be known he'd be glad of it. Just one less mistake for him to feel guilty over.

Not that Max Hollinsworth had felt guilty over anything since Jack Broussard had found him buried between Maureen's legs.

"Chantz?" The voice called softly from the dark.

"Ah, hell." Frowning, he descended the porch steps and struck off down the path toward the slave shacks.

Phyllis ran after him. "Please, Chantz. I don't blame you for being angry—"

"I'm not angry, Phyllis. What gave you that idea?"

"You looked angry enough that afternoon at the *salon*."

"You were mistaken, *chère*. I was simply annoyed at myself for believing that the woman I'd made love to the night before had wrapped her legs around me out of fondness and not because she had an itch I could scratch better than most."

She grabbed his arm, stopping him in his tracks. "I've tried to explain. I sent you notes by Andrew—"

"I got your notes. I guess if I gave a damn about what you had to say I would have read them."

"I think your mind has been occupied elsewhere," she said as her fingers twisted into his shirtsleeve.

"What's that supposed to mean?"

"Juliette Broussard. That's what I mean."

He stared down into her pale face and big, dark eyes. The image to come to his mind was not of her naked with her long brown hair spilling over her breasts but the vision of her standing at Juliette's side on the gallery. The difference between them had been as vast as the sun and the moon and he'd known with the flash of Juliette's challenging eyes that there could never—would never—be another who could compare. Suddenly all the hunger he'd once felt for Phyllis had coelesced into a gnawing ache that even now made him feel like a man losing the grip on sanity.

"All of Baton Rouge has been talking about it," Phyllis declared desperately. "How you and she were found together after the storm. How she was barely dressed and in your arms. I suppose if she's anything like her mother she's got you mesmerized by her charms. And I don't mean her pretty eyes."

"I believe you're jealous, Miss Buley."

"Yes, I am. I'm spitting jealous, Chantz. I can't stand the thought of you with another woman."

She ran her hand up his chest, to the deep opening of his shirt, slid her fingers over his bare flesh to the nub of his nipple.

He caught her wrist.

She leaned against him and slid her free hand down the ridge in his pants. "I've missed you something terrible, Chantz. I toss and turn in my bed at night thinking of us together. Thinking of all the things you do to me, and for me. Sometimes when I'm just drifting off to sleep I awake with a jolt, thinking I feel you whispering in my ear. I wake up crying, Chantz. I really do.

"Chantz. You can't deny it, you know. We're very good together."

"*Were* good together, Phyllis."

"We'll always be good together, Chantz. Twenty years from now we'll still make each other happy."

He drew her hard against him. Her fingers plucked at the buttons on his breeches, eagerly slid under the taut material. She pressed her lips to the base of his throat, scattered kisses over his neck and chest, licked his skin, until he buried his hand in her hair and forced back her head.

"Let me understand you perfectly, Miss Buley. Are you telling me that you intend to tell Horace Carrington to go to hell? Are you telling me that you're ready to shout to the entire world that you're in love with Chantz Boudreaux? Are you telling me that you're willing to sacrifice your luxuries to move into that house yonder and spend the rest of your life living for the moment that I crawl between your legs and make you scream in pleasure?"

Twisting his fingers harder in her hair, he said, "Well? I'm waiting."

"I . . . I can't do that, Chantz."

"Then what you mean is, you want me to linger in the background of your existence, at your beck and call like a damn step-and-fetch-it, there to satisfy whatever urges Horace Carrington can't or won't satisfy. Is that what you mean, Phyllis?"

"Please," she whispered. "I love you, Chantz. I can't bear the thought of living without you. Do you want me to beg?"

"I want you to get your hand out of my pants. I want you to march back up to that house and don't look back. I want you to remember one thing. Chantz Boudreaux might have to break his back for a living. I might eat sorry cornmeal and maybe I won't ever own a suit or eat at fancy coffee houses on pretty linen table cloths, but I won't ever be anyone's step-and-fetch-it. Because unlike you, Phyllis, I've got my pride."

He shoved her away and buttoned his breeches.

Phyllis drew back her shoulders and lifted her chin. "We'll see how much pride you have when Juliette Broussard gets through with you. That look you gave her this afternoon wasn't so prideful, Mr. Boudreaux. You looked positively sick with wanting her. If she's anything like her mother, I suspect she'll have you and every other man in this parish on his knees by the time she's finished using you up."

"Go to bed, Phyllis." He turned and started down the path again.

"I see you don't even bother trying to deny it," she yelled after him.

"Good night, Miss Buley."

He walked hard through the dark, until he was certain Phyllis hadn't followed him. With the night pressing down on him and the insect noise pulsating in his ears, he dropped onto the steps of a slave shanty and smoked and tried to get his temper under control. He could control what was going on in his pants a lot easier than he could what was going on in his head—had been going on in his head since he'd ridden up the drive that afternoon and come face-to-face with Juliette—barefoot, flushed by the heat, her hair tangled and flowing. The desire he'd felt the instant she'd elbowed her way between Max and Phyllis, her presence a blatant challenge, had set his teeth on edge.

The door creaked open behind him and a sliver of yellow light spilled over his shoulder. Little Clara, her eyes big, peered out at him.

"Boss Chantz, what you be doin' there in da dark? You 'bout sceered me plumb to death. I thought dat old bull gator done come knockin'." She smiled. "You brung me some ho'hound, Chantz?"

He fished into his pocket and withdrew a chunk of candy.

Clara sat down beside him, stuffed the candy in her mouth, and settled back on her elbows. Her knobby knees opened and closed like butterfly wings.

"Dat is mighty good ho'hound, ain't it?"

He nodded and smoked. Christ, what he wouldn't give for a breath of cool air to kiss the heat from his body.

"Granny gonna stir up some prawlins tomorra. Miss Julie gonna help her. Miss Julie say she better learn her way 'round dat kitchen 'cause when she move to Belle Jarod she won't be havin' no slave to cook and clean. Miss Julie don't believe in slaves. Ain't dat somethin', Boss Chantz? She a strange white lady. What got you so ruffled, anyhow?"

She sniffed at Chantz and shook her head. "You's been nippin', ain't you? You know what Granny say 'bout dat. Ain't no good can come of nippin' too much."

Chantz looked at Clara squarely. "You sound more like your granny every day, Little Clara."

"I know." She beamed him a big white smile.

He looked around, into the house that was apparently empty. "Where your folks?"

"Catchin' turtles. Granny say Fred Buley want turtle soup tomorra. Granny say Fred Buley be a pain in d'ass."

"Your granny would be correct." Chantz crushed the cigar stub out on the step. "As a matter of fact, all the Buleys are pains in the asses, Little Clara."

Her cheek bulging with candy, Little Clara gazed up at the night sky thoughtfully, her knees wing-beating back and forth. "Most white folk are, come to think 'bout it," she said, then added as she glanced at him slyly, " 'Cept'n you, Boss Chantz, 'cause you brings me ho'hound."

Nine

S he stood in the dark, tense as some cautious bird, fragile as the golden bloom of the night jasmine nearly obscuring the window in which she peered, eyes wide, lips parted, hands curled into pale fists. The dim light through the part in the window curtain barely brightened Juliette's face as she watched, spellbound, the goings-on inside his house.

"Oh." She gasped. "Oh . . . my . . ."

The breath rushed from her and she pressed the back of her hand to her forehead, stepped closer to the window, touched her tongue to the corner of her mouth, as if she were tasting something intoxicating and delicious. A sheen of moisture kissed her cheeks, inviting a tendril of hair to cling to her skin.

There came a whimper, a masculine groan, the bump bump rhythm of the bed beating the wall.

What the hell is she doing here? Chantz thought.

The ache for her started again, down low—not that it ever left him, he acknowledged with a razor edge of anger. His mother was right, damn her. Juliette's smell and taste had oozed into his blood and no amount of working himself to death in the mud and sun was going to sweat her out of his system. She had become as his flesh, and God help his soul.

As if the ghost of her mother walked the very grounds that she had loved with the same passion as she had worshiped a man's hands on her body, Juliette's image shimmered in the night, limned by the yellow light from his window. Something foolish and dangerous roused in Chantz. The hot pain pulsated like white anger in his chest, and in his loins. Sweat rose to the surface of his skin and he was forced to plant his feet hard to control the urges or God help him he would do something that he would regret for the rest of his life.

Chantz eased up behind her. She didn't notice, too spellbound by the tangle of two moving, naked bodies on his bed, white and brown, straining, flesh glistening with oily sweat. Andrew's hands twisted into Liza's hair, holding her head firmly as he kissed her mouth and thrust his hips, hard, making her dark hands claw at his white skin, her nails leaving red trails across his buttocks and back.

If he was smart he would dissolve back into the darkness and spend the remainder of the night pacing like a prowling animal, doing his damnedest to sweat her out of his soul.

Obviously, he wasn't smart.

Obviously, he was headed for the sort of trouble that would ultimately get him in waters deeper than the Mississippi, and far more dangerous.

Closer to the window Juliette moved, until the jasmine bloom brushed her hair. She touched her lips with her fingertips; they were trembling, down they slid, lingering on her breast, down to grasp fistfuls of her skirt.

Her skin, heated by her arousal, smelled sweet as the

flower-scented air. And that other scent, the one that had burned into his senses since the night he'd fished her out of the river—warm and earthy, spicy enough to make men mindless fools. He could hear her breathing, feel the heat of her body rising so it seemed the very air around her steamed. It made his own body ache. Badly.

Andrew moved his body down Liza's, and Chantz focused on Juliette, knowing well enough without looking what was going on in his bed. Juliette made a sound in her throat. Her fingers clutched at her skirt and she took a quick step back, as if anticipating a hasty retreat.

Chantz slid one hand over her mouth, the other around her waist, silencing her startled cry as he drew her hard against his body that was, he noted in that instant, painfully aroused. The sudden pressure of her buttocks against his erection felt like the thrust of a dull knife blade.

"Hush," he whispered against her ear.

Her body stiffened. Her shallow breaths felt warm and damp against his palm.

He moved back, away from the house. Still, he didn't loosen his grip. She felt too damn good. Her body molded along his, supple curves and heat that made the air unbearable to breathe.

"*Chère.*" His grip tightened. "Had you been any other woman I might feel shocked over finding you watching lovers in the throes of such pleasure."

Tighter. His voice lower, deeper, rougher; his shaking hands twisted into her dress. "Somehow I'm not surprised. As I recall, your mother was quite shameless and uninhibited about lovemaking. Anywhere and any time she felt like it."

No movement. No response. The back of her head, fragrant jasmine-scented hair, nestled against the curve of his throat. Her moist lips parted against his fingers. Her breath formed steam against his flesh. He felt overwhelmed with the need to end this certain madness before, like her mother, she destroyed every man who loved her.

She relaxed against him, as if she had melted, was melting, little by little like soft warm wax pungent with the smell of arousal and jasmine.

His hand moved up, slowly, and curved around her breast, the other gripping her so fiercely her ribs felt as if they might shatter. The need to lay her down in the night's dew-kissed grass raced through him with a violence that turned his every nerve raw and his mind maddened. Made him want to rip the dress from her body and bury his face between her legs. Made him want to tongue her until she thrashed in delirium.

"In case you haven't noticed," he said through his teeth, a whisper in her ear that disturbed the fine curls at her temple, "this isn't a convent where you can sashay around all hours of the night and not expect to invite trouble. Then again, maybe you were looking for trouble. That it, Miss Julie? Grow bored with listening to Hazel Buley mewl on about her lumbago and Fred's dyspepsia? Or maybe you just wanted to find out yourself what it's like to come face-to-face with a rutting bull with a mean hunger for sweet human flesh."

She wrenched free and backed away. Her eyes flashed as she shoved her hair back from her face. A jasmine blossom, caught within the lush, wild curls, rested near her cheek.

"I was looking for you," she confessed in a dry voice.

"Well." He narrowed his eyes and shifted his weight, pelvis thrust slightly, one knee bent. "You found me."

"I saw Phyllis leave the house earlier, and I thought—"

"Regardless of what you might have heard, darlin' "—he shook his head, spilling hair over his brow—"I don't fool with married women."

"She isn't married . . . yet."

"Good as, as far as I'm concerned." He reached for the blossom in her hair. She skirted back, beyond his hand.

"She's in love with you, you know."

"I know." He reached again.

She backed away. "Are you in love with her?"

His grin stretched and his eyes narrowed. "A gentleman never tattles, Juliette."

"But you're no gentleman. Remember?"

"Obviously. Or I wouldn't be contemplating what I'm contemplating. Then again, if you were a lady you wouldn't be slinking 'round in the dark, smelling like temptation, inviting such ungentlemanly contemplation."

Her chin lifted. "I had to . . . speak with you on a matter. You're a difficult man to corner during the day."

"I have a job to do. Some of us don't have the leisure of idling our days away watching steamboats paddle up and down the river."

He tipped his head and allowed his gaze to slide down her body. "I hope you're wearing shoes. Padding 'round barefoot on the gallery during the day is one thing, wandering the grounds at night without shoes is something else. There are snakes who find the warmth under a woman's skirts highly inviting."

She squared her shoulders and took another step back. "I didn't come here to discuss shoes or snakes."

"All right. Why did you come here, I mean other than to catch me in the act of making love to another woman?"

She flashed a look toward the house, her expression pained and flustered. "I want you to take me to Belle Jarod."

He frowned. "Why?"

"It's my home. I have a right to see it."

"When Max is ready for you to see Belle Jarod again—"

"Max Hollinsworth can go to hell."

"Tsk, tsk, *chère*. Not nice to bite the hand that feeds you. Especially when it's Max Hollinsworth's. He'd sail his own flesh and blood down the river if it suited his purpose. And speaking of that . . .

"I know you thought you were doing Liza a favor by giving her that dress. Trust me, darlin', that was no favor. Allowing her a taste of those kind of fineries can and will lead to problems."

"I hardly think that a little enjoyment over a dress can lead to problems."

"Once a woman enjoys the feel of silk against her skin, she's hardly gonna appreciate burlap, is she? That kind of dissatisfaction invites intolerance, and intolerance invites anger, and anger invites resistance to authority. Resistance, to a woman like Liza, invites reprisal. I don't think either of us wants to see her whipped. Or worse—"

"I can't imagine there being anything worse than whipping," she interrupted, her tone as biting.

"Then you *are* naive, Miss Julie. There are far greater terrors these people face if they're forced to leave Holly House. Woman like Liza sold in the market, no telling where she would end up. A whorehouse maybe. Maybe sold to a breeding slaver. And in case you aren't familiar with that, let me tell you. Men and women thrown together in a pen where they copulate under the watchful eye of their master. She works the fields on her hands and knees until she gives birth, most times right there in the dirt. Month later she's bred back, and the same old filthy ritual starts again. She'll most likely be dead by the time she's thirty-five."

Her eyes widened. She flashed a worried look toward the house.

He moved toward her; she hardly noticed until he

reached for the jasmine blossom in her hair. Turning her gaze up to his, she held her breath as he slid the flower along her lip, dusting it with fine yellow pollen.

"*Chère*," he said more gently. "You don't want to go to that haunted old place of shattered dreams and passions— not yet. Might stir up memories best left buried for a while."

"I'll go with or without you."

There it was again, the challenge.

He crushed the jasmine bloom between his fingers and the burst of fragrance scented the night air thick and sweet as cane nectar. Sliding the oil along the warm nape of her neck, he said simply, "Jasmine suits you, darlin'."

His feet propped on the gallery balustrade and crossed at the ankles, Tylor sat in a wicker chair on the night-cloaked balcony, drinking bourbon, staring hard through the dark, sweating. Max reined back his urge to wring his neck—at the least shake some sense and backbone into him.

"My patience with you is at an end, Tylor. It's time for you to behave like a Hollinsworth and the future master of Holly Plantation. By God, you're going to take an active role on this farm or—"

"Listen to those damn dogs, Daddy. Something's got them spooked. Howling and howling all night long. They don't ever shut up. It's enough to drive a man out of his mind."

Tylor stood and leaned his shoulder against the column and drank his bourbon. He closed his eyes and swallowed. "There's something out there. I feel it. Like cold fingers crawling over my skin."

"It's too damn much bourbon in your blood and yellow fear for a backbone."

Tylor gave a short laugh. "Whatever you say, Daddy."

Max moved up behind him. "You're going on that gator

hunt with Chantz and Andrew. You're going to start acting like a man around here."

Tylor turned and looked into Max's eyes. "You trying to get me killed?"

"That damn gator isn't going to kill you, Tylor."

"I ain't talking about the gator. I'm talking about Chantz Boudreaux."

Max walked away.

"He's got every reason in the world to kill me, Daddy."

"I don't know what the hell you're talking about, Tylor. Why would Chantz want to kill you?"

Drenched in night shadows, Tylor gazed out into the dark as he listened to the hounds bay. "If I'm dead there'll be nothing more standing in his way. You wouldn't have much choice, then, would you? You'd have to acknowledge him as your son or what the hell will happen to Holly Plantation when you die?

"I suspect you've long regretted your decision to turn your back on Emmaline, considering how Chantz and I turned out. Hell, you might treat him like dirt, but it isn't because you don't respect him. If you ever looked at me with a modicum of the esteem you feel for him, maybe I wouldn't have turned out like I did. How the hell am I supposed to live up to a man like Chantz?

"He'd like to kill me. No doubt about it. I see it in his eyes every time he looks at me. All that hatred and resentment. And I don't blame him. Hell, I'd like to kill him, too, just so I can be rid of the man who reminds me every day of my life that I don't measure up to my father's bastard son.

"Maybe I *will* kill him. What would you think about that, Daddy? What if I just drink enough of this damn courage to march out there and put a bullet in his handsome head?"

Tylor walked toward him, drinking his bourbon. "No

comment? Still won't acknowledge him when slapped across the face with the truth? That would mean admitting a mistake and Max Hollinsworth is too damn proud to admit his mistakes. Then you'd have to admit that you've been a son of a bitch to him and Emmaline for thirty years. You'd have to acknowledge to the world that you allowed your own flesh-and-blood son to live barely better than one of your slaves." Tylor grinned. "I know the truth about Emmaline, that she's nothing more than some little mud dauber you came across one night. I heard the two of you talking, how you got drunk and forced yourself on her, encouraged by your equally drunken cohorts. That was a pretty story she concocted for Chantz. Fine old Carolina family, my aching butt."

Max glared into Tylor's drunken eyes and said through his teeth, "You're to keep your mouth shut about that, Tylor. You hear me?"

Tylor raised both eyebrows. "Why, Daddy, I'm starting to believe you care more for that bastard than you're willing to admit."

He hurled away the empty glass; it shattered below. "You make me want to puke. I'm tired of your bullying me. I'm tired of your constant reminders that I don't live up to your expectations, as if I could as long as Chantz is alive. I'm declaring war, Daddy. And when the dust settles there is going to be one of your sons left standing. Winner takes all. Holly Plantation, Juliette Broussard . . . and Belle Jarod."

The sudden silence pressed down on them, and Tylor turned away, walked several paces down the gallery before stopping stock-still to stare out through the dark toward the hound pens. No howling, now. Not so much as a whir of an insect interrupted the stillness.

A movement amid the shadows. From the darkness,

Juliette ran toward the house, starlight reflecting off her flowing hair and lightning bugs streaking and flashing around her as if brightening her path.

Tylor looked around into Max's eyes, his face pale amid the night shadows.

Then the roar rose up, belly thunder, the deep, sensual solitary grunt of the bull gator staking his territory.

"I feel compelled to discuss a situation with you, Maxwell. A situation that Miss Julie might find a touch discomposing."

Fred Buley looked over at Juliette where she stood at the window, her back to Maxwell and Fred as she stared out through the dark in the direction of Chantz's house.

She could see their reflection in the glass—the way Max and Fred regarded her. Not so long ago she would have felt discomposed and furious by their blatant appraisals. Then, of course, she'd had every reason to feel outraged by such disrespect. But here she stood with the fire of conflicting emotions crawling up her throat and burning her face. How could she continue to pretend to herself, and to Chantz, that he meant nothing to her? More importantly . . .

How could she continue to hide her feelings from Maxwell when the hunger for Chantz drove her to risk, not just her reputation, but Chantz's as well.

Max said, "Juliette's presence at Holly House is to prepare her completely to mistress Belle Jarod when the time comes. If there is business to discuss, I feel she would benefit from participating in the discussion."

Fred sucked on his cigar and continued to focus his attention on Juliette. "Of course, Maxwell. I understand *completely* her reasons for being here."

There was something in the way Max looked at her tonight; his dark blue eyes were hooded as a hawk's. He knew, of course. He'd known even before she'd been willing to admit it to herself—since the morning after Tylor had returned her to Holly House he'd suspected that she'd fallen under Chantz's spell. The certainty of it had swept her like a wave when coming face-to-face with him on the stairs moments ago. Standing half in and half out of the shadows, he had stared down at her with glazed eyes and the expression of one slightly mad. Saying nothing, he had gently caught her arm and directed her to this room where Hazel and Fred appraised her like she was the condemned headed for the gallows.

Juliette turned from the window and met his stare directly, refusing to allow herself to be intimidated. Her hands were clasped at her waist. Too tightly. Much too tightly, she realized. The sharp pain of her nails digging into her palms crept up her arms like threads of ice.

His cheeks flushed by bourbon and the sweltering heat of the close night, Max set aside his glass. Turning his bloodshot eyes up to hers, he didn't so much as blink. Dear God, he was toying with her, like a cat with a pitifully exhausted mouse.

She had to warn Chantz. Prepare him. Panic beat in her chest as furiously as her racing heart. Suddenly the *whoosh whoosh* of the punka overhead sounded loud as a windstorm.

Fred tapped his cigar ashes into a glass bowl. "We have a concern over Liza."

Juliette stiffened. She did not, however, look at Fred where he sat in a chair, his muddy booted feet propped on an ottoman, watching her through a stream of smoke.

Max cleared his throat. "I can't imagine what sort of problem you might have with my Liza. She's a good girl. Works hard and knows her place."

"I won't mince words with you, Maxwell. We're all

adults here. Or most of us. We know the ways of men and women." Fred shot a glance at Juliette.

"For heaven's sakes get on with it, Frederick," Hazel blurted without looking up from her needlework.

"Very well," Fred declared. "I fear Andrew has become involved with the woman."

Juliette moved slowly, almost cautiously behind Max and walked again to the window. The nerves along her spine felt raw and the air in her lungs suddenly felt thick as the humidity. The image to rise in her mind's eyes of Liza slumped and weeping into her hands caused a chill of dread to sink to the pit of her stomach.

"Andrew is a robust, healthy young man, Fred. And Liza is exceptionally beautiful." Max focused his gaze on the coils of dark red hair lying against the pale skin of Juliette's exposed shoulders. He drank again before adding, "Andrew would hardly be the first to succumb to his base urges when it comes to finding his sexual gratification along shanty row, would he?"

"Agreed. However, my concern rests not in the physical relationship that he shares with the woman. Our concern is for the emotional relationship that might have developed between them." Fred dropped his feet to the floor and sat forward. "Rumors have reached me that Andrew has become overly fond of the woman."

"And who would be spreading such a rumor, I wonder?"

"Horace Carrington, that's who," Hazel announced, coming out of her chair and spilling her hoop and skeins of thread to the floor. "He's seen them together. At that dreadful little shanty your overseer occupies on his days off. Where Tylor found Chantz Boudreaux with her."

She thrust a finger at Juliette. "Do you think we don't know what sort of wickedness goes on there? Why, Juliette's own mother carried on dalliances with her lovers in that house. I won't have my precious son corrupted by the likes of that insidious woman. Such a relationship will ruin him. We won't be able to show our faces in town. In this entire state, for that matter."

"The way I see it," Fred said, "we've both got an unseemly situation that must be nipped in the bud. First, your overseer is obviously turning a blind eye to Liza's wanderings. I would venture to say that he's in fact encouraging this relationship between Liza and Andrew. The fact that he would allow the coming and going of your slaves willy nilly is outrageous and sets a dangerous precedent."

"He deserves to be whipped right along with Liza," Hazel declared in her most self-righteous voice. She lifted her chin and stomped her foot. "I want her gone, Maxwell. As soon as possible. Before this sordid attraction they have for each other grows completely out of control."

Juliette rounded on Max so fast her heavy coils of hair spilled like a wave of red water over her shoulders. "You wouldn't dare. Tell me you wouldn't sell Liza, Maxwell. Swear it!"

"What on earth is going on in here?"

Phyllis entered the room. Her eyes appeared red and swollen and she gripped a lacy kerchief in one hand. She flashed Juliette a telling look before gliding to her mother, dropping to the floor in a mushroom of bird's-egg blue taffeta and crinoline and began collecting Hazel's sewing.

"Mama, you've over excited yourself again. You're flushed as a plum. Shall I call Rosie to fetch you a lemonade?"

"I don't want a damn lemonade," Hazel barked, and snatched the tambour from Phyllis. "I want Maxwell to take care of his responsibilities."

Phyllis slowly stood. What little color had touched her

cheeks when entering the room drained from her face. "What are you talking about, Mama?"

"Your brother's relationship with Liza."

Phyllis walked to the open French doors—looked out in the darkness toward the distant twinkling lights scattered through shanty row. "Andrew is a grown man. Why don't you leave him alone? He's happy. Is that so bad?"

"Andrew has responsibilities, for heaven's sake. Time has come for him to settle down with a respectable young woman and get about the business of raising cane and children. Your father isn't exactly a young man any longer."

"And God forbid that anyone in our family actually marry out of love instead of financial convenience."

With a thin smile, she turned to her mother. "Would you prefer that he marry that drab little mouse of a woman— let me see, what is her name? Myra Howell? Looks a bit like yonder fence-post with the intelligence of a catawba worm? I suspect their children would have resembled opossums. Not that any of that would have mattered, of course. Ralph Howell has no sons and therefore Myra's husband will eventually inherit every one of Ralph's thirteen thousand acres. Why don't the two of you leave Andrew alone? He's an intelligent man. He knows what his responsibilities are . . . as do I."

With that, she twirled on her heels and exited through the French doors.

Hazel huffed and glared at Fred. "You've spoiled them rotten, Frederick. They're disrespectful, spiteful, and disobedient, thanks to your molly-coddling them all their lives. You've allowed Andrew to socialize with that sorry, no-account white-trash riffraff Chantz Boudreaux, and now it's come right back to bite you in the behind."

Wagging her finger at him, she said, "If you don't do something to stop it now—"

"Hush!" he shouted.

Hazel's mouth snapped shut and her eyes widened.

"For the love of God Almighty, woman, you squawk like a damn crow. I'm doing all I can. Your harping on isn't going to help our situation."

With a furious flurry of skirt and petticoat and squeak of her corset, Hazel flung the tambour and threads on the floor and stormed from the room.

Fred shook his head and tamped out his cigar, stood and adjusted his coat as he appeared to contemplate his next words.

"You and I have been friends a great many years, Maxwell. We've helped each other out in bad times. I once took your family in when the flood waters were so high they washed these furnishings right out through those doors and down the river. And believe me, I understand your hesitancy where Liza is concerned. But Andrew is my only son. I want him married and settled with a respectable and acceptable young lady. That won't happen as long as he's emotionally tied to that woman."

Max finished his bourbon and put down his glass. He did not look at Fred directly, just licked the bourbon from his lips and nodded. "I understand completely. I'll speak to Liza first thing in the morning."

As Fred left the room, Max shifted his attention to Juliette. The night breeze through the open window flirted with her hair, and the heat from the globe lamp beside her torched her cheeks with hot color. The outrage she felt boiling up inside made her shake.

"You needn't look so shocked and outraged," he told her as he stood, swayed, bumped against the table causing the crystal prisms on the lamp globes to tinkle musically. "Business is business. Fred is an old and valued friend."

"I'll speak with her." Juliette did her best to keep the nervous desperation from her voice as well as her escalating fury. Judging by the look on Max's face and the tone of his voice, antagonizing the situation would undoubtedly make matters much worse. "I'll tell her that her relationship with Andrew must stop. I'll explain the consequences."

"She knows the consequences."

He walked from the room, onto the gallery.

Max stood with his hands on his hips, looking down toward shanty row. Juliette's petticoats rustled softly as she moved up behind him, watched as he breathed in deeply and slowly released his breath.

"You look like your mother tonight, Juliette. All full of fire and ready for the devil. Jack always swore that if there was any human who could stand toe-to-toe with Lucifer and make him back down, it would be Maureen."

"I don't care to talk about my mother tonight. We're discussing a woman's life and happiness."

He turned unsteadily and looked down into her eyes, his own little more than blue slits. The smell of bourbon from his sweating skin made her stomach turn.

"Your hair a riot of curls and blaze. Smelling like flowers—jasmine tonight, not magnolia. You have the flushed look of a woman who would slink through the dark to meet a forbidden lover. What's this?" He touched her cheek and regarded his fingertips. Lips curving in an emotionless smile, he said without meeting her eyes, "Night jasmine. I do believe it cascades over Chantz's bedroom window . . . doesn't it?"

He lifted his head. The smile slid from his mouth. "No doubt you find it all rather romantic."

Juliette backed away, her hands clenched. "We're talking about Liza. We're talking about a human being whom you intend to send down the river like she's an oak barrel of cane syrup."

Drawing back her shoulders, she added, "You're her father. How could you behave so inhumanely to your own flesh and blood?"

He rocked, as if struck by her words. "While I welcome and encourage your involvement in Holly business, there are certain matters which should never concern you. The disposition of my slaves is one of them."

"Disposition? Dear God, you are heartless. No wonder Tylor has the conscience of a snake. You're as cold-blooded and mean as a viper."

His hand struck her face with enough force to snap her head back and electrify the night with blinding spears of pain; she stumbled against the column, her mind at first refusing to acknowledge what had just taken place. Tears rose. She forced them back, along with the emotion choking her breathless.

At last, she looked into his face, thought she saw a flash of some emotion in his eyes. Shock? Regret? Anger? Whatever it was, it swam behind a red, watery curtain of inebriation.

Like a wooden puppet, his movements jerky and disjointed, Max stumbled away and covered his face with his hands. "I told you to stay away from him, Juliette, yet I see you out there in the darkness . . . here you stand bathed in night jasmine and looking for all the world like a woman who has just fled the arms of a lover."

Voice dropping, trembling, slurring, he stressed, "I'm concerned only for your reputation, you understand. A woman like you can't be found with a man like him. You simply cannot continue to behave in such a way, Maureen."

"My name is Juliette." *And I am not my mother!* She wanted to shout, but the sobering realization struck her as fiercely as Max's hand across her cheek. She had become her mother with the touch of Chantz's hands on her body and she was too damn tired to fight it any longer.

Max closed his eyes briefly, shook his head; his shoulders drooped. "Of course. Of course you're Juliette."

As he reached out to her, she backed away, returned his look with all the defiance and outrage she could muster.

"What can I do to make it up to you, Juliette?" The words were raspy.

"Leave Liza alone. Allow me to help with the situation before you act so extreme as to send her away."

Maxwell nodded wearily. Without another word, he turned on his heels and entered the house, leaving her slumped against the column, her face numb and the sickening copper taste of blood in her mouth. Her eyes burned and her throat convulsed. Dear God in heaven, could this day get any worse?

"I admire your tenacity," came the feminine voice from the shadows, then Phyllis moved into view.

Juliette blinked and swallowed her emotions. Drawing herself up, she lifted her chin and did her best to ignore the tendrils of fire working down the side of her neck.

Phyllis moved closer, extended a kerchief. "Your lip is bleeding. There at the corner of your mouth." She pointed to her own mouth and her gaze softened. "There'll be swelling. Slight bruising. I have some rice powder that will hide it well enough."

Pressing the cambric to her lip, Juliette frowned. "You act like this deplorable brutality is commonplace."

"Are you surprised that a man who would whip a child

would think twice about slapping a woman? Our skin may be white and we might live in the big house but that is where the differences end between us and them."

She nodded toward the distant shanties. "We're all chattel, Juliette. Oh, they dress us in pretty clothes and parade us up and down the boulevards like we're fine warm bloods, but our one purpose in life is little more than providing them with sons they can lavish with attention, impressive educations, and ultimately bestow on them mostly undeserved prosperity."

Tipping her head, she looked at Juliette askance. "Can you imagine what will happen to Holly Plantation when Maxwell dies and leaves it all to Tylor? Although Maxwell would never admit it, I'm quite certain he shakes in his bed at night, imagining what will happen to all this after he's gone. Everything he and his father worked to build will crumble into that damn river or rot in the fields."

"Chantz won't allow—"

"Chantz will be long gone from here by then." Her voice softened as she moved down the gallery, into the dark. "I'm surprised he's stayed at Holly this long. He's biding his time is all. Saving every hard-earned coin he's made all these years, dreaming of buying his own land. He'll succeed, too, knowing Chantz. He never starts anything that he can't finish . . . one way or another."

Her step paused. She looked down at her hands and her shoulders rose and fell with a heavy sigh. "He's so very passionate about his dreams."

"You're very fond of him."

"I admire him. Most everyone along this river admires Chantz Boudreaux."

"You're in love with him."

Silence. Slowly, Phyllis turned and looked hard into her

eyes. "I'm marrying Horace Carrington in three months."

"But you don't love Horace Carrington. Do you?"

"No." She lifted her chin. "I despise him."

The pressure around her heart began to squeeze again. As it had the first time she had witnessed the longing in Phyllis's eyes when she stood on the gallery next to Juliette and watched Chantz ride up the drive on his lathered bay horse.

Phyllis stepped closer. "If I were a stronger woman and hadn't a family to consider I would risk everything I am and ever hoped to be to spend the remainder of my life with Chantz Boudreaux." She swallowed and took a fortifying breath. "There's nothing a strong woman couldn't accomplish with him at her side. And if he loved her . . . dear God, he would move heaven and earth to see that her dreams were realized."

Ten

The kitchen walls were of *bousillage*, a mixture of moss and mud that, unlike wood that would too easily burn, absorbed the heat—a good thing on winter days, but on a day like this one, Juliette suspected that hell's fire wouldn't have felt as hot.

The fact that she hadn't slept a wink didn't help. The side of her face where Maxwell had struck her had throbbed all night. The cut inside her mouth had frequently bled. She had been relieved, come dawn, to see in the mirror that the swelling was minimal and the mark upon her skin little more than a vague shadow. Briefly, she had considered running to Chantz and warning him that Maxwell suspected . . .

Suspected what?

That she cared more for Max's overseer than she should? How did one do that without confessing to him that her feelings ran deeper than just fascination over the forbidden?

Furthermore, she had boldly asked him if he felt love for Phyllis, and he'd refused to answer. What could be worse: knowing that he loved Phyllis or knowing nothing at all?

So as the sun had crept up over the eastern horizon, she'd waited impatiently for Liza—needing her confidante. Together they would determine a way out of their predicaments and it all came back to one blaring reality.

Belle Jarod.

Juliette's sore mood and anxiety only surged all the hotter when Rosie, arriving with her breakfast tray, had informed her that Liza had been sent to the fields to work.

Considering how poorly Liza had been feeling, toiling in the boiling sun would only worsen her sorry situation. Then Julie reasoned that the fields would be better for Liza than the slave market. At least until Juliette could devise a plan to help her—help them both.

Somehow she had to speak with Andrew. Alone.

As heat poured from the open hearth and radiated from the *bousillage* walls, Juliette, dress drenched with sweat, eyes stinging, nostrils feeling as if they were being singed, stood over the big copper pot and stirred the thick, bubbling praline concoction of butter and sugar. Rosie poured a stream of bourbon into it. Little Clara waited for Rosie's nod then dumped in a bowl of pecan pieces.

Her eyes closing, Rosie inhaled, smile growing in her round face as she shook her head. "Chantz be one happy man tonight. Yassa, that man love his prawlins."

"He be moanin' with a bellyache agin," Little Clara said, shaking her head and causing her numerous braids to bob. "Dat man just don't know when to quits when it come to prawlins."

Rosie waved Juliette away. "Best you git yonda, Miss Julie, whiles we move this pot to the table. If you wants, put them onions in that turtle soup and check on my corn bread. Fred Buley don't like his corn bread brown. Ain't ever hearda such a thang. That man be mule headed and mean."

Juliette dumped the cut onions into the simmering caldron of cooking turtle as Rosie and Little Clara hefted the pot off the fire and placed it on the big square table greased with butter and sprinkled with sugar and pecan chips.

Moving to the open doorway, hoping for a breath of air to cool her, Juliette watched as Rosie grabbed a ladle and proceeded to spoon the thick liquid confection into mounds that spread into golden discs. She tried to imagine Chantz eating *la cuite* until he got a bellyache. Hard to imagine him as a child. Hard to imagine him any way other than hard and dark and turbulent, capable of making her body hurt.

She looked down the cart road toward the fields. Excitement over the night's hunt electrified the air today. Throughout the morning timber for bonfires had been built near the swamps. Boats had been moved into place and weapons prepared.

Little Clara waved a praline under Juliette's nose and grinned. "Dat's some fine prawlin, Miss Julie. You done good. Have a bite. Gonna make Chantz's eyeballs roll right back in his head."

Juliette grinned and took the candy that was warm and soft. She nibbled it, her eyebrows lifting and her smile stretching.

"Tolds ya." Little Clara beamed. "Ain't nobody 'tween here and N'awlins gots prawlins like dat."

Rosie pointed to the massive sugared ham on another table. "Clara, you be cuttin' that hock. Hurry now. Chantz be up soon and wantin' food. Lawd, that man can eat. Wonder he ain't big as a house. Hurry now. I ain't gots all day. Child is slow as cold molasses."

Juliette grabbed another praline from the table and left

the kitchen. She dropped on the cypress step and stretched her legs out, bare feet crossed at the ankles, and indulged in the warm confection so sweet it made her teeth ache.

She saw him then, Chantz, walking up the path, Andrew at his side. Both men were hot and mud covered from their toils with the levee, sleeves rolled up above their elbows. The workday finished at noon on Saturday. Slaves were given the rest of the day and Sunday to rest and take care of their own gardens.

As the confection melted in her mouth, Juliette took a deep breath and forced herself to relax back on the steps, elbows propped, legs stretched, the hem of her thin cotton dress hiked halfway up her shins. Hazel's eyes at breakfast had virtually popped when seeing her not just corsetless but petticoatless as well. With her hair bound up under one of Rosie's tignons, her skin running with sweat, the image she portrayed was hardly that of refinement. Lord help her, but she was starting to enjoy it.

As Chantz and Andrew walked to a water trough near the tall cistern located next to the milk house, Little Clara burst from the kitchen with toweling in one hand, her other full of pralines. Her skinny legs carried her at a run down the path, scattering the big gray guineas scratching the dirt for bugs.

As Chantz removed his shirt, Andrew looked around, smiling broadly at Little Clara. He made a grab for her; she skirted by him, howling in laughter, and flung herself on Chantz.

Juliette couldn't hear what was being said. Didn't matter. She'd learned soon enough that a person could know exactly what was going on in Chantz's head by the look on his face. His fierceness melted like the warm praline in her mouth the minute a child smiled up into his eyes.

She'd heard once that a man's hidden character could be

judged by the way he was accepted by a child or an animal. If that was the case, then buried deep beneath Boudreaux's hard, occasionally intimidating façade must have resided a saint.

Little Clara shoved a praline into Chantz's mouth, then stuffed one into Andrew's. Then she pointed at Juliette. Both men turned and looked at her.

While Chantz plunged his head and torso into the trough to bathe, Andrew sauntered toward her, thumbs hooked in his waist band, mouth smiling. "Well, well, Miss Julie, I didn't recognize you."

"I can well imagine," she replied.

He glanced at her naked feet and raised one eyebrow. "Nice pralines. You know what they say: The way to a man's heart is through his stomach."

She looked past him to Chantz, toweling the water from his head and shoulders.

Andrew dropped onto the step beside her. His expression became serious, and he lowered his voice. "I understand that you're aware of my relationship with Liza."

"Yes." She nodded and forced herself to look away from Chantz and Little Clara. She lowered her voice. "I have to speak with you. Privately. As soon as possible."

Sitting forward, elbows on his knees, Andrew watched Little Clara and Chantz do a tug of war with the towel. "Is this about Liza? Because if it is, I'm well aware of the risks—"

"You should know that your parents are aware of your feelings for Liza. They've demanded that Max remove her from the house and send her to the fields."

His head slowly turned and his brown eyes locked with hers.

Her gaze swung back to Chantz as he tossed the towel over his broad shoulder and started toward her. "I'm coming to realize," she said in a thin voice, "that too often our better judgment is overridden by something far more powerful."

"That is . . . ?"

"Urges that have nothing whatsoever to do with intellect."

Andrew focused on Chantz. "Well, there are certainly a great many of those urges running amok in Louisiana these days."

Chantz wore sinfully low-slung pants that exposed his navel that was surrounded by downy black hair that formed an arrow into his pants. His scuffed boots were knee high. His nipples were like copper coins and his stomach flat and rippled as a washboard. And his hair, dark and damp, full of long, wild waves, coiled over his brow and around his ears.

His mouth curled as he regarded her, lazed upon the steps, her bare feet and shins exposed, nibbling on her praline. Saying nothing to her, he mounted the steps and entered the kitchen.

Juliette shifted her gaze to Andrew, who grinned as if he knew exactly what was going on in her mind and body. Of course, he would, she reminded herself. His own sister had fallen under Boudreaux's spell. If a woman like Phyllis Buley found herself incapable of resisting him, what was a woman such as herself supposed to do?

"Git outta them prawlins!" Rosie shouted. "No prawlins till after you eats some decent food. Take this ham and corn bread and git out. I can't be havin' no foolin' in my kitchen today. Fred Buley gots a hunger on for turtle soup and this damn turtle is tough as bo' hide. Lawd, that man is gonna fuss. I declare he 'bout turnin' my old head white. Git!"

Chantz exited the kitchen at a half run, laughing, his hand full of pralines.

Rosie followed, dumped a cloth-wrapped bundle of ham and steaming corn bread into Andrew's and Juliette's laps, then slung one at Chantz.

Hands on her wide hips, her sweating face a scowl, she declared, "I gonna put the lot of you to work on soap if'n you don't git. Don't be lookin' at me that way, Chantz Boudreaux. I whupped your butt for less when you was a young'un. You might be bigger than me now but I kin swing a mean skillet. I be whuppin' you upside your head before you kin sneeze scat."

Juliette sat up and looked back at Rosie. "You whupped him, did you, Rosie?"

"I did. Least two time a day. Boy a mess. Filchin' my prawlins. Filchin' my pone. Agitatin'. Always agitatin'. And sass-mouthed. Least once a week I has to wash his mouth out with lye soap. Wonda he even gots a tongue left."

She shook her head and pursed her lips. "You still a mess, Chantz Boudreaux. Still agitatin'. Still sassin'. Still filchin' prawlins."

"But you love me anyway, don't you, Rosie?" He winked at her.

Rosie puffed her cheeks and looked away. "I reckon I ain't gots no choice in the matter. I's stuck with you whether I likes it or not."

With that she reentered the kitchen and began to sing at the top of her voice: "Well I mighta gone afishin' but I gots to thankin' it over, and the road to the river is a mighty long ways."

Chantz walked toward the big live oak dripping moss in the distance. Andrew caught Juliette's arm and helped her to stand. They followed Chantz down the path, sun beating down on their shoulders, the heat and steam of the corn bread turning the cloth wrap dark and damp. Juliette noted

Andrew looking toward the big house. A cloud passed over his face.

As they settled on the ground in the shade and proceeded to eat Rosie's ham and corn bread, Juliette announced, "Andrew has agreed to drive me to Belle Jarod tomorrow afternoon."

She looked up to find both men staring at her with their cheeks bulging with corn bread.

She shrugged. "We'll be safe enough. Maxwell and the Buleys are calling on neighbors in the morning and will be gone all day. Maxwell need know nothing about it."

His face going darker, Chantz turned his blue eyes on Andrew, who swallowed hard and appeared to mentally stumble as he considered his response.

Putting aside her food, Juliette said, "I understand you feel that it could be disturbing for me, Chantz. And I appreciate your concern. But it's time I put my life in order. I should know what sort of task is ahead of me—"

"Task doesn't come close to describing what's ahead of you," he declared with an undercurrent of anger, "if you intend to rebuild Belle Jarod. Such an undertaking borders on absurd. It's an impossibility, Juliette. At least for an unmarried woman with no money. As I recall your father spent somewhere around three hundred thousand dollars on Belle Jarod—"

"But that was the initial costs," she argued. "The purchasing of the land, the building of the house, the mills, the equipment, the slaves. As I understand it, my mother had extravagant tastes when it came to furnishings. I don't care about those things, Chantz. As long as the house is livable—"

"The house burned. Or most of it. The mills are falling in and grown over. And as far as crops: It would take every one of Max's hundred slaves and then some to turn that much ground over before it's time to plant ratoons come January."

He looked at the corn bread in his lap. "Get you a wealthy husband. Belle Jarod will be the Jewel of the Mississippi again in no time." Flashing a hot look toward Andrew, he said, "Or maybe that's exactly what you're doing."

"I'd rather plow that ground with my own bare hands before I marry a man just for his money," she declared, tossing her food aside.

Stretching her legs out and leaning back on her hands, Juliette gazed up through the heavy oak branches, at the streams of frilly moss and the spatters of pale blue sky between the leaves. The grass, crushed under her palms, gave off a sharp scent like mint.

"As a very young woman I would lie in my bed at the convent and imagine what my future home would look like. I suppose there must have been memories of Belle Jarod buried in my mind. There were towering Doric columns and wide shaded galleries. *Parterres* with colorful flowers. Honeysuckle and jasmine dripping in golden clouds from the trees. Silver doorknobs and spiral staircases, ceiling frescoes and murals depicting the French countryside. I could see out my big windows to a lake where swans swam. Twelve of them, gliding like boats in a breeze, the sunlight reflecting from the water ripples as if from thousands of tiny mirrors.

"There were times when I walked the convent grounds on crisp, breezy mornings that the touch of wind on my face and through the trees would stop me in my tracks, as if the feel and sound of the wind were somehow awakening dormant memories."

Reluctantly, she forced herself to look at Chantz. Food forgotten in his lap, relaxed against the gnarled tree trunk, his face moving with tree shadows, he regarded her with an intensity that stole her breath, that brought all the hunger he had ignited in her the previous night into a flame that made the heated air unbearable against her skin.

His hand reached for the loose tignon on her head—his rough fingers brushed her cheek, tugged on the blue scarf until it drifted toward the ground, freeing her heavy hair that flowed like dark red water around her face and over her shoulders. In a breath his blue eyes turned deep as indigo.

She felt lost in that moment—lost in those intense blue depths and the upsurge of warmth that surrounded her heart, making it ache with a fierceness that brought sudden tears to her eyes.

I love you, she thought, the acknowledgment snapping some final gossamer of denial inside her.

Jumping to her feet, spilling her food over the ground, she fled down the path toward shanty row.

She sat cross-legged in the dirt between two tall green walls of sugarcane, her elbows on her knees and her face buried in her hands that were muddied by dust and tears. Cicada calls vibrated the air, pulsing in rhythm with the shimmering waves of heat reflecting from the cane leaves. The drone somehow exaggerated her overwhelming sense of despondency.

How foolish she felt. And desperate. She could flee the length of the Mississippi, she could swim the ocean back to France, but she couldn't escape the fact that she had fallen in love with Chantz Boudreaux.

A shadow fell over her face, and she looked around, felt her heart skip with excitement and fear. Somehow she had known—at least prayed—that he might follow her here.

"Oh." She swallowed and averted her gaze from Chantz's. "What are you doing here?"

He moved around her, his broad shoulders momentarily blocking the sun. How tall he seemed, even amid the towering cane. As usual his very presence stole the air from her lungs that felt, suddenly, as dry as the silt beneath her.

Chantz eased down on one knee and closely regarded her face. "You've been crying. Why?"

She forced a smile. "I don't dare tell you, Mr. Boudreaux. You would think me quite scandalous, I fear."

"I already think you're scandalous." His mouth curled— again with that charming lopsided smile that made him look boyish. He sat down close, swiped the dirt from his hands, then plucked a sliver of grass from the base of a cane stalk. He looked at her through a strand of hair that fell over his eye. "Everything about you is scandalous, darlin'. Your pretty face. Your pretty hair. Your body. The fact that you run around this place in bare feet, wearing no petticoats—"

"It's too hot to wear petticoats." She sniffed and wrist-wiped her running nose.

"The fact that you come to my house at midnight—"

"I explained that—"

"You lied." He tipped his head to one side to better look into her face. "The fact that you would come here and play in the dirt like a child." He pointed to the scribbles in the sand. "You don't strike me as the sort of young woman who cries easily."

"I despise tears." She sniffed again and looked away, tears rising and dripping, streaking her hot cheeks. Her brain was beginning to burn with her pent-up emotions. She wanted to crawl in a hole and disappear—like the doodlebugs burrowing in the sand near her feet. "Tears give away secrets."

Catching a tear on the end of his finger, Chantz regarded it intensely. "No secrets here that I can see."

She frowned. "Don't treat me like a child, Chantz. I couldn't bear it."

"Seeing you sitting here with your cheeks tear kissed and your toes sandy I'm reminded just how childlike you are, darlin'. You're just too damn naive to know what the sight of you can do to a man."

Raising her gaze to his, she said, "What, exactly, do I do to you?"

His face darkened and his blue eyes bored into hers with an intensity that made her tremble. Yet, he did not respond. The set of his shoulders remained still and his hand, resting upon his knee, tightened into a white knuckled fist. Suddenly her heart pumped wildly, and she lifted her gritty hand and placed it over his.

"Would you like to touch me?" she asked softly, without blinking. "I wish you would. Touch my face. My hair." She lifted his big, heavy hand in her own and placed it against her cheek. Her eyes drifted closed. "You smell like sunshine," she whispered. "And feel like . . ." She nuzzled—felt his fingers quiver upon her cheek. "So hard. So very hard. And so gentle. It's what I recall about you at night, how gently you touched me. And your lips? So hot and wet and tasting like spirits. My heart races . . . like now. I hold my pillow to my breast and pretend that it's you. I kiss it sometimes—pretending that it's you, that if you kissed me again I would know better what to do." Opening her eyes, looking into his, she admitted, "I had never been kissed before, you see."

Shifting onto her knees, her gaze holding his, Juliette took his face in her hands, searched his eyes that reflected some emotion—a turbulence that reminded her of storms.

"I think I should die soon if you don't kiss me again, Chantz."

Nothing. No movement. Only the beating of heat on their shoulders and the singsong cadence of the cicadas. "Do you want to kiss me again, Chantz?" she finally asked.

"I want . . ." he began in a rough voice, then stopped, swallowed, looked, for a moment, as if he might jump to his feet and stalk away. "You," he finally whispered—the sound like a surrender.

She leaned into him, pressed her mouth upon his, nothing wet, nothing parted, nothing hot, just a light brush of her lips upon his that felt surprisingly soft. Again, lingering, lips against lips, his breath a quick rush of air upon her cheek as he exhaled. A sound in his throat. A tensing of his mouth. Now a parting of his lips and pressure—sweet pressure as he kissed her back. Her lips opened and his tongue slid inside her—slightly salty and sweet, hot and wet—oh oh but it felt good—just like she remembered—a flurry of feelings winged up within her—she drew him in, closer, arms slung over his shoulders as their bodies moved together, as his hands slid around her ribs and up her back—opening wide, fingers curling slightly into her body to grip her with barely constrained desire.

At last, he turned his head away, eyes closed, every nuance of his face etched in a sort of pain she was only beginning to understand. She felt it too, in her heart, and lower, a colliding of emotion and hunger—something primitive, something moving, thickening, a force as powerful and demanding acknowledgment as the love wing-beating in her heart.

"Touch me," she heard herself murmur, her head falling back, face turned up toward the hot sphere of sun overhead.

His hands cupped her breasts, and the pressure shimmied like heat waves through her body. He lifted her. He lowered his head, buried it in the swell of her bosom, breathed in sharp, short pants that felt warm and moist through her blouse.

Twisting her hand in the dark, thick waves of his hair, she pulled back his head and looked into his eyes that were blue as flames. "I like your hands on me," she confessed breathlessly. "And your mouth. And your body. Does that make me wicked, Chantz?" She didn't allow him to answer, but kissed him again, forcing his head back further. With a quick tug of her blouse from her skirt, his hands slid beneath the frail top, shoved the shirt up to expose her breasts barely concealed behind the barrier of her ecru, lace-edged shift.

Gently, so gently, he eased his mouth over one.

She gasped.

Breathed upon it.

She groaned.

Tugged the shift down with his rough-tipped fingers, down over her aching peak, freeing it so he could slide his moist lips over it and draw it deeply against his tongue that caressed it like a finger.

"Oh." She sighed, feeling the hot sun beat upon her closed eyelids, the same heat pulse in her heart, and her body, low and deep, making her breathless. "Oh yes."

Then his hand lifted her skirt, brushed upon her thigh, danced, flirtingly, over the slit in her short drawers before sliding inside the clothing, inside her body that felt, in an instant, in sublime pain. White heat and electricity. Lightning at his fingertips.

"Sweet God, Juliette," Chantz murmured, stroking her, licking her, nuzzling, his teeth ever so slightly into her sensitive flesh and suckling like a child, igniting her every raw nerve.

"I love you," she heard herself confess, knowing the instant that she said it that she had erred. His body tensed. His hands stilled. Wrapping her arms around his shoulders, one hand tunneling through his hair, she held his face hard against her breast, felt the sharp stubble of his unshaven cheek burn into her flesh.

"I love you," she repeated as her gaze lifted to the towering tops of the cane that glistened in the sunlight. "I know it's wrong. That I shouldn't. And perhaps you'll tell me I'm too young to know what love is. That I shouldn't love you, of all people. And you're right, of course. I don't want to hurt you. I just think you should know." She looked down, on his head, his hair a rich dark brown tumble of lazy waves upon her pale skin, and a swell of pain filled her at his silence. "I just thought you should know," she repeated, and closed her eyes.

Eleven

Anticipation of the hunt hung in the air heavy as the humidity, as did the smell of burning cypress bonfires that, by now, would be turning the hot summer night into something infernal. He should be mentally preparing himself for the hunt. Instead, Chantz focused on the big house where lights burned in the dusk and tried not to think about what nearly happened that afternoon. Tried not to recall how sweet Juliette had tasted . . . or how her confession of loving him had shaken him. Even now, with rum pulsing behind his eyes like drums, her words had the sobering effect of a fist punch in his gut.

"I'm afraid, Chantz," Emma said as she moved up beside him and followed his gaze to the big house. "Here you are set to hunt a man-eater and you're half drunk. Don't do it, Chantz honey. Don't go out there tonight in this frame of mind."

He thought of telling her that some damn bull gator with a hunger for human flesh was the least of his disquietude—that he'd been seduced by Juliette Broussard's body—not just her body, but her heart and soul, and he was beginning to feel . . .

What, exactly, was he beginning to feel?

Desperate. *To hold her again.* Desperate. *To taste her mouth again.* To smell the sun on her skin and the flower scent of her hair. To look into her sparkling eyes, and float on the odd, seductive innocence of her smile. Desperate to close his eyes at night and dream of sugarcane instead of her flood of dark red hair sliding like a silken breath over his body.

Desperate, desperate, *desperate not to love her.*

Without looking again at Emmaline, he left the house, stood on the bottom porch step, and briefly covered his face with his hands. Damn, if he couldn't still smell her on his fingers. Damn if he couldn't still taste her on his lips, despite the rum he'd downed in an effort to obliterate her from his thoughts and body.

Someone moved toward him through the darkness. Liza. Turning on his heels, he headed down the path toward the swamp. She ran to catch up with him, saying nothing for a while, which screamed louder than words ever could.

Finally, he said, "If you've got something to say, say it."

Nothing.

"I assume you've seen Juliette."

"I seen her all right. What in this heaven was you thinkin', Chantz? What you gonna do now? That girl is just plain crazy 'bout you and don't you think it don't show. She float around that house like she got wings on her feet. What you thinkin' to go lovin' her in that cane patch? What if Maxwell found you? Or worse. Tylor. Lord, sittin' in the same room with Miss Julie and Miss Phyllis like sittin' in a room full of gunpowder—Juliette flashin' Phyllis looks and Phyllis flashin' her looks. There sat Phyllis on one side of the dinin' table and Juliette on the other. Both women glared at each other throughout the meal like two hungry cats over a rabbit carcass. I expected them to leap out of their chairs at any minute and collide atop Rosie's ginger cake. Can't think of why you'd do such a silly thing as to let yourself get seduced by that child."

Chantz stopped abruptly and faced Liza, watched as she took a cautionary step back, her eyes wide as walnuts. "You about to preach to me, Liza? Because if you are, don't bother. Heard it already. Besides, you're not exactly a fine example of good judgment when it comes to affairs of the heart. If yours and Andrew's relationship don't wind up with you marched off to the market and him disinherited it'll be a miracle."

He regretted the words immediately. The darkness did little to mask the distress on Liza's features. "You know good and damn well what you're riskin' by foolin' with Julie," she argued. "Ain't but one other thing that Maxwell has wanted more than Maureen Broussard and that is Belle Jarod. He ain't gonna like anyone gettin' in the way of his plans. If he got to get you gone from here, he'll do it." She stepped closer and lowered her voice. "Makes no difference he's your daddy, Chantz. He got only one son in his mind and that is Tylor, sorry excuse for a man that he is. I don't like to think what gonna happen to us if you leave."

She was right and he knew it. That didn't make the situation any easier to stomach, however. He continued toward the swamp, Liza trailing. Smoke from the bonfires stung his eyes and the rum in his blood made his head pound in rhythm with his rapid heartbeat. There was an edge to his nerves tonight. Judging by the expressions of the collected men who turned to acknowledge him as he entered the firelit camp, he wasn't the only one who felt the tension in the air. Normally there would be lively chatter, perhaps storytelling, singing, dancing. The only sounds tonight were the hiss and crackle of burning wood and the throaty growl of the fire that fingered high into the night sky. Heat shimmered in the air and as Chantz glanced around the silent black faces that were painted by sweat and flames he got the uncanny feeling he had just sauntered straight into Hell . . .

And there was the devil himself, leaning against a tree, face pale in the night shadows as he watched Chantz. Tylor. The son of a bitch had actually shown up. By the looks of him he was none too happy about it, either.

Louis moved up beside Chantz. "Boss, we all thinkin' maybe we oughts to wait 'til another time for this hunt. My Tessa done read them coffee grinds and she say we is in for trouble. There be spooks in the air tonight. I can feel 'em."

"You're too damn big to be so superstitious, Lou." Andrew moved out of the dark, grinning. He flashed a smile at Liza, then toward Tylor before crossing his arms over his chest and adding in a quieter voice, "The only buggers batting around Holly Plantation is up at the big house. Phyllis boldly confronted me tonight, demanding to know if there is anything between you and Juliette."

"That be none of Phyllis's business," Liza snapped at Andrew, causing the smile to slide from his face as he turned his gaze down to hers. "Can't have it both ways, Andrew Buley. You love somebody or you don't. Phyllis done made her choice. As my mama used to say, Phyllis done made her bed, now she gonna have to sleep in it—with Horace Carrington, God bless her soul. Best you remind her of that, Andrew. And while you're at it you best think long and hard 'bout it yourself. We all got choices to make in our lives and we gots to accept the consequences of our actions."

Liza turned on her heels and marched away. Andrew stared after her, frowning. "I swear I could live to be five hundred and I would never figure out a woman's moods."

Louis shook his head and lowered his voice. "Tylor gonna bring bad luck to this hunt. Don't much care for that look in your eyes either, Boss. I gots a feelin' you gots more on your mind than gator huntin'. "

Placing a big hand on Chantz's shoulder, Louis lowered his voice. "Now ain't the time to be lettin' your personal feelin' for Tylor git in the way of what we gots to do."

Louis was right, of course. He must focus. Think coherently. He'd always been so damn good at remaining logical, undaunted, and steady as the Rock of Gibralter during the most stressful of times. But in that moment logic did not exist in his mind—not that logic had played a great part in his life since he first set eyes on Juliette Broussard.

Tylor moved toward them in a halting stride, as if he were forcing his reluctant legs to move. Despite his sorry attempt to hide his nervousness, his white shirt clung to his skin by sweat.

Forcing a tight smile, Tylor said, "Judging by your glances my direction, I must be the topic of conversation."

"Suffice it to say," Andrew began, "that when I challenged you to join us in this hunt, I didn't actually believe you would do it."

Tylor's eyes narrowed. "Ask anyone. I'm quite the hunter, Andrew. Nothing I love more than to track down prey, close in for the kill, and pop it with a bullet right between its horrified eyes."

"Your idea of prey is anything that can't bite back. Helplessness incites your manhood, Tylor. Defenselessness empowers you into believing you actually have a grand pair of balls between your legs."

"One of these days I'm going to show you just how big my balls are, Andrew," Tylor replied with a smug smile that didn't reach his eyes. "One of these days you're going to regret the manner with which you insult me."

"Kill that bull gator tonight and my opinion of you will immensely improve, Tylor."

Lowering his voice, his eyes narrowing, Andrew added, " 'Course you know the risks of this hunt. That bull's got a special sense in him—an ability to detect weakness. You've got bait branded smack across your forehead." Jutting one finger at Tylor's sweating brow, Andrew declared, "Right there. Says 'Eat Me' in big salty red letters."

Tylor swatted Andrew's hand aside.

His eyebrows lifting, Andrew said, "I suppose there's no time like the present to discuss the best plan of action to take in case that bull comes sliding out of the water to snap you out of that boat like you're a peach ripe for the plucking. Of course, you already know that once he closes his jaws on you it would take two men the size of Louis there to pry them open, if you're lucky. First he'll roll to his back to get you off your feet, then he'll carry you under and keep you there until you drown, give you a few shakes to break your neck or back.

"I understand that you don't have to worry much about pain. You go into shock immediately. Just feel a pressure mostly. About the only way you can save yourself is to put out his eyes. That'll be his only vulnerable place. You take your thumb and jab just as hard as you can into his eyeball. Of course we'll be there for you in case something happens. Won't we, Chantz?"

Tylor backed away; a pearl of sweat slid down his jaw as he turned his gaze on Chantz. "If something happens to me, you'll be answering to Daddy. That's for damn sure. You best keep that in mind, the pair of you."

Louis shook his head as Tylor stalked away. "That man is

just mean to the bone, Boss. And crazy. I declare, he be the craziest white man I ever seen."

"Obviously you haven't spent a great deal of time in the proximity of my future brother-in-law," Andrew pointed out. Reaching into his shirt pocket, he withdrew cigars, handed one to Chantz, the other to Louis.

As Chantz lit the cigar, he watched Tylor settle against the cypress, shoulders slumped and lower lip drooping like a chastised child's. Fear radiated off his features as glaringly as the firelight.

Chantz knew well enough that Maxwell was behind Tylor's presence at this hunt. He could imagine Max shaking his fist in Tylor's face, declaring, by God, that Tylor was going to show some backbone for once in his life and how better to do it than this.

As he moved away from the firelight and muted conversation, night sounds pulsed and the air turned cool against his hot face. Weeds scraped his boots and frogs splashed the black, stagnant water where he wandered the shoal, trying to focus his mind on his objective and not on the nagging idea that he wanted—needed—to see Juliette again. Desperately. As if his damned life depended on it.

The boats were lined up side by side, half in, half out of the water. The stench of bait, rotting meat, and blood strewn over the water and shoals made Chantz's stomach queasy. Or perhaps it was the rum that was lying in the bottom of his belly like a pool of kerosene.

He wasn't a superstitious man—never had been—but something, some sense of foreboding, was working up his backbone in that moment, making the beads of sweat on his brow sting like bits of ice.

Odd. There had been few times in his life when he had experienced anything remotely like fear. Rosie had often teased him that he'd been blessed or cursed, depending on her mood at that particular moment, without the ability to experience the sort of distress that could turn a man into a cowering animal incapable of reason—like Tylor, quaking yonder in his fine boots and drenching his tailored shirt with the sickly sweet sweat of bone-chilling dread.

Idiot. Tylor wasn't afraid of that damn gator, he was afraid of Chantz.

Maybe Tylor wasn't so stupid, after all.

Louis was right.

Tonight was not the night to look a reptile demon in the eye. There were too many of his own scratching around in his head.

Too late.

The belly roar of the bull rolled out of the darkness like a menacing storm. The sound vibrated inside Chantz, shivered up the back of his neck so it seemed that every hair on his head crawled on his scalp.

There it was. The challenge. The taunt. It was as if the son of a bitch could read Chantz's thoughts.

He turned his gaze up the long, narrow bayou of scum-covered backwater. Blackness stared back at him, then the sound again, closer, deeper, echoing against the walls of cypress trees so he couldn't tell from what direction it came.

The hunting party moved to the water, every other one carrying lit torches. Two by two they climbed into their boats.

Chantz tossed his cigar into the water, then slowly turned to Tylor whose expression was frozen into something almost comical.

As Andrew and Louis joined Chantz, he said, "Tylor goes with me."

Andrew and Louis exchanged concerned looks.

Chantz crooked his finger at Tylor and Tylor moved toward him as if he had weights on his feet. Louis thrust a torch at him. Tylor, his hands shaking badly, took it and stared past Chantz toward the water.

The boats moved soundlessly over the water's surface, barely leaving a ripple behind them. Torchlight cast yellow pools onto the black water. The high rushes and cypress knees reflected the illumination like slivers of glass. Then came the mist, vapor fingers reaching out from the scum-covered shoals in tendrils that coiled and twisted like pewter ribbon.

As Chantz poled the boat beneath the canopy of trees, Tylor crouched with both hands grasping the torch, jaw clenched so tightly every muscle along his neck stood out in tense cords. Up and down the bayou the boats scattered. Their torches burned in a burst of flickering golden light that floated in the blackness like celestial bodies. Taking up their spears, the men waited, silent, popping the water occasionally to draw the bull in.

"What do we do now?" Tylor asked, voice trembling with nervousness.

"Keep your mouth closed and your eyes open and the torch high." Chantz glanced at Tylor where he crouched in the boat bottom shaking so badly the vibrations sent tiny ripples across the water.

"Mind telling me just what it is I'm looking for?" Tylor asked.

"A bull gator around fifteen feet long."

Tylor curled his lip. "You're a smart ass, Chantz. Anyone ever told you that?"

"You, every chance you get. I said to keep the torch high. Higher."

"My damn arms are getting tired."

"You might try occasionally to lift something heavier

than a glass of bourbon. Higher. The light will reflect off his eyes like two burning coals."

"Maybe he high-tailed it—"

"He's here." Chantz searched the water. "Hear the silence? No frogs. No crickets." He shifted, gripping the weapon tightly as he placed it across his knees.

"Got to be crazy to be in this boat with you," Tylor muttered, his voice trembling still. "You'd like nothing better than to see me dead, wouldn't you, Chantz?"

He looked at Tylor, felt his fingers tighten more on the spear shaft as he studied the man's profile.

Tylor's head turned and he stared into Chantz's eyes. "I can certainly understand how you feel. Your existence in my life, after all, has been like an infected wound that won't heal. Sometimes I think you thrive on suffering."

Still, Chantz said nothing. He pressed his hand across his brow, tried to force himself to concentrate on the task at hand, to keep his emotions in control—refuse to allow Tylor to antagonize his anger. At some time during the last tense hour of waiting for the bull to appear, a bone weariness had crept into his body—a draining exhaustion and mounting despondency which, no matter how he tried to ignore it, wouldn't shake away. He had the odd, discomfiting sensation of sinking in quicksand every time he thought of holding Juliette that afternoon.

Tylor relaxed, shifted the torch from one hand to the other, flexing his cramped fingers by opening and closing them as he searched the water with apparently little concern, at least for the moment.

"I have to hand it to you, Chantz, you've managed to hold on to your dignity quite well, considering the circumstances of your birth, not to mention your heritage."

Again, Chantz closed his hands more tightly around the

spear, focused his attention on the dark water and not on the niggling of disconcertion squirming in his gut.

A grin curving his mouth, Tylor slowly turned his gaze back on Chantz. There was something in his expression now. Something sinister and confident—not like Tylor at all. Not the nervous buffoon who trembled and perspired under Chantz's hard blue stare. He leaned forward and fixed Chantz with his calculating gaze. The smile slowly disappeared and his expression became hard and intent.

"I imagine growing up a nameless bastard is bad enough. The fact that your mama was nothing more than a mud dauber Daddy crawled on when he was too damn drunk to know what he was doing would be enough to shame most men to their death. Oops. I forgot. You were under the assumption that your mama was some banker's daughter from Carolina."

Suddenly Tylor smiled again, broadly. Chantz stared at him—forgetting the bull gator and Juliette—and for a moment he considered that Tylor must surely have totally lost his mind. Or perhaps Chantz had simply misunderstood him. Tylor would never have been such an imbecile to insult Chantz's mother in such a way, not if he cared for his life.

But a gleam of confidence burned in Tylor's eyes.

"The closest your mama ever came to Carolina was the west bank of the Mississippi River. I believe that's where Daddy stumbled over her outside that tarpaper shanty she was living in with her no-account mother and several snot-nosed younger brothers and sisters."

"You're a filthy liar." Chantz raised the spear and pressed the sharp tip against Tylor's throat.

Tylor scrambled back, nearly dropping the torch and causing the boat to tip dangerously side to side. He clutched at his throat, his eyes widening as he looked at his fingers smeared with blood. Slowly, slowly, his eyes, bright with the torchlight, shifted back to Chantz.

Chantz felt the weight of the spear balance in his two hands as he looked Tylor in his eyes and prepared to kill him. Wanting like hell to kill him. Happily prepared to burn in Hell for all eternity for the pleasure of watching him squirm in death throes.

The boat lifted out of the water as if plucked up by some invisible hand. For an eternal moment it hovered there, half in and half out of the water, and as Tylor let out a howl of fear and jumped to his feet, flinging the torch so it streaked through the dark like a meteor, the bull gator sank again like a stone. The boat hit the surface with a smack and tilt that caused Tylor to pitch over the side, into the water.

With frantic shouts the men in the closest boats paddled toward them.

Chantz jumped to his feet, balancing his weight as the boat rocked and bounced, spear raised as he searched the dark water for any sign of Tylor. He surfaced then, gasping and wailing in terror as he thrashed the water in a feeble attempt to reach the boat.

"Help!" Tylor choked as he looked up into Chantz's eyes, Tylor's face a mask of horrifying acknowledgment.

Reality blurred in that moment, flashes of memory: taunts and jeers through the years, the stones glanced upon his flesh and the pain that had choked him breathless as he'd stood on the outside of Max's world looking in—always into Tylor's face that haunted him like a nightmare.

Then that world came sharply back into focus and there was Tylor with his hand outstretched, the hate turned to desperation and helplessness.

"Son of a bitch," Chantz cursed, then tossed down the

weapon and dropped to one knee, grabbed Tylor's hand and hauled him partway into the boat.

Tylor scrambled, kicked, and clutched. The boat rocked perilously, and as Chantz danced momentarily in an effort to regain his balance, Tylor rolled onto his side, blinked water from his eyes, and drove his foot into the back of Chantz's knee.

He hit the water hard. His weight drove him deep into the dark, wet void where the only sounds were the muted shouts of men and the rush of air bubbles by his ears. His hands clawed aside the tendrils of vegetation coiling around his arms and throat, and he fought his way to the surface and the wavering glow of approaching lights that seemed a thousand miles away.

And there was Tylor's pale face staring down at him with eyes wide and dark as chasms.

Breaking the surface, gasping for air, Chantz lifted one hand to Tylor.

Tylor, his expressionless face streaming with water, only stared.

The first thought that streaked through Chantz's brain as the bull gator took him was that Andrew had been wrong. Dead wrong. There *was* pain. A great deal of pain, then the pressure—crushing as the bull rolled over and dragged him under . . .

Twelve

She had learned about desire from the doxies who frequented the village cockfights. She had watched them rub their bodies together—the whores and drunken farmers—acknowledged the pleasure they found in touching. Occasionally, she would hear the other girls at the convent whisper, sharing secrets, but none of the things she had seen or heard had prepared her for the feelings that had taken hold of her that afternoon. The urgency of it all had been razor sharp and sweet—mindlessly pleasurable, equally painful—for her as well as for Chantz.

Daft ninny. What had she been thinking to confess her feelings? What had she been thinking to seduce him? Right there in the cane field. Right there in broad daylight. A kiss. A forbidden touch—that's all.

A confession of love.

It had angered and frightened him, of course. He had put her away from him and stalked off even though she had called out his name. Even though she had run after him with tears burning her eyes and embarrassment biting her sunburned cheeks.

Chantz Chantz Chantz.

Juliette paced in the dark, up and down the gallery, thinking she might go insane if the hounds didn't stop their barking.

"You really should attempt to be less obvious," came the voice behind her, and she turned to look into Phyllis's eyes. Phyllis gave her a tight smile. "Granted, there is something about Chantz that crawls into a woman's blood and won't let go. But most of us attempt to hide it . . . at least in polite company."

"I don't know what you're talking about," Juliette replied, turning her back on Phyllis.

"Very good. Keep on denying it. Perhaps, eventually, you'll come to believe it yourself. But that will require you to leave Baton Rouge and never see him again. Are you willing to do that, Miss Broussard?"

"I've nowhere else to go."

Phyllis moved up beside her, her arms crossed over her bosom as she looked out over the dark terrain. "I almost envy you for what you are. I wish I had your courage and willfulness and spirit—not to mention your pride. I wish I had even the tiniest portion of your strength and humanity. It's why he admires you." Leaning against the pillar, Phyllis regarded Juliette's profile. "I suspect that his . . . admiration isn't exactly what you have in mind. No doubt you desire his love and undying devotion."

"You do love him," she said, feeling loss loom around her, and within her. "Don't you?"

"Yes."

She swallowed. "And does he love you?" Her voice trembled.

Phyllis remained silent as the hounds' barking sounded louder and more frantic. "And if I said yes? Would that change how you feel about him?"

"No."

Phyllis smiled. "Isn't it a shame that we can't simply turn love on and off at will? Our hearts would hurt far less. Perhaps our lives would be spent in contentment instead of remorse over what might have been if only . . ." She sighed. "If only I was marrying Horace because I loved him. If only Chantz's eyes weren't so blue or his grin so cute and his kisses so soft . . . I might actually, eventually, fall in love with Horace. If only Chantz wasn't forbidden . . ."

At first the shouts sounded like a night bird's, faint and static in the distance.

Juliette and Phyllis exchanged looks before hurrying to the far end of the dark gallery. Some instinct made Juliette reach out and catch Phyllis's hand, as if the connection would somehow force a strength back into her legs that felt, suddenly, as trembling as pudding.

The sound again. Closer.

"Dear God." Phyllis drew in a quick breath. "Something's happened."

A figure moved swiftly through the darkness toward the house.

"It's Liza." Phyllis covered her mouth with one hand.

Lifting her skirt, Juliette descended the steps and struck out running to meet Liza whose gulping sobs made Juliette's thumping heart climb her throat.

"Liza!" she cried. "Liza, what's happened?"

Stumbling, Liza fell into Juliette's arms. Her fingers clutched with desperation at Juliette's dress as she sank to her knees. Her words were incoherent, and as she covered her face with her hands, she rocked back and forth.

Juliette eased to the ground and took Liza's tear-streaked face between her hands. "What's happened, Liza?" Her voice shook and dread filled up her chest with such force she felt as if she might explode. She wanted to shake sense into the woman. "For the love of God, Liza, calm down and tell us what's happened. Please."

She gave Liza a sharp shake that snapped Liza's head back. Something in her dark, grief-stricken eyes struck Juliette with a fear so immense she couldn't breathe.

"Chantz," she choked. "Something's happened to Chantz." Liza nodded and sobbed.

Phyllis fell to her knees, her hands clasped to her bosom.

"Is . . . is he dead?" Juliette demanded. "Is he?" She shook Liza furiously. "Tell us, damn you."

"Gator got him," she finally managed. "Took him clean under."

Juliette stared at Liza as if hoping to find some indication in her face that this was all a mistake.

"Is he dead?" she heard herself ask.

"Don't know. Louis done gone in the water after him." Swiping the back of her hand over her cheeks, Liza looked at Juliette squarely and said, "Tylor sat there and let it happen. Chantz done reached out his hand for help and Tylor done sat there and let that damn bull take him."

Several men emerged from the dark. One shouted, "Fetch the doctor! Best git him quick. Chantz bleedin' bad!"

Juliette stood, glanced at the others, like wooden statues with their mouths open and their eyes big and as glazed as china. The only thought to beat at her brain was that Chantz was alive.

Someone on a horse went tearing by, popping a crop frantically against the animal's haunches.

Juliette started down the path toward the bayou, tripping on her skirts, forcing her to lift them as her stride stretched into a run down the narrow, stone-littered path, tripped over tufts of prickly sedge until her ankles and shins felt as if they had been raked by knife blades.

The blazing bonfire cast light over the group of men huddled near the water. Louis looked up and saw her.

She froze as he stood and moved toward her. His drenched clothes clung to his skin, the white shirt soaked by blood and his hands shining wet with it. Sickness and fear rolled in her stomach as she forced herself to look up into his anguished face.

"Best you gits on back to the house, Miss Julie. This ain't no place for a young lady. I done sent Elijah to town to fetch help and soon as Doc gits here ever'thin' gonna be just fine."

"He's alive?" She swallowed and tried to breathe. Impossible. The air radiated with heat from the bonfire making her skin feel as if it were being seared from the bone.

Louis nodded but looked away.

"I want to see him. I want to see for myself—"

"Don't be wantin' to see him now. Not 'til the doc been here and—"

She moved around him.

Andrew came out of nowhere. The damp streaks of blood on his face made him look savage as he took her shoulders in his hands. His fingers felt slick and damp with blood and a shudder passed through her. A scream crawled up her throat and she fought to restrain it. Those last moments in Chantz's arms rushed over her like the incinerating heat from the bonfire.

His arms sliding around her, Andrew pulled her close, held her hard. Only then did she realize she had begun to cry. Her body shook and she buried her face against his shoulder.

"Hush now." His voice sounded thick and the words wavered. "We'll have to be strong for him, Julie."

"I want to see him, Andrew. Please."

After a moment's hesitation, Andrew took her by the arm and they walked together toward the huddle of men on their knees, some talking in soothing tones while others appeared to be working feverishly on Chantz's leg.

Chantz lay on his back, his eyes closed, and for a horrifying moment she believed him to be dead. She clutched at Andrew's arm as he said, "He's in shock, in and out of consciousness. I think he doesn't know a damn thing about what's happening."

She eased to the ground, just by his shoulder. His face, though damp with sweat, looked pale and smooth as wax.

Andrew dropped down beside her. "How is it looking, Matthew?"

The black man shook his head. "Gots the bleedin' most stopped. He done bled fierce, though."

Chantz groaned.

Juliette touched his cold brow. His eyes opened and for an instant she felt impacted by the blue of his eyes. He might well have been asleep, just awakened, drowsy and barely aware of where he was.

She pressed a kiss to his forehead. Lingering there, her eyes drifting closed, she allowed her senses to absorb the feel of his flesh against her mouth, the soft brush of his hair against her cheek—his scent—oh God, his scent. It rushed through her body with a heat greater than the fire burning in the distance. She felt desperate to press her body against his.

Andrew touched her back. "We have to move him now, Julie. Come away."

As he pulled her aside, she struggled, briefly. Chantz turned his face away, and as the first spasm of pain flashed through him his hands dug into the dirt, shaking and suddenly sweating. A sound rolled inside him. His teeth clenched.

Louis and Matthew situated a stretcher beside him, and as the men moved to lift him, Andrew forced Juliette away. "Have Rosie prepare us plenty of hot water and clean linens. And bourbon. I suspect Chantz is going to need a great deal of that."

Turning on his heels, he moved to assist with the careful lifting of the stretcher.

Shifting her gaze toward the water, she looked directly into Tylor's eyes.

He stood in the shadows, partially behind a tree, his cheek pressed against the tree trunk and his fingers curled into the bark as if he would tumble to the ground should he loosen his grip.

Moving toward him, she watched his eyes widen. The expression on his face reflected a sickly mixture of suppressed excitement and mounting fear. He wanted to run, she could tell. Yet, he stood there as if anchored, his legs shaking, defying his own alarm as much as her intimidation.

His bloodless lips parted, and he croaked, "It was an accident. I swear to Almighty God, I didn't mean for Chantz to go into that water. The boat was rocking, back and forth, and he lost his balance. That's all. I tried to help—"

"You're a liar. You're a spineless, good-for-nothing wastrel unfit to lick Chantz's boots. If he dies, Tylor Hollinsworth, I'll see you hang for murder."

"You best be careful how you threaten me," he shouted in a broken voice.

She forced herself to curve her lips in so cold a smile Tylor took an awkward step back.

"You're friendless. Loveless. Without character. I pity

you, Tylor Hollinsworth. If that were you on that stretcher there wouldn't be a man or woman in this entire state who would give a damn if you lived or died. That's what bothers you most, isn't it? That a man like Chantz would be so highly regarded by your peers, while you, on the other hand, are considered worthless and laughable."

Moving closer, she said, "For the remainder of your life on this earth, Tylor Hollinsworth, you'll see his face every time you close your eyes to sleep."

Juliette fled up the path, back to his house where the few windows shone with light. With her heart in her throat, she ran up the steps, hearing Chantz's groans before she saw him twisted on his bed, his hands ripping at the bloody sheets as Andrew and Louis fought to keep him still.

Flinging her body over his, Juliette stopped his thrashing. She felt his heart slamming against her breast, felt the heat and sweat of his body penetrate her clothes.

Pressing her cheek against his, she whispered in his ear, "Hush. Hush now. You must lie as still as possible, Chantz."

My darling, darling Chantz.

Her eyes burned, whether from her own sweat seeping from her scalp or from the tears she tried desperately to ignore, she couldn't tell. Her existence in that moment centered on the roughness of his unshaven cheek against her tender flesh, the harshness of his frantic breathing, the low suffering groan that rattled in his throat.

He stilled.

His breath brushed her ear. His lips touched her temple, moving the damp tendrils of hair there, tasting the salty trail of the tears she had been crying.

"Juliette," he murmured.

Andrew pulled her away and suddenly Rosie was there,

opening her arms and taking Juliette against her massive soft breasts, hugging so hard it seemed her ribs would snap.

"Gonna be fine," Rosie said with a composure that almost, but not quite, convinced Juliette that she had imagined the extent of Chantz's injuries.

"Hush now," Rosie crooned, rocking her even as Juliette felt the deep silent sob constrict the dark woman's chest. "He gonna be fine. Just fine."

Odd how she wished in that moment for the Reverend Mother who was as devout in her belief in miracles as she was in her belief that each soul was God's gladiator against evil.

Andrew stepped from the house, face white as flour, his eyes dark sockets of worry. He searched the shadows before finding Juliette, alone in the darkness, huddled against the wall with her knees drawn up to her chest and her hair falling over her brow and eyes, as if it somehow curtained her away from the bedlam going on inside Chantz's house. Jumping to her feet, she hurried to him, throwing open her arms as he reached for her, drew her against his chest, and held her so hard she felt his heart pound against her. With her head on his shoulder, she closed her gritty eyes and swallowed back her emotions.

"Please tell me he's not dead, Andrew. *Please.*"

He stroked her hair and smiled. "He's not dead, Juliette."

"Will you let me see him now?"

"We've got the bleeding stopped. He won't lose his leg. But he's in a great deal of pain. You should be prepared. The man in that bed . . . he's not Chantz. Not the Chantz that you and I have known."

She pulled away and searched his eyes.

He nudged a wild hair from her cheek. "I only meant

that his suffering . . . such suffering takes a toll on a man, and on his spirit, and on his sanity."

"Where is Emmaline?"

"She's with him."

"And the others? Maxwell and Phyllis . . . ?"

"Bed. Long ago. You should get some rest yourself."

"Not until I see him."

"Before you go in . . ." Andrew cleared his throat. "Emmaline is . . . despondent. You should be prepared."

Juliette nodded and turned away, too weary almost to stand, too heartbroken. Falling against the cool porch column, she covered her mouth with her hand and closed her eyes. Dear God, give her strength.

Drawing back her shoulders, Juliette started toward the door. Suddenly Emmaline was there, moving toward Juliette, eyes wide and glassy and her dress smeared with blood. Her hair drooped in thin gray strands around her gaunt face.

"I won't allow you to destroy him further," she sneered. "I told him what would happen if he succumbed to you. He wouldn't listen."

"Get out of my way, Emmaline," Juliette declared.

"You'll see my son over my dead body. He doesn't want to see you." Emmaline planted herself in the way, her hands fisted and her legs braced. "What have you done to turn him against me, Juliette?"

Juliette frowned, confused by Emmaline's sudden accusation. "I don't know what you're talking about."

"He doesn't want me in the room. He refuses to look at me and when he does . . ." Emma pressed her bony fist against her mouth as if that would help her swallow back her rising hysteria. "You've somehow turned him against me. I won't allow it, do you hear me? He's all I've got in this world."

Lifting her chin, Juliette met the woman's gaze directly. "Place the blame for this tragedy where it belongs. At Tylor Hollinsworth's feet."

Her stoic façade crumbling, Emmaline's shoulders slumped and she covered her face with her hands. As she appeared to totter, Juliette grabbed her, held her fiercely as the woman struggled weakly, then collapsed against her, as if every bone in her small body turned to water. Juliette gently stroked Emmaline's coarse, lank hair, feeling her own outrage dissipate. A flicker of emotion tickled her— pity, no doubt.

No, she realized in an instant. Not simply pity. Compassion?

The woman shaking in her arms was Chantz's mother whether they liked each other or not.

Closing her eyes, she turned her lips to Emmaline's forehead and kissed it. "Hush. Hush now, and listen to me. Despite what you believe, Emmaline, I care for Chantz. I truly care for him."

Emmaline backed away, faded eyes flashing with fresh anger, her lower lip trembling as she stared at Juliette. "I knew there would be trouble. I felt it here." She thumped her heart with her fist. "I saw it in his eyes—I heard it in his voice. You were there, in his head the whole time. His thoughts were all tied up with you—not on that damn gator. If you cared for my boy—truly cared, you would leave him alone. He was happy until you came here. We all were. You've done nothing but brew discontent since you arrived and we all want you gone—before you end up killing Chantz like your mother destroyed Jack."

Juliette rocked back, fought the urge to slap the hysterical woman.

"That's enough, Emmaline." Andrew took Emmaline

by her shoulders and moved her aside. Emmaline, too weary to fight him, shuffled clumsily down the stairs at his side.

Juliette focused on the open door and forced herself to move, paused at the threshold while her gaze shifted from Rosie's tired, shadowed, and distraught features to Liza, who sat in a chair near the window, head hanging wearily between her shoulders as she napped.

Rosie cleared her throat.

Liza looked up, blinked sleepily.

Juliette looked from one to the other, her heart beating painfully in her throat.

Her legs shook as she crossed the floor and stopped by the bed, the sheets deep red with blood. She reached for Chantz's hand that felt so very big and hard and heavy in her own—so heavy she was forced to hold it with both of hers.

Bending her head, she pressed the back of his hand to her cheek, closed her eyes, and recalled how it had stroked her the day before—so gently despite its power.

Absolute stillness hung in the room, and absolute silence—thick as always on the cusp of dawn, before the first dim gray rays broke through the dark to awaken the birds.

"Julie."

Her eyes opened and she raised them to Chantz's. Her heart beat fast as she acknowledged the hollows of his face and eyes—so different from the feverish passion for life that had always burned there.

"*Chère*," he whispered, his dry lips curving.

She stroked his brow, willing herself to remain stoic. She smiled into his eyes and pressed a kiss on his cheek.

His mouth curved. "Still love me?" he asked, drifting, drifting, his eyes closing, brow furrowing with pain.

Juliette forced herself to look at Liza. "Is it true?" she whispered. "Is this my fault?"

As Liza averted her eyes, Juliette turned to Rosie. "Answer me, Rosie."

Rosie exhaled a deep breath and shook her head. "Can't say what was in the man's head, Miss Julie."

"Dear God." A sob worked up her throat as she looked again into Chantz's pain-etched features. Suddenly her body felt cold as ice. She wanted to run away, as fast as her legs would carry her. Run away and not look back. She touched his cheek, briefly, then turned and fled the house, down the steps and through the scattering of dark bodies huddled together on the ground, waiting for assurance that Chantz would survive.

She ran until she could run no farther, until the river yawned before her and her feet sank in the deep cool mud. Sinking to the ground, her legs crossed beneath her, she stared out through dawn's gray mist. She lifted her face toward the sky, in which the stars were no longer visible and a white sun was just rising, its edges shimmering and casting streaks of light through the fog.

Slowly, the river materialized, a splash of fiery yellow set ablaze by the rising sun, and on it she glimpsed a pair of night herons rise from their perch, the measured beat of their wings a muffled pop in the quiet. The night jasmine began to furl their golden petals from the light and the trees moved with birds that fluttered and warbled and took to the awakening sky in dark masses.

Bowing her head, she began to cry.

Maxwell closed the bedroom door behind him, his gaze fixed on Tylor's nude form on the bed, body slick with sweat and shaking so fiercely the bed bumped against the wall. The air smelled of bourbon and was so thick with the stink of fear Maxwell was forced to breathe through his mouth.

Tylor sat up abruptly and stared through the mosquito netting. He didn't bother to reach for a sheet.

"Daddy," he croaked before Maxwell cut him off.

"Shut up, Tylor. I didn't come here to listen to your excuses for doing what you did."

"But it was an accident, I *swear* it."

Maxwell crossed the room and turned up the flame in the globe lamp, then he reached for the netting and tucked it behind the hook on the bed post.

"The boat was rocking, Daddy. Back and forth, and Chantz lost his balance. I don't care what they said I did, I swear I tried to save him. I reached out my hand for him—"

"I don't want to hear it. I want you to shut up your drunken, cowardly mouth and listen to what I have to say."

Maxwell withdrew a cigar from his pocket and, putting it in his mouth, bent to light it from the lamp flame. His eyes drifted closed as he inhaled, drawing the smoke deeply into his chest as he straightened and rolled the fat cigar between his lips. Finally, he exhaled the smoke and turned his gaze on Tylor.

"Do you know what you've done to us, Tylor?" Max sat down on the bed and, removing the cigar from his mouth, studied its smoldering tip. "I don't think you do. Because you're stupid, Tylor. You are and always have been, too stupid to walk straight. You're a lot like your mother. She was a stupid woman. Good for little more than spending my money and swooning from the heat. She wasn't even pretty. There was as much character in her face as a gator pod. But she came with a decent dowry—decent enough to pay for the draining of the back three hundred acres and the purchase of fifty decent slaves.

"Hell, she couldn't even deliver me a decent crop of children. First one died, you know. Premature. I put another one in her right away and that one died too when she was only four months gone. Then came you, and I had such high expectations. I needed a strong, brilliant son, but what I got was a tiny, mewling, and sickly runt that squalled day in and day out until I was forced to move to the old *garçonnière* in order to sleep."

He smoked and regarded Tylor's face, slack and tear-streaked, his eyes glazed by bourbon. "I was determined, of course, to get me a decent boy, but your mama wouldn't have it again. Put a lock on the door and wouldn't receive me. Said she'd done her damn duty—given me an heir and that was enough. She sat in her room month after month, rocking you in her arms, singing the same damn song over and over, 'Jesus Is the Light and My Salvation.' Is it any wonder I turned to Maureen?"

Smoking, puffing so hard the tip of his cigar shone red-gold as a flame in the dim light, Maxwell looked around the room, his thoughts scattering over the last many years. "It didn't help," he finally said, "that Emmaline had planted herself out yonder, reminding me every minute that I had undoubtedly made the biggest mistake of my life. Oh, I don't mean that I made the mistake of lying down with her—though I'm not proud of the deed. Men will be men.

"No, I'm talking about Chantz. But what could I do, really? I briefly considered taking the boy, but what would that have accomplished? Nothing, really. He wasn't legitimate, you see. I could have adopted him, but there was you to contend with. You were the legitimate heir, Tylor. No getting around that issue. Why, do you know I actually considered a time or two stuffing you in a tow sack and tossing you in the river, right along with your mama.

"But then there was Maureen, and God help me I actually got all caught up in the fantasy that perhaps one day she would leave Jack for me. I imagined she would give me the kind of son I wanted and needed for Holly House. I imagined she would lift this sorry plantation out of mediocrity and turn it into something as grand as Belle Jarod. For a while, I even imagined murdering Jack to get my hands on them both. My God, what thoughts desperation encourages in a rational man's mind and heart. It's frightening as hell, Tylor. But I digress . . ."

Turning his head, he looked into Tylor's eyes that were wet and gold with lamplight. "Every day of the last twenty-seven years I've looked into your eyes and felt the bitter bite of disappointment because you weren't more like Chantz. One has to wonder what it is that can make one son a fighter, handsome, strong, possessed of a spirit that raises him to a level of excellence, and the other a weakling of mind, body, and character. I suppose there's no need to dwell on it now. What's done is done, alas."

"What the hell are you trying to say to me, Daddy?"

"Only that you're a damn fool, Tylor. Not only have you possibly destroyed Chantz, but you've destroyed me as well. Not just me, but us. This plantation. Now I ask you, should Chantz quit me, what the hell am I supposed to do about my sugarcane?"

"I'll see to it." Tylor's voice sounded dry and hoarse. His soft shoulders slumped as he looked into Maxwell's eyes. "I can do it, Daddy. I just need you to believe in me for once in your life."

"Believe in you?" Maxwell frowned and left the bed, walked to the open French door and looked out on the dark Holly grounds. "Believe in you," he repeated without turning. "Hell, Tylor. The idea of setting eyes on you again makes me want to vomit. Believe in you? I doubt it."

Thirteen

The pain was ceaseless. How many hours had he lain there in his sweat-sodden sheets, sliding into blessed sleep only to experience again his reaching for Tylor who stared down at him with his face still and smooth and emotionless as a china doll's, and realizing in that instant that he was damned . . . and dead. Then the blast of pain and heat, his last desperate gulp of air as he was dragged under. It was *that* moment's fear and pain that continued to awaken him over and over, heart slamming in his throat and fresh torture spearing through his body.

Then there was his mother.

Emmaline sat rigidly in a ladder-back chair near the open window, her thin weathered hands clasped in her lap. She appeared to have aged years—her body wraithlike, too thin and ashen—her eyes too large for her sunken face. In his rational moments, he stared at her—the stranger he thought he knew for nearly thirty years. Tylor's words turned over and over in his mind, cutting as sharply and brutally as the bull's teeth into his leg.

"I know what she told you . . . she was nothing more than a mud dauber Daddy happened upon when he was drunk . . ."

He almost wished the gator had killed him. Existing in Maxwell's vacuum of denial for thirty years had been bad enough. At least he could rally his dignity by reminding himself that he walked the earth because, however briefly, Emma and Maxwell had shared a common fondness. He could have felt pride over the fact that Emma had come from a respectable mother and father.

What an idiot he'd been. And blind. Of course, it all made sense now. Even in his fever state and overwhelming pain, the truth glittered as pure as gold . . . why Maxwell turned his back on Emma—and on Chantz. There had been no fondness between them. No mutual respect. No nothing. No doubt Max had awakened the morning after with little, if any, recollection of Emmaline Boudreaux at all. Chantz wondered whether to despise Max or to pity him.

Chantz stared out the window. The hot summer air shimmered off the waxen green leaves of the magnolia tree. The heavy blooms were starting to die—browning around the creamy petal edges. Yet, their perfume wafted sweetly. He felt intoxicated by the sensuality of the fragrance, and of the memories it evoked.

Juliette. Juliette. Juliette.

The moist sweetly scented pulse of her throat against his mouth. Her hair wrapping around him, brushing his cheek, exciting his senses with its smell. Midnight Magnolia. Her body heat had radiated with it as he slowly moved his hand up her leg, and he recalled thinking that the soft skin of her inside thigh was as smooth and pale as a magnolia petal.

Juliette.

What irony that the greatest experience of his manhood

had been spent in her arms in that cane field—was she a last gift from God? Or was she the reason for this tragedy? Was this agony in his leg God's punishment for his succumbing to the seduction in her magnificent eyes and lips?

Dear God, even now the ache for her was as sweltering as the summer heat. He felt maddened by it.

The pulsating whir of the cicadas had a way of intensifying the heat and the silence that fell heavily when the insects ceased their mating calls. Yet there was no silence today. Just as well. The chorus was as soothing as a lullaby.

He floated on images of Juliette interspersed with those of vast flats of high green cane and the rattle of their leaves in the wind. He imagined himself walking down the long furrows, encouraging the women and children who plucked the grass from the base of the stalks, tignons dark with sweat, their voices harmonizing as they sang, "Onward Christian Soldiers."

Voices drifted to him: Juliette's and, more rarely, Maxwell's—the sorry bastard—more concerned over when Chantz would be up and around again . . . then Liza's, Rosie's, Little Clara's . . . and Andrew's.

Andrew and Juliette . . . together. Andrew holding Juliette. Her smiling up into his eyes.

When he awakened, the air felt cooler on his body. How long had he slept? The sun that had earlier splashed in golden pools over the oaken floor faded to gray shadows that slowly crept toward his bed.

His mother turned her head and looked at him. She left her chair and came to the bed, peeled the bandage back from his leg and nodded, apparently satisfied by what she saw. "Thank God for your boot. You'll hurt awhile, but you'll heal. Maybe now you'll listen to me, son. You'll listen when I tell you that dwelling on thoughts of that woman—"

"Who are you?" he said, cutting off her words and bringing a sudden flush of color to her wan cheeks. "Or rather . . . what are you?"

Her shoulders stiffened. Her gaze touched his briefly before she turned away—walked again to the window and looked out. "Maxwell and the Buleys rode over to the Fairchilds' this morning after church. You'd think with his overseer, not to mention his son, lying up in a bed with his leg—"

"Maxwell doesn't give a damn about me and I'm beginning to understand why at long last." Clenching his teeth, he pushed himself up on his elbows and glared at her back. "All these years we've lived a lie, haven't we, Mama? Your parents weren't from Carolina. Were they? Who was your mother? More importantly, who was your father? Or don't you know?"

She wheeled around and stared at him, her eyes straining with anger. Her mouth opened and closed, saying nothing.

"Tylor told me," he said. "Now I want to hear it from your own mouth. And I want the truth."

"He's a filthy liar," she cried, and fled the house, knocking over the old ladder-back chair in the process. Falling back on the bed with a groan, Chantz stared at the ceiling, reason and pain a swirl of confusion in his mind.

Hands touched his brow and he opened his eyes to look up into Louis's face, marred by deep lines of distress. "Best you keep quiet now, Boss. Can't be havin' that leg bleed agin. Doc say you gonna be just fine long as you lay quiet for a few days." He smiled broadly and shook his head. "Reckon that ol' gator thought he done met his match when I go jumpin' in that water. Give him a good jab in the throat with my knife. Thought I done had me that bounty money for sure." He chuckled.

Chantz searched his friend's eyes. "Where is Juliette?"

"Gone with Mistah Drew. Out to the Belle. Left soon as Massa Maxwell and the Buleys took off to church. Now you rest. Rosie done got supper nearly done. Sooner you gits food in your belly the better, Doc says. More food and less rum. You be back on your two legs in no time."

Closing his eyes, Chantz said nothing as Louis left the house. He listened to the man's footsteps ring down the porch steps, listened to the rise of voices singing church hymns in the distance. "Swing low sweet chariot coming for to carry me home."

What the blazes was Andrew doing? He'd specifically forbidden Andrew to take her to Belle. If Maxwell found out . . .

You one of those bees, Drew?

Stay rational.

Hell, he should be focusing his thoughts on the son of a bitch who'd tried to kill him. More than that . . . what was he supposed to do now? Close his eyes to the fact that his half-brother had attempted to murder him? Was he to simply go on pretending that nothing had changed?

Sensing a movement, he looked around into Little Clara's big eyes. She held a praline in each hand, one of which she slid into Chantz's mouth. The sweet candy momentarily replaced his pain with pleasure.

"Why aren't you at the sermon?" he asked.

"Done had my Bible readin', Boss Chantz. Miss Julie read me verses ever chance she have. In the mo'nin when she gits up. Aftanoon when she suppose to be nappin'. She read all us young'uns Bible verses." She dashed to his chest of drawers and collected his tattered lambskin Bible and brought it to the bed, flipped it open and held it in her hands as she squinted to study the words. A braid tied with a dark blue ribbon bobbed over her forehead.

"And the Lord said . . . let there be light . . ." Turning her face up, her smile stretching, she said, "Ain't that somethin', Boss Chantz? 'Cept you can't be tellin' Rosie I can read 'cause she gits all to flappin' like an old mad hen."

Chantz reached for the Bible, tugged it from her hands as her smile faded and her face became somber, as if she'd just been caught filching pralines without Rosie's approval. "It's against the law for you to be learning to read, Little Clara. You know that."

Her lower lip pouted and she shrugged. "Miss Julie say that what stupid folk don't know don't hurt 'em none."

Throwing the Bible as hard as he could toward the end of the bed, Chantz declared, "If Miss Julie isn't careful she's gonna find herself hanged. Same for you. The law doesn't abide slaves learning to read, Clara. The first one of you I find with your head over a book I'm gonna lock in the hot-house for a week. You hear me?"

She nodded and her lower lip protruded further.

He reached and caught one of her braids, gently tugged her closer, lowered his voice, and did his best to muster a smile, despite his mounting irritation and frustration and the throbbing heat in his leg. "I love you, Little Clara. And I love Simon. And Louis. And Liza. And Rosie. And I would rather have both my legs and arms cut off and my eyes plucked out than have any of you punished for reading. Understand me?"

She nodded again and started to smile.

Pushing up on one elbow, he said, "Now I want you to get me a pair of pants. And my pair of old boots out by the back stoop. Then I want you to go down to the stables and have my horse saddled."

Her eyes widening, Little Clara said, "What you think

you gonna do, Boss Chantz? Can't be gittin' outta bed. Your leg gonna fall right off."

"Just do it," he said, and fell back on the pillow.

"Come away from here, Juliette. If Maxwell doesn't shoot me then Chantz will. In case you aren't aware, he forbid me to bring you here. I don't mind telling you, I'm feeling a bit like a traitor—we're friends, after all. Hell, had I realized you were sincere about exhuming Belle Jarod I would have refused to bring you here. Besides, I thought the true point of this jaunt was to discuss privately my situation with Liza."

"We'll get to that," she declared over her shoulder before focusing again on the tangle of wild vines and trees forming a dense green wall before her. "Surely there's some mistake, Andrew. You've brought me to the wrong place. There's nothing here. Nothing at all but wilderness."

Turning on her heels, her frustration mounting, Juliette regarded Andrew where he remained by the buggy, straw hat in his hand and his buff-colored broadcloth jacket sprinkled by dust and dandelion fluff. The whir of the cicadas punctuated his silence as he focused on the lair beyond her, his frown response enough.

Some distance below, the river glistened like a ribbon in the sun. Evidence of the recent high water was scattered along the banks, splintered trees and dead river grass, the carcass of a deer that had become caught in the tow and drowned. It was the relic of rotting timbers jutting up out of the water that caught her eye and held it, made an ache settle deep in her chest so she couldn't breathe. Ghost memories roused: wide verandas over the water where paddleboats with gingerbread adornments docked, women and men in gay-colored clothes laughing, musicians greeting guests with lively tunes that added to the festive air.

No mistaking, she realized with sinking despair . . . Andrew had brought her home, to Belle Jarod. Except, there seemed to be no Belle Jarod any longer.

Her face sweating, her hands and arms scratched and beaded with blood, Juliette struggled for a breath in the still air. Behind her, Andrew fought through the copse, his mild curses muted by the increasingly loud whir of the cicadas and the shriek of crows that moved in a black cloud from tree top to tree top. Panic set in. Perhaps there was nothing left, nothing at all. Perhaps all that remained of Belle Jarod was buried beneath the humus of rotting leaves beneath her feet, humus that smelled like the fresh, upturned earth of a grave.

Her foot caught on a root and she went down hard. Lethargy stole through her and she closed her eyes, welcoming the coolness of the earth that embraced her damp body and made her shiver. Suddenly she didn't want to go on. She wanted to curl up with her knees to her chest and sleep. And dream.

"Juliette." Andrew took her arm.

"Chantz was right. It's hopeless," she spoke against a dry oak leaf.

"Get up. Last thing I need is for you to get snake bit. Come on, now. Rosie is going to have a mess of a time cleaning that dress."

Wearily, she lifted her head.

There, through the break in the tangle of blackberry vines dotted with green berry nubs and ground ferns with violin-shaped fronds, Doric columns shimmered in a swath of sunlight. The ache that had tightened her chest rushed through her body with unbearable lightness.

Taking Andrew's hand, she struggled to her feet and pushed her way through the mire, distantly aware of the briars and twigs clawing at her exposed skin. Nettles bit at her ankles and sent tendrils of heat up her legs. Grasshoppers sprang in flurries and birds burst from their roosts with popping flaps of their wings.

The remains of Belle Jarod gaped like a bleached skull in the dim light, her walls eroded by weather and chewed away by flora crawling up the columns and into the glassless windows. The front door hung from its hinges.

Cautiously, she moved up the cypress steps, weathered but rock hard, to the gallery littered by leaves and mildew and moss that had formed a dense green covering over the shaded planks.

She paused at the doorway, looking into the cave of dark ruined rooms, then moved into the shadows. The heavy scent of rich humus permeated the air, along with the underlying stench of damp, old ash.

Her skirt hem flurried the scattering of dry leaves on the floor as she wandered first into the *salle de compagnie,* slippers leaving imprints in the settled dust. The disconcerting sense of abandonment hung over the room like a pall.

Everything remained just as it had been the evening her father had returned from New Orleans unexpectedly to find his wife with another man: The once fine furnishings, faded by years of dust and leaves, plush satin and velvet cushions ravaged by burrowing animals. The settee sat at an angle to the marble-manteled fireplace where the rusted iron grate held logs. Mirrors hung lopsided on the walls.

Juliette ran her hand over the back of the settee. "Well." She sighed brokenly. "I'm not sure what I expected. It wasn't this, I assure you."

She managed a dry laugh and gave a slap to the settee, sending a cloud of dust into the air. "He simply walked away, didn't he? Too painful for him to even return for the furnishings."

Turning, she collected herself enough to square her shoulders and lift her chin. Forcing a smile, she looked into Andrew's eyes, her own swimming with emotion. "It must have been very beautiful, once."

"It was." He glanced around, his look nervous. "I don't think it's a good idea our being here like this. I shouldn't have brought you. Maxwell, not to mention Chantz, will have my hide, I'm afraid."

Between the dark green patches of lichen on the dining room walls were glimpses of fading frescoes, images of France again. She might have been looking out the clerestories at the convent at green hills dotted with sheep. Her exploration carried through the butler's pantry, again down the central hallway and into the ballroom. Slowly, slowly, she turned around while looking up through the open charred rafters crowded by tree limbs and cascading moss. A pair of ruby throated hummingbirds darted from one gable to the next, feeding on the blooms of honeysuckle.

The tears rose at long last. She couldn't stop them. They trickled down her cheeks, burning like scratches.

"Julie," Andrew said with a gentleness that only exacerbated the pain in her chest. "Don't do this to yourself. Best you can do is just walk away. Chantz is right. No amount of wishing and dreaming is going to bring back Belle Jarod."

"Funny what love can do to people, isn't it, Andrew? Lately I've been thinking I was happier in that dreary old convent with Reverend Mother barking with every other breath that my soul was doomed to perdition. I don't know what I was thinking, believing there was actually something here for me."

Frowning, she knuckled a tear away and focused on her friend who remained in the foyer, his hat in one hand, the other slid into his trouser pocket.

"Love is supposed to be gentle, isn't it?" she asked. "Well? Isn't it?"

He nodded, his frown deepening.

"Love is supposed to be the giving of one's heart and soul. The ultimate sacrifice of self. Isn't it?"

Shifting from one foot to the other, Andrew swallowed and said, "Yes."

"Then tell me why the hell it hurts so badly. Why does it appear to cause more suffering than war and disease? Why does it crumble dignity and shatter hearts and bring hope and faith down into ashes?'

"I don't know." He shook his head.

Drawing back her shoulders, she said, "Emmaline was right. My presence at Belle Jarod has been nothing more than a bother for Chantz. Now he's lying in that bed suffering because—"

"Because of Tylor. Not you."

"They all warned me. Liza and Rosie and Maxwell. Stay away from Chantz. Leave him alone. Yet I allowed myself to get all swept up in what was going on here—" She pointed to her heart. Focusing on Andrew again, she asked:

"Are you in love with Liza, Andrew?"

Emotion crossed his face and the skin around his eyes appeared to tighten. "Yes," he finally declared in a tight voice.

"Your parents are aware of your . . . relationship. They've demanded that Maxwell send her away. They want her gone so you can marry properly and beget children who look like opossums. What are you going to do about it? Answer me, damn you!" The words bounced off the walls and caused the hovering hummingbirds to dart away through the trees.

His face bleached gray as the walls. "What can I do—"

"She's expecting a child."

The hat dropped to the floor where it stirred up a puff of dust and caused a leaf to startle. He stood there, stock-still for a long moment, in the cool blue shade of the rafter overhang, looking out the door at the still, wild tangle of trees and brush and tall wild flowers that crowded the rotting gallery floor. A dragonfly hovered in the air between them and she watched the sun catch the spectrum of colors on its wings as it whirred, hovered, then streaked out through the window in a blur. Finally, Andrew closed his eyes. "Oh my God," he said . . . just before Chantz moved up behind him and grabbed him by the scruff of his neck.

fourteen

*J*uliette gasped. "My God, Chantz, what are you doing here?"

Andrew turned, stumbled back, crunching his hat underfoot.

Twisting his fingers in Andrew's coat, Chantz said through his teeth, "I've got several good reasons to beat the hell out of you. One is standing yonder looking like she's been in a cat fight. As I recall, I *forbade* you to bring her here. The other is Liza. You've put a baby in her, Drew, now I want to know what you intend to do about it."

"Chantz, please . . . let him go," Juliette pleaded.

"It's all right," Andrew declared, his gaze fixed on Chantz. "Chantz has every right to throttle me. It wouldn't be the first time, I assure you. I recall as boys we spent more time rolling on the ground bloodying each other's noses than we did talking or fishing."

"I'm not in the mood to reminisce, Drew. My leg is hurting like hell and I'm about two blinks away from passing out—or dying. Either way I'm going to hurt you—"

"I'll take care of her, Chantz. You know I'll take care of them both."

"How?"

He clutched tighter, jerking Andrew closer so they stood nose-to-nose. His hands shook and the pain that splintered through his lower leg made breathing impossible for a moment.

"Tell me how you're gonna keep her off the auction block when your daddy discovers she's about to deliver him a quadroon grandbaby. How are you gonna keep that child from experiencing the ache of rejection and the hunger for acknowledgment when he lies in his shanty mattress and looks out at the big house wondering what it would feel like to go to bed with a full belly and a fond good night from his father?"

Andrew shook his head. "I don't know, Chantz. I've got to have time to think."

"You should have done your thinking long ago, Drew. Before you ever decided to fall in love with her."

"Don't go climbing on your high horse with me, Chantz. You're not exactly an example of good judgment. Fact is, you're here right now because your jealousy and suspicion got in the way of your common sense. Look at you, for God's sake. You can barely stand up. You look as if there isn't another drop of blood in your body and sweating so fierce you might have just climbed out of the damn river."

Chantz eased his grip on Andrew's coat and stepped back.

Andrew smoothed his lapels and bent to retrieve his hat. He glanced toward Juliette as he situated the Panama on his head. Dark color blotched his cheeks and he forced a tight smile.

"Chantz will see you back to Holly, Miss Julie, if he doesn't die first. I'm sure you won't be bothered, will you?"

He gave a dry laugh. "Of course not. I suspect that stupidity is as rampant around here as the mosquitoes are blood-thirsty. At least when I burn in Hell I won't do it alone."

Andrew's footsteps rang on the old floor as he exited the house. Chantz stared after him, a reluctance to refocus his attention on Juliette an annoyance that fisted low in his belly. The son of a bitch was right, of course. Considering what was going on in his heart and mind—not to mention his body—in that instant he had no room to throw stones at Andrew.

Through the paneless window, Juliette watched Andrew fight his way through the brush. "You were very cruel," she said. "You had no right, considering . . ."

"Considering what?"

Her head turned and her eyes held him. The thought struck him that those eyes had never looked so green, green as the ivy climbing the wall at her shoulder, greener than the lizard sunning in a streak of light on the sill.

"That you risked your life and Phyllis's reputation on an affair that was doomed from the very beginning, of course."

She moved toward him, passing through shafts of yellow sunlight that made her hair blaze with color. His discomfort increased and he turned his face away, into a shadow that felt slightly cool upon his sweating cheek.

"I'm coming to the conclusion that love and commitment are less a state of heart than they are of mind," she said in an oddly sleepy voice—as if she were weary. "Take my father, for instance. Had he married a respectable woman, demure, plain, vaporish, he would undoubtedly be alive today. Belle Jarod wouldn't be little more than a worthless pile of rubble."

"There wouldn't *be* a Belle Jarod," Chantz pointed out as he leaned against the doorpost and closed his eyes, made breathless by pain. "Nor would there be a Juliette," he finally added, thinking:

And that would be a crying damn shame.

Her arm brushing his, she gazed across the foyer strewn with damp leaves and shadows. "You won't let Maxwell send her away, will you?"

He looked down at her arm next to his. "I can't stop him, if that's what he decides to do."

The staircase curved up into a fallen wall of charred wood. Chantz caught her wrist. "It isn't safe—"

She turned on him. Her eyes blazed and her chin quivered. "I only wish I had done this years ago. Seen for myself what sort of complete destruction of a man's life my mother accomplished. What dreams she razed. I suppose it wasn't enough that she shattered his heart . . ." Her voice broke and she drew in an unsteady breath, turned to look up the staircase. "Please, Chantz. Let me go."

Sunlight spilled in hazy shafts through wide holes in the ceiling where blackened beams thrust toward the sky. There were animal nests in the joints. Honeysuckle formed a sweet cloud of red, yellow, and white blooms that tumbled in streamers from the highest peak.

Her shoulder brushed the honeysuckle streamers, sending a flurry of butterflies rising into the air. Like a wraith, Juliette moved through the streaks of sunlight, to the threshold of the nursery—the room Chantz himself had fought to reach through the flames in order to save her those fifteen years ago.

The fire had eaten its way through most of the floor, the ceiling, even the cypress timbers in the walls, leaving odd breaks in the plaster where plants had taken root and sent long green tendrils climbing toward the sunlight. As she walked to the tall window opening, the slanting rays of sunlight limned her body as she gazed out at the distant lily-covered lake.

There were no swans, of course. They were long gone.

Limping, Chantz moved up behind her—not quite touching. Wouldn't be smart. Too damn weak. His control felt as fragile as the lacy web fluttering from the near rafter. He should insist that they leave now, before the afternoon shadows lengthened and dusk settled amid the bones of the old house. Darkness came swiftly beneath the copse. Yet, all he could do in that moment was stand near her enough to feel the heat of her body on his, the vibrancy of her presence, and fight with all his remaining strength not to reach out to her. If he did . . . he would regret it.

Then she leaned back against him, as if her legs would no longer hold her.

A heartbeat passed before he slid one arm around her waist, felt the trembling in her body that worked up her throat in a painful little cough. Turning his lips into her hair, he breathed in the moist fragrant heat of her and closed his eyes. Ah, the surrender. More blood letting than his injuries. If he died now, he would, at least, be happy.

She sighed. "I was foolish, believing there might be something left. Something worth saving. I wonder if she ever loved him? My father, I mean. Just for a day. An hour. A moment. What madness could take over a woman and make her sacrifice all this?"

"Love is illogical. It makes a man believe in the impossible. Makes him a damn fool." *He should know.*

"It wasn't all fantasy, was it? There *were* swans."

"Twelve of them." He smiled into her hair.

"The heat in my dreams . . . fire. This fire. I wish I could remember."

"What's done is done, *chère*. The memory won't bring your parents back or rebuild these walls."

"It's who I am, Chantz, and what I was. I don't want to repeat the mistakes . . ."

She sank closer and he felt the length of her body along his, warm supple curves beneath the thin cotton of her dress. The slow pulse beat began in his groin. Slivers of pain spread through his belly and thighs in threads of heat. "I intend to love only one man," came her whisper. "And I'll give him everything I am and all that I own . . . on one condition."

"And what is that, *chère*?"

Turning, her body still pressed against his, her head tipped so she could look up into his eyes with an intensity that winded him. Her vermilion lips curved and her lashes lowered, just slightly, so the green of her eyes was slightly shadowed. "That he love me in return, of course."

Sliding from his arms, she left him staring out at the pool of brackish water. An egret hovered with white outstretched wings, long leg extended as it grasped a turtle from a log and lifted again into the air.

Her footsteps bounded down the stairs, and, forcing his body to move, he followed, knocking aside the spray of honeysuckle as he stumbled against the doorpost, hands clenched as he willed back the pain.

She hesitated briefly as she searched for the clearest path to the distant kitchen, then struck out at a trot, forcing Chantz to grit his teeth and lengthen his stride to keep up.

Chantz threw his weight against the kitchen door before it sprang open, releasing a rush of hot air. He moved clumsily into the deeply shadowed room before her. Mice scattered. An opossum, hanging from an overhead rafter by its tail, blinked at the sudden burst of daylight and scrambled for cover.

Various shaped bottles, the colors bleached by years of dust, lined the shelves on the walls. There were iron pots and long-handled utensils and several tables similar to that on which Rosie had spooned the pralines yesterday morning. The high ceiling remained solid as did the fireplace that took up the entire north wall, along with the ovens.

Juliette turned round and round, searching every nook and corner. "It's perfect. It needs cleaning of course and minor repairs. I'm certain the mortar will need replacing here and there, those tables refinished."

She moved up beside him, her body close as her gaze swept the grounds, the distant outbuildings; the storehouse, stable, smoke-house, the line of slave shanties that were little more than gray, precariously leaning roofs peeking out from under tall brush.

"What are you thinking?" he asked, taking her arm to add emphasis to his question, knowing as he did so what touching her would do. He drew away, back against the doorpost, and waited for her response.

Yet, without responding, she pulled away and ran back toward the house. By the time he caught up to her she was back in the living room sweeping her hand over the settee cushions, allowing color and pattern to emerge.

"It was red. The settee. I remembered. And that chair, the one by the window, I'll bet it's green." She gave it a kick, sending a fresh cloud of dust into the air. A flurry of moths rushed up, causing her eyes to brighten.

"It *is* green! There used to be a table there with a pink marble top." She dashed into the dining room and back again through the door, the lamp table scraping the floor, leaving narrow trails through the dust. She placed it by the chair before facing Chantz again.

"You're a mess, *chère*." He shook his head. "Come here."

He moved to the mirror on the wall, rubbed enough dirt away so she could see her face streaked by dust that frosted her hair and eyelashes. Then she lifted her hand and enlarged the circle to include Chantz. How dark and hard and weathered he looked beside her. Like that rusty old kitchen pot set next to a Dresden figurine. She was sunlight and he was shadow. She was silk, and he was burlap.

Turning away, he ran his callused hand over his face. The heat rose again—not the simmering air in the room but the fire inside him. He felt angered by it.

She touched his back. "Chantz."

"Damn place is a wreck," he said, shifting from her hand. "Might as well tear it all down and start again. That's gonna take some doing. And money. Which brings me back to what I said before.

"Best you marry a wealthy man, Julie. It's gonna take a king's fortune to repair this house and those grounds. As I recall your daddy owned close to two hundred slaves. Hell, you'd need twice that to reestablish Belle Jarod."

"The house is livable," she replied. "Or most of it."

"Maybe now." He moved across the central hall and into the remains of the library. Sun poured down through the charred rafters, forming a butter yellow pool of light on the floor. He stepped into it and lifted his face into the sun. Its heat oozed through him, dulling the pain in his leg but doing little to alleviate the ache in his heart.

"You'll be thinking otherwise come winter and rain. Young woman like you who doesn't know what it's like to be cold or to watch the rain pour through your roof will have your sensibilities offended the first time your toes get so cold you can't feel them."

Looking over his shoulder at her, he added, "If I were

you, I'd sell Belle Jarod. Take that money and go back to France where you belong."

"I belong here, Chantz. Belle Jarod is my home."

Juliette wandered out onto the gallery. A breeze moved the shadows and scattered leaves around her ankles. Dandelion tufts lifted in the air and caught within the coils of her hair as she eased down the steps and picked her way through the wildflowers and weeds. Buried amid the tangle of growth peeked the blood-red blooms of Cherokee roses. Juliette touched the silken petals carefully, as if they might shatter.

"*Was* your home," he told her with an edge of the rawness he could feel in his chest. "Back when your mama dressed you up in bows and bonnets and paraded you around like you were a princess. When you tried to do handstands in that *parterre* yonder. When you chased butterflies and hummin'birds and believed, if given the opportunity, that you could ride swans off into the clouds. Back when you stole ho'hound candy from young men's pockets and believed night fairies sprinkled dust in your eyes to make you sleep."

She turned, slowly, and regarded his face. Her cheeks bloomed with color as deep as the rose petals at her fingertips.

"In case you're not aware, Juliette, you're not a child any longer. Time to see this world through an adult's eyes. And the reality is, you're nineteen years old and you have no money. Your only means of support is Max Hollinsworth until you're twenty one, or marry. You're gonna be just as penniless at twenty-one as you are now. What then? Unless you're willing to sell your body and soul to a man with a great deal of power and money, Belle Jarod and you don't have a future together. Unless, of course, you're willing to settle for this." He nodded toward the rubble.

Juliette walked toward him, her step slow, never shifting

her eyes from his. "And if I sold my body and soul to a man with great power and money that would make me no better than my mother, wouldn't it?"

"Oh, I don't know, *chère.*" Touching one fingertip to a smudge on her cheek, he traced it to the tip of her mouth. "If you're lucky you might actually fall in love with him."

Fingers curling into a fist, he shoved his hand into his pocket and drew in a breath. "I imagine he'll consider your body and soul a very nice investment indeed. A man might believe he's purchasing himself a fine plantation by wedding you, but in reality, it'll ultimately be your heart he'll desire more than all the sugarcane in Louisiana."

Her lips curved. "Or I could end up like my mother and Phyllis Buley. Married to one man and loving another." Placing her hand against his chest, she said softly, "It was you, wasn't it, Chantz?"

The touch burned. He frowned.

"It was you who saved me that day from the fire. You were here. Those features in my dreams—never clear enough to see them, they were yours. Do you know how many times I reached out for you these last years? You offered me comfort, Chantz, and security. If it hadn't been for you—"

Backing away, he turned on his heels and reentered the house.

"Why were you here, Chantz?" she called, following hard on his boot heels, her fingers plucking at his shirt. "You saw it all, didn't you? You saw everything that happened—"

"Leave it alone, Julie—"

"I won't!" Clutching his arm, she sat back on her heels, stopping him in his tracks and spinning him around to face her. Her wide eyes fixed on his and her breath rushed in and out of her lips in audible little pants. "Dear God," she gasped. "It wasn't you and my mother—"

"No." He yanked his arm away and backed toward the stairs. "I didn't see anything, Julie. I was down at the kitchen when the fire broke out."

"You're lying."

"There were storms. I took shelter with the others in the kitchen. By the time we saw the smoke and flames—"

"What others?"

"The house servants."

"Why weren't they in the house?"

"Because your mother always sent them out when she entertained her . . . gentlemen friends."

"I see." She swallowed. "I take it she had several?"

Releasing a weary breath, Chantz shook his head. "I don't know, darlin'. Just leave it alone, Julie. Take a good look around you and get it into your head that all the drudging up of memories and wishful thinking isn't gonna change the past. Put it behind you and get the hell away while you still can. Before all these old ghosts rise up to destroy you, too."

A flash of emotion brightened her eyes—tears rose though she fought valiantly to deny them. Then her shoulders slumped and she looked at him with a dawning that only added to her despair. "Oh Chantz. Look at you. Hurting so badly and trying so desperately to hide it. And as usual I've been too caught up in my own thoughts and emotions to see clearly—too damn overwhelmed by all of this." She swept one hand around her, blinked and knuckled away her tears, brows drawing together as she looked at his leg.

"You're bleeding," she said with a rip of despair in her voice. She ran to him, dropped to her knees before him, and oh so gently touched him where his pants leg had become blotched with blood. Her head falling back, she gazed up at him from her cloud of dark-fire hair, her eyes and face illuminated by the afternoon sunlight. "I love you, Chantz. I have since the first instant that I opened my eyes and looked in your face the night you pulled me from the river. I think I have since I was a child and you saved me from the fire. Always you were there, a tower of strength and bravery. My security. Someone who made me laugh through my tears. It was always you I reached out for in my dreams . . . and in my worst nightmares."

He touched her hair and her cheek with his fingertips.

"I never want to hurt you, Chantz. *Never.*" Closing her eyes, she pressed her face gently against his thigh, her hands easing around his leg to stroke it—lightly so lightly and gently it felt like worship.

He knew, even before he reached for her, that his life would never be the same after this. Lifting her, pulling her against his hard body, Chantz slanted his mouth over hers with a force that made her whimper, made her shake, made her small hands clutch at his shirt as if she were tottering again on that precipice above the raging Mississippi. He wanted to hurt her. Frighten her. Make her believe in that instant that the emotions burning in him were anything but what they were.

There was no room in his life for love. Women were simply a convenience, necessary upon occasion to assuage his base hungers—cane was his true mistress.

Yet her mouth . . . Christ, her mouth. Any other woman would have wilted to the floor under the fierceness of his kiss.

Not Juliette.

Curling her arms around his neck, burying her hands in his hair, she drew him deeper into the kiss, molded her body into his, inflaming him with the feel of her loins pressed against his.

Lifting his head, he stared into her eyes, wanting like hell to teach her a lesson she wouldn't soon forget, teach her that a man like him would lead her straight down the path to damnation.

"What the hell do you think you're doing?" he demanded roughly, and shook her, then lowered his mouth again to hers, more gently at first, then harder as he brushed his fingers across her breast, felt the nub of her nipple rising up high and hard beneath the thin fabric of her dress.

She moaned; her mouth parted; her tongue danced with his as she pushed harder into his hand, offering her breast to his caress that went from gentle to hungry. The control he'd held over his body since the moment he'd dragged her out of the river eroded like sand in turbulent waters.

Easing her down onto the floor, amid the clutter of dry leaves and the tattered remains of ruby-red carpet, he slid his hand under her skirt, eased his fingertips up her calf to her thigh. A sudden wind gust groaned through the empty rafters, stirred the branches high overhead so the leaves clattered like a sprinkling of pebbles on a tin roof. As dust lifted and danced in the spear of sunlight pouring through the glassless window, reason felt as gossamer as the crepuscular rays pouring over Juliette's face and hair. The hunger to possess her, not just her body but her soul, made him urgent, made him shove her knees apart with his leg and draw the skirt up her thighs, made him slide his hand through the slit in her drawers to the warm, moist, and feminine flesh within.

She gasped. Her arms slid over his shoulders and her hands curled into his shirt.

"Damn you," he whispered as she unashamedly opened her legs, lost in the bliss of what his hand ignited in her body. Turning it hot. Turning it liquid and silken and redolent with a scent that sluiced to his brain and incinerated his ability to reason. The world in that moment became Juliette's eyes, green as the leaves on the trees shifting shadows over the floor, her mouth, lips parted, full, quivering, her face, pale amid the wild, tangled shock of red hair—

He slid his body partially over hers, so she could feel his weight and the hardness of his penis against her thighs—needed her to know how badly he wanted her, that his control had bled from him through the ragged holes in his flesh. He wanted to tell her that in those last frantic moments before he had gone black with shock she had been the only image to rise up in his mind. His only regret. He had wanted to turn back the clock to that bright hot afternoon in the cane field and not walk away in fear. He wanted to lay her down in the warm silt and possess her, body and soul. He wanted her to know that he ached more for her than he ached for legitimacy.

She moaned as she felt his mouth against her throat, her face, her lips; his hands fumbled with the buttons on his breeches and once he was released he caught her hand and moved it to him, reluctant at first, then her fingers closed around him and his eyes drifted closed in such sweet agony he could only groan and tremble. His fingers found her, between her thighs, touched her lightly, parting the lips of her sex, and she cried out at first, startled by the sudden sensation and the ecstasy of the gentle invasion. Yet, her eyes watched him with heat and yearning—no embarrassed coyness from her, and he hadn't expected any; her legs opened farther, inviting, and he moved between them, fighting the hunger to move too fast—she was a virgin, after all, and he entered her gently—though he didn't *feel* gentle, he felt violent—allowing her body to open, little by little, knowing the instant he breached her—the cry was soft, the gasp sudden, the darkening of her eyes like a passing of one life to another.

Her hands clutched him and her lips parted, eyes lit by emotion, fire, and wonder. "Oh," she sighed against his mouth. "How . . . wonderful."

Wonderful, he thought, sinking closer, deeper, drifting in the cloud of her scent and the music of her words. Wonderful. Wonderful. Christ, wonderful would be never leaving her body again.

"Now isn't this cozy," came Tylor's voice from the door.

Juliette stiffened and her eyes flew wide.

Chantz froze.

He eased his body out of Juliette's and pulled down her skirt, adjusted his pants, then struggled to stand, hopping up and down on one leg as new pain, sharpened by his escalating anger, washed over him. He swung around to face Tylor, his fists clenching as Tylor, smirking, walked into the room, riding crop in one hand, tapping at his leg.

"I declare, Chantz, but this is getting to be a bit redundant, finding you with your hands on that young woman. And that"—he pointed his crop at the bulge in Chantz's breeches—"is positively vulgar."

Chantz straightened, keeping his body between Tylor and Juliette. "If you have something to say, Tylor, say it and get the hell out of here."

Tipping his head to one side, Tylor grinned. "Juliette, certainly you're aware I have every right to demand satisfaction. In most cases that might be a duel to the death. But on second thought, an exchange of gunfire at dawn is a gentleman's way of settling such distasteful matters. For a piece of mud dauber trash like Chantz Boudreaux we simply tie him to a post and whip him until he bleeds to death."

Juliette gasped—Chantz cut her off with a quick shake of his head.

Tylor moved in close, his blue eyes never leaving Chantz's. "I'm gonna make you regret your sorry existence . . . more than you already do, of course."

Chantz narrowed his eyes and said through his teeth, "Go to hell, Tylor. You just go straight to hell."

fifteen

"What have you done, Chantz? Look at me, son. Something's happened. Something dreadful."

Chantz poured rum into a glass and considered how he should break the news to his mother that he had become, in the blink of Juliette's green eyes, a man as stupid as Jack Broussard and Maxwell Hollinsworth and God only knew how many others—all emotionally blinded by a madness that made him ache harder for Juliette than he dreaded the consequences of his behavior.

"What gives you that idea?" he said, aware his voice sounded rough and tight and there wasn't a damn thing he could do about it.

Emmaline moved up behind him and placed her hand on his back. "Your refusal to look me in the eye for one. You know you never could lie to me, Chantz. Those damn blue eyes give you away every time.

"Second, that's the third drink you've had the last hour. You're not a stupid man, normally. You wouldn't be swimming in that rum if you weren't bothered by something."

She took the bottle from his hand and put it on the table, next to his shaving cup and brush and Bible that lay next to a clear jar of colored pebbles the children occasionally presented him. Emmaline's eyes were lined by worry and bright with the fierce, desperate protectiveness of a mother for her son. He'd seen that look far too often not to recognize it now. Hell, he could lie to the world, lie to himself, but never to his mother.

"You can't do it," she said. "You can't look me in the eye. You've got guilt stamped all over your face. No. Not guilt. Something more frightening than that. It's her, isn't it? Juliette? Folks was talking, Chantz. They say Andrew drove her out to Belle Jarod today and that when you found out about it you climbed out of your sick bed and rode out of here like a mad man. They say Andrew came back alone. What happened there, Chantz?"

"Leave it alone, Mama."

He turned away and drank his rum. His leg hurt like hell and he was one deep drink away from inebriation. Just as well. The damn rum would make facing the inevitable a little easier. It was only a matter of time . . . minutes, probably. He could almost hear the seconds ticking by in his head.

Standing in the open doorway, he swirled the liquor in the glass and focused on the big house where lights burned in the dusk. The whir of crickets had begun along with the occasional *garump* of a bullfrog.

He wanted to wrap his hands around Juliette's beautiful throat and strangle her for turning him into the kind of man who could so easily lose control, not just of his good judgment, but of his body. He wanted to press her down in the grass, climb between her beautiful legs and finish what they had started at Belle Jarod, and that's what angered him most.

He stepped from the house, into the dark and humidity. His mother was right on one count. Too damn much rum in his blood. Among other things.

The bell began ringing.

The doors along shanty row opened, spilling yellow light down the steep stairs. Louis came first, hurrying up the path. Behind him filed others, their expressions grooved with concern as they moved toward the big house. Louis's dark eyes touched upon Chantz's briefly as he walked by. Normally he would have stopped. There would have been discourse on the reason for the call bell, but Louis knew as well as Chantz did what hell was about to break loose, and why.

Little Clara exploded from the big house and tore through the dark. The converging men parted to allow her through, watching with mounting concern as she barreled toward Chantz, eyes wide and mouth turned down, a wail of despair erupting from her as she flung herself against him with her face buried against his belly. Behind her came Simon in a frantic limp, then Liza.

The darkness did little to mask the distress on Liza's features as she approached.

"What's happening?" came Emmaline's voice behind him. "Chantz? Why is that child crying so? Chantz—"

"Hush," he said, cutting her off. Looking down onto Little Clara's ribbon-coiffed head, he soothed the trembling child with a hand on her shoulder. "Mama, I want you to go in your house and close the door. I don't want you to come out for any reason. Understand?"

Her footfalls thumped down the steps and he felt her move up behind him. "Lord God in heaven, son—"

Looking around into his mother's haggard face, he said more softly, "Please. Don't argue with me. Don't make this any harder on me than it need be."

Her face ashen, Emmaline searched his eyes, resignation and acknowledgment weighing her shoulders and turning her jaw hard as stone.

"Damn you," she muttered as drops spilled down her cheeks. "You were always too muleheaded for your own good. I told you . . ." Her voice broke and choked to a tight sob. Drawing back her shoulders, she turned away and, heels dragging, moved toward her house.

Liza, her fists pumping at her sides, stalked toward him wearing the same dress she'd worked the fields in, the same sweat-stained tignon that had held her hair off her neck as she hoed weeds from around the cane stalks.

As Little Clara looked up, tears spilling and nose running, he allowed her a dry curl of his lips and said, "Don't look now but here comes trouble."

"You knew good and damn well what you was riskin' by foolin' with Julie," Liza declared as she approached. "But like a stubborn-headed jackass you gone and done it anyway, hadn't you?"

Shaking so hard her teeth chattered, Liza took hold of Little Clara and peeled her off Chantz, shoved her toward shanty row and shouted, "Git! Git them young'uns—all of em—inside and don't be stickin' your nose out f'nothin'. You hear me, Little Clara? First ones I see peekin' is gonna get a whuppin' with a willa switch."

She covered her face with her hands and tried futilely to hold in her emotion. Finally, she shook her head and her voice rose in mounting hysteria. "He gonna whup you, Chantz! Tylor. He gonna do it!"

He nodded and looked past her. "Where is Juliette?"

Dark eyes flashing with disbelief and anger, Liza shook her head. "Didn't you hear what I just said? Tylor is comin' here with a whip. He gonna cut you up—"

"Is she all right, Liza? Because if either of them touches her . . ."

Liza covered her trembling lips with one hand and tried to breathe evenly, to swallow the short sharp sobs closing off her throat. Closer, she reached one quivering hand out and clasped his arm, fingers twisting into his shirtsleeve. "Ever'thin' just goin' to hell, ain't it? For you. For me. For Miss Julie. What gonna become of us, Chantz?"

The bell tolled. On and on it went, like the death knell for Sister Eve, ringing and ringing for what felt like forever, until Juliette had been forced to cover her head with a pillow or start screaming.

She paced as Rosie sat on the ottoman, skirt hiked to above her big knees to allow her thighs to cool. With her crossed arms nestled beneath her massive breasts, the Negress stared at the ceiling and moved her lips as if carrying on a conversation with angels.

Planting herself in front of Rosie, her hands clenched and buried in the folds of her shirt, Juliette declared, "For the love of God, will you stop muttering and tell me what's happening? Why did the Buleys leave so suddenly? Why have I been locked in this room like some prisoner—"

" 'Cause you done wrong, Miss Julie." Rosie pursed her brown lips and shook her head. "Shouldn't have talked Andrew into takin' you to Belle. Shoulda known that would stir up a hornet's nesta trouble with Massa Max and Tylor. That man just been waitin' to make trouble fo' Chantz."

Falling to her knees before Rosie, Juliette grabbed her dark, plump hands in her own. "Tylor wasn't serious about whipping him—"

"He know what he was doin' when he ride to the Belle after you and Andrew. Tol' him myself—'you be askin' for a whuppin' if'n they finds out.' Sho'nuff his dust ain't settled fo' Tylor show up from church, like he knowed somethin' was gonna happen."

Heaving herself to her feet, her gait like a boat rocking side to side, Rosie moved to the curtained and locked French doors. She peered between the drapes, out into the night, her face somber as she began humming low in her throat. Tears welled over her dark eyes and beaded on her lashes.

Juliette crossed the room and gripped the sleeve of Rosie's dress with her trembling hand. "What's happening, Rosie?"

"I 'spect it over by now."

Frantic, Juliette looked around, swept the lush fern from the bowlegged marble-top stand.

"Lawd!" Rosie shouted and clutched her hands to her bosom, "Chile, what is you doin'—"

"I'll damn well find out for myself!"

Juliette heaved up the table, swung it as hard as she could toward the glass doors that exploded from the impact in shards over the dark gallery.

Her slippered feet slid on the glass slivers and she fell hard amid the knife-edged debris, felt it cut through the thin cotton of her skirts and into her knees and shins, into her forearms and wrists, and the faint thought flashed through her mind that she might well bleed to death, realizing in the same moment that she wouldn't care, not if she had in some way caused more harm to Chantz.

No mournful baying tonight, the hounds, they filled the charged air with maddened chesty yaps as if frenzied by the scent of bloodied quarry. As Juliette descended the steps to the ground the distant wail of weeping added to the horrifying cacophony of the dogs. With her skirt lifted to her knees she ran down the path, down through the shanty row where groups of black-skinned men, women, and children clustered on the steps or in open doorways, their gazes following her as she passed through the shafts of light from their houses, toward the group of huddled men.

"Out of my way," she cried, shouldering through the men who turned to stare at her with shocked expressions. Stumbling into the clearing, she froze.

Liza moved in front of her, took her shoulders in her hands, and looked hard into Juliette's eyes. "This ain't no place for a young lady like you, Miss Julie. Best you git on back to the house afore—"

"Tell me that isn't Chantz!" Her head shook and a rip of sound worked up her throat. "Tell me that isn't Chantz hanging from a pole with his back—"

"I tol' you, Miss Julie. I tol' you what would happen if you didn't leave him alone."

She stumbled back. Oh my God. Oh my God . . .

"Nothin' you can do here, so git on back afore Maxwell find out—"

Shoving Liza aside, Juliette moved toward the dreadful image, her legs like water suddenly and her heartbeat sinking. Only then did she notice Louis at Chantz's side. His dark face turned toward hers, eyes full of firelight. His tears stopped her cold.

Tylor paced the length of the drawing room, the coiled whip in one hand, his shirt smeared with blood and his brown hair plastered to his brow by sweat. His face shone with the heat of his excitement. His smile, however, appeared as painted and mirthless as a marionette's as he turned his eyes on Maxwell.

"Are you satisfied, Daddy?" he demanded. "Are you proud of me? I do believe I handled the situation in a manner that would make a Hollinsworth proud."

Maxwell turned away from Tylor and looked off into the dark toward the river. The moon was high and reflected off the wide brown water. A breeze touched his face, cooling the sweat from his brow.

Tylor moved up behind him, close enough so his smell of sweat and bourbon made Maxwell frown. Tylor slapped one hand on Max's shoulder, and Max glanced down at his son's blood-stained fingers. He forced himself to look harder at the river.

"You should have waited—" he began.

"Waited? Why ever for, Daddy? Am I not a Hollinsworth? Am I not your son and therefore in charge of this plantation in your absence? Let me refresh your memory. Just recently, on the veranda outside my bedroom, you said that I was to act like a Hollinsworth. Were those not your exact words? You want me to act like a Hollinsworth, and I have. Was I to look the other way once I discovered the young lady being handled by that piece of trash?

"Shall I describe to you in detail what he was doing to her? He was making her moan and move her hips like she was one of Meesha's girls. Hell, he was buried so far inside her it would've taken a pair of strong mules to drag them apart.

"What's wrong, Daddy? You're white as a sheet. I'm wondering if you're looking sick as an old dog because somebody has got to her before you or because I just laid open the back of a man whose existence in your life you supposedly tolerate out of some twisted sense of responsibility."

Closer, so his breath brushed Max's cheek and his lips moved against his ear. "Guess what else I did, Daddy. I told the bastard that he was finished at Holly. Told him to clear out and take his sorry ass old lady with him."

Max turned his head and looked down into Tylor's eyes. "You did what?"

"I already talked to Boris Wilcox and he'll come to work for Holly for half of what you've paid Boudreaux."

"Boris Wilcox? That goddamn paddy runner who practically drove his last planter to bankruptcy?"

Maxwell wrapped his fingers around Tylor's throat. "In case you haven't paid close attention, there is only one thing keeping Holly from sinking into that goddamn river and that's Chantz. If he walks away from this farm that's the end of me. Do you understand, Tylor? There isn't another overseer in this state who grows the kind of cane he does or who gets the kind of respect and cooperation out of his slaves as Chantz."

His face white, Tylor clutched at Max's hand and tore himself away, stumbled back, gulping for air. He gagged hard enough so his body convulsed, then he turned on Maxwell with his teeth bared.

"Just what the hell do you want, Daddy? You want your sugarcane or do you want Belle Jarod? Because you're not gonna get both. Juliette's never gonna give up Belle to either of us as long as Chantz is around. Sorry to tell you this, but she won't spread herself for you like Maureen did."

Juliette stood in the open French door, her fingers gripping a willow switch. She looked past Tylor into Maxwell's eyes.

"It was you," she whispered. "Of course. It all makes sense now, why my father grieved so. He not only lost his wife, but his best friend as well. It was you he found with my mother, wasn't it?"

She moved into the room. "All this time I wondered why my father would bury me away in that remote, dreary, and detestable old convent—I thought it was because he hated me—he was simply trying to protect me, wasn't he? To hide me. From you."

Tylor dropped into a chair and began laughing.

"Because of you my family is dead and my home is in ruins. I'm orphaned and penniless—"

"It doesn't have to be that way," Maxwell declared in a flat tone.

She slashed his face with the willow switch. He didn't flinch, just stared down at her as emotionless as a corpse, a thread of blood rising to the surface of his pale cheek.

Again, and again, tears blinding her, fury beating in her chest and mind like frantic bats. "Detestable, hateful creature! Fiend! I would blow out my own brains before I allow you to set foot on Belle grounds again much less own it!"

The switch cut into his face and neck until blood soaked his shirt collar, turning it dark and glistening wet. Tylor's laughter reverberated in the air, driving her fury to a maddened fever pitch, washing her reality into a surreal haze as horrifyingly crimson as Chantz's open bloody wounds.

"I should kill you," she hissed through her teeth, into his eyes. "But I intend to watch you suffer, you and your despicably cruel son. I'll see you despair every day for the remainder of your sorry, miserable existence on this earth— just like my father despaired, driven to absolute madness by his heartbreak. If it's the last thing I ever do, Maxwell Hollinsworth, I'll see you driven to your knees and everything you hold priceless devastated."

"And how do you propose to do that?" he said. "I'm a well-respected planter in this state, Juliette. There won't be another man of any consequence who will touch you, regardless of your inheritance, should I inform them of your promiscuity with my overseer."

"I hear Meesha is in need of a few good whores," Tylor

blurted with another howl of laughter. "Even better, I noted a camp of mud daubers down the river a ways. Considering the glimpse I got under your skirts this afternoon, I suspect there would be plenty of daubers willing to offer you a blanket on which to sleep."

With a whirl of her skirt around her ankles, Juliette turned on Tylor and lashed out with the willow switch, slicing his face as keenly as with a razor edge, turning his laughter into a screech of pain that jolted him out of his chair and onto the floor, clutching his cheek and nose and staring up at her like one who had just witnessed a portent of his own demise.

Again, she struck, and again as he curled his knees to his chest and covered the back of his head with his hands that were fast becoming bloody. "This is for Chantz," she declared. "This is for every slice in his back, for every horrible fiery mind-shattering bolt of pain he endured at your hands. For his humiliation of being strapped by his wrists. For your sending him into that water so he was nearly killed by that gator."

"For the love of God, Daddy, make her stop!"

"Chantz didn't beg, Tylor," she declared, striking harder and faster until the switch whistled and the back of his shirt became thin stripes of dark red. "He made not so much as a whimper, Louis said. Is that why you beat him so mercilessly? Were you trying to break him? Drive him to your level, a whimpering miserable excuse for a man? Chantz Boudreaux could be driven to crawl on his knees begging for mercy and still not be so weak and unmanned as you."

The switch snapped in two at last, one end partially wrapped around the back of Tylor's neck, the other jutting from her fist like a stob.

Maxwell caught her wrist. His fingers bit into her skin like the steel jaws of a trap sending pain splintering up her arm.

"While your anger is justified, Juliette, cold-blooded murder is not. You're far too pretty to hang, and besides . . . I'm certain you wouldn't risk Belle Jarod falling into the hands of the courts upon your death. No telling who would get their hands on Belle . . . ultimately."

He released her and she backed away.

"I refuse to spend one more night in this house."

"That's up to you, of course."

Maxwell glanced down at Tylor who looked up at Juliette through his bloody fingers covering his face. "I'll remind you that you had nothing upon coming to Holly House, nothing, that is, except the few pitiful rags you wore at the convent. You have no money. You should think prudently before rushing to any rash decisions."

"I would die of starvation before I take another crumb of bread from you." She tore the combs from her hair and threw them at his feet. "I would spend the rest of my life burning in hellfire rather than breathe the same air as you."

She exited the house the way she had entered, through the French doors and along the gallery, down the steps, one hand clutching the balustrade while the other curled against her stomach as if that would stop the fury and disgust churning there.

In the distance shanty-row lights sparkled and lightning bugs pulsed like tiny torches in the darkness. Juliette ran along the path, her skirts sweeping the short hedges and flower clusters of lavender and primroses, her focus on Chantz's house and the crowd converged on his porch, all straining to see into the room in which Louis had carried Chantz in his arms like a baby.

Liza moved out of the dark, into her path. Her hands reached out and closed around Juliette's arms, gripping her, forcing her to look into Liza's face.

"Listen to me," came Liza's words that sounded little more than a hum behind the roar of blood in her head. "You don't wants to be goin' there now, Miss Julie. Emmaline done takin' care of it all. Just leave it alone right now, hear me?" Forcing a smile, Liza softened her voice. "He a strong man, Miss Julie, but he don't wants you to see him like this. Understand what I'm sayin'?"

She backed away, pushed Liza's hands away, and walked off into the dark. The oppressive night settled upon her skin in a warm film of moisture that beaded upon her breasts and ran down her sides beneath her clothing.

Away from the house and the press of anxious bodies, the night sounds began to hum and pulsate. Night birds cried out, like a woman screaming. The cacophony of frogs became a chorus that given any other circumstance might have sounded like music. Tonight, however, with every nerve raw and sensitive, the sounds scratched painfully at her. Running down the path, she covered her ears with her hands and forced herself to keep moving. Her need for revenge felt as vast as there were stars in heaven and she realized that only one other time in her nineteen years had she felt so overwhelmed by a compulsion beyond her means to control it.

Covering her eyes with her fists, she wondered what was happening to her. She felt raw with emotion, helpless with an inability to control her thoughts and actions. Her body had become a stranger to herself, as if possessed. Yes oh yes. The Reverend Mother's demons most assuredly had, at long last, taken her over. They were lust and hatred, and as she stood there in that darkness amid tall weeds and brush, her heart pounding in her ears, she felt as wild as the creatures that no doubt stared out at her from the black shadows and tangled lairs.

A confusion of memories flashed behind her eyes—all

images of Chantz Boudreaux—as if she had not existed until that stormy afternoon when she opened her eyes and saw his face beside hers on the pillow. In a spellbinding instant her world had narrowed into a painful pinpoint—a universe of sensations that expanded inside her as she drew in the scent of his skin that had been intoxicating to her blood, as she touched her trembling fingertips to dark coils of hair that lay upon his broad tanned brow.

She realized now that she truly had not lived until that moment, had not known the true essence of desire. What she had experienced during her secret forays into the village to watch cockfights with smelly, drunken farmers and their gangly sons with black teeth and ravaged complexions had been foolish adolescent curiosity. True desire, once ignited, could not be extinguished. It could not be ignored. Despite all that had transpired the last hours, the heat burned yet. If she allowed herself to succumb to its lure, even as she stood there sweating with fear and fury, the fire would consume her as it had at Belle Jarod.

She swallowed and lowered her fists from her eyes, recalling the very instant that she realized that what she felt for Chantz was more than some forbidden attraction. The emotion vibrated inside her and filled her with new desperation.

At last she came to the water—the wide still strand of swamp thick with reeds and lily pads that reflected the moon like mirrors. She stood in the dark, shaking, sweating, listening to the drone of mosquitoes and feeling them light upon her bare skin to draw blood, their bites like stinging thorns on her arms and shoulders, yet she did nothing but tremble in the deep shadows of the broad oak tree and stare through the streams of Spanish moss at a dilapidated shanty in the near distance.

Chantz. His arms around her, his mouth kissing her, his body inside her. What sweet sublimity.

The musty scent of the moss and swamp mud made the air nearly impossible to breathe. Then she realized, 'twas fear, not the bayou smells—the stink of rot—that made her lungs feel as if they were being gripped by cruel hands.

Dear God, she ached to hold him again. To kiss away his pain. She had brought this upon him. Her inability to deny her own desires.

Is this what drowning feels like? she wondered. This desperate need to draw in a breath—so desperate her head felt as if she'd been caught up in a whirlwind and spun and spun until the world had become a blur of movement so she could hardly stand without falling.

She moved on trembling legs, drawn by some inexplicable force toward the shanty with its weathered and warped wood shimmering in the moonlight. The streamers of moss trailed over her shoulder, scratching like fingernails and tangling in her hair that adhered to her face and neck by sweat.

At long last she reached the steps. In the moonlight they looked steep and rotten. There were no banisters to grip and as she focused on the black, weed-infested space beneath the house her mind raced with thoughts of what might lie hidden there; what, should the rickety old lumber give beneath her weight as she climbed to the door, might wait there in the murk and dampness.

As if in response to her thoughts, the low grunt of the bull gator resonated from the swamp.

The night sounds bombarded. Something moved in the nearby rushes, and spinning around she fled, fast, with the high weeds stinging her arms like tiny whiplashes. Her foot caught on a tree root and she fell, hit the ground hard so pain streaked through her face and the moment Maxwell struck her flashed again through her mind as did fresh disbelief and panic. Tears rose, hot and stinging, and for an instant she felt too sad to move. Perhaps this would prove to be a nightmare—just another dream like so many others over the years that would, thankfully, dissipate the moment she opened her eyes to find sunlight pouring in through the tiny clerestory near her cell's ceiling.

But as some insect crawled over her face, she slapped it away and pushed herself up. The world careened; stars and earth collided momentarily. More carefully, she moved up the path until she reached shanty row. All doors remained open spilling light down the steps where children continued to huddle, staring out at her sleepily.

Suddenly Little Clara came out of nowhere and threw herself against Juliette. Her frail arms clutched fiercely—so fiercely Juliette's ribs felt as if they might shatter. Her head, with its odd spikes of plaited hair, fell back and the child's dark damp eyes looked up into hers, face streaked with tears and her full brown lips pulled down at the corners.

"He gonna die?" she cried, fingers clutching at Juliette's dress.

Juliette took Little Clara's face between her hands and did her best to steady her voice. "No," she declared, stunned by her resoluteness.

Burying her face against Juliette, Little Clara wailed all the harder, and Juliette felt more arms encircle her, more small hands fisting upon her skirts. Suddenly there were a half-dozen faces peering up at her, all eager for reassurance.

She moved clumsily to the nearest shanty, climbed partly up the stairs before allowing the weight of the little bodies to pull her down. They climbed onto her lap. They wrapped themselves around her shoulders and on her knees. She wanted to be strong, for them, yet she felt the fear inside, welling, clawing at her throat and slamming against the back of her eyes.

Don't think of Belle Jarod and the awful emptiness and disappointment she'd experienced as she stepped through the wild tangle of shrubs and weeds and stared up at the charred skeletal remains of her hopes and dreams. Don't think about her father's pain of discovering his wife in the arms of his best friend. Don't think that her own inability to contain her need for Chantz might well have destroyed his future, and his life.

Small, cool hands bracketed her face, lightly pressed upon her cheeks. She opened her eyes and Little Clara smiled at her. There were tears in her eyes and her pug nose was running. One of her heavy braids, tied with a tiny blue ribbon, bobbed over her forehead and between her eyes.

"I'm thinkin' you needs to rest, Miss Julie. You looks white as Rosie's cone stach."

"No." She shook her head and attempted to stand—she must help with Chantz if Emma would allow her—she must put her thoughts in order and think what she would do now, where she would go and what she would do to survive.

Yet, there was no strength in her legs.

The children surrounded her. Their hands grasped her clothes and in unison they gave a collected grunt and lifted her to her feet. They pushed and pulled her into the shanty that was lit by two lanterns. The room was small. There was a fireplace on one wall; its glowing embers intensified the oppressive heat of the night.

The ceiling was high with exposed rafters where hung drying garments and herbs and a meager collection of cooking utensils. There were no beds, just makeshift mattresses stuffed with Spanish moss strewn over the floor. When Juliette moved over the floor it seemed the entire house swayed and her footsteps resonated like thumps on a goatskin drum.

A child, she recollected her name was Sally, ran ahead and busily plumped a mattress. Her shoulder blades protruded under her gingham nightgown unnaturally. But her smile stretched broadly and when she looked up, her eyes sparkled. As Juliette dropped onto the bed another child hurried to unbuckle her shoes while another then briskly rubbed her bare feet, kneading them with adept little fingers as she lay on her back and stared up at the ceiling.

She tried not to think about Chantz and the horrible pain he had endured—all because of her, again. But the effort was useless. As useless as denying the emotion that filled up the entirety of her soul when she thought of him.

She wondered what she would do—what she would become if she never held him again.

Sixteen

ᘓᔆᘓ

Dust hung in the air, kicked up by an occasional hot wind that rattled the oak leaves and caused the hanging moss to dance like shapeless green marionettes. For the last two days, rain had threatened.

Something shameful, deep in Juliette's soul, prayed to God Almighty to bring another fierce flood and wipe away Holly House completely and forever. She imagined Maxwell's precious home tumbling end over end down the river, wrenched apart plank by plank by the roaring force. She imagined him on his knees, weeping into his hands, as her father must have wept upon burying his wife. Upon watching his beloved home, all that he had toiled to build over the years, go up in flames, his dreams and life incinerated. With each rumble of thunder and spit of rain, Juliette visualized the driving wave of water leveling every last stalk of cane from Holly soil, and leaving in its wake a desolation of mud.

She prayed that lightning would strike Maxwell Hollinsworth and his worthless son.

But no. That end would come too swiftly. Maxwell must

know the sting of her retaliation. It would cut as deeply as the whip into Chantz's back. It would bury as deeply and devastatingly into Maxwell's heart as a bullet had buried into her father's brain.

But how? *How?*

But for the meager roof over her head and the sagging, rotting old settee beneath her, there was nothing with which to strike but the certain satisfaction that Maxwell Hollinsworth would never get his hands on Belle Jarod.

Or would he?

Here she lay with hunger gnawing at her insides, thirst raking at her throat, and she felt like one on some precipice of death.

For the last days since fleeing Holly House and coming home, to Belle Jarod, she had feasted on pecans that had lain buried beneath debris, the meat as dry as old leather or so rancid it was all she could do to chew it. She had tasted the bitter green berries that cramped her stomach so cruelly she screamed profanities into the dark.

To her mounting dismay, Juliette realized that she had become as wild as the animals that moved about her in the night, that burrowed in nests within the fireplace hearth and scratched inside the chimney. She no longer felt . . . human.

Her senses expanded so she detected the tiniest rustle amid the brush, the chattering of field mice and, occasionally, the rumble of the old bull gator. At twilight she smelled the ash smoke drifting from the planters' shanty rows, the damp moss crawling along the north sides of the deeply shaded trees, and the pungent scent of rotting marsh grass.

The sun had become a vibration of heat waves that reflected off the leaves and water and dark earth. She caught the slightest movement of a twig from the corner of her eye. The clouds were no longer simply white and dark billows, but swirling, creeping outstretched hands of sunlight and shadow.

Taste had become a mixture of tantalization and repulsion.

If she died, Maxwell would win. If she died he would know the satisfaction of profit at the cost of all her father had worshiped.

Therefore she would fight until her last breath to witness the final blur of defeat in Max's eyes as all he had ached for was swept from his life.

Juliette lay on the tattered settee and allowed her gaze to wander the room. Belle Jarod's walls were once again the color of pale butter thanks to endless hours of scrubbing the last days. They reflected the daylight pouring through the glassless windows and she imagined her mother, stretched upon this settee as she was now, hair flowing over the cushion to pool upon the floor. How very far Juliette had come, she realized, from loathing the thought of Maureen to comparing herself to her.

Had Chantz suffered because of Juliette's actions? Because, like Maureen, she could not contain her emotional and physical yearnings?

She deserved to be lost!

It was she who should have been strapped to that damnable post and whipped! No torment she could inflict upon her body would satisfy her own aching need for penitence.

Yet, despite it all, she continued to hunger for Chantz.

During the daylight hours she had worked her fingers to the bone as if by doing so she would sweat away the memories of his mouth and hands on her flesh. But at night . . . she must lie here in the dark, a prisoner of this room and of her body that was a host both for torment and for pleasure.

With mounting desperation, she attempted to focus her thoughts on Chantz as she last saw him, unconscious and bleeding, and she fought with all her energy for the hate she felt for Maxwell and Tylor, for Max's deceit and Tylor's cruelty, to replace the burning for Chantz that continued to mount.

"Miss Julie?"

Juliette opened her eyes.

"Lord, girl, you is a mess," Liza whispered, and touched Juliette's cheek. Wild gladness and relief flooded Juliette and she wanted to take Liza in her arms and clutch her—even more, she wished for Liza's strong, dark arms to encircle her.

Yet, she felt too weak and sore to move.

"Can you sit up?" Liza asked gently.

"Liza, is that truly you?" Juliette asked, despising the weakness in her voice. "Am I hallucinating again?"

A rush of wind whipped through the shutters, scattering leaves around the ball and claw legs of the settee, bringing with it smells of impending rain; a coolness in the air sent a sharp chill down her spine. No, not chill, but the surge of energy that both invigorated and frightened her. A storm threatened. Its energy moved against her flesh.

"Is it you?" she repeated.

Liza nodded and took her shoulders, tugged her to a sitting position on the settee. She smoothed Juliette's hair back from her face and regarded her with an intensity that brought hot discomposure to her cheeks.

"Gots to hurry. Can't be gone long. Can't be havin' Boris Wilcox findin' me gone from the field. I woulda come sooner but Boris been watchin' us like a hawk the last days 'spectin' one of us would try to see you. Maxwell done sent him to the levee today, though, what with the threat of rain comin' on.

"Look here. Rosie done sent you some food for now—she be sendin' more tonight, once the sun go down. By that time Wilcox be so far into his rum he don't know his tail from a hole in the ground."

"Boris Wilcox?" She watched as Liza spread a napkin over Juliette's lap, revealing a portion of ham and corn bread and a half-dozen pralines. Her jaws spasmed and hurt so badly she could not open her mouth.

"What do you mean, Boris Wilcox?" she said through her teeth. "Where is Chantz? What's happened to Chantz?"

Panic crushed down on her again, as did guilt and the suffocating emotion that had tormented her since she stood in yonder *parterre* of wild Cherokee roses and elderberry bushes and discovered upon looking into his eyes that she had, in some way, loved him and ached for him since he saved her from the fire that destroyed her home.

Liza dropped onto the settee beside her, and her hands lay limply in her lap. She stared at the window, her face expressionless.

"He and Emma done gone from Holly. Tylor fired him but Max try to undo that real fast, 'cept Emma told him to his face that she wouldn't be havin' her boy misused no more by him and Tylor. Chantz still be unconscious when she had Louis load him into a wagon along with their few belongin's and rode him right out of Holly and into the dark.

"Boris showed up next mornin'. All hell done broke loose. When he ain't strappin' us for not workin' proper he be cussin' the babies. Three of the boys done took off. Boris done turned his paddy roller friends on 'em. I 'spect they be found soon enough," she said sadly and with a heavy sigh.

Juliette stared down at the food on her lap, her spasm of hunger having passed. Her face burned and her eyes felt raw. She covered her face with her hands.

"This is all my fault. All of it!" she cried angrily.

"Not all of it, Miss Julie. Tylor what done the worst." She shook her head. "It been comin' a long time. Chantz as much at fault as anyone. He a grown man. He got more self-restraint than anyone I know. Had he wanted to keep his distance from you, a dozen strong mules couldn't have dragged him into your arms."

"Where is Chantz, Liza? Where did Emma take him?"

"To the shanty, I s'pose, 'til Chantz can get back on his feet."

Liza looked around the room at the leaves Juliette had swept into piles and at the walls from which she had scrubbed years of dust and soot. "You been workin' these last days."

At last, she forced herself to pick at the dark pink pork, carefully placed a sliver on her tongue, and, closing her eyes, savored it before chewing. Like an angry fist, her stomach clenched and she forced herself to breathe evenly.

"There are four livable rooms. This one, the dining room, and two west bedrooms upstairs."

"You been sleepin' here?"

"On this settee."

"Rosie be right about you. You crazy as a betsy bug. Surely the craziest white lady I ever seen. Ain't you scared by yourself at night?"

She nodded and reached for the bread. Her mouth felt full of water and she was forced to swallow twice before sinking her teeth in the sweet baked cornmeal.

"Not since the first night," she finally replied, then swallowed. Her eyes drifted closed in pleasure. Rosie had buttered the corn slab and drizzled it with honey. "There are raccoons at night. And birds roost. This morning when I awoke there were two dozen black-breasted grassets lining the rafters."

Juliette smiled wearily. "From one of the upper rooms I can see the marshes. At dawn a low purple mist covers them so only the tops of the highest trees can be seen. And the pond—blue herons float just above the water and hunt for frogs. At dusk there is a yellow-crowned night heron that perches on the trunk of the dead gum near the water's edge."

"You can't just sit here alone doin' nothin' but clusterin' leaves and scrubbin' walls, Miss Julie."

"I don't intend to."

"What you gonna do, then? Go back to Maxwell and Tylor? That's what they is waitin' on. They think you gonna come back soon as you git hungry enough."

She chewed the ham, her thoughts on how sweet and salty it tasted. Overwhelmingly salty. At last, she swallowed and looked around, into Liza's eyes. "I'm going to rebuild Belle Jarod, of course."

She bit into the ham again, a bigger bite, so big she could hardly chew. Hunger suddenly became a beast yawning inside her. She could not think beyond feeding it as quickly as possible.

"You gonna what?" Liza asked without blinking, her gaze following Juliette's hand as she grabbed a praline, pinched off the pecan on top, and tossed it away. She had eaten enough damn pecans the last three days to last her a lifetime.

She shoved the confection into her mouth, along with the ham, and her eyes rolled closed and the sugar and salt melded into a mélange that made her whimper and her eyes tear.

"Can't be rebuildin' the Belle alone, Miss Julie. One thing to sweep up a lot of leaves and trash, another to put a roof on this house—"

"I'll see Belle rebuilt if it's the last thing I ever do."

She nearly choked on the declaration as she attempted to swallow and speak too. The words reverberated angrily in the room, causing Liza's eyes to widen and her body to shrink back slightly against the settee.

"I'll sell my soul if I must, Liza. I'll see this house rise up above the river again. I'll see those fields lush with cane and the docks stacked high with Belle's hogsheads."

Liza waved the statement aside with her hand and shook her head, a scowl pulling down the corner of her mouth. "That as likely to happen as my marryin' Andrew."

Pulling her skirt snug over her belly, Liza studied her flat stomach and her voice dropped to a bitter tone. "Can't see me raisin' no baby without a daddy. Can't see me raisin' no chile to watch him sold down the river to spend the rest of his life workin' like a damn mule in the sun, gittin' whupped by no-account folk like Boris Wilcox or Tylor Hollinsworth."

"You won't."

She placed a praline between two slabs of corn bread and pushed it into her mouth with great relish. From the corner of her eye she saw Liza's head turn as she stared at Juliette as if she were a lunatic. She *felt* crazy in that moment. She felt like the village idiot—a farmer's wife the Reverend Mother was forced once a month to lock in the cellar while the sisters took turns praying for her tormented soul through the door.

"You're leaving Holly," Juliette declared between chews, cheek bulging with bread and praline. "You're coming here to live with me."

Liza's eyes grew large and her hands clasped harder in her lap.

"I don't know how yet, Liza. Just trust that I shan't allow you to remain at Holly with Boris or Tylor or Maxwell now that Chantz is gone."

"I can't be leavin', Miss Julie. I gots Simon to care for. He cripple—"

"Then Simon shall come, too. And Little Clara and Rosie . . ."

Wiping her mouth with the back of her dirty hand, she gazed out at the wilderness that moved forward and back as if shifted by ghosts. Thunder rumbled and leaves tumbled over the floor. Again she felt the energy of the approaching storm. It centered like a hot spark in her chest and something crawled inside her, a sense of destiny, perhaps: a destiny that had brought her back to the place of her birth, to surround herself with this destruction while she considered her fate.

How long did she sit there, watching the storm weave its way through the wild growth, tossing the tupelo gums and maypop vines and live oaks to and fro?

When she looked around, she discovered Liza had gone. Carefully, she tied the napkin around her food, reason telling her that should the weather turn very bad Liza would not manage to bring her more despite Wilcox's drunken oblivion.

The first taps of rain sounded upon the trees. Harder and harder the drops fell as Juliette moved out of the salon into the foyer and watched the rain drive in spears into what had once been her father's library. The drops bounced off the old cypress floors and sprayed her bare feet.

Memories stirred again—ghost images of rosewood furnishings and book-lined walls, a deep chair sitting before the window of open shutters, the evening sun pouring over a woman's face that was troubled and tear streaked. She looked sadly toward her husband who was focused on ledgers open on his desk, and when she spoke to him he didn't notice.

"*Si seulement vous ressentiez autant d'emotion pour moi que vous eprouvez pour votre maudite canne, Jacques. Ma solitude vous émeut si peu?*" I wish your passion for me burned as fiercely as that for your damned cane, Jack. It matters so little to you that I am lonely?

There came a sound behind her, and she slowly turned.

Several Negroes stood shoulder to shoulder at the open door. Water beaded on their hair and dripped from their clothes. There were three men, one with a scrawny chicken on his shoulder, and an old woman with very fat cheeks that almost hid her watchful and suspicious eyes.

They all stared back at her, their faces a mixture of fascination and fear.

Odd that she experienced no fear. Odd that they did not feel like strangers to her. Or mayhap she'd simply been alone too long.

"Lawd have mercy," the woman finally said, the words followed by a deep rumble from the clouds. "Done tol' you I seen a haint."

A young man little older than herself moved forward. His old shoes were held together with twine and there were holes in the knees of his pants. He half crouched as he stepped over the threshold, into the foyer, as if he anticipated having to make a quick getaway. He inched closer, one black hand lifting and stretching toward her, eyes widening, body beginning to tremble so fiercely the rain spat from his hair onto his shoulders.

His finger poked at her and he jumped back.

Juliette frowned and raised one eyebrow.

Again he prodded. At her shoulder, then her breast.

She jabbed him back and he skittered toward the door, his shoes leaving muddy marks on the floor.

"She real?" the old woman asked the quaking young man.

"Real as I is!" he declared excitedly.

"I'm Juliette," she said, and they all gasped and retreated a step. The chicken, with a flap of its wings, landed on the floor and strutted toward Juliette, making a low cluck in its throat.

The woman elbowed her way between the men. Her girth took up most of the entry as she paused, looked Juliette up and down with her lips pursed and her brow deep folds of contemplation. Her skirt looked sewn from a flour sack, her blouse of the poorest quality cotton. She wore a man's boots with buckles on the sides and her thick stockings sagged around her ankles.

"Juliette," she repeated in so heavy a dialect Juliette could hardly understand her. "Done go un growed like yo mama. Yassum. Like d'lady Maureen." Her smile stretched over her broad, black-as-night face exposing ivory yellow teeth that were long and rectangular as piano keys.

Suddenly her arms stretched wide and she lumbered at Juliette, swept her into her plush bosom with a grip that cut off Juliette's breath. Her face nestled into the rolls of fat in the woman's neck where a piece of what smelled like nutmeg hung from a string. Again, memories emerged. Her hands, of their own accord, twisted into the woman's dress and she felt overwhelmed with a sense of elation that confused her.

"Lawd lawd," the woman repeated. Conversation snapped back and forth between them, working the men into an excited frenzy punctuated by spurts of loud laughter.

The big woman squalled, crushing Juliette to her. Her hot tears leaked down onto Julie's cheek as she rocked her from side to side and stroked her matted hair.

Her name was India. Her sons Jasper and Custis—twins, though they looked nothing alike—called her *Mamaloi* which in the West Indies, Juliette learned, was a noted priestess of voodoo. Though Jasper stood tall and reed thin, Custis stood no higher than India.

India's brother was named Gaius, and though he was younger by a number of years than India, his hair had already begun to gray. It was he who proudly owned the chicken, or *koklo*, that he called Jesu.

Juliette learned they were free blacks, thanks to her mother. India and Gaius were brought from the West Indies to Louisiana by her father even before he knew her mother. Before he placed the first brick of the Belle's foundation, before he planted his first ratoon—when he was barely more than a boy himself, perhaps Juliette's age.

As the storm raged, Juliette curled upon the settee with her head resting in India's lap. She labored to understand her words while from the other rooms came the murmurs of India's sons and brother, an occasional clatter, the swoosh swoosh of leaves being swept into a pile. Gaius entered with his arms full of wood and proceeded to stack it into the fireplace, withdrew a Lucifer match from his pocket, lit it, and ignited the dry tinder.

Juliette learned her father had become consumed with his desire to make the finest cane outside of the West Indies, that his slaves were imported from the Indies and knew the secrets of growing exceptionally good cane.

Jasper and Custis returned with skinned squirrels they had somehow killed. They skewered them on sticks and situated them over the fire so their grease dripped and flames spat in response. The smell of the cooking meat made her jaws ache.

She learned that her mother would not abide slavery, and would marry her father only on the condition that he allowed them the opportunity to buy their freedom by repaying the money which he had spent to purchase them. They did so by providing labor. To entice them to remain at Belle after attaining their freedom, he offered them a plot of land on which they were free to sow their own crops, a portion of which they gave back to Belle in exchange for the land. They came to be known as sharecroppers.

Along with the cooked squirrels came wild onions and cabbages plucked from the old gardens. Custis, having scrubbed an iron pot from the kitchen, boiled the onions and cabbages over the fire. The aroma mixed with that of the rain and the wet, earthy smells of decay heightened her senses and her appetite.

She learned that India cared for her mother. Her face glowed with the memories and Juliette watched with perverse curiosity when India's entire body shook with mirth as she related Maureen's trials and tribulations of running the largest cane plantation in the area. Juliette was struck by the realization that she had never seen an expression of appreciation associated with her mother. She felt . . . unbalanced by it. As if her solid world tipped slightly under her feet. Perspective became warped.

Custis used the drippings from the squirrels to season the cabbage.

She learned that her mother taught India how to read and write. She learned that once, when her mother discovered Harlan Carrington, Horace's father, beating a child she wrestled the stick from him and thrashed Harlan so severely she was taken to jail and her father forced to pay a heavy fine for her release.

She learned that her mother helped to secrete abused slaves away from their masters and bring them to the North to freedom. Juliette learned that had Maureen been caught . . . she would have hanged.

The meat of the squirrel was tough and stringy, but delicious, the cabbage somewhat bitter, but she ate it regardless along with the remaining corn bread Liza had brought her.

At last, her belly full and mind drowsy, she lay with her

head on the settee support, her arm thrown over her eyes to hide her tears as she allowed the gossamer memories to curl like smoke in her mind—images of her mother sitting in a swing below the old oak, her perched on Maureen's lap with her arms around her mother's neck, the scent of magnolias filling up her world of Cherokee roses and violets and lavender.

She awoke, alone. The shadows were long and the rain slashed. Had she dreamed them, India and Jasper and Custis and Gaius?

Struggling, she sat up and looked at the fireplace, at the glowing ashes, the pot of cabbage and the plucked carcasses of eaten squirrels.

What should she do now? How should she proceed?

Then, as the thunder shook the house and the lightning briefly brightened the room, casting shadows upon the walls and floor, she knew what she must do. She had known all along.

Seventeen

❧

Once again, the dreaded pain drove him from his bed.

Chantz tried his hardest to focus on something *other* than the deep gnawing fire in his flesh. He couldn't wear a shirt, yet even the air scalded him, so there was no relief even in nakedness. The bourbon pulsed in his blood, hot and thick, and the thoughts in his head swarmed like angry bees.

Twice the last days his mother stopped him from riding hell-bound for leather back to Holly and killing Tylor at long last—should have done it the minute Louis pried him out of that bull gator's mouth. But the pain had been too damn bad—not just the punctures in his leg. Not just the fact that Tylor would pull something so stupid—he'd been half expecting it, after all.

No, for the first hours he'd been too immersed in his panic that Tylor, for once in his sorry life, might have been truthful, that Chantz was nothing more than a damn mud dauber. One of the very people that he had both despised and feared all his life—despised for their worthless, wandering, thieving ways. Feared them because, should Maxwell have decided to cut Emmaline off completely, there would have been little choice but to become one of them— begging for food, clothes, shelter.

Hell, illegitimacy was an indignity enough.

But Emmaline had assured him—sworn on his tattered old Bible that Tylor had been lying.

And Christ, oh Christ, he wanted to believe her.

No, it hadn't been Tylor's display of stupidity during the hunt that had filled him with such blinding hate. Whatever minuscule thread of familial responsibility and tolerance Chantz might have held for his half-brother had been obliterated the moment Tylor forced Louis to strap him to that whipping post.

Closing his eyes against the sweat oozing from his hairline, against the heat building in the shanty room from the cooking fire, Chantz tried not to think about the long excruciating minutes he had hung there, helpless, anticipating each knifelike strike of the whip. He'd known humiliation in his life. He'd tasted hate. But never as he had in those moments. Perhaps he'd deserved punishment for succumbing to his base needs—for plucking Juliette's prized virginity, for loving her—but not to the extent that Tylor had inflicted. He was lucky there was any flesh at all left on his back.

He glanced toward his bedroom door. At long last, driven to exhaustion by her despair and worry, Emmaline had reluctantly taken to bed. Occasionally he could hear her weep in her sleep. Not for the first time, of course.

As a boy he would lie sleepless in the dark and listen to her cry. He would drift to sleep and imagine growing to be a man who would somehow rectify the mistakes of her life, who would rise up from their squalor and become a man more powerful and successful than Max or Fred Buley or Jack Broussard. He'd imagined cutting the highest, sweetest stalk of cane on the final day of harvest, wrapping it in the traditional blue ribbon and placing it at her feet. Then they would lift bumpers of rum in toast to success, and Little Clara and Simon and Sally and all the other children would dance to the pleasant popping of goatskin drums.

Now, however, Emma cried, not over weariness or hunger or even anger. She wept for his stupidity.

Juliette.

Dropping into the husk-seated chair, his elbows on his knees, he buried his head in his hands and stared at the floor. As thunder shook the house, he imagined Juliette sitting in this very chair those many nights ago, after he had pulled her from the river, staring down into the fire, cheeks tear streaked, her hair a wild red spray and her scent swirling in the air as forcefully as the raging river roaring in the dark.

Desperation and frustration mounting, he futilely tried to refocus his hate for Tylor and Maxwell on his concern for Liza and Louis and Little Clara—all who would surely suffer now that he was gone from Holly. Boris Wilcox would murder them, eventually. Everything that Chantz had built the last years would rot from Boris's neglect and ignorance and slothfulness.

Tylor and Maxwell deserved to suffer from Boris's stupidity.

Maxwell's Negroes did not.

Juliette.

She'd be ruined now.

She deserves it! Emmaline had argued and wept as she ministered to his wounds and held his head.

Because of him. Because of his weakness, she would suffer.

She used you, Chantz! His mother had wept with fury as, even in his excruciating misery, he had risen from his red haze of pain to call out Juliette's name. *She used you just like Maxwell has used your intelligence and ethics the last years to succeed. Just like Phyllis used you for her own pleasure caring little for your feelings. Just like the other planters along this river who came to you for advice over the years, and what have any of them done for you in return? A tip of their hat occasionally when they see you on the street?*

Standing, he paced again and tried to think of the incomplete levee and what would happen to Max's sugarcane if the river rose due to the storms. All that they had toiled to rebuild the last weeks would crumble. Perhaps this time Maxwell's beloved home would be obliterated. That thought should have given him satisfaction, yet . . .

Juliette.

What had happened to her?

If Tylor harmed her in any way . . .

If he touched her in any way . . .

Chantz would hang for certain.

Yet, if she were to show up on his doorstep at that very moment . . . he feared he would kill her himself.

Chantz!

The wind moaned like a woman's cry.

Chantz Boudreaux!

"Christ, leave me the hell alone," he hissed through his teeth, and squeezed his eyes closed.

Still, the siren howled for him, taunting and tempting amid the gale winds that suddenly drove with a force that smashed the door open and back against the wall with a thunderous crash.

Spinning toward the door, he stared out into the night, into the vague light that poured through the open entry into the dark.

The winds rushed over the threshold, whipping leaves

and brush and bits of grass around his bare feet. He hardly noticed as his vision sharpened on the image standing just beyond the light like a haunting, hair a mass of wind-whipped banners and her thin dress molded to her body, legs braced apart as the hem of her skirt lifted above her knees and clutched her thighs, outlining their long slim contours that had so easily parted for his hands.

Her big eyes stared at him in fear and anger and the same passion that even now aroused his body to a pain more unendurable than the cuts in his back or the wounds in his leg. All the desperate fury he'd felt for her the last days flared like the fire in the hearth fed by the hot winds whipping through the room.

Chantz.

Her lips moved yet he could not hear her. The words were dashed aside by the wind.

As he moved toward the door, she backed away. Her face glowed ghostly in the dark; her cheeks were hollow, the set of her chin resolute. There was no child left in her now. There was only madness in her eyes.

"Don't do it," came his mother's desperate voice behind him, and looking over his shoulder he saw Emmaline silhouetted in the bedroom doorway, her eyes frantic and tear-filled. "Don't do it," she pleaded. "She's got you just where she wants you now, Chantz. She'll play on your sympathy, on your conscience. She'll offer you marriage. She may even offer you love. All she wants is Belle Jarod, Chantz, and you're her only way to get it."

Forcing his legs to move, he stepped from the house, into the wild wind that clawed at his wounds and robbed him of breath . . . or perhaps it was *her* inflicting the pain and tearing from him the final shreds of his soul.

As the last of his dignity roused to war against her seduction, he looked into her face and suddenly all that he was, and had been, and might have been, crashed inside him with the ferocity of the storm. Now she stood on the precipice of darkness like a succubus sent from Hell to lure him over the final black abyss.

He ran down the damp and muddy steps, expecting her to dissolve into the night like a spirit. When he reached for her he expected his hand to grasp vapor.

Her body slumped heavily against his. Those eyes, murky green and turbulent as the churning Gulf waters, stared up into his. There radiated no fear in their depths. No fear in her body. Only challenge.

"Marry me," she said.

He blinked and frowned. His fingers curled more forcefully into her arms as his mother's warning slashed like Tylor's whip into his heart.

"Marry you." Chantz laughed sharply and without humor as he lowered his head over hers, head tipped slightly to one side as he looked deeply into her eyes. So easily he could crush her in that instant. Yet, as her lips parted, thoughts of fury and murder tumbled like the whipped debris over the earth. The memory of her taste and smell became his universe. The familiar hunger expanded to every bleeding nerve, raw pain, and exquisite fire.

"You're insane," he said, then he kissed her. His heart began its chest-hammering rhythm and the slow heat of his desire for her oozed through his body as white-hot as molten silver.

At last, he forced himself to move away before he lost total control.

Her eyes flashed. There was fight in her yet. Defiance. Absolute fury. "I won't beg you," she declared over the howl of the wind.

Leaves caught upon her exposed legs that were like soft polished gold in the light spilling from the shanty. "You can go to hell if you so desire, Chantz Boudreaux. You can live out the remainder of your life sweating, your hands bleeding for others. Watching others reap the rewards of your labor. Or you can marry me and Belle Jarod will be yours."

He looked hard into her eyes. Her skirt billowed higher, teasing him. She wore no drawers tonight. No petticoats. For the first time he noticed her cotton dress was soiled and torn.

What the hell had happened to her since his mother carted him away from Holly House? What had they done to her?

"You don't have to love me," came her words, drawing his focus away from her thighs and back to her eyes. There were scratches on her cheeks and her hair was a nest of tangles. "Your only obligation will be to Belle Jarod. I want her reconstructed, Chantz. I want cane in those damn fields. I want Maxwell Hollinsworth to suffer each time he rides by Belle and sees her flourishing."

"You're crazy," he shouted down at her. "It'll take a king's fortune to rebuild Belle—"

"It's the cane I want, Chantz. I'll live in a slave shanty if I must. I'll furrow the earth with my own hands if I must. I'll cut every damned stalk of cane with my own two hands if I must."

"Then what the hell do you need me for?"

"To teach me."

Turning on his heels, he climbed the steps.

"Obviously I was wrong about you," came her words.

Halting, he turned. Her hair blew partially over her face, nearly obscuring her eyes. The slant of smugness on her mouth replenished his desire to crush her.

"You struck me as a man with aspiration. Intelligence. Hunger to rise beyond mediocrity, not to mention poverty.

Instead, you would waste your life drudging to line the pockets of buffoons like Maxwell and Fred Buley because you're too much the coward to risk failure."

She moved toward him, into the light. Her eyes were like ice on fire and her cheeks aflame with color.

"I'll do it with or without you, Chantz." Lifting her chin a notch, she raised one eyebrow and added, "If for no other reason, just imagine how Maxwell would suffer over our union. I suspect the pleasure you would feel over such revenge would make marriage to Maureen's daughter worth the bite of bitter gall you may occasionally experience from compromising your healthy dignity by marrying me."

When he spoke his voice sounded level, almost matter of fact. Only the clenching of his fists, their trembling, betrayed the upheaval of emotion he felt in that moment—certain knowledge that his mother had been right all along. Suddenly all his faculties felt numb and the silence that followed, interspersed by the groan of wind, sounded intensely loud and seemed to stretch for a painful eternity. Every deep lash in his back hurt with new ferocity.

He looked down into her eyes for a long time, his face grave and still, then said, very deliberately, although his voice caught on the words, "In other words, darlin', I'm nothing more than a means to an end to you, right, Juliette? Get your hands legally on Belle Jarod and at the same time have your revenge on Maxwell, make him suffer over destroying your father."

Her expression stunned, Juliette said nothing.

More slowly, the deep throbbing ache in his leg and back causing sweat to rise to his brow, Chantz turned back to the house, paused in the threshold, fighting the desperate need for her to call out and deny his accusation, fighting his need

to walk back into her arms and forget his goddamn pride
and foolish sense of dignity . . . or what dignity he had left.

But there came no response.

Shutting the door against her, he pressed his forehead to
the barrier and closed his eyes, swallowed back the lump in
his throat.

Oh, God, he thought with sinking despair. *What have I
just done?*

India and her family returned again and again. More
frequently they remained, sleeping on the floor on mattresses they plumped with goose feathers and moss. They
strung ropes from tree to tree and over them tossed
Spanish moss. Drying, they turned black and were ready to
be stuffed into the old settee and chairs and between quilts
for mattresses. The window shutters were repaired. The
floors and walls were scrubbed.

Mounds of silt accumulated on the gallery were shov-
eled away, the bricks scraped of lichen, and though no
longer white but dingy gray, the high square columns,
without the mire of vegetation, were magnificent once
again. The bricks, each one hand-made and baked in the
sun, had been stamped with her mother's initials.

Sitting on the front gallery steps, her hair concealed
under a tignon, she stretched her legs out before her. The
back of her ragged skirt had been drawn up between her
thighs and tucked into the rope around her waist, revealing
her shins that had been scratched by briars and whelped by
mosquito bites.

She watched Jasper and Custis drive their old gray mule
Snapper with shouts and whistles. The animal lunged to
drag the weight of a fallen live oak from what once was the
long drive covered in crushed white oyster shells. At long

last, Juliette could see sunlight through the trees and, occasionally, flashes of sunlight on the river. The anticipation of revealing Belle Jarod to the world had driven her to work from sunup to sundown. Yet, she no longer ached. Her slim, hard body had become capable of hoisting weight upon her back and shoulders that would make Phyllis Buley and those like her pale in mortification.

Still, no matter that India and her family had been sent like angels from heaven to help her, the reality remained. Belle Jarod would never thrive again without a miracle. No matter the progress they made each day hacking away tupelo gums and maypop vines and elderberry trees, the thousands of acres crying for cane remained abandoned. Most of Belle's roof remained a charred and crumbled mess. Without money, there was no hope.

Chantz, of course, had been right about that, if nothing else.

Still, she stubbornly refused to give in. She would rather die of starvation or snakebite than return to Holly Plantation.

"Hello, Miss Julie."

Startled from her morose thoughts, Juliette looked around to find Andrew Buley standing near the tree edge, his Panama in hand and his shirtsleeves rolled up to his elbows. Sweat beaded his brow as he forced a tight smile, no doubt appalled by her appearance. His gaze slowly moved down over her bare legs, lingered, smile growing thinner, his eyes as dark as the rich earth under his boots.

Juliette reached for her machete, stood, and without so much as looking toward him again, dove into the copse of blackberries and young cottonwoods.

"I don't blame you for being angry with me," he said as he followed. "I haven't done right by Liza. But I'm here today to rectify that."

Whack. The blade bit deeply into the brittle cottonwood trunk.

Andrew cleared his throat. "You've done one hell of a job here, Juliette." He swatted at the cloud of gnats and mosquitoes swirling around his head.

Whack.

"I heard you found some Negroes—"

"They found me. And before you go getting on your high horse, they are free blacks. That means they are free to live and work wherever they so desire, Mr. Buley."

Straightening, the knife clutched in her hand, Juliette squared her shoulders and looked him in the eye.

"My mother freed them. I suppose that's another trait I share with her—I don't abide slavery. Nor am I a hypocrite. Now, tell me why you're here. As you can see, I don't have time for idle chitchat."

He followed her deeper into the brush, ducked back as she swung the blade high over her head and down, severing a sapling in two.

"I'm concerned about Liza," he said in a raised voice as he fanned away the insects with his hat.

"Do tell."

"Have you seen her?"

"Occasionally."

"And the baby?"

Turning on him, she placed the tip of her blade on his shoulder, causing new sweat to rise on his brow. "There is still a baby, if that's what you mean."

"I've given the situation a great deal of consideration." He swallowed and released a breath, relieved as Juliette turned again on the brush and began chopping. "I intend to tell my parents about the child."

"I'm sure they won't be bothered about the child,

Andrew. Liza herself is evidence that plantation owners care little whether they repopulate their flesh trove of slaves with half-caste children."

"I can't marry her. She's a slave. It's against the law. Besides, I have my folks to consider."

"You have your inheritance to consider, you mean."

"What the hell am I supposed to do, Julie? Without that inheritance I've got nothing. I was taught to grow cane, for God's sake."

"You can't grow cane and love Liza too?"

"I can't grow Buley cane."

"From my understanding, Buley cane isn't exactly special."

"What is that supposed to mean?"

"It means your father grows inferior cane."

His face flushed dark as the berries at her feet. "We can't all be Chantz Boudreaux."

She momentarily froze at the sound of Chantz's name, feeling the heat of Andrew's stare on the back of her neck. Reluctantly, she looked over her shoulder, into Andrew's dark eyes.

"How is he?" she asked, hating the quiver she heard in the words. She'd told herself a thousand times over the last days and nights that Chantz could go to hell. "Not that I truly care," she lied with another whack of her blade against a tree branch.

Andrew bent and plucked several berries. They stained his fingers before he popped them into his mouth and looked away. There was something about her expression, perhaps, that discomposed him.

"He's working the river. The pay is sorry but it feeds him and Emmaline . . . for the time being. In case you haven't heard, there is talk about quarantining New Orleans. There appears to be an outbreak of yellow fever, mostly in the shanty town along the river. Authorities have managed to keep it confined but the last week several people in the quarter have gone sick. If New Orleans is quarantined there won't be any river traffic."

Whack.

"The river. The idea is absurd. Chantz should be growing cane, Andrew. It's in his blood. He loves it. And he's good at it."

"It's not for lack of offers." Andrew grinned. "My own father offered him a job. I do believe Maxwell and Tylor underestimated his esteem in this parish. He could go to work for any of a dozen planters along this river in a heartbeat."

"Then why doesn't he?"

"I don't know. I don't think he does either."

Juliette flung the machete down so hard it knifed deeply into the dirt. Shouldering her way through a tangle of brush, she upset a covey of quail that exploded into the air with a popping of frantic wing beats. They disturbed a drove of water turkeys near the pond edge. Their enormous bodies rose up in a dark cloud, their thin black necks outstretched as they soared toward the low marshes.

By the time Andrew followed her into the house, Juliette paced down the long middle corridor that divided the destruction of Belle Jarod from the complete rooms she had called home the last weeks. India stood at one end, hands on her hips and her mouth a bend of disapproval as she fixed Andrew with her small black eyes.

"I don't understand," Juliette declared, words ringing in the open rafters high overhead. "I offer him marriage. I offer him Belle Jarod to marry me. I would think that he might not give a damn about me, and wouldn't blame him after the harm I've caused, but that he would give a damn about this." Flinging open her arms, she turned round and round, becoming dizzy.

"Chantz is a proud man, Julie. Too damn proud for his own good, mostly. He's worked for everything he's ever owned. He's not about to sell his dignity for a lot of sugar-cane. And if you offered it because of some sense of obligation you feel over what happened, or God forbid pity—"

"Pity?" Hands curled into fists, Juliette moved toward Andrew. "He accused me of manipulation, Andrew. He accused me of using him to exact revenge on Maxwell for destroying my father. After what took place between us . . ." She shook her head and willed back her escalating anger. "How dare he believe I would prostitute myself—"

"You've got Emmaline to blame for that. Not Chantz. She's a tired, bitter woman, Juliette, and she's afraid of losing him. I'm sorry to say she can't get over the fact that you're Maureen's daughter. She'll suspect everything you do."

She entered the salon and continued to pace, her frustration and irritation mounting.

Andrew followed, looking around the room. He walked to a glass jar India had filled with roses and honeysuckle that scented the air so there was little hint of the old decay. Then he glanced toward the stack of books on the marble-top table and picked one up, turned it over, before focusing on her again. His eyes no longer looked pleasant. "When will you see Liza again?" he asked.

"Soon. Tonight possibly."

"Does she come here?"

"When she can. Whenever she can get away without that idiot Boris finding out. Fortunately, he's often away in the evenings."

"I know. He and his paddy roller friends came by our place last night."

"Oh?" She flashed him an askance look. "Are you harboring runaway slaves?"

"They're not after runaway slaves. There is a rumor running amok that someone is teaching our slaves how to read."

"Imagine that." She sniffed and crossed her arms.

"I don't care to think about what will happen to such a tutor if she . . . he is discovered."

She raised one eyebrow. "Then don't think about it."

Juliette moved again into the foyer and dragged the tignon from her head. Her hair fell in a mass around her shoulders.

"India!" she called. "I'll need my good dress. The one Liza brought me last week. And I'll want a bath. Will you have Jasper heat me water?"

"Yassum." India smiled, radiating her pleasure at doing the menial chore.

"And have Gaius cool down the mule. I'll be riding Snapper into town."

Eighteen

❧

*I*ndia perched behind Juliette on the broad rump of the old mule while Jasper and Gaius walked beside her, one on each side. Jasper carried a cottonwood switch with a tuft of leaves on the end. When Snapper stalled, refusing to budge a hoof further, Jasper popped him on the haunches with the switch until the mule bared his long yellow teeth in displeasure, brayed, and returned to his ambling gait.

Gaius carried a *macoute* strapped over his shoulder. He had brought it from the islands so many years ago, and he kept it always within reach. Within the satchel made of leaves of the bourbon palm, he carried a small vial of *eau sirop*, a *garde*, and *paquett* . . . as well as Jesu. The head of the scrawny old chicken stuck out through the *macoute* flap as she looked out upon the world with frighteningly intelligent eyes.

Numerous boats lined up along the docks, stageplanks securing them to the piers that teemed with shouting, whistling, singing roustabouts loading freight: feed, flour, sugar, and other supplies for the plantations up and down the river. They sang as they lifted:

Ol' roustabouts ain't got no home.
Makes his livin' wid his shoulder bone!

One boat in particular caught her eye, especially handsome, with lofty smokestacks with lacy iron feathers decorating the top. Her name was scrawled boldly in gold leaf upon the side of her wheelhouse:

THE SASSAFRAS

Other boats floated by; their enormous stern wheels churned the placid water. Clouds of black smoke billowed upward from their tall smokestacks, some rising nearly fifty feet tall, tainting the air with an acrid stench that made Juliette's eyes burn and her stomach queasy. With a puff of steam and deep bells ringing that caused Snapper to flick his big ears in annoyance, the boats disappeared around the bend of the broad river.

Women in outrageously fancy dresses and coiffed hair beneath their frilly bonnets congregated along the *banquettes.* Juliette thought them like flocks of peacocks with their colorful plumes spread. They laughed as they conversed, sharing secrets that only the vapid minded would find interesting and amusing—mindless gossip and chitchat—no doubt most of it was about her. From behind their ornate fans, the women, young and old, flirted outrageously at the suited fancy men who paused to compliment them on their attire. Mothers hovered, concerned for their precious daughters' reputations should one of the dandies presume too much.

Little by little, however, the titter of conversation and laughter began to fade as they saw her.

One by one they turned, their expressions a mixture of

curiosity and contemplation. They knew her, of course. Her reputation, and her mother's, preceded her. The fact that she straddled an old mule, her robin's-egg blue taffeta skirt hiked above her knees, wouldn't help. Nor did she wear a pretty bonnet. Not that she would even if she had owned one, of course. Then, of course, there were her companions: India had lapsed into a low chant to ward off evil thoughts and Jesu had scrambled from the *macoute* and perched on Gaius's shoulder.

Still, Juliette gave the curious gawkers barely a glance. Instead, her gaze swept the long streets and *banquettes*, heart beat rising as she narrowed her eyes against the sun reflecting off the rutted and hard-packed earth and the storefront windows. From the river came the excited chatter of the market hawkers lining the wharves. The stink of the water and fish and tobacco as well as the chickens and pigs and cattle in pens near the river felt overwhelming, forcing her to cover her nose with her cambric as she searched.

Where was he?

She focused harder on the dozens of men moving up and down the docks, loading and unloading the big boats—some flat that were used to transport cotton bales down river during harvest, others multileveled with gingerbread ornamentation and brightly painted smokestacks and banners so they looked like floating carnivals.

Chantz. Where was he?

And what would she do if she saw him?

Ironic that the thought of him left her trembling, yet she could ride so easily down the street of Baton Rouge shamelessly straddling a mule, defying decorum, and care little that the pretty women were no doubt laughing behind their gloved hands and painted fans at her.

And the men, of course . . .

Ha! She knew what they imagined, especially the older ones who could clearly remember her mother.

They stepped from their businesses, some wearing long white aprons and others smoking fat cigars, leaned against the doorposts, arms crossed over their chests, and watched, expressionless, as she rode by. Her cheeks warming and her stomach fluttering, Juliette told herself that it was because of the intense afternoon sun and not because she imagined she knew what thoughts toyed with their memories.

At last, they stopped at the Mercantile. As India slid her girth off the rump of the mule, Jasper lifted his dark hands up and clasped her around the waist as she dismounted and set her lightly on her feet. Up and down the *banquettes* people moved closer, shoulder to shoulder, some of them.

Lured by the aroma of coffee, she entered the dark and dusty Mercantile. A young boy stopped his sweeping and stared at her while a woman with light bronze skin and wearing a brown satin dress cut daringly low sat at one of several linen-draped tables in the corner near a window overlooking the river.

As Juliette's eyes grew accustomed to the darker interior, the woman put down her demitasse and regarded her with a half-smile. She wore a hat on her head with a large feather swagging over her shoulder. The brown tips on the feather perfectly matched her dress.

A short bald man behind a counter peered at Juliette through his round spectacles. "May I help you?" he asked.

Indeed. She wondered what she was doing here, considering she hadn't so much as a penny to purchase coffee or any of the other goods lining the walls and tables. Again, the heat of discomposure and frustration rose to her cheeks as she wondered if there was anything on her person that she could trade for a solitary cup of coffee.

"The mademoiselle will have a coffee, I think," the dark woman said.

"No," she responded almost frantically—too frantically, she realized too late.

"My pleasure, of course," the woman hastened to add. With a graceful motion of her bejeweled hand, she pointed to the chair opposite her. "I've been eager to meet you, Miss Broussard."

Juliette looked back at the man. He rewarded her with a sharp nod then turned to retrieve a cup and saucer from a shelf behind the counter.

As she moved through the store, India, Jasper, and Gaius settled onto shaded benches on the *banquette*. Lapsing into their island dialect, they murmured among themselves as they watched the traffic move along the street—normal again since Juliette had entered the building and was out of sight. Jesu strutted into the store, cocking her head to one side as she watched Juliette between pecking insects from the floor.

As Juliette moved closer, she could see the woman was extraordinarily lovely, reminding her of Liza—rich brown hair and eyes dark as the coffee she was drinking. Suddenly the merchant moved to her side, drawing the chair back and placing the demitasse on the table. His expression appeared slightly dazed as he stared into her eyes.

"You should close your mouth, Baxter, before you swallow a fly." The woman gave a husky laugh, causing Baxter's cheeks to color.

"I beg your pardon," he declared, then dried his sweating hands on his apron. "But for a moment . . ."

"She's much like her mama, *oui?*" The woman's head fell back and she laughed again. The peacock feather brushed her shoulder.

"Yes." Baxter smiled, relieving the tension that had

momentarily stiffened Juliette's back. "Extraordinary. Your mother was a frequent customer. Yes, yes, she stopped here often. Sat right here, as a matter of fact. She enjoyed peppermint with her coffee. Would you care for one?"

Her gaze shifted to the glass container of colored candy sticks. How many years since last savoring the hot and sweet bite of peppermint? Her mouth watered and her stomach rumbled. Suddenly she detected every delicious aroma around her. She felt dizzied by them.

Baxter's smile widened. "You always enjoyed the pink the best, though your mother always assured you that there is no difference in flavor. Please. It will be my pleasure."

As he hurried toward the candy, the woman reached for her demitasse. "As I recall he became as flustered over your mama. Then again, so did every other man in Baton Rouge. My name is Virginia, by the way. It's a pleasure to meet you at last."

The coffee was thick and black and so hot it burned her tongue. Ah, but it was delicious. Her eyes closed in pleasure. Even the mention of her mother could not spoil her enjoyment of the drink. Then she realized that she rarely became displeased any longer by thoughts of her mother.

"I understand you've moved into Belle Jarod," Virginia said, then blew on her coffee to cool it.

"Yes."

"How are you surviving?"

"Well enough."

"You have your mother's tenacity."

"I suppose that's a compliment?" She hesitantly returned her smile.

"Of course. Your mother was highly regarded in Baton Rouge."

A frown crossed her brow and Juliette focused harder on her coffee.

"Does that surprise you?" Virginia asked, tipping her head slightly to one side as she regarded her.

"That depends by what you mean. In what way did they 'highly regard' her?"

Virginia relaxed against the high back of her chair. There was a choker around her long neck—a black velvet ribbon with a cameo of ivory and onyx.

Pulling a lace-edge cambric kerchief from between her full breasts, she pressed it to her cheeks as she watched Juliette sip the hot coffee. "There are a great many people in this town who are grateful to your mama for numerous reasons. She had a sharp mind for business."

Her lips curving sensually, she looked up at Baxter as he placed a demisaucer with pink peppermint sticks on the table. "Take Baxter," Virginia purred, her eyelids growing heavy. "I'm certain he'll tell you that it's thanks to Maureen that he enjoys the profits of this pleasant café. *Oui?*"

"Yes." He nodded. "Oh yes."

"Before there was no dignified place, other than *La Madeleine,* to enjoy this splendid brew." Lifting one eyebrow, she added, "Would you care to hear how Baxter's Café came to be, Juliette?"

She nodded and reached for the candy stick, eased it into the coffee and stirred. Jesu pecked around her feet and made low noises that sounded disconcertingly human. She tried to nudge the *koklo* away with her foot.

"I was twelve at the time," Virginia began, her voice soft and distant. "I arrived here from N'awlins with my mama who was very ill. It was December and cold and raining. I wanted a cup of chocolate. But mostly I wanted my mama out of the weather."

She lifted the cup to her lips, and her eyes drifted closed as the steam curled around her features. "She took me into yonda hotel. We sat at a table near the fireplace—the first warmth we had felt since leavin' N'awlins."

Virginia placed her demitasse on the saucer, stared into it a long moment before raising her gaze back to Juliette's. "We were asked to leave, of course. People of color are not allowed in such dignified establishments as *La Madeleine*.

"There was a beautiful young woman sitting at a table, close enough to overhear the exchange between my sick mama and the proprietor of the hotel. As I recall, she had just been served her meal. To this day I can still feel the ache of hunger in my stomach when I think of that food—hot bread and thick meat with sauce and peas with a goodly slab of butter melting atop it. She turned her head and looked at me and I recall thinking that I ain't ever seen eyes like that, green as a cane field in August.

"She smiled at me—so perty and sweet I forgot about my hurting belly and even the look of distress on my mama's face. She put down her fork and carefully folded her monogrammed napkin and placed it aside her plate. Then she stood and in a voice that cut through the room like a knife blade declared that she would not patronize an establishment that would put out a sick woman and a hungry child.

"The lady brought us to Baxter who invited us to sit at his own table. Your mama sat with us many times after that and, as far as I know, she never stepped foot in the hotel again.

"Maureen and my mama became very good friends over the next few months. She paid for burying my mama when she died.

"Child," Virginia said softly as she leaned toward Juliette. "No need to look so angry when I mention your mama. There are two sides to every story. Ask ten people what they think about a person and you get ten different opinions. You like peppamint. I don't. You sit here and share a demitasse with me and there are a dozen ladies yonda who will not. Don't make me crazy for not liking peppamint any more than it make you crazy for liking it. Understand, Juliette?"

As Juliette nodded and slid the peppermint into her mouth, Virginia narrowed her dark eyes in contemplation.

"You come to town looking for Chantz?"

She thought of lying. What good would it do? Some instinct told her that the woman sharing her company would recognize more clearly than she her excuses for coming to town.

"Heard what Tylor done," Virginia said. "Ever'one heard what Tylor done. Chantz got a lot of friends in this town. Best Tylor watch his back. He and Horace Carrin'ton and Boris Wilcox."

She touched her lip and for the first time Juliette noticed a cut there, just a slight one that was mostly healed except for a pinkish scar. When she spoke again her voice sounded low and thoughtful, with a razor edge of contempt that she had not voiced even when discussing *La Madeleine.*

"Some getting tired of them rough-shodding over folk. They liable to wake up some night with a knife at their throats."

Juliette's hand tightened around the hot demitasse; the steam wept against her palm, yet she could neither look away from the light in Virginia's eyes nor speak. Emotion closed in her throat and she could not swallow it.

Standing, the chair scraping the floor causing Jesu to scramble toward the door, Virginia reached for her parasol made of the same material as her dress. Her striking height made her even more beautiful as she appeared to float around the table.

Bending over Juliette's shoulder, Virginia whispered near her ear, "The man be worth fighting for. Man who risks a whupping to be with a lady gots to be feeling love whether he know it himself or not."

With that, she turned, murmured something to Baxter, then proceeded out of the store.

Only when she was gone did Juliette look around, up into Baxter's kind eyes.

"As I recall," he said, smiling. "At the time of your mother's unfortunate demise . . . I owed her money. Will you allow me to repay you with food?"

She looked toward the door again.

India craned to look around the doorpost into the store. Her smile beamed, and Juliette smiled back.

"Yes," she replied, and nodded. "Food will be fine."

Gaius slung the cotton sack of food stuffs—flour, salt, cheese, and coffee, a hock of sugared pork and a small prized tin of tea—over his right shoulder, the *macoute* with Jesu over his left. Still, Juliette hung back. Flour and sugar and salt and such were very nice and greatly needed, but they were not the reason she came to town. And while there was a part of her heart that tingled with the awakening of admiration she was beginning to experience for her mother, the slow aching throb of disappointment remained.

Where was Chantz?

Why was he wasting his time working the river when his passion was for cane?

When her passion was for him?

"Who have we got here?"

Turning, she looked up into the countenance of a man

with pale blue eyes and a complexion like wheat paste. His blond hair was slicked back from his heavy brow, giving him a hooded, hawklike appearance.

Jasper and Gaius stepped back and diverted their gazes to the ground, less out of respect, Juliette suspected, than aversion.

India, her heavy jowls aquiver, glared at him with a hatred hotter than the afternoon sun baking their shoulders. She did not step away, however, but placed herself at Juliette's side with her feet planted firmly apart.

His lips thinned as he smiled and reached for her hand—gloveless, he noted with a hesitation and a lift of his oddly arched brows. His eyes narrowed as they appraised the roughness of her fingertips and the scabbed abrasions over her knuckles. Yet, he lifted her hand toward his lips as his discomposingly pale gaze shifted to hers.

"*Mademoiselle* Broussard, I assume?"

She slipped her hand from his and wiped it on her skirt. She'd heard enough about this man the last weeks to feel repulsion at his touch.

"Carrington." She stepped away. "Your reputation precedes you."

"*Merci.*" He straightened.

"There's no reason to thank me, I assure you. 'Twasn't meant as a compliment."

His smile didn't falter. His eyes burned more brightly as he curved his soft white fingers around the snakehead crook of his stepping cane. The eyes of the snake were faceted emeralds, the carved scales tipped with gold. She tried not to imagine that for what Carrington spent on such a frivolous object she could eat for a month . . . if not longer.

"I understand you've moved onto your father's estate.

You're wasting your time, Miss Broussard. Belle Jarod is as dead and buried as her namesake. If you care to sell her—"

"Impossible. She's not yet mine to sell."

"Ah, yes. There is that little matter of age or marriage." His gaze slid down her body. "I wouldn't be opposed to assisting the matter along in one form or another."

"Considering Phyllis Buley is as we speak planning your wedding, I hardly believe you're in a position to contemplate other 'forms or another' regarding marriage."

"But you misunderstand me. I mean only to . . . shall we say, provide for you in a manner that would keep you comfortable until you're of age to sell the Belle to me."

"I would rather my Belle rot completely to the ground before I allow her to fall into the hands of a man who so unconscionably whips human beings and cheats on his fiancée."

He didn't so much as blink, just lifted his chin slightly and looked at her down his sharp nose. "How very sanctimonious coming from one who so recently was discovered compromising herself with the likes of Chantz Boudreaux."

Replacing his hat on his head, he glanced up and down the street before adding conversationally, "Take care in your activities. 'Twould be a shame if something untoward happened to you and the Belle became a disposition of the courts. No telling what sort of scoundrel would get his hands on her then. Until we meet again, *adieu, Mademoiselle.*"

She glared at his back as he moved down the *banquette*, the snake eyes on his cane glittering back at her. There were people watching, men and women. Baxter peered out through his dusty storefront window, his expression somber.

Raising her voice for all to hear, she called, "The next time you proposition potential mistresses and threaten women's lives, Mr. Carrington, consider a less public venue."

There came a blink of a hesitation in his step, but he did not look back.

"Bahd mahn," Jasper said close to her ear. His voice quavered, and as she looked around into his eyes she witnessed a tumult of emotion there that made her blood run cold. "Don't wants to make enemy of Carrin'ton, *Maîtresse*. He a bahd, bahd mahn."

India muttered something under her breath then spat in the dirt, in his footsteps, murmured something again, and backed away. Fixing her eyes on Carrington's back, she whispered through her teeth: *"Poussé allé! Poussé allé, Commère!"* She removed the string with the nutmeg and amulet from her neck and slipped it over Juliette's head.

"Arrêt!" India declared, and placed her big hand upon the amulet that rested between Juliette's breasts. *"Arrêt, Maîtresse. C'est bien bon. Bien bon."*

The cloud of anger on India's dark face was again replaced by her beaming smile that, even in that moment with Juliette's anger boiling more hotly than the sun, with the dust slightly suffocating her lungs, uplifted her spirits.

Placing her hand upon the amulet, she smiled and looked again toward the busy wharf, and repeated softly, *"Oui, Mamaloi. It is very good."*

Chantz had watched Juliette that day from the deck of the *Sassafras*, watched her ride into town on Snapper, Jasper and Gaius at her side and India behind her. He'd felt the stares of the other men on him as he watched her ride among the staring crowds, her head held high as if she were as royal as a princess. He'd been forced to go below and remain there in the hot box of burning coal and steam or surely he would have allowed his emotions to get the better of him.

What emotions?

Standing there watching the sun turn her hair to a flame and kiss her face—the very face that he could still imagine when he closed his eyes at night, the very face that he focused his thoughts on as Tylor whipped him—he had been forced to fully acknowledge what he had tried so hard to deny.

He was in love with Juliette Broussard, her spirit, her soul, her mouth and laughter and eyes . . .

Damn those eyes that had stared up into his with a soul-rending passion. He could almost imagine that he could see, even from the deck of the *Sassafras*, their passion and fire. He had never felt so full up with a hunger to conquer since he'd last stood in a barren field and imagined turning it over with his bare hands.

He rode the horse hard through the dark, through the splashes of white moonlight on the road, through the shadows scattered here and there making the lathered animal quiver with the fear that those shadows were bottomless pits straight to Hell. He dug his heels into the gelding's flanks, driving him on as he sank into the saddle in case the horse veered at the last minute. The river stretched out beside him, smooth as bottle glass and as reflective. Starlit mist hovered over the water like ghosts so humanlike occasionally his heart gave a leap. The same fear stabbed at him over and over . . .

What if he was too late? The possibility sent hot, fresh panic through him.

Word had arrived only minutes before the *Sassafras* was to have set off for New Orleans. The quarantine had been established. No boats would be allowed into New Orleans, nor would they be allowed out because of what appeared to be an escalating outbreak of fever. For once in his life he thanked God for such fate or he would have been miles down the river when the Negro child had come scrambling down the dock looking for Chantz, running up the stage-plank yelling at the top of his voice:

"Missive fo' Boss Chantz!"

The note had read simply:

"There will be trouble tonight at Belle Jarod."

What kind of trouble?

Didn't matter.

Didn't matter who sent it, though he had his suspicions. He'd received enough of Phyllis Buley's letters over the last months to recognize her handwriting, signed or not. He'd suspected for a long while that Horace Carrington was involved with Boris Wilcox and his group of troublemaking paddy rollers, and that's what frightened Chantz most: Horace's love of pain, and inflicting it.

Since he'd watched Juliette dismount that cantankerous old mule, watched her stand there in the street with the hot sun beating on her while she searched the docks for him, he'd needed one tenuous thread of reason to walk away from the *Sassafras*.

With a measure of disquietude and relief, he'd crumpled the note in his hand and walked away from the sweating, glaring, cursing *Sassafras*'s captain and didn't look back.

Please, God, please, whatever the trouble, don't let him be too late.

He'd known that eventually Maxwell or Tylor would be forced to make a move. They had expected Juliette to crumble when faced with the hardship of surviving with no money. They had boasted among the townsfolk that she would come crawling on her knees and be grateful for any crumb of food or pittance of money they might provide her if they would only take her back. She would eventually

come to her senses when she realized just what sort of goliath task she faced in rebuilding Belle Jarod—with no
money or manpower.

But days had passed. And rumors had surfaced that free
blacks had moved into Belle to help her.

Then the other whispers had surfaced. Someone was tu-
toring the slaves at night. Not just Holly slaves, but others:
Buley slaves and Carrington slaves. The secret had been
breached when one of Carrington's slave children had picked
up a chore list and commented on it. The boy had refused to
tell Horace where he had learned to read, though Chantz
suspected the child had suffered greatly for his silence.

Chantz knew, of course. That certainty and fear expanded as vastly as the night sky overhead as he drove the
horse like a bat out of hell toward Belle Jarod. The pounding of his horse's hooves and the whippoorwills' calls were
the only sounds in the dark.

At last, he came to the gates—not long since lost amid
the tangle of wild growth—now standing like gray sen-
tinels in the moonlight. Atop each perched bleached
horse skulls—India's work, of course: island magic
against evil.

There was still no riding up the drive. The horse
wouldn't have it even if the thick copses had been entirely
cleared away. As if sensing something amiss the big sweating bay danced on his back feet, slung his head with froth-
covered bit, and threatened to unsettle Chantz from his
back.

At last, Chantz managed to dismount, and the horse
heaved himself backward, yanking the reins from Chantz's
hand, spun on his haunches, and, giving a side kick toward
Chantz, sprang off into the dark like all the hounds of hell
were snapping at his hocks.

As the thunder of retreating hoofbeats was swallowed by the whirring of crickets and the continuing calls of the whippoorwills, Chantz moved beyond the ghostly brick entries into the lair of heavy trees and brambles, footsteps silenced by the carpet of dead leaves and moss. The smell of honeysuckle and jasmine perfumed the air. Occasionally the ranker odor of morass near the river's edge intruded.

At last, he broke through the tangle and stood looking at the house lit by moon and stars. For a moment, just a moment, he was swept back in years to when the Belle had stood like a glowing palace above the *cyprière*. When, as a boy, he had looked upon her massive columns and graceful arches and imagined that some day he would own something as grand as Belle Jarod. For a moment, however brief, he was that boy again, left breathless by her majesty. She looked . . . reborn.

Then as the clouds eased over the moon and the light dimmed, the bones returned—empty black eyes and exposed rafters. Nothing had changed except there was no longer the flesh of wild growth to shield her scars.

He heard it then, the weeping. A cold dread centered in his belly and he forced his resistant legs to move. Sweat formed on his brow like beads of hot ice as he moved up the steps, over the gallery, through the open door, and into the foyer. Every sense attuned to the silence, to the dark.

"Juliette?"

The word came out sounding little more than a dry rattle of fear.

"Juliette?"

The sound again. The soft weeping. Then a man's voice. Chantz moved down the foyer toward the back room where the faintest light of a candle interrupted the dark. The only sound he could hear in that moment was the explosive pounding of his heart in his ears.

India lay on her back, arms and legs splayed, her mouth open and her eyes wide, fixed on the ceiling. A scrawny chicken perched on her big belly, clucking softly while Jasper, Custis, and Gaius knelt beside her, shoulder to shoulder and hands clutched to their chests as if praying.

Andrew, on his knees as well, clutched Juliette to his chest. Her arms lay motionless in her lap.

A frigid pain seized his bones; he couldn't move; he couldn't breathe. His gaze inched up her body, to the pale skin showing under her torn bodice, fear pressing outward from his chest so he thought he might be dying. There was a smear of blood on the side of her face that was turned into Andrew's white-shirted shoulder which shook as he wept.

As if sensing Chantz there, Andrew slowly turned his head and looked into Chantz's eyes.

"Oh, sweet Jesus, Chantz."

Juliette's head turned and her eyes speared him.

Chantz sank against the doorpost and closed his eyes briefly. Hot relief flashed through him and the sudden need to vomit turned his flesh cold as ice. He covered his face with his hands.

"There were five of them," came Andrew's words, "wearing hoods to cover their faces. They had clubs and knives. I was upstairs . . . with Liza when I heard the racket. By the time I got down here . . ."

Chantz lowered his hands and turned his gaze back to Juliette's.

"What have they done to you, Julie?" he demanded

through his teeth, his relief and fear replaced by a mounting storm of fury. Every tender tendril of hate he had carefully contained the last years began to fray in that instant. Murder tasted sweet as syrup on his tongue and he hungered for it more than he wanted to breathe.

"What the hell have they done?" he repeated in a choked voice.

"She's fine, Chantz." Andrew stroked her hair that lay as dark red beneath her as a spreading pool of blood. "India stopped them. Had it not been for her . . ." He briefly closed his eyes and shook his head. "One minute she was roaring at them like a bull, her body planted between theirs and Juliette's, the next she was clutching her heart and dropping. I suspect she was dead before she hit the floor."

Jasper shook his head and wiped his nose with his shirtsleeve. Custis looked away and Gaius stood, tottered, plucked Jesu off India's belly, and walked off into the dark.

Chantz glanced around the room. "Where is Liza?"

"Gone." Andrew's voice thickened with anger. "They took her. I suppose back to Holly. Hell, Boris Wilcox could wear ten hoods but I'd know those damn eyes anywhere. I tried to stop them. I honestly did. I imagine they would have killed me if . . ."

He squeezed his eyes closed and turned his face away. Tears ran down his cheeks and dripped on Juliette's breast.

"One of them was my daddy, Chantz. I suspect he was as shocked to see me come thundering through that door as I was to look into his eyes and recognize my own father.

"They took Liza. Boris went up after her, dragged her

kicking and screaming down the stairs. It was so damn awful and I was so goddamn impotent to do anything but stand there and stare into my daddy's eyes. My God, Chantz, I wanted to kill him. I wanted to kill him with my bare hands."

Chantz moved across the room, refusing to look into India's dull eyes. Closer into the light he could detect pages of books ripped from their leather bindings and scattered over the floor. He eased to one knee beside Juliette who continued to watch him with her odd eyes, her body limp in Andrew's arms.

"Darlin'," he said softly, and reached for her hand. It felt cold and limp and so damn small in his a new ache started in his chest. He had never truly noticed how small she was, how fragile she felt, like a delicate marsh sparrow. Perhaps because she had never realized it herself. Perhaps because he had been so damn swept up in his lust and fear of her that he could think of nothing beyond losing himself—his priorities, his identity . . . his heart.

Gently, he took her in his arms and stood. Her face nestled against his throat as he carried her out of the room, down the corridor, and up the winding flight of stairs to the room that had once been her nursery, to the room he had fought through flames to reach, where she had bravely stood in the middle of her bed with her little arms outstretched for him.

He carried her through the shell of charred lumber and fallen rafters, to the window where moonlight spilled in a vaporish white pool on the floor. There he sat on a fallen cypress beam, Juliette in his lap, her breath falling softly upon his cheek.

Silently, they looked out at the pond that appeared as smooth and silvered as a mirror, sparkling with the reflective blooms of the water hyacinths. The night odors coiled around them: the musty decaying vegetation from the swamps, the sweet night-blooming jasmine and the wild magnolias.

His arms closing more tightly around her, Chantz rested his cheek upon her forehead, watched a night heron lift off the lightning-struck stump of the old live oak near the water's edge, recalled the night of storms and fear and how the bolt had streaked out of the sky striking the earth the moment the woman in his arms had taken her first breath of life.

"Some day," he said softly, "I'll buy you a dozen pretty swans. Big ones so you can sit on their backs and ride right off into the clouds if you want."

Her head moved slightly and he felt her look up at him, felt the first shiver of her body as she clawed her way out of her shock.

"What are you trying to say to me, Chantz?" she asked with a catch in her voice.

Chantz swallowed, took a breath, curled his fingers into her torn robin's-egg blue skirt that she had worn so proudly into town just a few hours ago.

If he hadn't been so proud and stubborn he would have marched down that damn stageplank, right down the middle of the goddamn street and gone on his knees and thanked her in front of God and all mankind for the opportunity she had offered him.

What did it matter that he was simply a means to an end?

It's all he had ever been, anyway.

"Darlin'," he heard himself say, "I'm asking you to marry me."

Silence. An eternity's worth. It beat like heat upon his face. Surely every human and animal ear within shouting distance could hear his heart slamming against his ribs.

At last, her trembling hand lifted and cupped his cheek, drew his face around. Her wonderful mouth curved, just slightly, despite the sparkle of moon-kissed tears in her eyes.

"I should have known a man like you would need to do the asking," she said.

Nineteen

 ~~~

Maxwell walked the long row of cane, a stick in one hand, his sweat-damp kerchief in another. Tylor dragged along behind him, tripping on a runner of grass that had taken deep root and was choking a slender stalk of cane that stood shoulder high to Max. With all the strength he could muster, Max sliced at the cane stalk with his stick. The stalk snapped with a spray of sugar sap over Maxwell's cheek.

"Sorry, worthless shit is what it is. All gone to hell, Tylor. All of it."

Wheeling on his son, the stick gripped hard in his white-knuckled hand, Maxwell stared into Tylor's sunburned face.

"The whole goddamn place has gone to hell. Eight of my slaves have took off. These fields are fast getting eaten up by trash grass and the other . . ."

Grabbing Tylor by the scuff of his neck, Maxwell shook him like a dog with a river rat.

"Take a good long drink of that air, Tylor. Smell it. What does it smell like, son? I'll tell you what it smells like. Smells like shit, don't it? Smells like rot and chickenshit and morass. Can't even sit on the damn gallery in the evening because the mosquitoes have grown so thick. And why have they grown so thick, Tylor?"

Tylor struggled and Max gripped him tighter, shook him harder. "I'll tell you why, Tylor. Because since Chantz has been gone and that moron Wilcox has took over the ditches haven't been cleaned. There's enough morass swamping this place to invite every goddamn mosquito in Louisiana to breed here. Listen. You hear that? That's mosquitoes, Tylor. Goddamn mosquitoes. Have a look yonder. You see that dark haze in the distance? That's mosquitoes, not a goddamn mirage. Are you willing to admit yet that you're a goddamn fool for doing what you did to Chantz?"

"I did what I had to do, Daddy." Tylor yanked loose of Maxwell's hold and backed away, rubbing the nape of his neck. "You'd have done the same," he snarled, "had it been anyone else."

He shook his head and ran one hand back through his sweaty hair. "I place the blame over this fiasco at your feet. It's your damn obsession over Belle Jarod that's brought us here. Had you not gone sailing off to France and dragging Juliette back to Holly we wouldn't be in this predicament."

Max swiped at another cane. "Cane should be standing higher than this by now. At least to the top of my head. We've got maybe two more months of growth before harvest and we both know right now is the prime growth period. If I don't get another five feet out of this cane by October you might as well kiss Holly good-bye. Goddamn flood took half of my crop as it is. As it is, I'll be lucky to inspire these lot of slaves to mill what cane we do harvest.

"Well? What have you got to say for yourself, son?"

Hands on his hips, blinking the sweat from his eyes,

Tylor stared at Max's feet. Gnats landed on his face and adhered to his skin.

"I'm saying this for the last time, Daddy. You're mixing up Chantz Boudreaux and God again. This cane would be as shitty if Chantz was here. What do you think, he goes around sprinkling fairy dust on each cane so it grows taller and sweeter? Cane is cane. This crop ain't as good as some and it's not got anything to do with Chantz Boudreaux."

"No? Well, let me tell you something in case you haven't been paying close attention the last twenty-seven of your miserable, lazy years. It's what happens in that goddamn sugarhouse that will make or break me. Chantz could take this lousy cane and squeeze every last drop of blood from it."

He shook a cane piece in Tylor's face. "Now you tell me how Boris is going to do that. He's an idiot who can't find his ass in the dark. And what about my levee? Louis doesn't know squat about building levees. Next water rise we get and this plantation is going to settle someplace out in the Gulf of Mexico."

"Next flood we get, Chantz or not, and your precious Holly House is going down the damn river. Chantz told you so himself." Tylor shoved Maxwell aside and made for his horse.

"I want Boris gone from Holly, Tylor!" Maxwell yelled after him. "The lazy pig is good for nothing but stirring up trouble."

"He's your damn overseer, you fire him!" Tylor glanced over his shoulder and grinned. "Last time I fired your overseer I got my ass whipped."

"I want him gone and I want Chantz back!"

Tylor froze.

Max moved up behind him. "Did you hear me, Tylor? You're going to Chantz and if you have to get down on your hands and knees and beg, you're going to convince him to come back."

"You can go to hell," Tylor declared coldly, his gaze fixed on his grazing horse. "Chantz would tear me in two with his bare hands if I was to go knocking on his door."

"Boris Wilcox is trouble. Louis told me that he's sniffing around the women. Not just the women, but the children, too."

Tylor's head turned and his eyes narrowed. "You're growing too damn soft. Everybody thinks so. You've drowned yourself too often in your fine bourbon so you can't think straight any longer. You haven't thought straight since you got word that Jack Broussard spattered his brains with a bullet. What happened, Daddy? Did your conscience finally get the best of you?

"If you were thinking straight, Juliette Broussard would be buried as deeply as her mother now. That's the only way you're ever going to get your hands on Belle Jarod."

"No harm is to come to Juliette, Tylor. Do you understand me?"

Tylor's mouth curled.

Maxwell swallowed and stepped closer. "You didn't have anything to do with that attack on her those nights ago, did you, son? You weren't part of that group that caused that old woman to die of fright, were you? Because if you were—"

"What do you think?" he sneered.

Tylor mounted his horse and spurred the mare toward the big house. Maxwell followed, whipping his horse to a lather with his cane stalk.

By the time he arrived at the house, Tylor had dismounted. He stood on the gallery, staring at the front door as Simon struggled with Tylor's agitated horse. Max's gaze swung wider and fixed on the big bay gelding hitched to a post.

Chantz!

Max slid out of his saddle even before his horse skidded to a stop near the stairs. He took the steps two at a time, flinging the cane stalk at Tylor's feet as he swept by him, into the house where he found Little Clara beaming and her cheek bulging and her every braid bouncing up and down as she danced on her tiptoes. From her hand spilled long ribbons of every color. Her eyes widened the moment Maxwell entered the house and she dashed off down the hallway, her skirt flapping and her braids bobbing.

"Boss Chantz be back!" the child squealed as she ran.

Max expected to find Chantz in the foyer—after all, the hired help was never allowed in the formal rooms until admitted.

But Chantz wasn't there.

Frowning, Maxwell entered his office, swept the room with a glance.

But Chantz wasn't there.

Then he moved back into the foyer and found Tylor, staring into the drawing room, his face white under blotches of sunburned skin. Maxwell walked to the open doorway and looked in.

A man stood there, before the high open windows. Tall and distinguished looking in his smart-fitted brown suit coat and trousers to match. He wore a brocade vest and a soft doe-colored cravat around his throat, cinched with a ruby broach.

He was drinking Maxwell's best bourbon. From Maxwell's finest crystal. Both of which Maxwell laid away for any dignitary who might visit.

He turned from the window and looked at Maxwell. His mouth curled and he tipped the glass slightly, as if in toast.

"Hello, Daddy." His smile widened, white teeth against bronze skin, blue eyes like hard sapphires. "What's wrong? My actually acknowledging you as my father somehow left you speechless?"

Chantz drank then regarded the bourbon. "Very nice. I often wondered how the good stuff you reserved for your peers would compare to the garbage you gave me."

"Chantz?"

"That's right, Daddy. What's wrong? Don't recognize your own son when you see him?"

Tylor shoved Maxwell aside and glared at Chantz. "Where the hell did you get that suit?"

"If it's not my own brother—"

"Shut up. What the hell are you doing in this room like you're the king of England or something? Where the hell did you get those clothes? They must have cost—"

"A gift."

Chantz's blue eyes narrowed and he took a short drink. "I resisted at first. You know me. Never was good at accepting the generosity of others. Felt it somehow lessened my manhood. I finally decided I had too damn much pride for my own good."

"Who the hell cares where he got the damn clothes," Maxwell declared as he moved further into the room. "What matters is you're back. We can sit down like grown men and discuss this sorry situation in which we find ourselves these days."

Maxwell motioned toward the side door. "We'll go to my office—"

"We'll stay right here . . . *Daddy.* I believe this is where you entertain your more distinguished guests."

Tylor coughed a deep laugh. "You're no guest, Chantz, and you sure as hell aren't distinguished, suit or no suit."

Chantz's black lashes lowered so his eyes were mere slits of dark blue as he regarded Tylor.

Maxwell cleared his throat and moved to a high-backed chair, pointed to another and watched as Chantz eased into it and crossed his legs. His fingernails were well manicured and clean and his hair fell in a rich dark wave over his brow. The light through the window reflected from the broach at this throat. The blood-red ruby winked like a flirtatious eye into Maxwell's face.

Then Max's gaze shifted to Chantz's left hand where it rested casually on the chair arm. He swallowed and focused harder. Heat rose to his cheeks and his scalp began to sweat.

"Why are you here?" Tylor demanded as he moved to Maxwell's side.

"A number of reasons." Chantz held Maxwell's gaze, not so much as glancing at Tylor.

"Bring me a drink, Tylor." Maxwell settled back in his chair.

Tylor glared at Maxwell. "Get your own damn drink. What do I look like, a slave?"

"And while you're at it, Tylor, refresh Chantz's drink as well."

Tylor's jaw went slack.

"You heard me," Maxwell said in that tone that brooked no resistance. "Get us a drink. *Now.*"

Maxwell took a steadying breath. "Heard you to be working the river, Chantz."

"I was."

"Can't see you enjoying it much. You're a cane man."

"I am."

"I'm hoping your reasons for coming here today are to ask for your job back."

"Boris Wilcox has taken my old job."

Maxwell's mouth thinned and he fisted his hands. "I won't play games with you, Chantz. Boris is an idiot."

He glanced unwillingly toward Chantz's hand again.

"We both know that if I'm going to survive this last flood I'm going to need help in getting everything I can out of that damn crop. There is also the levee. We both know soon we'll be face-to-face with that damn equinox. We get another hurricane boiling in from the Gulf and there won't be anything at all left of Holly House."

"I didn't come here to discuss cane or levees."

Chantz drank again, regarding Maxwell over the lip of his glass.

"I'll up your salary, Chantz."

"I don't want your money . . . *Daddy*."

"Then what *do* you want?"

"Louis."

Maxwell frowned.

Tylor turned from the cellarette, decanter in hand, and stared at the back of Chantz's head.

"And Rosie," Chantz added as he swirled the fine bourbon in the glass, lifted it toward the window, and studied the golden glow of the sunlight through the amber drink. "And Liza. Were you aware she's with child? I hate to think what I might do to Boris should I discover that he harmed her in any way when dragging her kicking and screaming from Belle Jarod. And there's Simon, of course. And Little Clara."

His gaze shifting again to Maxwell's, Chantz said, "I want them all. Right now. I want you to sign their papers over to me . . . and once that's done, we'll discuss the possibility of my seeing you through this upcoming harvest."

"You're insane," Tylor began, but Maxwell silenced him with a lift of one hand.

"What do you need with a lot of slaves, Chantz?"

"I don't need slaves. I fully intend to release them from their bondage. When they join us, they'll do so as free blacks."

Maxwell gripped the chair arms fiercely as he said through his teeth, "I'll repeat myself. What do you need with a lot of Negroes, slave or not?"

"To work my plantation, of course. A man can't plant and harvest cane by himself. Can he?"

"I'm not a game-playing man, Chantz. You know that. So why don't you just say what you came here to say."

"You want my help to harvest that cane or not?"

"You married her, didn't you?"

"As it is, you won't reap enough profit from that crop to see you through winter. Not with Boris spending more time in his rum than he does in the fields."

"You married Juliette."

"I want them. All of them. Rosie, Louis, and his wife, Tessa, of course. Liza. Little Clara and Simon."

Maxwell sprang and grabbed Chantz by his suit lapels. The bourbon in Chantz's glass sloshed onto Max's white shirt and the glass shattered on the floor as Maxwell heaved Chantz out of the chair. Teeth clenched and fists shaking, he stood nose-to-nose with his bastard son and searched his cold eyes.

"Answer me, damn you. You've taken her, haven't you? Juliette? Belle Jarod? You're wearing his ring, Chantz. Jack's ring."

"Yes. I married Juliette this morning."

Chantz peeled Maxwell's stiff fingers from his lapels and backed away. His voice dropped, throaty with fury. The former coolness of his mien transformed into something dark and dangerous, a tumult of emotion that electrified the air.

"You're gonna know now what it's like to watch ever'thing you ever wanted and needed sift through your

hands like Mississippi silt. Every meanness you did to me
and my mama is gonna come back to haunt you every day
for the rest of your life. You reap what you sow, Max. And
you've done nothing over the last thirty years of my life but
sow neglect and humiliation. You ruined my mama. And
you tried to ruin me. No more. I won't allow you to hurt
my dignity any longer."

Tylor fell back against the cellarette, knocking the decanters over so Maxwell's fine bourbon poured in a rich
golden stream onto the floor. He filled the room with a roar
of laughter.

"I—I don't know what's funnier," Tylor managed, gulping for air as he straightened and flung spilled bourbon
from his hands. "The look on Daddy's face or the ridiculous comment about your dignity, Chantz. You have no
dignity, for God's sake. You've just sold your dignity for the
price of a rundown, weed-infested property and a wife who
looks at you as nothing more than a workhorse. A glorified
overseer. Instead of paying you with money she's gonna
spread her legs. I don't know which of you is the bigger
whore."

Chantz didn't so much as flinch, just continued staring
into Maxwell's eyes. "Do we have a deal or not, Hollinsworth? I want those people and their papers and I want
them now. Else you and your cane and your goddamn levee
can rot into the river and good riddance."

"You're a son of a bitch, Chantz."

Chantz grinned, just a cold curl of his lips that didn't
reach his eyes. "Like father like son, *Daddy*. Don't you ever
forget that."

Liza fell into Andrew's arms and covered his unshaven
face with kisses. Together they stood in Belle's library with

the twilight sky a wide flush of melon pinks and reds and the gold flame of sun heat cast over the floor. Tears slid down Andrew's face as he pressed his lips to Liza's cheek and whispered: "God oh God, I'm so sorry. Please forgive me. I swear I won't ever leave you again, Liza."

Chantz turned away, moved out onto the gallery where Rosie, Louis, and Tessa sat. Little Clara and Simon stood amid the blackberry vines and stuffed their mouths with ripe berries.

Where was Juliette?

They all looked around as Chantz leaned against the gray column, hands buried in his pockets and his coat caught behind his wrists. Perhaps they could sense his mood better than he.

What, exactly, was his mood?

The spiteful pleasure Chantz experienced at watching the shock of his news cloud Maxwell's eyes had burned hotly, but briefly—just long enough to ride his horse to the Belle's entry and face, once again, the astronomical challenge of resurrecting a dream with little more than the sweat of his own brow to help him.

A niggling fear of failure had bothered him. Still bothered him. Along with the acid sting of Tylor's words.

And that made him angry as well. Fighting angry. This was his wedding night and all he could experience as he stood there looking out at a wall of wild growth and listening to the whippoorwills' calls was gnawing frustration. He felt suffocated by it.

No one spoke. The bewildered and shocked expressions on the Negroes' dark faces said enough. Rosie's eyes were red and swollen from crying. Tessa clutched at Louis's big arm as if she expected to plummet off the edge of the earth just any minute.

Finally, Rosie shook her head and pressed her plump hands together at her breasts. "Lawd lawd. Never thought I'd see the day I was free. Lawd have mercy. Wokes up this mo'nin fetchin' Tylor his coffee and wonderin' what I be fixin' Massa Max fo' his suppa. Now you tellin' me I gots a house yonda I can call my own and a fine plot of dirt as well—all fo' doin' nuthin' but what I done befo'."

Tessa straightened and her eyes widened. "I can be havin' a baby now, Louis. A little chile I can hold in my arms and knows for a fact he won't be wearin' no stripes on his skin from a whuppin'."

Louis shifted and turned his eyes up to Chantz's. Still, he said nothing, just curved his lips in a quivering smile that made Chantz walk away, back into the house.

Liza and Andrew were no longer in the library.

Then he heard Liza—womanly giggling from the rooms at the top of the stairs, followed by Juliette's huskier laughter.

His wife's laughter.

Andrew moved up behind him.

"I don't know about you, but I need a drink, Chantz." As Chantz looked around, Andrew lifted a champagne bottle and two glasses. "I think a toast is in order. Several of them, by the looks of you." As Chantz looked again toward the top of the stairs, Andrew grinned. "There will be time for acquainting yourselves later. I think we should talk."

Reluctantly, and with a last glance up the stairs, Chantz followed Andrew out the back door where they sat on the rotting gallery and looked out at the rows of crumbling brick houses once used as slave quarters. Beyond those rose the tall, vine-covered sugarhouse chimney and the dilapidated roofs of the storehouses. And beyond that, fifteen thousand acres begging to be planted with sugarcane.

Andrew poured them each a glass of champagne,

handed one to Chantz, and smiled into his eyes. "Here's to Belle Jarod, my friend. You'll be the envy of every man in Louisiana now."

Chantz looked down into his glass, watched the effervescent spray dance in golden bubbles over the top. "Or a laughingstock," he replied simply, then drank, hoping to swallow the tight knot of anger rising up his throat.

Andrew leaned back against the column and drank as he regarded Chantz closely. "I was hesitant to mention this, Boudreaux, but you don't exactly look like a man who was just married to the finest plantation in this or any state."

"I didn't marry this damn plantation, Drew." He looked into Andrew's dark eyes and said more forcefully, "I married Juliette."

"One and the same, Chantz." Andrew stretched his long legs out and crossed them at the ankles. "Remember when you and I would boat down the river at night, sit there in the dark, and look up top of that *cyprière* and stare at the Belle. She shone in the night like a star cluster. We'd sit for hours trading tales about what we'd do if the Belle were ours. Now she's yours and you look like a dying calf in a hailstorm."

They looked out over the vast land that would have to be turned over completely by January if they had any hope of harvesting in October. The impossibility of it closed around Chantz's throat. What would happen when the reality sat in? Juliette believed him capable of working miracles—of saving her father's dream. What would happen when she discovered that he was just as human as the next man?

"We're a right pair, aren't we?" Andrew shook his head and set his glass aside. "I've turned my back on my father for his involvement with paddy rollers. While I can't blame him completely for what happened to India, I cannot simply ignore the fact that he would be involved with the virtual crucifixion of individuals who are attempting to lessen the plight of a group of people. The irony of it is, I haven't got a damn thing I can offer Liza now. Except me."

"That's enough." Chantz looked at his friend askance. "You're a fortunate man, Drew. Liza loves you very much."

"I declare I detect a thread of envy in your voice."

Chantz shrugged, sipped his champagne before saying, "Have I thanked you yet for the suit and broach?"

"Several times."

"And for standing up with me?"

"Yes."

"A shame my mother refused to join us."

"Emmaline is stubborn. You know that. Regardless of her anger over this marriage and her feeling that you've been disloyal and are headed for a life of hell . . ." He laughed. "She'll come around because she loves you. Give her time, Chantz."

They sat in silence while the last threads of gray twilight succumbed to darkness. One by one the stars came out, twinkling like a breath-blown candle flame. Occasionally murmurs of conversation drifted to them from the upstairs windows and the ache in Chantz's body expanded.

Jasper, Custis, and Gaius wandered up from the fields, looking tired and sad and lost without India. Jesu perched on Gaius's shoulder, not having made so much as a squawk since their laying India in the ground.

Eventually they were joined by the others, all who appeared as lost as India's family. The idea occurred to Chantz that the people clustered together like survivors adrift on a raft had never been off Holly Plantation but for the occasional jaunt into town when Maxwell was feeling particularly generous.

Little Clara climbed on Chantz's lap and smiled into his eyes, her own twinkling like bright, star-kissed buttons.

"Granny say it time fo' you t'be makin' a baby with Juliette."

Chantz lifted his eyebrows. "Your granny talks too much."

"My granny say you done set us free. That I ain't gots to fetch Massa Tylor's rum no mo' or rub his stanky old feet. Is that a fact or is you just pullin' my leg agin?"

"It's true, Little Clara. No more rubbing Tylor's feet."

"You still gonna bring me ho'hound, ain't you?"

"I am." Chantz nodded. "Every day, I promise."

Little Clara looked at Simon where he stood in the dark, his bullfrog tucked under his arm. "You heah dat, Simon? No mo' stanky feet and ho'hound too. I 'spect life can't get much better'n dat."

Rosie lumbered by and swatted at Clara.

"Git on, now. You still gots my hand on yo' backside if'n you don't watch out. Lawd, what is gonna become of that chile, I jes don't know."

Little Clara squirmed on Chantz's lap until she could take his face between her little hands. Looking at him intensely, she said, "I gonna say a special praya fo' you t'night, Boss Chantz. Gonna tell God he betta be right nice fo' ya now and bring ya lotta perty young'uns with Juliette, and cane what reach right up to d'sky so high angels be dancin' on 'em. Can ya imagine dat, Boss Chantz? Angels dancin' on each and ever' cane stalk, sweet as d'sugar fairies Miss Julie tell me about."

"Sugar fairies?" He grinned.

"What makes yo' cane so sweet. 'Cause ya got d'sugar fairies on ya shouldas. Miss Julie say so."

Liza moved out of the house. "I 'spect you all best git on now and stop usin' up Chantz's weddin' night. Man fit to be tied, I imagine. If he ain't he will be soon enough. Soon as he gets a look at his new wife."

Her smile wide, Liza moved against Chantz as he stood. She nestled her face into his neck and sighed.

"Felt my baby move today," she said softly. "Right after you come and tell me I'm a free woman. I swear she be flutterin' in happiness."

He kissed the top of her head and looked into Andrew's eyes. Chantz wondered if he looked that sick in love when he watched Juliette. God, God, what a woman could do to a man . . .

Liza pulled back. "She waitin' on you, Chantz. Got her bathed and dusted with sweet-smellin' powder. She got magnolia blossoms in her hair. We done plumped up that old mattress with fresh moss and goose down. Gonna feel like you're floatin' on a cloud."

She turned and reached for Andrew's hand. They walked down the stairs together, toward the old shanty they would share for this night only. Tomorrow they would move into the spare room at the top of the stairs. Tomorrow Andrew Buley would start to work for Chantz Boudreaux.

It all felt crazy, as if the world had gone topsy-turvy.

With his hands in his trouser pockets, Chantz looked off into the dark. In the flood of moonlight he could almost imagine that the reflection of silver in the distance was the moon glancing off the endless rows of high, sweet cane.

This time next year.

He sat again on the stair and reached for his glass of champagne. Elbows on his knees, his long hard fingers gently tracing the rim of the glass, he watched the dance of fireflies and listened to the whir of crickets. The ring on his finger felt heavy and cold. The heart in his chest ached. Ached so badly he could hardly breathe. Why?

Why?

Chantz Boudreaux—bastard who this time yesterday didn't have a pot to pee in—had married the most beautiful woman in Louisiana. He now owned the jewel of the Mississippi. Soon folks would be moving off the *banquettes* and doffing their hats in respect when he walked by. It was going to be *Mister* Boudreaux from now on.

No more goddamn infested cornmeal.

Great God, he had ached for Juliette with every bone and muscle in his body the last weeks. He'd thought of nothing but losing himself in her scent, in her body. The memory of her heat in his hand had driven him mindless—walking his floor night after night, wrenching him from his dreams with his body so full and hard between his legs he'd groaned in pain.

Now here he sat in the dark on his wedding night, sweat oozing from his pores, his body so tight he was afraid he'd never make it up the stairs to hold her, and he could think of nothing but Tylor's words:

"You've just sold your dignity for the price of a rundown, weed-infested property and a wife who looks at you as nothing more than a workhorse. A glorified overseer. Instead of paying you with money she's gonna spread her legs. I don't know which of you is the bigger whore."

A sharp pain bit his fingers.

He looked down, at the broken glass stem, snapped in two by his sudden fierce grip of anger. Blood beaded on his flesh—black in the moonlight against his palm, spreading like thick molasses.

Hurling the glass into the dark, Chantz stood, moved into the house where the moonlight poured through the roof and onto the stairs. Slowly, he ascended. The bourbon and champagne beat at his skull.

Convince yourself that you care for nothing but the cane.

That your heart hasn't chipped a little each time you look at her.

That it doesn't matter that she doesn't really love you. That she may never really love you. That her greatest burning desire is also for the cane.

The goddamn cane.

A wild fire.

A tempest.

A siren's song.

Love had nothing to do with it. Jack knew it. Didn't matter.

Chantz knew it.

Shouldn't matter.

He removed his coat, carefully tossed it over the banister as he climbed, slowly. Then his vest, only then realizing as it slid off his shoulders how badly he had sweat in it. Though the air was warm, it chilled his damp skin, making his entire body quiver. He paused, looked up through the exposed rafters at the heavy moon, and tried to even his breathing.

Merciful Mary, he hurt.

Leaning against the banister, gritting his teeth, he ran his hand down the ridge in his pants. His eyes rolled shut. The pressure of the buttons bit into his sensitive flesh sending sharp pain through him.

Again, he climbed.

The hint of magnolia drifted to him. It seeped into his blood like fire.

The bedroom door was ajar. Quietly, he let himself in, stood for a moment in the threshold, doing his best to ignore the rising throb in his loins, to ignore Tylor's words that kept rapping rapping rapping at his brain, at his heart, at his damn pride.

The moon through the window painted the bare floor and walls in silvery splashes and shadows. Her scent washed over him in a wave of floral and musky sweetness.

He found her at last, lying on the mattress.

Reaching for his shirt buttons, he silently crossed the room, to the bed where she lay with her head on a down pillow, her eyes closed. Her skin looked milky soft in the moonlight. Her hair sprayed over the bed like a dark copper fire. There were magnolia petals scattered around her head.

Her arms and shoulders were bare. Only the sheet tossed over her body shielded her from his eyes that suddenly ached to absorb her every lovely nuance. Still, the thin linen molded to every curve and peak, accentuating her most intimate places—highlights and shadows.

With the heat rising in his body, he stooped and, with trembling hand, reached for the sheet, eased it down her body, exposing her high, proud breasts with their dusky nipples, down, beyond her tiny waist, down, revealing the downy mound that appeared mauve in the shimmering light.

A groan sounded in his throat. His fingers curled into fists.

If only . . .

If only she would open her eyes and see him as something special. Her husband. No damn overseer. No damn means to an end. Only a man who, since the moment he dragged her out of that river, would happily offer his heart in his hand if she would but cherish it. Christ, he had nothing else to give her, after all.

Had Chantz Boudreaux actually become one of the very men he had despised for their inability to deny a woman?

What the hell had happened to him?

Cane had been his passion. Planting it. Growing it. Harvesting every last tall green stalk.

Now he seemed little more than a ghost, as if he were slowly becoming a mist of what he had been—obstinate, willful, and so full of bitterness his life had become a twisted irony.

It was that bitterness that bit at him still, fighting to take control. To remind him that, once again, he was nothing and she was . . . everything.

Everything.

Standing, he removed his clothes slowly, piece by piece. Let them fall where they may as he watched her sleep. Her cheeks still bore the bruises of the attack those nights before. Even as she drifted in her light dreams, her mien appeared drawn with her fear and despair over India's death.

Oh, she had grieved over the loss of her friend. She blamed herself, of course. Had she not involved herself in teaching the darkies how to read . . .

She stirred, turned her head so the moonlight through the window found her face. The long curve of her lashes painted shadows upon her skin.

A shiver of emotion passed through Chantz, a sudden swelling of ecstasy and pain.

Naked, he carefully slid onto the mattress beside her. Motionless, his body heavy and full, he refrained from touching her. The need felt too great. His every nerve felt on fire, the heat centering between his legs and his brain.

Instead, he allowed his gaze to absorb her, half wanting her to open her eyes, half praying she wouldn't. Not yet. He wanted the moment to last an eternity.

The minutes ticked by. Perhaps an hour.

He reached for her, hands brushing her flesh, lightly tracing her moist lips that parted so her warm breath and sigh touched his fingertips. Down, he moved, tracing the curve of her throat, farther, to cup the fullness of her breasts and the peaks that hardened at his caress.

Lowering his head, he pressed his lips against hers— briefly, more like a flutter of a hummingbird's wing, fast as the beating of his own heart. "Sweet God," he murmured, his eyes drifting closed. "I must be dreaming, darlin'. Ever'time I look at this ring on my hand ... ever'time I reach for you and you don't dissolve into air. Have you any idea how many nights I've lain in my bed imagining this and aching so damn bad because I never believed it would happen?"

She sighed. Her lips curled. Still, however, she did not open her eyes, as if she were playing at being asleep now.

Sliding lower, he took the rose-colored nipples between his lips, sucked them gently, first one then the other, nuzzled them with his tongue, round and round until the peaks became hard as pebbles and her scent rose up to inflame him.

Closer, so his thigh nestled against the curve of her hip. His hard, erect body lay upon her leg, and he felt the first ripple of excitement pass through her. Her breathing quickened. Her body warmed.

"Chantz," she murmured so softly he barely heard her. "Husband."

She moved her body toward his and her arms came up around him. Suddenly her wide eyes full of moonlight and sleep were looking up into his. He felt her thighs shift, opening, inviting, quivering. His fingers tangled in the triangle of hair at the cleft of her thighs, then slid further, into the hot moist soft-as-silk folds, the memory of which had driven him mindless.

Mindless.

The abyss was there, waiting, deep and dark and bottomless. As his fingers sank into the very hot heart of her it seemed in that moment that he had leaped from a precipice, down through the eye of a storm of senses and emotions that whirled and beat at him.

Her legs parted wide, and as he shifted he accomplished the breach with an easy thrust that was sublime. She gasped. Her fingers sank into the flesh of his back as he joined her, hot steel within hotter silk, a cocoon of heat wrapped so tightly around him he wouldn't dare move. Didn't dare breathe.

Another push; her body resisted. Again, gently, though the hunger felt unbearable, more unbearable than the whip cutting into his back. More unbearable than looking into his father's eyes for the last thirty years and knowing that he didn't matter—would never matter.

Burying his face in her hair, he drank in the perfume of magnolias.

The heat mounted.

She moved against him, taking him in, deeper, tilting her pelvis up, lifting her legs high around his waist until she had all of him, until her mound ground against his. Soft, urgent words touched his ear, "My love. My life. My husband. All that I am and all that I have is yours."

Sliding his hands into her hair, he parted his lips over hers, drank her breath, her life, allowed the frantic wing beats of need to at last overtake him.

"Juliette. Juliette. God, how I've burned for you."

They moved, together, flesh against flesh, heartbeat

against heartbeat, until the passion for her consumed him and he lifted heavenward, helpless to stop the fall when it came, a knife tearing, letting his life and blood—the death, the little death. He would die in her arms . . .

"I would die before I would lose you," he groaned. "For any reason."

Twenty

❧

The whistle and shouts of men sat Juliette straight up in bed, her heart racing in fear as the memory of that dreadful and horrifying night only the week before came winging at her.

Little Clara burst through the doorway, cheek bulging with ho'hound and eyes round as coins. Her hair bobbed like springs with the multitude of ribbons Juliette had given her.

Naked still, Juliette snatched up the sheet to cover herself as Little Clara, eyes dancing with excitement and her smile stretching from ear to ear, shouted, "Best ya come quick. Folk heah with hosses and mules and stuff piled high in wagons."

From below came Rosie's voice, snapping out orders to Jasper and Custis. Suddenly Jesu let out a kadoodle that resounded through the house and made Rosie yell: "Lawd have mercy, be gittin' that damn bird outta this house. Ain't no place for a damn chicken I be eatin' for suppa if'n you ain't careful! Out!"

"Where are Chantz and Andrew?" Juliette asked Little Clara.

"They done gone to d'fields fo' day break. Louis, too. Won't be back, I 'spect, 'til suppa."

Jesu squawked again and Rosie let out another curse that was followed by Gaius whooping and Jasper responding with a burst of frantic island babble.

As Little Clara dashed from the room, Juliette quickly pulled on her dress and, with hair wild and tumbling over her shoulders, ran barefoot down the stairs.

A group of men stood in the foyer, talking among themselves and pointing to the fallen rafters and the charred walls.

She froze as they looked around. Faces somber, they regarded her in silence.

Then Baxter elbowed his way through the wall of men and adjusted his glasses as he smiled at her and extended a handful of peppermint sticks. "Madame Boudreaux. Do you remember me?"

"Yes." She nodded and eased down the stairs, her gaze still moving from face to watchful face, alert for any hint of animosity. She reached for the candy, a smile touching her lips.

"We've brought a few supplies—"

"I didn't order supplies."

"Necessary items. Lumber. Hammers. Saws. Nails. Pots and pans."

Her cheeks warmed. "But I haven't any—"

"All gifts, of course. For your housewarming. Wedding gifts."

"From—?"

"Friends. Of Chantz. And of your parents, of course. As you recall, they were highly regarded in Baton Rouge. They did many of us a favor here and there. As you'll soon learn, folks in Baton Rouge rarely forget a kindness."

A man stepped forward, broad of shoulder and with a wild thatch of yellow hair. Rolling his old hat in his hand, he averted his eyes when he spoke.

"Chantz done me a good turn back when my wife took sick. Rode two hour ever day in the dead of winter to work my job at the mills so I can stay with my wife who done passed on now, God rest her soul."

"Helped me rebuild when the fires took most ever'thing I own year before last," another man said.

Baxter nodded and adjusted his glasses on his nose. "Fact is, Mrs. Boudreaux, your mama loaned me money when I fell behind with the bank. No telling where I would be now if it hadn't been for her generosity. All of us owe something to your parents or Chantz. This is our way of saying thank you to you both."

Emotion choking off her words, Juliette sat down on the step, watched as the men dispersed through the house.

Liza moved up the stairs and sat down beside her, slid her arm around Juliette's shoulder and hugged her tightly. "Like a dream, ain't it? A real sweet dream."

"If this is a dream, Liza, I don't ever want to wake up."

"It only gonna get better for us both. You gots Chantz and the Belle. I gots Andrew and a baby growin' inside me. Ain't love wonderful?"

Liza cocked her head to one side and studied Juliette's profile. "You awful quiet."

Juliette looked into her friend's dark eyes. "It's Chantz, Liza. I fear he isn't happy."

"Chantz? Not happy? Lord, girl, you shoulda seen him go outta this house bright and early this mornin' whistlin' like a mockin'bird. Don't think I ever seen that man smile so big."

Grasping Liza's hands in hers, Juliette gripped them fiercely. "I want to make him happy, Liza. I'll do anything to make him happy, to make him . . ."

She looked away.

"To make him what, Julie?"

"Love me."

Liza sat straighter, curled her dark fingers around Juliette's. "Love you? Why, Juliette, that man loves you so much—"

"He loves Belle Jarod. He loves sugarcane. He burns for both. I want him to burn for me, Liza."

Liza grinned. "You tellin' me he wasn't burnin' for you last night?"

Averting her gaze, her cheeks warming, Juliette smiled. The memory of those hours in his arms—her body learning passion and her heart wrapped up with a fulfillment she had never known—all flurried in her mind like gossamer butterflies.

"I suppose he burned a little." Her smiled widened.

She did not recognize the man at first. The sun cast a glare over the freshly scythed grounds of scattered, wilting sunflowers and into Juliette's eyes, forcing her to lift her hand and cup it over her brow. Her step froze while around her the cicada calls pulsed like the summer's heartbeat and heat rose from the earth to penetrate the thin soles of her kid slippers.

"Tylor." She drew in a breath to steady her nerves. "I don't recall inviting you to Belle Jarod."

"I felt it my duty to drop by on my way to New Orleans and offer my well wishes to the happy couple."

"Chantz won't be pleased that you're here. I would leave immediately if I were you."

"I'm not afraid of Chantz, Juliette. Hell, every man in this parish is aware that you've castrated him. He's about as lethal as a toothless rattlesnake now."

"He'd just as soon kill you as look at you, Tylor. And so would I, for that matter."

She swept by him, clutching the basket of wild onions and yams and clutch of sunflowers she had bundled together with a ribbon from her hair.

He fell in behind her, walked right on her heels.

"No need for you to stay so snippy. It's not like I'm any threat to you any longer. Me and Daddy want to make peace. We're neighbors now."

"You are and will always be my enemy, Tylor, and you'll never be welcome at Belle Jarod. Neither will your father."

She bounded up the back steps and entered the house. The sounds of the hammering and sawing and the men's jovial laughter were like music to her ears—sweet enough to extinguish somewhat her outrage at finding Tylor Hollinsworth on Belle soil.

Refocusing her thoughts, she imagined Chantz's face when he got home, tired and hot and aching from work to discover these friends reshaping his home. Already the pungent aroma of fresh lumber sweetened the air. Already many of the trees between the house and the river had been felled. Her heart beat double-time as she ran onto the front gallery and swept her gaze over the wide, long alley that had once been paved with crushed oyster shells.

With a snap and crack the final tree standing between her and the river slammed to the earth. Before her glistened the wide Mississippi. A pair of boats passing in that moment let out a whistle and a ring of their bells.

Odd that it wasn't her father she thought of in that moment, but her mother. How Maureen would have thrilled over this accomplishment—as meager as it seemed.

Tylor moved up beside her, stood at her shoulder, and looked down the shadowed alley.

"I'll be damned," he remarked softly, more to himself than to her. "As a betting man, I'd almost consider wagering on your success at rebuilding Belle Jarod." His mouth curled as he looked at her. "But regardless of what my father thinks, I'm not an idiot. You can fell trees for the next year and every man in Louisiana can line up to repay Chantz for past favors—rebuild that roof and those walls and shore up that old sugar mill with mortar and bricks—but unless you've got something to mill, that being sugarcane, of course, you're never going to make it, Juliette."

"We'll make it."

"Took your daddy nearly two hundred slaves to keep this place up. You expect to do it with a half-dozen?"

"We'll do it, if for no other reason than to spite you and your father."

"You never struck me as a spiritual woman, Juliette."

"And what is that supposed to mean?"

"It means only a miracle is gonna help you resurrect this place. The last time I checked, God didn't necessarily favor the lascivious."

Turning her head, she looked at him squarely and said in a soft, threatening tone, "You're welcome to leave any time, Tylor."

Reentering the house, Juliette paused to watch several men winch a rafter up high.

"I take it that Chantz isn't here," Tylor said.

"Obviously or you would have already been escorted off Belle by the scruff of your neck."

"I would think his priorities would be on his pretty new wife, at least for a few days. Then again, it's not like this is a love match, right? Chantz's priorities are, and always will be, sugarcane."

She exited the back again, her stride lengthening. A machete sat propped against a column. Sweeping it up as she descended the steps, she marched toward the copse of elderberry bushes that had overgrown what once had been an herb garden.

Little Clara and Simon were to have begun the task of clearing the plot. They were nowhere to be seen, alas, and Liza and Rosie and Tessa were down at the kitchen scrubbing the floors and walls and preparing the evening meal. The smell of boiling pork and onions made her mouth water, despite her mounting irritation at Tylor.

Where were Little Clara and Simon?

Surely Chantz and Andrew and Louis would be home directly. Suddenly she wanted them home—desperately. She wanted Tylor gone. His presence on Belle soil exhumed something dark and frightening deep inside her and she clutched at the *arrêt* hanging from her neck.

Liza's and Rosie's laughter brushed her ear and she looked toward the kitchen, thought of joining them, then saw Tylor from the corner of her eye—noted his smugness, as if he realized that his existence infuriated and disgusted her and took pleasure in it. Caution stiffened her spine. Instinct told her there was more to his motivations than simply offering neighborly well wishes.

"What do you want?" she demanded, fingers wrapping more tightly around the machete. "Tell me and leave, Tylor. You're not welcome here. Ever."

"You really should try to put the past behind you, sister. We're family now."

"What do you mean, we're family?" she fired back. "You're no family of mine, Tylor Hollinsworth, and you never will be."

His eyebrows rose and his smile stretched. "So, he obviously hasn't broken the news to you yet."

Slowly, she turned to face him. There was something in his mien that sent dread through her chest.

"We're brothers," his lips said as his eyes—frigid as ice, yet mocking—bored into her, into her heart that felt in that instant as if it was being twisted from her chest.

She looked into his eyes—his blue eyes and the rich wave of hair spilling over his brow, not so dark as Chantz's but with the same wild lushness.

"Liar," she heard herself say, her reasoning arguing with bare-teeth fury at the horrifying truth that slowly materialized before her.

Dear God, how could she have missed it?

"You've married a Hollinsworth after all, Juliette. Were something to happen to Chantz . . ." His smiled flattened. "Or if something were to happen to you both . . . who do you think will inherit Belle Jarod?"

Chantz looked from face to face, Liza's pinched and her eyes red and Rosie with her brown lips pressed as she stirred the big pot of beans over the low embers. He should have known something was amiss the moment Rosie allowed him into her newly scrubbed kitchen without having washed the day's sweat and grime from his body. With the heat and steam of the hot corn bread oozing between his fingers, he felt the first wave of fury roll through him as the import and impact of Rosie's words sank in.

Tylor Hollinsworth. *Here.* At Belle Jarod.

As Chantz stepped from the kitchen, he flung the bread

as hard as he could to the ground. Dusk hovered. Fireflies danced. He hardly glanced toward the scattering of lumber and tools around and in the house as he moved through the house to the stairs and paused.

"Juliette!" he yelled, and a flurry of grassets lifted off a new rafter overhead and rose in a dark cloud into the gray sky.

No response.

Slowly, he climbed.

She would feel betrayed, of course. She would believe that he had intentionally misled her.

Of course he should have told her even before they took their vows. Told her that he was Maxwell's bastard son. He should have assured her that there were no ulterior motives for his marrying her. That Max Hollinsworth had never acknowledged him and never would . . .

But he should have known Max would have the last laugh. He should have seen it coming. If for no other reason than pure revenge on Max's part.

Juliette was not in their bedroom. He found her in the nursery, sitting before the window overlooking the pond that glittered gold in the last rays of daylight.

"Juliette?" he called softly.

"Last night," she said, her back straight and her hair a copper curtain that pooled around her hips on the floor. There were strands of dying honeysuckle surrounding her, fallen from the old rafters. "While you were sleeping, I left our bed and came here, sat right here in the moonlight as I must have done as a child, and gazed out at the lake watching the fireflies dance. The water was so smooth and mirrorlike their bursts of light reflected from the water's surface. I imagined that one day our own son or daughter would sit here looking out at the pond and the swans you promised to buy me. I prayed very hard that you put a baby in me. I don't think I've ever prayed so hard for anything . . . until now.

"Now I'm praying that Tylor was just being mean again. I'm praying that Tylor was lying to me about you, Chantz. That you're not Maxwell's son."

He eased down to one knee beside her. Tears streaked her face.

"Don't touch me," she said calmly, without looking at him. "If you're Maxwell's son, you won't ever touch me again."

"Julie . . ." He lifted his hand to touch her hair—her glorious hair that had slid over his body last night like fragrant silken water, drowning his senses. But she moved away, just slightly, and he curled his hand into a fist. "What am I to say, *chère?* How do I acknowledge a father who won't acknowledge me?"

Her head turned and her big eyes were anguished and angry. "So this is your revenge? *I* am your revenge? That's all?"

"No. No." He shook his head. "No." Still, those eyes pierced him, to the hard core of him where those dark, turbulent emotions roiled, all the anger and hate that had festered over the years. He looked away, knowing she saw them, knowing it would do no good to deny them.

"How do I make you understand, Juliette? Maxwell is nothing to me."

"He's your father."

"Since when?" His voice cracked with anger. "Since I married you, that's when. I made the choice between you and Maxwell the day I made love to you." He raked one hand through his hair, hardly believing the torn words he could hear coming from his own mouth—so choked with emotion he could hardly speak.

Standing, he began to pace. Something monstrous tore

at his insides, a rage that slashed at him like knives. And helplessness. Not just that, a need to murder. Maxwell, the son of a bitch, even now would not allow him the smallest thread of contentment.

He paced up and down the room, glancing toward Juliette, her silence growing deeper with every passing minute, the air colder, the night sounds a cacophony that became crucifyingly loud as his each raw nerve inflamed with his mounting fury.

Finally standing over her, glaring down on the top of her head, he said, "You want the truth, Juliette? Hell, yes, there is a part of me that wanted to shove this marriage down Max's throat. I wanted it to choke him. I needed him to feel it all the way to his gut. I wanted the reality to grow there like a goddamn cancer. His bastard son whom he would never acknowledge, his own flesh and blood whom he treated little better than dirt, had taken from him the only thing other than Maureen Jarod that he every truly loved."

Dropping to one knee again, he grabbed her shoulders in both his hard, soiled, and bleeding hands and shook her, said through his teeth, "Damn you, listen to me. More than I ever ached to make Maxwell suffer, I ached for you. More than I gave a damn about my dignity, I ached for you. Max Hollinsworth can burn in Hell, Juliette. Tell me you believe me, Julie." He shook her again. "Tell me you won't let him destroy us. Because if you do, darlin', he wins. The bastard will have stripped me of every dream I ever clung to."

Tears rose to her eyes again and her lower lip trembled. "If I thought you truly cared for me—"

"Care?" His fingers tightened so hard he felt her flinch. "I love you, Juliette. Don't you know that? More than I ever wanted my father's love and respect, more than I want to see Belle Jarod thrive, I want you to love me, too."

The pain and anger that had marred her brow softened as she looked into his eyes.

The shouts rose up, causing the night herons along the pond to lift with sharp wing beats that sounded like muffled gun shots. Before Chantz could stand and turn for the door, footsteps banged up the stairs and down the hallway. Tessa staggered into the room, gulped through sobs as she clutched at her skirts.

As Juliette scrambled to her feet, Chantz crossed the room and took Louis's wife by her shoulders. "What's happened?" he demanded.

She babbled incoherently and pointed toward the stairs. Without looking back at Juliette, Chantz struck off down the staircase, his mind scattering with reasons for the woman's hysteria, his thoughts coming back to the previous week's attack—where were Andrew and Louis? How would he fight off a mob were they to confront him?

A group of men stood in the foyer, their faces somber, their eyes turned up to Chantz as his step slowed. Andrew turned to look up at him. His face appeared colorless.

"What the hell—"

"It's official," Andrew said, and the words seemed to vibrate along the rafters like a death knell.

Juliette joined Chantz on the stairs. He reached for her, took her hand, and drew her close against him—unable to hold her close enough in that moment. Some gut deep and frightening instinct told him that the news was not good— what he and everyone else had feared had at long last come to fruition.

Andrew passed one hand over his eyes and appeared to sway. His voice thick, he said, "No doubt about it now, the fever has taken hold of New Orleans. But that's not the worst of it . . ." Turning his eyes back to Chantz's, he said, "There's been an outbreak just south of here."

Chantz moved slowly down the stairs, his gaze never leaving Drew's eyes. "How far, Drew?"

"Ten miles."

"Ten . . . Jesus, Drew, that's near your father's . . ." Chantz swallowed as he watched Andrew turn away. "Not your family," he finally said.

"My parents. Both of them. Phyllis is with them. She isn't sick. Yet. But I've got to go to them—"

"No!" Liza stepped out of the shadows, her eyes wild with fear. Chantz moved into her path, took her in his arms, though she struggled then buried her face against his shoulder. Her body shook in an effort to contain her emotions.

A man stepped from the group. "We're closing the roads just south of Baton Rouge. We need volunteers to stand them, make certain nobody comes or goes beyond those points. Chantz, we need your help. I know you're just married and all—" He glanced toward Juliette as she carefully moved down the stairs, her face pale as Andrew's. "But if we don't quarantine the area we'll all be in a world of hurt. That damn fever take hold here and there won't be a family left standing."

"How bad is it?" Chantz asked, fearing the answer.

"The last three days have seen over five hundred people die. It's gone out of the river district like a brush fire. Folks are scattering for their lives and we've been forced to send out posses to stop them before it's spread over all of Louisiana." The man released a bone-weary sigh and turned his sad eyes toward Juliette. "I won't lie to you. It's a bad one. Promises to be the worst in twenty years the way it's traveling. I suspect you'll be gone awhile . . ."

The words faded as Chantz looked into his wife's eyes,

and for a moment he attempted to remain detached of emotion—of the dread that rose up in his chest in a horrible heat, that made his entire body wet and clammy, like that instant he had looked up through the water into Tylor's cold and calculating face—just the moment that the bull gator slammed his mouth down on Chantz's leg.

Damned fate.

The moon filled the bedroom with a radiance that painted their bodies with shadows and highlights. Juliette, her face turned toward the window to hide the fresh tears in her eyes, tried to breathe as evenly as possible, though her heart felt shattered and her body soulless. She had not experienced such despair since getting word of her father's death.

"It isn't fair," she whispered to the silence.

Liza's weeping floated through the night, a cry of loss. Andrew was gone, and though his leaving had been quiet and there had been promises that he would return as soon as possible, the fear rang as brightly as bells. If Andrew's family had been stricken by the fever, the chances of his returning to Belle Jarod were slim.

Finally, she rolled again to Chantz, who lay on his back, staring at the ceiling. She drew him to her with a kind of desperate urgency, melting her body against his as his arms slid around her and his body into her. Closing her eyes, she imagined him as he had been the day before, dressed in the suit that Andrew had given him, a nervous bridegroom stumbling over their vows and making her cry out of happiness. She imagined his surprise when she pulled out her father's ring to slide it on his finger. She recalled her own pleasure as he'd produced the tiny silver band he had purchased from Baxter that morning . . .

Then she thought of nothing but the beauteous glow of

love he inspired in her body, in her soul, the mindless pleasure that lifted her up beyond the high rafters, beyond the soaring tree-tops where the night birds glided against the stars. And when he cried out her name, when the cataclysm shook him, quivering and groaning, she reached for his face and took it between her hands, looked into his eyes that shimmered with tears.

"I love you," she told him. "You believe me, don't you? That I love you? Tell me that you do, Chantz. Promise me that you know that I need you, and want you, and desire you more than all the cane fields in all the world. More than my father desired wealth, and my mother love. More than I desire to breathe . . ."

He said nothing, just looked into her eyes and reached for her.

"No!" she declared with an edge of raw anger. "You must swear it. Swear that you believe me. Promise me that you do. Promise me that you'll remember that while you're away from me. That I'm waiting for you, Chantz. And I'll wait forever, if I must."

"I believe you, Julie," he finally said, his voice deep and broken, his eyes burning with relief . . . and gratitude.

Stretching her body against his, she laid her head on the pillow beside his and stroked his cheek and searched his face. Yet, the desperation remained. She listened to Liza's soft weeping, knowing tomorrow that she, too, would pace and worry, knowing that those who came face-to-face with the horrible yellow plague rarely lived to tell about it. Even as they lay there in the night shadows, listening to the occasional hoot of the owls and the constant high-low trill of the whippoorwills, they felt the night compress as if the monster loomed. As if its foul fingers were sliding silently and malignantly around them.

At long last, her eyes drifted closed, and she allowed her mind to slip into the dark, to dream of the man who had saved her from the fire, the man who held her now, his arms once again her sanctuary.

But when she awoke in the morning, the bed beside her was empty, and, turning her face into his pillow, she sobbed.

Twenty-One

She tripped down the gallery steps and ran hard down the old path, on and on until the path gave way to weeds and bramble that tore at her meager skirts and shins, beyond the crumbling old shanties and storehouses and liveries, beyond the sugar mill virtually lost under the tangle of wild blackberry and honeysuckle vines.

On and on and on, she ran until the breath burned like fire in her lungs. On until the wild growth gave way to a clearing on a hill with a solitary ancient oak whose twisted limbs spread like some palatial emerald roof overhead. And there, rising from the earth, a blur of white amid the shadows, was a carved marble angel, naked, with cascading hair and her wings outstretched. She overlooked the valley like a goddess.

MAUREEN JAROD BROUSSARD
1817–1837
WHOM THE GODS LOVE DIES YOUNG

Juliette approached the high angel, touched her finger-tips lightly to the smooth, hard planes, traced the deep etchings in the feathered wings and the coils of her hair tips—a wild array of wind-tossed curls that draped over one naked breast like a toga. It was her own face, her own eyes and lips lifted toward the heavens.

No, Maureen's face, caught in its youthful eternal beauty.

A month ago, she might have fled in disgust.

Instead, she sank upon the blanket of close-cropped grass and wild primroses, her cheek pressed against the earth as she curled her legs up under her skirt. Dear merciful God, she felt tired.

"Mama, what shall I do now?" she asked softly. "How will we survive? What will I do if Chantz never comes home again?" She squeezed her eyes closed and the pain swelled in her chest. *Dear God, let him come home again.*

She drifted.

Gliding through the tall drifts of marsh cattails and top-heavy sunflowers rode a woman on a tall white horse, her hair a blaze of banners behind her. Closer and closer she came until it seemed that the ground thundered with the hoof falls and the wind groaned in a rush of noise like a thousand storm clouds colliding.

"Mama?" she cried, watching herself—a child—raising her little arms up to the advancing steed, a sense of jubilance lifting her tiny feet from the earth as if she were flying.

"Lady? Lady, you awright?"

Juliette opened her eyes and blinked away her tears.

A grizzled face with a long white beard and bushy eyebrows peered down at Juliette. She thought briefly that she had died and gone straight to heaven. How else could she explain the images of her mother—now this face, ancient as time immortal with kindly eyes and lips, what she could see of them, tipped up in a smile?

Except God's breath wouldn't smell as if something had crawled in his craw and died. Nor would his body reek with so sour an odor she felt her stomach roll.

Scrambling to her feet, Juliette backed away, stopping short as the angel's toe jabbed into the small of her back. Beyond the man materialized others, all moving slowly through the morning heat, through the knee-high grass, clothes in tatters and filthy. Children followed, hanging on their parents' skirttails, hollow-eyed and young faces streaked with river muck. They all stared back at Juliette with equal curiosity and suspicion as they looked first at her, then up at the angel, then back at her.

Whispers scattered through the groups, turning their expressions all the more somber.

"Who are you?" she finally demanded. "What are you doing on Belle Jarod?"

The old man pointed toward the river. "Been yonda campin' now on a month, I reckon. Come up from N'awlins way. Got out before the fever took hold. Before folks started dyin' like flies. Be lookin' for work."

Juliette frowned and glanced over the crowd, now more than two dozen at least and more arriving, old and young, their Caucasian skin dark and rough as old leather. She supposed there were women as young as her nineteen years, though you couldn't tell it, judging by the suffering grooved into their gaunt features. The boys, too, had a shadow of misery in their eyes. Old before their time, like dead men walking. It was all enough to make her forget, momentarily, about her own fear and sadness.

"Why have you come here?" she asked in a dry, rough voice. "Why have you come to me?"

"You need help. You be needin' planters to turn this valley. Turn it over for sugarcane like it used to be."

"How do you know what Belle Jarod used to be?"

"Seen it with my own eyes, lady. Cane tall as two men and fat as my arm. Good cane, and sweet. Sarah yonda done cut her teeth on Belle cane."

Juliette glance toward the woman with long golden hair not much older than herself.

"I haven't any money," she said wearily, feeling the tears threaten again.

"You have land," came the voice, and Juliette turned to find Emmaline standing knee high in dark green grass.

Startled, Juliette sank against the monument—its sharp edges biting into her back. Yet, some emotion—not grief—assuaged the onrush of despair and replaced it with a numbing sense of befuddlement. What in Heaven's name was Emmaline doing here with these people?

Her eyes red and swollen from crying, Emmaline moved closer, lifting one hand to point toward the cluster of silent onlookers. "There are a hundred men here, Juliette. A hundred families. They're accustomed to making do with very little. There are some folk who will try to tell you that these people are worthless and lazy. Well, they're wrong. They simply need someone willing to trust in them. To believe in their worth. Give each of these families ten acres to do with as they wish and reap the rewards of their appreciation and loyalty for the remainder of their lives."

Juliette looked beyond the scattering of men, women, and children, to the stretch of green land where once her father's cane had grown. In the silence that stretched out in that moment, she felt, as she always did in moments of such immense grief and confusion, an odd sense of calm—like one must feel the very moment of one's death—a calm acceptance of the inevitable. Often in those moments reason arose more clearly—as it did now.

She had begun this journey with one dream in mind. That Belle Jarod would rise from the ashes.

And so it would.

When Juliette jolted from sleep she had been dreaming of Chantz—that she had awakened to find him walking up the long alley from the river road—sauntering in that long slow stride that made her heartbeat quicken. His eyes were blue as April skies.

Covering her nose and mouth with her kerchief, she tried her best not to gag from the awful stench of burning Spanish moss—Louis was convinced that the acrid smoke would keep the pestilence at bay. The smoke from the bonfires infiltrated the house and trees; indeed the entire sky had become like the foul clouds of coal smog that suffocated London.

What had awakened her?

Her bedroom door opened and Little Clara stood there, her eyes watering and swollen from the smoke. "Best you come quick, Mistress Julie."

"What's happened, Little Clara? Has Chantz—"

"It be Miss Phyllis. She in an awful mess."

Juliette pulled on her dress and hurried down the stairs. Through the haze of smoke, she could barely make out the figures in the salon. Phyllis sat hunkered over on the settee, her face buried in her hands. Liza watched her from the doorway, her hands clasped at her waist.

"What's happened?" Juliette asked, her gaze locking with Liza's.

"It's horrible." Phyllis wept and shook. "My parents . . . my parents are dead—"

Liza grabbed Juliette's arm. "Leave her."

"What do you mean, leave her?" Juliette demanded, yanking her arm away. "She's distressed—"

"She just come from a death house. She got it on her."
Her eyes slightly wild, Liza glared toward Phyllis and cried,
"What you doin' comin' here? Bringin' that pestilence to
Belle Jarod? And where is Andrew? Why ain't he with you?"

"I've . . . got no place else to go—"

"What's wrong with Horace Carrington? If anybody deserves to die then he does."

"Please." Phyllis looked into Juliette's eyes. "Don't send
me to Horace."

Liza made another grab for Juliette, but Juliette shoved
her hand away and hurried across the room, stood by the
settee where Phyllis rocked in her fear and grief, and stared
down at the wreck of a woman who only vaguely resembled Phyllis Buley. The soiled black mourning dress hung
on her thin frame. Her hair trailed in limp strands around
her ashen face.

Sinking back against the settee, Phyllis wearily shook her
head. "Everyone is dying. Hundreds. Thousands."

"Where is Andrew?" Juliette asked as steadily as possible.

"I . . . don't know. After Papa died . . ." She shook her
head as a new rush of tears rose and fell. "Volunteers were
needed, he said, to collect the dead and to secure the quarantine. He left me there . . . I couldn't stay," she cried frantically. "I couldn't stay there another minute. So I ran. I ran
until I couldn't run anymore." She clutched Juliette's arm,
her broken, dirty nails cutting into Juliette's flesh. "Please
don't send me away, Juliette. I know you despise me—"

"I don't despise you, Phyllis." She glanced down at her
arm.

"Well you should," she said angrily, her dark eyes flashing. "You should because I've despised you since the moment I heard that Chantz had married you. I'm ashamed to
say that I wanted you to die. I wanted you to be struck by

this horrible fever. I imagined that Chantz would come back to me and . . ."

Covering her face with her hands, she sobbed in a broken voice, "I'm so sorry. I didn't mean it. Will you ever forgive me?"

Juliette sank onto the settee and took Phyllis in her arms. "There's nothing to forgive, Phyllis. Hush now. I'll have Rosie prepare you a meal—"

"You're not going to allow her to remain here, surely."

Juliette looked around.

Emmaline stood at Liza's side, her face soot streaked and sweating. "Look at her." She pointed at Phyllis, her hand trembling. "She's just come from a death house. She's brought the pestilence into this house and you're holding her in your arms."

"Liza," Juliette said. "Have Rosie prepare food for Phyllis. I'll put her in my room—"

"You're sentencing us all to die," Emma declared furiously.

Standing, one hand resting on Phyllis's shoulder, Juliette shook her head. "If you disapprove, Emmaline, you're welcome to leave Belle Jarod. I've extended hospitality and respect to you because you're Chantz's mother, but you're to remember above all else that you're a guest here. I know in my heart that if Chantz were here, he would do the same."

"Chantz isn't here," Emmaline shouted. "He's out there somewhere. He might be dead already—"

"Stop it." Emmaline backed away as Juliette moved toward her. "I won't hear you talk like that again, do you understand me? Chantz is going to come home. He's going to walk in through that door at any moment."

Emmaline shook her head. "No he isn't and we all know it. People are dying by the thousands out there. I've heard the stories. Bodies stacked one on top of the other, entire families, hauled away in wagons like slaughtered sheep. It's here already. I can smell it." She glanced from Juliette to Phyllis then Liza. "You can burn all the damn moss in the world, incinerate the air with heat and suffocating smoke, but if it's here already, in one of us, we don't stand a chance of whipping it. Once it takes hold, we're all dead people. And inviting her into our midst is suicide."

Turning on her heels, Emmaline stormed out through the front door.

"She's right." Phyllis stood, swayed, drew back her shoulders, and forced a tight smile. "I shouldn't have come here. I've put your lives in jeopardy. I'll leave—"

"No." Juliette frowned, and without looking at Phyllis or Liza again, walked to the open front door and onto the gallery. Though the smog bit at her eyes and burned her nostrils, she looked down the long alley toward the distant river—empty the last days of steamers. Emma had been right, alas. Some stillness had crept over Belle Jarod the last day. The eerie cries of a drove of screaming crows in the trees near the pond only added to the consuming loneliness, the sense of despair and impending loss.

"Mistress Julie?"

Wearily, Juliette turned to find Louis standing at the far end of the gallery. A Negro child stood at his side. He held her little hand in his massive one. A moment passed before she recognized the child as Sally. Then, beyond Louis, others stepped through the bushes, faces frightened and wary of Juliette's response. They were Maxwell's Negroes, she realized, and she stared at them one by one in confusion until a sudden realization struck her like a fist. Her gaze flew back to Louis.

"Dear God," she whispered.

"They runnin', Miss Julie. Gots to git away from Holly.

Massa Max be sick. Real sick. Folk say it come on him yesterday. Boris Wilcox done took off last night." He turned Sally toward her fretful mother and gave her a gentle pat on the head, watched as Sally scurried off through a cluster of wildflowers to her mother's side. Then he turned his big, soulful eyes back on Juliette. "Gots to go, Mistress. Gots to git out whilst we can. Folks be movin' north fo' d'stockade paddy rollers close us off. That happen and we is all dead."

"Where is Tylor?"

Louis shook his head. "Went to N'awlins and ain't come back. 'Spect he stuck now that the paddy rollers is out. They is shootin' anybody who try to cross the barricades." In a gentler voice, he repeated, "We gots to go. Fo' it's too late."

Juliette sank against the pillar and closed her eyes. Where was the elation she thought she might feel over Maxwell's misfortune?

"Yes," she replied without opening her eyes. "Have Rosie and Tessa prepare food. Tell the others. You must remove the children as quickly as possible. Now hurry. Put as much distance as you can between you and Belle Jarod before nightfall." As Louis turned to leave, she asked, "Who is left at Holly, Louis? Did anyone remain behind to help Maxwell?"

"No," he said, then turned and joined the others.

"You stayin', ain't you?" came Liza's voice behind Juliette.

Juliette sat down on the gallery step and propped her elbows on her knees. She looked off down the alley, toward the river. "I'll wait for Chantz."

"What if he don't come home, Julie?"

"He will." She forced a smile.

"Then I'm stayin' too."

"No. You have to go, Liza. There's the baby to think about. Besides, Little Clara and Simon need you. Louis needs you."

"He ain't comin' back and you know it. Just like I know I ain't ever gonna see my Andrew again."

"I won't give up. Not yet. You mustn't either."

She sat on the rafter in the nursery, sat at the window and peered down on the dark green pond. The fires, little by little, had dwindled now that Louis and the others were no longer there to stoke them. The smoke had cleared, inviting the rush of smells to return, and she didn't realize until that moment how much she had missed them. Yet, with their resurrection came memories that made her chest ache and the tears rise.

"Please, God, please," she whispered with her eyes closed. "Please let him come home. Chantz. My darling Chantz. I'll give anything. My dreams. My home. My life if only you will bring him back."

Then she prayed silently, willing the impossible with every seed of faith that the old Reverend Mother had planted in her soul over the years. *Please God.* She recited all the prayers she could remember, but they sounded to her immensely loud in the silence. *Please God.*

Rising, she ran down the stairs and stood on the gallery, her gaze fixed on the long alley. *Please God.*

Nothing moved. No stirring of air. No birdsong. No wild rabbit scurrying through the brush. No Little Clara begging for ho'hound. No Simon with bullfrog. No Rosie fussing about burning their supper. No Jasper or Gaius carrying on lengthy conversations with a scrawny old chicken. No Liza dreamy with pleasure over her baby moving.

No Chantz.

Only the silence and the milky sky, lit by a thin sun and diffused by banked pale clouds dusted by a hint of impending rain.

* * *

She rode Snapper to Holly, right up to the gallery floor where a blue-tick hound lay sprawled on its side in the shade, barely lifting its head to look up at her with droopy eyes. Solemnly, she looked around, over the wide flat grounds stretching toward the river, remembering that a short while ago the grass had been lush and kept. Guinea hens scratched at the dirt and roosted on the lounges in the gallery shade, scattering feathers everywhere.

Upon sliding from Snapper's back, Juliette moved into the open threshold, into the foyer, and stood looking up the curving staircase, listening to the quiet clicking of the guinea hens as they strutted over the gallery planks, the excessively loud case clock ticking away the seconds of the dying day.

"Hello!" she shouted.

The hound moved to the doorway and stood silhouetted against the bright light pouring over the threshold. His head held flat, his eyes somber, he stared at Juliette while a thread of drool drained from his lip and pooled on the floor.

She made her way slowly up the staircase, the sense of dread pressing more heavily on her chest with each passing minute. On the landing above, she paused, listened, watched the dog move to the bottom stair and sit, panting as he watched her, then she continued, walking on the balls of her feet, caution expanding with her every breath, until she stopped at Maxwell's bedroom door.

The door of the room was partially open. She eased it back. The shadows were deep, and there were no candles burning. Beyond fear, Juliette stepped into the room, immediately assailed by heat and smells that took her breath away and stung her eyes and nostrils. The pungency of it all coiled in her stomach, forcing her to fight her need to retch. She had experienced the stink before. Soon after her arrival to the convent, her first assigned chore was to assist Sister

Margaret in the preparation of a body for burial. The old woman had lingered for months with her illness. The stench of death and decay had permeated the walls of her sickroom and as Juliette had stood there staring down at her parchment thin skin, at first refusing to touch it, hating her father for abandoning her to such an existence, certain she would never smell anything again but that dreadful scent of . . . dust.

Here it was again, wrapping around her, so repellent she was forced to set her heels to stop herself from fleeing. She heard his breathing—a wheezing rasp of air, animal-like sounds, an attempt to communicate.

In the rays of the late sun coming in through the shutters, she saw Maxwell in his bed, naked, his body shaking, his flesh flushed and sweating. His head turned and his glazed eyes stared at her. The pain that twisted his features momentarily eased, and his mouth curved into a grotesque smile.

"Maureen? Honey, is that you?" He lifted his hand toward Juliette. "Oh my sweet lady. My darlin'. Look at you, pretty as a rosebud. I've been praying you would come for me."

Her legs trembling, Juliette moved closer, fear and sickness rising up her throat as the man's blue eyes held her. His raw, blackened tongue protruded from his mouth slightly. Yet, something drew her closer—her gaze shifting from his mad eyes to his hand outstretched to her.

"Maureen . . . darlin', pretty as the day I first saw you. Like an angel. Lord God, I've missed you."

She reached for his hand. It radiated with heat and curled around her own with a fierceness that made her gasp and struggle.

"I've suffered, darlin'. Suffered every day of my life for what happened. I tried to stop him. He was like a madman." His eyes drifted closed, yet he continued to hold her.

His grip sent cold, crushing pain up her arm and her panic mounted. A scream worked up her throat, cutting like a sliver of bone. "I tried to warn him. I tried to tell him that you were lonely, that you desired love more than you desired cane. I wanted to thrash him for his blindness. God, oh God, if you had only been mine . . ."

He gasped for air and his body twisted in pain. His lips pulled back, exposing his teeth and bleeding gums. For an instant his eyes appeared to clear and he stared up at her with an insight and horror that made the scream slice more sharply, expanding and closing off her ability to swallow.

"Chantz," he growled. "Chantz, where are you?"

"He's not here," she heard herself reply through her teeth. The pain in her arm had become like burning ice.

"Ashamed . . . so ashamed. Should have done right by you. Holly . . . is yours. Don't let Tylor destroy it. You hear me, boy? Do what you've got to do to save her." Suddenly his ferocity melted into despair and his eyes filled with tears. His body relaxed and sank into the bed as if boneless, releasing his grip on her arm.

"Maureen, darlin' . . . hold me."

She backed away, toward the door, her legs shaking and her heart beating frantically.

The bed began shaking, tapping on the floor as Maxwell's body trembled with the fever. She tried to turn, to run, yet as she stood there a feeling of realization washed over her. Suddenly it wasn't simply Maxwell Hollinsworth lying there, twisted in his death sheets, but Chantz. How easily she could see him now, his face strong and intelligent and handsome in a sharp, forbidding sort of way. Was Chantz lying helplessly sick and alone somewhere?

Was he, perhaps, dead already?

Her shoulders sinking and her chest constricting,

Juliette returned to the bed, untangled the sheet from his shivering legs, and gently laid it over his hips. She sat on the bed beside him, stroked his wet hair back from his brow.

"Maureen?" he called weakly, staring at some point beyond Juliette. "Honey, is that you?"

"Yes," she replied softly, and pressed a kiss to his hot forehead.

The rain began at just before twilight. Juliette drove the stubborn old mule through the downpour, whacking his haunches with a willow switch when he stopped, hoping the rain would wash the stench of sickness from her skin. As a chill ran through her she whipped the mule harder, desperate to reach Belle Jarod before nightfall, before the waters turned the road into a mire. The river churned, a certain sign that there were heavy rains further north, driving high waters toward the Gulf.

Dear God, she was tired. Her arms felt like lead and her head throbbed deeply from crying. She didn't want to think of Maxwell's last hours—of his awful suffering. Yet, it was there, the memory burning behind her eyes and filling her up with a fear that made her want to flee with a desperation that caused her to lash at the plodding animal beneath her and curse.

At long last, Belle Jarod materialized through the rain and night shadows. A light beamed from her bedroom window.

A light. A light! Someone was there.

Chantz?

She saw a horse then, near the front gallery, standing with his head down as rain pummeled it. Upon sliding from the mule, Juliette ran along the alley of live oaks, hands clutching her sodden skirts, her toes catching on the exposed roots of the fallen trees she and India's family had labored to haul away.

The front door hung open.

Her muddy feet slipped on the gallery planks as she ran into the house, first to the salon that was empty, then back into the corridor, paused to catch her breath—a sound from up the stairs, a clattering. Running to the staircase, she looked up toward the dim light, excitement squeezing her breathless.

"Chantz! Husband, is that you?" She ascended, her feet feeling oddly as if they were weighted. "Chantz?"

She hurried to the bedroom, shouldered open the door, her smile fading as her gaze swept the room. Empty. "Chantz?" she called softly.

Nothing.

Slowly, confusion mounting, Juliette turned, searching, her eyes aching as they focused on the night shadows. She reached for the burning lamp, held it high as she slowly moved toward the stairs and allowed its light to spill to the lower landing.

"Where is she?" came the deep, rough words behind her.

Wheeling, causing the light to sputter, she stared toward the shadowed figure. Little by little Horace Carrington materialized from the dark. The whites of his eyes, like Maxwell's, were blood red. His skin shone with oily sweat, and the same repulsing stench washed over her: fever and death.

"Answer me, goddamn you!" he shouted, making her jump and back away. "Where is my goddamn fiancée? How dare she leave me. I know she's here. I found her hat yonder. Where are you hiding her—"

"She's gone," Juliette said, backing again as he stumbled toward her, tottered like a drunk before drawing himself up and blotting his cheek with his filthy coat sleeve. "She left with the others—"

"You're a lying bitch." His tearing eyes assessed her. His lips parted, exposing his black tongue. "A damn shame that a piece of trash like Chantz Boudreaux got you. Son of a bitch. Thought he could stop me from crossing that barricade—"

Her heart leaped. "Chantz? You've seen Chantz?"

"Thought they were going to keep me from going home." He moved toward her. "Like I was going to remain in that death pit, people dying everywhere, corpses stacked like firewood along the streets."

Knees suddenly weak with relief, Juliette sagged against the wall. Dear merciful God. Chantz was alive . . .

Her eyes shifted downward momentarily to Horace's hands that were fisted and shaking, then back to his eyes that were like two pits of fire.

He lunged. She screamed and jumped, a sharp, brief awareness falling on her too late as she realized that the stairs dropped away beneath her.

Twenty-Two

~

The rain beat furiously against his shoulders as Chantz rode the bay hard down the river road. In the last few hours the river had risen, driving timber along the banks where the fallen trunks with their low-sweeping limbs festooned with Spanish moss left deep ruts in the mud. Word had arrived just hours ago. It was every man for himself. Married men were encouraged to return home as quickly as possible. The yellow death had somehow made its way beyond the quarantine and was spreading like wildfire and Baton Rouge lay directly in its path.

None too soon. He'd long since grown weary and sickened by the job—forced to keep men from their families by threat of death, burying women and children found dead by the side of the road. The last days had been a blur of sulfur-smelling smoke, death, and putridity. Every young woman he had placed in a pit and covered with dirt had filled him with a desperate ache to climb on his horse and go home, to hold his wife and kiss her sweet mouth. To convince her that he loved her more than life.

He smelled the smoke before the red-gold glow of fire shimmered through the trees. As the horse tucked its haunches and slid to a stop, Chantz hit the ground running, his heart climbing his throat as the long tongues of fire lapped at Belle's windows. Black smoke billowed through the open doorway, fueled by the old lumber and the rain driving through the new rafters.

"Juliette!" he shouted, his panic mounting. *Where the hell was everyone?* Shielding his face from the heat, he edged along the trail of flames toward the staircase. He saw her then, at the bottom of the stairs, lying face up, her face reflecting the advancing flamelight.

Diving through the line of fire, he fell to his knees and scooped her up in his arms.

Shouts arose. Louis came barreling through the smoke and flames, pounding the fire with wet flour sacks, while behind him came others—strangers, with rusty buckets of water and whatever else they could use to douse the fire.

Chantz carried Juliette out of the house and partially down the alley where the trees formed a cathedral over their heads against the rain. Falling to his knees, her limp body clutched to his chest, he closed his eyes, afraid to look, afraid she would be dead—

Liza fell down beside him, choked by sobs. She grabbed Juliette's hand and pressed it to her cheek. "Shouldna gone," she cried, and rocked on her knees. "Shouldna gone and left her."

"What the hell are you saying?" Chantz stared at her.

A movement—just slight, in his arms. Then she made a sound and Chantz gently laid her on her back and smoothed the hair from her face. "Juliette? Darlin', open your eyes." He patted her cheek then shook her. She drew in a deep breath, coughed, then her eyes opened wide and looked into his. Fear, then confusion touched her features, then her arms lifted around his neck, and with a cry of gladness she threw herself against him. Her fingers twisted in his hair and her lips touched his cheek, his eyes, his mouth.

"Am I dreaming?" she cried.

His eyes closed, he crushed her to him. "No, darlin', you're not dreaming. "God oh God, I'm sorry for leaving you. I should never—"

"Kiss me," she wept, and taking his face between her hands, kissed him passionately, tasting like tears and smoke.

As Liza sank back on her heels, Juliette held Chantz closer, as if she would dissolve her body into his, if possible. Only then did she appear to notice Liza. She blinked and said almost angrily, "What are you doing back here, Liza? You should have been long gone—"

"We couldn't leave you, Juliette. And it's a damn good thing we came back. What happened here?"

She turned her face into Chantz's shoulder. He felt her struggle to hold back her emotions. "Horace," she said. "He came looking for Phyllis."

"Son of a bitch."

Chantz tried to stand. Juliette clung, her desperation showing in her flashing eyes.

"He's sick, Chantz. Desperately. He might well be dead already."

"What the hell is going on here?"

Andrew walked out of the dark, his hair and clothes plastered to his body by rain. Liza jumped to her feet and with a scream threw herself into his arms. Eyes closed, he lifted her off her feet and rocked her.

Louis joined them. He dropped heavily onto the damp

ground and wiped his face with his shirtsleeve that was singed and tattered. Smiling into Chantz's eyes, he said, "Sho' glad to see you, Boss. Done believe you gone over the bridge."

Chantz said nothing, just held Juliette, felt her heart beat against his and tried not to think about what might have happened had he not come home when he had.

"Chantz? Chantz, honey, is that you?"

Chantz stood as his mother ran down the alley, her thin arms thrown open wide. She felt light as a bird in his arms, and he found himself holding her more tightly than he had held her in a great many years. The last days pressed down on him—the frailty of life, how quickly it could be snuffed. He had seen enough tragedy the last days to fill his remaining lifetime with nightmares.

Lifting his head, he stared at the dozens of strange faces, the men who stood shoulder to shoulder holding lanterns high so light painted their features. He felt his mother stiffen.

"Who are these people?" he demanded, though some gut instinct turned over inside him. His hands curled into fists as he waited, shifting his focus back to his mother's stricken features.

Emmaline backed away, but as she opened her mouth to speak, Juliette pushed herself to her feet and caught his arm.

"I've employed these people. They're hard workers, Chantz, and all they ask is ten acres each to call their own— theirs as long as they work for Belle Jarod. Husband . . ." She closed her trembling hand around his arm and moved against him, took his face in her hand and smiled into his eyes. "I prayed for a miracle and God sent them. They're the answer to our prayers, Chantz. They're going to help us rebuild this house and replant those fields. They're going to help us prosper."

He looked at his mother who regarded him with a defiant lift of her chin and set of her shoulders. Mud daubers. The sick reality of why they were at Belle Jarod rolled in his empty stomach.

As if Emmaline could sense his thoughts, her eyes filled with tears. "I'm sorry to shame you, son. But I can't run from it any longer. I brought them here to help you. To help your wife realize her dreams. And yours. Folks shouldn't be blamed for where they came from, Chantz. You've suffered from the bigotry yourself. You worked hard to become the man you are now, but chances are it might never have happened had Maxwell not extended the pittance of charity that he did." She turned her gaze on Juliette and her lips quivered with a faint smile. "I should listen to my own advice sometimes."

Emmaline turned and, joining the others, moved off into the rain drenched darkness. Liza and Andrew followed as did Louis.

Juliette's warm hand touched his cheek, and he looked down into her face that looked smooth as pearl in the darkness. The last days of fear and anguish rushed over him then, fierce as the moving water in the river, driven by a force beyond control. Taking her in his arms, he crushed her to him and buried his face in her hair—held her while rain ran in cool streams through the overhead trees and sprinkled their heads and shoulders.

With his eyes closed, he tried to swallow. Held her tighter. Heard her breath catch and her body shiver. "God, I missed you," he whispered upon her ear. "I was so damn scared, Julie, that I would never see you again. Or hold you again. So many people dead. Entire families, men and women and little babies. We took to burying them in pits one on top of the other because there are no more coffins—last count was ten thousand dead. Can you imagine?"

"Hush now." She kissed his cheek and pulled away, and when he reached for her again, she backed away further.

"What's wrong?" he asked. "Are you mad because I went—"

"No." She shook her head and turned away, moved to the gallery out of the rain that had begun to spear harder from the night sky. Thunder rumbled and somewhere near the river came the sound of splintering wood. She sat on the bench seat Louis had built from old lumber, buried her clasped hands between her legs, and looked off down the long alley.

He eased to one knee before her, took her hot hand in his. Her palm felt moist with sweat. "Are you certain that fall didn't—"

"My head hurts a little." She smiled and touched a place above her right eye. "Actually . . . it hurts a lot. But it's so very inconsequential compared to what's happening to so many others." Her voice caught and for a moment she simply sat in silence, her shoulders oddly slumped, her head down as she stared at her hands.

He touched her hair and took her small chin on the crook of his finger, lifting her face so he could look in her eyes. "Still love me?" he asked with a faint curl of his mouth.

"Oh, Chantz, I fear you'll never know, truly know, how very much I love you."

"I'm depending on you to show me."

He grinned.

She grinned.

Then, as if the dam burst in her heart, she covered her face and began to shake. Chantz sat down beside her and took her in his arms. She shoved him, jumped to her feet, and backed away.

"What the hell is wrong, Julie—"

"Chantz, your father is dead."

Thunder rumbled and the sky momentarily brightened. "Maxwell is dead?"

"I was with him. I sat with him for the afternoon. I couldn't simply leave him, you see. He was so . . . pitiful. And alone."

"Where the devil is Tylor—"

"New Orleans."

"Jesus." Sinking back against the wall, Chantz stared off through the dark. "Does my mother know?"

"No."

He closed his eyes. Some emotion turned over inside him, hot pain and hotter anger. Standing, he paced. He walked to the far end of the gallery and fixed his gaze on the distant dark pond, vaguely aware of the spray of rain covering his face. His fists shook. "Bastard," he said through his teeth. "All I ever wanted was a single nod of acknowledgment, and bastard that you are you went and died on me . . ."

"I left him there," came Juliette's tired voice. "He needs burying, Chantz."

Nodding, running one hand back through his damp hair, Chantz laughed and shrugged. "Well, I guess it's the least I can do. After all, thanks to his *charity* I wasn't brought up a damn mud dauber."

Juliette touched his back. "Forgive him, husband. I did. He died alone and frightened and begging forgiveness for his sins. He called out for you. He wept for you. He said that you were his finest accomplishment and if he had his life to live over he would not make the same mistakes again where you are concerned. Forgive him," she said softly, "or you'll never know peace in your life."

He turned slowly back to his wife. How small she looked in the dark, little more than a child, it seemed, with her long hair wild about her shoulders and her eyes very big. So many years ago—she wouldn't remember, of course—they had stood here similarly, she barely four and with ribbons in her hair, hand outstretched pleading for sweets, and him thinking her a pain in the butt. Later she had played amid the Cherokee roses while butterflies had danced around her shoulders.

She swayed.

He jumped to catch her in his arms, his heart racing with fear.

"Julie . . . darlin', what's wrong?" He kissed her hot dry brow, fear expanding inside him.

"I'm tired," she said wearily. "And sad. Very sad. Max's death was . . . dreadful."

He carried her into the house, over the scorched floor and up the stairs to their bedroom, placed her gently on the mattress. The lantern on the near table cast her face in gold planes and blue hollows. Her eyes looked dark and sunken. Her flesh radiated with heat.

Smiling, she reached for his hand. "Don't look so fearful. I'm fine. Really. I've simply been so worried about you, then your father . . . say you forgive him, Chantz. All my prayers won't do us any good if you won't in your heart of hearts put the anger and resentment from you."

Smoothing the hair back from her brow, he bent and pressed a kiss to her forehead, lingered there, absorbing the faint hint of magnolias on her skin. Her eyelashes brushed his face. Her fingertips caressed his cheek. "Go," she whispered near his ear. "Take care of your father. I'll sleep and when I awaken we'll start again. Go," she repeated, looking into his eyes. "And hurry home. I've missed you long enough."

Her eyes closed and suddenly she was asleep. Chantz kissed her dry lips, her closed eyes, then forced himself to stand, to walk to the door where he stopped and looked back. "Julie?" he called softly.

Nothing.

"Darlin', I love you," he said, then stepped from the room and closed the door.

The others waited at the bottom of the stairs, their faces somber and frightened. Liza cried softly as Andrew held her. Rosie stepped forward and wrung her hands.

"She sick, ain't she?" Rosie said, her voice aquiver with worry.

"No." He shook his head in denial and moved toward the door.

"Are you sure?" Liza demanded.

He turned on her. "She's not sick. She's tired is all. Hell, she tumbled down a flight of stairs—"

"I'll sit with her."

Phyllis moved out of the salon, paused at the threshold as everyone turned to stare at her. But for two bright red spots of color on her cheeks, her face appeared white as goose down. He might not have recognized her had he bumped into her in town. The black mourning garb she wore gave her the look of a corpse.

Her gaze locked with Chantz's, Phyllis did her best to straighten her spine and smile as nonchalantly as possible. "She might rest better with someone near. It's the least I can do, after all. She did open her home and her arms to me when I came here. For that matter, it's the least I can do for you."

She marched by Chantz, going partially up the stairs before pausing and looking back. "Rosie, will you bring me a bowl of fresh water and linens?"

"She's not sick," Chantz declared with a rise of anger and panic.

Andrew stepped forward. "Of course she's not. You know women. She'll feel much better once she's cleaned up a bit."

"She's not sick, Drew." The words rattled in his throat.

Andrew forced a tired smile as he looked hard into Chantz's eyes.

The river roared and the rain drove hard upon Chantz's shoulders as he slogged through the deepening mud and water and climbed the gallery steps, flinging the shovel hard to the ground where it disappeared in a puddle. Dawn fought its way through the dark clouds as Chantz looked out over Holly grounds. Already deep gulleys and broad chasms fanned out all directions, a growing plain of dark silt strewn with debris. By now, without the levee, the river would have risen to the lower cane fields, already decimated by the last flood. If he didn't start back to Belle soon, he wouldn't make it until the water subsided.

He came face-to-face with Tylor in the foyer.

Soaked by rain and sweat, his teeth chattering, Tylor stared at him with glazed eyes and blue lips. "My, my, look who we've got here. Just when I thought we had got rid of you for good."

Chantz mopped his face with his damp shirtsleeve as he looked Tylor up and down. The whites of Tylor's eyes were red and his skin sickly yellow. "How the hell did you breach those barricades?" he asked.

"Like I do everything else, brother. What Tylor Hollinsworth wants, Tylor Hollinsworth gets. Except for one thing.

I've always wanted you dead. Guess we can't always get what we pray for."

Tylor unsteadily turned on his heels and staggered into the parlor, to the cellarette where he clumsily knocked against the decanters of his father's good bourbon and rum. Chantz watched him from the door, the hot core of hatred that had burned in his chest over the years turning into something else. Pity. It felt like a cold stone in his belly.

"Where the hell is Daddy?" Tylor demanded as he poured himself a drink. "No doubt down at that damn levee trying to sweet-talk the river out of his sugarcane. Bet he's pissing his pants right about now."

Chantz swallowed. "Maxwell is dead."

Tylor slowly lifted the glass to his mouth and drank deeply.

"Did you hear me, Tylor? Maxwell is—"

"You're a goddamn liar, Chantz."

"I just buried him."

Turning, the blue of his eyes a shock of color against the bloody whites, Tylor glared at Chantz and began to shake. "Son of a bitch. You killed him, didn't you?"

"The fever killed him."

"That's why you're here, isn't it? You think you could kill Daddy, and then me and get your hands at long last on Holly."

"You're crazy, Tylor. And you're sick."

Tylor flung the glass to the floor and stumbled toward the door, ramming Chantz with his shoulder. "Daddy!" he shouted. "Daddy, where are you? Where the hell is everyone?"

"Gone," Chantz said. "They all took off when Max came sick."

"Daddy!" Tylor shouted up the stairs. "Get down here. Your bastard son is up to something again."

Silence but for the drumming of rain on the roof and advancing thunder.

Tylor frowned and closed his eyes. He swayed, toppled toward the wall before catching the stairpost and shoving himself upright. When he turned back to Chantz he bared his teeth and inflamed gums that were tinged with black. "I won't let you get your hands on Holly. I'll kill you, Chantz. Do you hear me?"

"I don't want Holly. I don't need her anymore."

Chantz turned for the open front door. Already water had climbed to the first gallery stair. Rain fell in a dense gray sheet, obliterating the river in the distance. Still, its roar vibrated the air. The gallery planks trembled beneath him.

"Come back here, goddamn you!" Tylor yelled. "How dare you turn your back on me. Chantz! What the hell are you doing? Where do you think you're going?"

"I'm going home, Tylor."

Ducking his head against the downpour, Chantz descended the stairs, sank to his shins in the rising water, and headed for his horse tied under a shed.

"Home to what?" Tylor shouted from the door. "Home to that pile of rubble and trash? Home to your whore of a wife?"

The water swirled around Chantz's boots as he untethered his horse. He mounted, struggled momentarily with the wild-eyed bay that snorted and fought the bit. He took one last glance toward the house—a mirage behind the wall of rain. Tylor stood in the door, pale as a ghost, face a mask of fear. Chantz could no longer hear him. The growl of the river and rain drowned him out.

Little Clara and Simon lay curled together on the floor before the fireplace. Little Clara gripped a handful of bright ribbons to her chest. Liza sat on an overturned wood crate, staring blindly into the fire while tears coursed down her cheeks. As Chantz stared at the children, then Liza, the air turned hot, his blood hotter. He felt it rise up behind his eyes and pound at his temples. Briefly closing his eyes, he tried to swallow the lump of dread congealed in his throat. *Oh Julie, Julie. Not you too. Please God . . .* This was a nightmare.

"Phyllis is with her," Andrew said in a rough voice that seemed to come to Chantz from a hollow well.

Clumsily, Chantz moved around him, mentally cursing his legs that felt weak as old straw, as if they would snap at any moment.

Andrew caught his arm. "Don't, Chantz. You don't want to see her like this."

"Get your hand off me, Drew."

"You won't do her any good by getting sick yourself."

"If I was gonna get sick I would be sick by now."

"Chantz—"

He turned on Andrew and shoved hard enough to send him sprawling to the floor on his back. Liza leaped to her feet and ran to him, her eyes flashing with anger.

Chantz mounted the stairs, moved woodenly to the door that stood ajar. Phyllis sat at Juliette's side, lightly bathing her flushed brow with a damp cloth. Startled, she looked around.

"I'm sorry," she said sadly.

Chantz moved to the bed and Phyllis stood. "She's been unconscious since dawn."

"Leave us."

"Chantz—"

"I said to go. Now. My place is with her."

Phyllis folded the linen and put it in his hand. She moved to the door, then stopped, looked around, her dark eyes reflecting her sadness and concern, then she silently left the room.

He had never felt so inadequate in his life, never so full with helpless fear. The suffering he had experienced over the last days ill prepared him for the fever that filled up Juliette's small frame and racked her with pain.

Climbing onto the bed, he took her in his arms and held her, hour upon hour. He bathed her sweating body with cool water. Covered her with blankets when her teeth chattered. Flung them from her body when she burned.

Twice the sun rose. Each time daylight, dim as it was through the rain clouds, crept through their window he cradled her in his arms and stroked her hair.

"Another day, darlin'. One more day. You can make it, Julie. You're a fighter. Hold me, darlin'. Hold me tight as you can. I love you, Juliette. I'll cease to exist without you . . ."

Tylor awoke with a jolt. The fire that had burned his brain for the last days was gone. Lying in his bed, the filthy sheets twisted around his naked legs, he stared at the ceiling and listened to the . . . silence. The rain had stopped.

He started to laugh. He howled roughly, his body contracting and his lungs wheezing. Son of a bitch, he had beaten it.

"Now who's the big man, Daddy?" he yelled at the ceiling and beat the bed with his fist. "Here I am and where are you?"

He coughed and pain sliced through his belly and chest. Groaning, he rolled and clutched his stomach that felt hollow and cramped. God, he was hungry. He thought of yelling for food.

Impossible, he realized with a groan. Everyone had deserted him. Everyone had taken to the woods like scattering guinea hens in the presence of a fox. Well, he'd show them. He'd hunt them down and drag them back by their damn ears if he had to. He'd nail their ears to a post and whip them dearly. They'd think twice before they ran away from Holly again. They'd soon learn that, unlike his idiot soft-headed and soft-hearted father, when dealing with the *new* master of Holly Plantation there would be hell to pay for their betrayal.

He rolled from the bed, and sank into water.

"Jesus," he croaked, staring down at the swirl of muddy water around his knees. Panic mounting, he slogged weakly toward the bedroom window, leaned upon the sill, and stared with horror at the landscape of water.

A sound crawled up his throat, and he groaned in fear as a water snake slithered around his leg. Frantic, he turned and looked around the room. Yes, yes, he was in his room. This was no sinking ship. There was no escaping without a boat. There was no food, no water . . .

"Help!" he shouted out the window. "Help!"

The chicken coop floated by, bobbing up and down while clucking, flapping chickens balanced on its peaked roof.

With a yowl of outrage, Tylor slammed his fist into the wall. "Son of a bitch Chantz Boudreaux, this is all your fault thanks to that sorry excuse for a levee . . ." He hit the wall again, then waded through the deepening water to the open door, out into the corridor and to the top of the stairs that disappeared beneath the brown surface. A turtle paddled by and Tylor momentarily thought of clubbing it with something. God, he was hungry. How many days had passed since he'd last eaten?

"I'll get you for this, Chantz. I'm gonna make you suffer

for this. Probably did it on purpose, envious bastard that you are."

He returned to the room and retrieved a tin of matches from the fireplace mantel. He struck three before one lit. With shaking hands, he ignited the lantern by his bed while shadows crept in. Scrambling onto the high mattress, pulling his knees to his chest, he watched the water level creep up, up, turning darker as night closed in.

Drained of strength, he dozed.

He awoke suddenly, his heart hammering. The stench of river water filled his nostrils. The lamp fuel had burned low. The wick cast a weak light over the murk.

With a whimper, he realized the bed was wet. The water crept over the top of his mattress, lapping at his feet and legs. Staring at the tester overhead, he wondered frantically if it would hold his weight.

A bump.

He glanced toward the window where moonlight flooded through the panes and silvered the watery floor, turning it into a calm lagoon.

Bump.

His hands shaking, Tylor crawled onto his knees and reached for the lantern. He clutched at the wick screw, cranked it high so the flame momentarily licked upward, casting light upon the far walls and on the water surface. Something splashed near the foot of the bed, and staring, his eyeballs bulging, he watched a pair of mud catfish swim into the halo of light near his feet, then dive with the blink of an eye out of sight. The idea that they were probably crawling along his daddy's prized oriental carpet made a bubble of hysterical laughter rise up his throat.

Then the lamp flame flickered and dwindled.

Bump.

Slowly, slowly, he moved his gaze over the water, toward the door.

"What the hell?" His vision sharpened on the two small glowing coals that appeared suspended just above the water's surface. They began to move toward him.

And the realization struck him then.

It sluiced through his mind more horribly than the fever pain—like a knife blade, tearing with such torment the body could not fully comprehend. Cold shock turned his chest numb.

"No." He scrambled to his feet, ramming his head against the tester, stumbling, grabbing the mosquito *baire* and ripping it off in his fist.

The bull gator rose, snout breaking the murky surface, water swirling around its body as its tail drove it smoothly through the water, toward the bed.

Staring down into the bull's eyes, Tylor dropped the lantern, heard it crack as the heated glass hit the water. Then there was nothing but the moon through the window, and he let out a crazed, terrified wail as the bull lunged and snapped . . . rolled to its back and took Tylor under.

The fever peaked. It burned her body throughout the day. She shook uncontrollably, thrashed in her delirium so Chantz and Andrew were forced to tie her hands and feet to the bedposts.

Crying, she begged to die.

Crying, he begged her to live.

The slightest touch of her clothes upon her skin sent shock waves of torment through her, so Chantz stripped her of clothes and fanned her body, her skin that became mottled with oozing bruiselike discolorations. Then the black vomit began. Like one possessed with a demon her body fought the cloth ropes binding her to the bed.

Phyllis, going to her knees beside the bed, prayed, "Omnipotent and eternal God, the everlasting Salvation of those who believe, hear us on behalf of Thy sick servant, Juliette, for whom we beg the aid of Thy pitying mercy, that, with her bodily health restored, she may give thanks to Thee in Thy church. Through Christ our Lord. Amen."

Curling up on the bed beside her, Chantz took Juliette into his arms and held her. Exhausted, he fell asleep and when he awoke again the sun was high and pouring through the open window. A mockingbird sat on the sill, head cocked to one side staring at him. The trees moved with birds and their warbling echoed like angel songs through the room.

His eyes drifted closed again, and for a moment he believed himself swept back to the morning after their wedding night, their bodies kissed by morning's chill. Only, as he opened his sleepy eyes and turned his head, the heart-wrenching reality greeted him.

Juliette lay still as death in his arms.

Groaning, he rolled away. He covered his face with his hands.

The door opened and Andrew moved across the room to Chantz's side. "You've got to rest and eat. You're not going to do her any good if you're half-dead yourself."

"I'm afraid," he said, his voice soft and rough with fatigue. Staring out the window, at the pond, he said, "I'm afraid she'll slip away from me while I'm gone." He cleared his throat and turned his face away from Andrew. "I don't want her to go alone."

"One of us will stay with her. Please." Andrew laid a

sympathetic hand on his shoulder. "I know how helpless you're feeling. I watched my own parents die, Chantz . . . I'll call you if there's any change."

Chantz nodded.

He descended the stairs and left the house, sat on the gallery step and looked down the long alley of trees, to the high water obliterating the river road. Belle Jarod might have been an island. The only evidence of land beyond Belle were the far tips of trees protruding from the water. For the first time, he thought of Holly, and of Tylor. He thought of the unfinished levee, then told himself that levee or not, there would have been no holding that river back. Something like pity touched him, and he mentally shook it away. Now wasn't the time to dwell on his confused feelings for Maxwell's passing—the anger, frustration . . . and even sadness. His wife was dying. His precious wife. Juliette with laughing, flashing eyes. Juliette who touched him like no other person had ever touched him. Who gave him hope. Who inspired belief in miracles . . . and in himself.

Leaning back against the pillar, he turned his face into a shaft of sun. Over the last dreadful days he had focused his thoughts on their plans for Belle. Of tall green cane. Of filling the new rooms with laughing children, of escorting her into *La Madeleine* where he would buy her the finest champagne. He would dress her in the most lavish gowns and emeralds to match her eyes. He'd make damn certain that she would never regret marrying a mud dauber's boy.

Someone touched his shoulder. Startled, he looked around, into Louis's face.

His mouth stretching into a smile, Louis pointed to the pond. "Look yonder, Boss. Right fine, ain't they? Perty as a dream."

Slowly, stiffly, Chantz struggled to his feet, his gaze fixed on the sun-golden pond, still and reflective as glass. Upon it floated two white swans.

His heart stopped. "Julie," he whispered, pain choking off the word, his body going cold. Wheeling, shoving Louis aside, he ran into the house and up the stairs, slowing as his mother looked down at him, her lower lip trembling and her eyes pouring tears.

"Hurry," she wept. "I fear she's leaving."

The others gathered around the bed, Rosie and Liza holding Juliette's shaking hands while everyone else rested on their knees with their hands clasped. Andrew put his hand on her forehead and closed his eyes.

"Almighty and everlasting God, preserver of souls, who dost correct those whom Thou dost love, and for their betterment dost tenderly chastise those whom Thou dost receive, we call upon Thee, O Lord, to grant Thy healing, that the soul of Thy servant, at the hour of its departure from the body, may by the hands of Thy holy Angels be presented without spot unto Thee—"

"No." Chantz shook his head and curled his hands into fists. Rage shook him.

Phyllis looked around. "He's giving her Last Rites—"

"The hell you are," he shouted, then shoved his way through the onlookers, to the bed where Juliette, pale as milk, began to convulse. He tore the bindings from her wrists and ankles, and scooped her hot body into his arms, turned on his heels and left the room. Her head resting on his shoulder, Chantz carefully descended the stairs, feeling every tremble of her body vibrate through him in waves of heat.

"Hold on, darlin'. Hold on for me just a little longer."

He left the house. His long, urgent stride carried him

along the gallery, then into the garden where his feet slipped on the damp grass, down the path along lush copses of honeysuckle that sweetly scented the morning air and bees buzzed from blossom to blossom. Beyond the flourishing magnolias and Cherokee roses, through the gray-green streamers of Spanish moss to the risen waters of the glassy pond where the white swans floated.

He walked into the water, sank to his shins, his knees, his thighs and hips, deeper, until the bracingly cool water swirled around Juliette's feverish body and her magnificent hair floated and spread like a fiery starburst in the water beneath her head. She gasped, and groaned. Her arms thrashed and her legs kicked. Her eyes flew open wide and she cursed him.

"Fight," he said through his teeth and immersed her deeper, until the water frothed around her neck, until, exhausted by her struggles she rested her head on his shoulder again and closed her eyes.

Stillness then, but for the big white birds with graceful arched necks and black bands around their eyes. The swans glided toward them, around them, stretching their necks and lifting their faces toward the sky as if . . . praying.

. . . *Back when you chased butterflies and hummin'birds and believed, if given the opportunity, that you could ride swans off into the clouds.*

Her trembling stopped, and with a soft sigh, she lay still and heavy in his arms.

The swans stretched their massive wings and lifted gracefully toward the pale blue sky.

His arms gripping Juliette, his chest aching with grief, Chantz watched the white birds rise up toward the clouds. "Don't go," he pleaded, feeling his chest heave as the sob swelled. His voice breaking and scalding tears rising to his eyes, he cried, "Don't go without me, Julie."

She stirred.

Her drowsy eyes opened.

"Husband," she sighed, her lips curving as she lifted her weak hand and touched his cheek. "I dreamed I was flying."

Epilogue

OCTOBER

Each day she grew stronger. Sitting in a chair on the gallery, each evening she watched for Chantz—counting the minutes until he returned home from the fields, wishing that she could join him and Andrew and the others as they turned the earth to prepare it for January planting. Soon, she told herself. Very soon.

Tonight, anticipation vibrated through her body like tendrils of electricity, and although she forced herself to relax, the eagerness made her antsy. She paced. Again and again she returned to the office where the missive lay on the desktop. She picked it up and held it to her bosom, eyes closed, heart beating wildly with gladness.

How should she tell him?

Over and over she rehearsed the words. "Holly Plantation is yours, Chantz. Maxwell acknowledged you long ago—in his Last Will and Testament. Long before he died. He's taken care of your mother, too . . ."

Could life possibly get any better?

She smoothed the papers with her hands and propped

them against the lamp. Decision made. He must learn the news alone. It was long awaited and far too personal. She would be there for him when he was ready. She would hold him and kiss him and they would fold their bodies together and love and dream of their future. They would try again to make a baby, and this time they would succeed. She felt it in her body, and in her heart.

Juliette left the house, paused on the shadowed gallery, and looked out over Belle's cleared grounds, the neat *parterres,* the long wide alley of ancient oaks, and the river beyond.

Lifting her cotton skirt, she danced down the steps and ran, exhilarated by the cool kiss of October air on her cheeks, the sharp scent of damp grass, and the rich aroma of dark, wet earth. Reaching the high-pillared gates, she stopped, turned her face toward the sky in which the stars were just beginning to twinkle. A pale fuzzy moon was just rising, its edges softened and blurred by a thin film of clouds.

A whippoorwill called, then another. Then, like a vapor, the white shapes of the swan pair drifted over the treetops, the measured beat of their wings a dull sound as they banked toward the pond and drifted gently down to the surface.

A warmth suffused her. A smile lifted her lips. The air grew colder, but she didn't care. The house, the river, the swans, her husband's love infused her with a sense of puissance. They could, they *would* accomplish anything and everything as long as they had each other. She held that emotion in her fast-beating heart, allowed the heat of love to ignite her every nerve, her every dream.

Chantz. Chantz. Chantz. My darling Chantz.

She felt him then, his presence, and she turned and saw him on the gallery, lit by the golden lights behind him, the missive in his hand. Elation filled her—for Chantz, for her father and mother, their dreams that would be realized at long last—for Belle Jarod that glowed like a jewel in the night.

"Husband," she whispered as he stepped from the alley, the papers falling from his hands as he ran toward her. "We shall accomplish miracles, you and I . . . together."

With a sense of lightness in her step, and a shiver of excitement over their beginnings, Juliette ran to meet Chantz, her arms open.

Return to
a time of romance…

***SONNET
BOOKS***

Where today's

hottest romance authors

bring you vibrant

and vivid love stories

with a dash of history.

PUBLISHED BY POCKET BOOKS